STAY WITH ME

nicole fiorina

STAY WITH ME

Stay with Me

First Edition | Paperback
Publication Date: August 3rd, 2019
ISBN: 978-1-0759698-8-1

Published by Nicole Fiorina Books | Poetry by Oliver Masters
Editing by Murphy Rae | Proofreading by Annie Bugeja
Cover & Formatting by Nicole Fiorina Books

10 9 8 7 6 5 4 3 2 1   USAZNFB

nicole fiorina

For the souls who feel lost or misunderstood,
this is for you. You are not alone.

Playlist available on Spotify:

https://spoti.fi/2ObKgcA

You can also stream from
https://www.nicolefiorina.com

PROLOGUE

"You stood before me, a memory,
but I was a stranger in your eyes.
Did you forget to remember,
or remember to forget?"

OLIVER MASTERS

Mia

would never forget the day you slipped away. A small lift of your chin and our eyes met. I only saw emptiness in a place where a wistful vulnerability used to collide with wonder. Now, a hollowness of a bottomless pit. In your eyes, I'd never seen your shade of green so dim. It caused my stomach to fall into the same somber eclipse, spiraling faster and faster with no end, no walls, only darkness.

And then you averted your gaze.

The flesh from my bones, the blood in my veins, the oxygen in my lungs, all of it crumbled, breaking into small pieces yet still holding on by a thread—the thread was my heart. It pumped on auto-pilot as if it couldn't associate with the rest of my body. It's thumping sounded in my ears, and I wished it would stop, but my heart was not ready to let go. It continued with the same steady beat, refusing to give up what was right in front of me. *Maybe your eyes will return to mine*, I thought—well, prayed.

And I waited.

Two seconds passed.

Then three—waiting as my body weakened from your disconnection, and my heart continued to pump.

Four.

And then your back was to me.

Whatever we'd had no longer existed, but I remembered everything clearly, and it wasn't fair. Could I have accepted the hollow look in your eyes over the wonder? Surely, anything you had to offer would be better than nothing. If only you had turned back around. Had you even noticed me?

And then you took a step in the opposite direction.

You were gone, left in obscurity and I couldn't bring you back, but my heart still maintained a steady beat, pumping along to a rhythm of crimson hope. *"Stay with me,"* you had said over and over. Who would have thought you would be the one to take a step into oblivion? *I'm screaming now, can you hear me?* Why didn't *you* stay with *me*?

I didn't get to kiss you goodbye. You were gone, and even though you were only twenty feet away, I missed you. It was entirely possible you'd wake up and turn back around, or I'd wake up.

Either way, it was a nightmare.

I forced my eyes closed. I couldn't watch you walk away, each step drawing more distance and less of a chance of you coming back. The darkness was better, anyway, and if I held my lids closed tight, I could see stars. I focused on the yellow and orange horizon behind my eyelids, pretending it was a sunset through the bitterness. The only warmth was the water gathering in the corners of my eyes. The tears struggled for a moment, fighting the same lie as my beating heart.

I wished I could switch places with you, because I didn't deserve a world once blessed by your light, and you didn't deserve this at all.

But this *was* what I deserved.

In the beginning, I'd thought you would be fun, that this would be a way to pass the time. And by the end, I'd thought I could leave you effortlessly. It was me who stomped on hearts, but now it was *my* heart left bleeding. The walls surrounding me had been durable, indestructible, before you.

And with no more walls, and no more you, I was slowly suffocating. When it came down to you and me, I'd never thought you'd be the one to slip away.

ONE

*"Falling down through the darkness.
She doesn't scream or cry for help,
lost her mind a long time ago.
She prefers falling down."*

OLIVER MASTERS

never took my stepmother seriously when she said I would one day be sent away for my reckless behavior after she found a boy in my closet, and I never really cared. It only fueled my actions.

So, one day, I stole the keys to her precious BMW 3 Series and drove it straight through the garage door.

Diane had grown tired of my acting out and blamed it on my father's increasing abandonment of the belief I could be cured. My father, the simple and passive-aggressive man he was, took each harsh word that poured from her perfectly made-up lips as he sat at the dining room table, staring blankly.

I didn't even like the boy, either. All I'd wanted was to feel something. Anything.

On the edge of nineteen, and at my stepmother's final straw and my father's last nerve, they both agreed to call the law after my BMW incident. Since it was my last warning, I would have been thrown into a mental institution, but my father pleaded with the judge to send me away to Dolor—the farthest reformatory college for *people like me.*

Don't get me wrong, I knew I wasn't normal, but I never thought there would be anyone else like me, especially not a school dedicated to my ... kind—if there was such a thing.

At what point had I taken a turn for the worst? I assumed I had always been this way. Allowing boys to use me had never been for their benefit.

It had been for mine.

I wanted to feel their hands on me, their mouths on mine, and the eagerness and lust as if it would rub off on me. It never did, but maybe, just maybe, it would light a fire inside me long enough to burn. Pain, lust, anger, passion, I would take anything at this point. My heart was stiff. Rigor mortis had already set in my soul, if I even had a soul. I could no longer be sure.

My suitcase lay half empty at the edge of my bed as I stood over it. Even with a brief list of acceptable items, I had nothing I desired to bring. No pictures, no attachment to a pillow or blanket. No interest in anything aside from my headphones that I was sure they would confiscate upon my arrival. I opened my nightstand to retrieve a box of condoms, because it wasn't on the list of "unacceptable items," and stuffed it into a secret pocket at the bottom of the suitcase.

Satisfied, I reached for the top of the suitcase, slammed it shut, and closed the zipper without an afterthought. I wasn't mad at Diane. If I had been, that would have meant I had feelings. Honestly, I didn't blame her. If I had a stepdaughter like myself, I'd call the police as well.

"Mia, you ready?" my father called out from the bottom of the stairs.

I didn't answer.

"Mia Rose Jett!"

"Two minutes!" I set the lightly packed suitcase beside my bedroom door and took one last look around at the bare walls of an old prison before I entered a new one. My walls were always empty, just like my bed, my dresser, my desk. No personality. Once I walked out the door, it would be like I had never lived here. This space could quickly become a guest bedroom, and I bet Diane already had a Pinterest board dedicated to it.

"Oh, no. You can't wear that." Diane scrunched her face from the bottom of the stairs. Her short bleach-blonde bob didn't move as she shook her head slightly from side to side. She always wore too much hairspray. Come to think of it, I'd ever seen her without her hair blown out, straightened, and sprayed in place. Even when she did her fifteen-minute workout videos after dinner in her room with the door cracked, I'd never seen her hair move.

"What's wrong with what I'm wearing?" My chin dropped as I straightened my oversized black t-shirt that read "cute but psycho" over my destroyed jean shorts, revealing my chicken legs. One would think I was naked underneath, the shirt was so big, but I wasn't. I was covered. *Promise, Dad.*

"Nothing's wrong. Let's move. We're already late for the airport," my father said, waving me down. He always avoided confrontation at all cost, and sometimes I wondered who he was more scared of—Diane or me? At this angle, I finally noticed the bald spot he'd been complaining about on the top of his head. I never believed him before, but now I didn't care enough to point out he was correct. He'd been a handsome man once, but even with Diane around, loneliness had sucked the life out of him. Bags scalloped under his brown eyes, and he'd lost all his muscle.

Marriage would do that to you.

The suitcase banged against each stair as I stepped down. "She could have, at the very least, brushed her hair," Diane said under her breath as she walked out the door ahead of my father and me. I pressed my lips together at the hypocrisy of her statement. At least I *could* run a brush through my hair.

"Not too much longer now," my father said as he gripped the handle of the suitcase and brought it behind him. He was right. Only eleven and a half hours longer, and I would be 3,447 miles away from both of them, give or take. He was choosing a perfect life, and I wasn't a part of perfect, and that was okay. I'd done my research. I knew what was waiting for me on the opposite side of the plane ride.

Dolor University was a reformatory college—a prison—specifically designed for troubled souls and delinquents who suffered from mental illnesses, addictions, and a poor parental guidance that led one to a career in crime, located in none other than the United Kingdom. I couldn't help but think the reason for the location was so they wouldn't feel pressured to visit, and I was okay with that. They could ship me wherever. I didn't want to be around people who didn't want to be around me, anyway. Isolation was my paradise.

I kept my attention out the window, twirling my dirty brown hair around my finger the entire way to the airport while my father went on about the curriculum.

"With Mia Rose's history, we should have chosen an all-girl reformatory," Diane scoffed.

"Mia Rose needs diversity," my father reminded her.

"Mia Rose is right here and can speak for herself," I informed both of them.

Diane conveniently stayed in the car as my father escorted me through baggage check-in and to the end of the line at security. He couldn't go any farther, and I was surprised he had made it this far.

I stood before him as his eyes glossed over. "I'm sorry, Mia."

He had never been good with words, but neither had I. Seconds passed, and he still couldn't look me in the eyes. He never could. Even when I talked to him, he'd look past me as if I were a ghost.

Look at me, Dad.

But, after a single nod, he turned and left me without so much as a second glance as I clutched my passport and plane ticket in my hand.

TWO

"It was instantaneous,
the mutual agreement between
her mind, heart, body, and soul.
All at once, they left her;
replaced by four walls.
Though inside, she's screaming.
The darkness was inevitable.
It was instantaneous."

OLIVER MASTERS

The flight wasn't so bad. No obnoxious crying children or Chatty Kathy's. Though, I didn't look like the type to entertain a conversation. People tended to stay away from me. Resting bitch face was real, and I wore my venom on my sleeve, not my heart—I didn't have one. Well, yes, I had the organ that was continuously flowing blood through my body. It did its job, unfortunately.

I spent the entire flight leaned against the window, looking out into the different shades of blue with my wireless headphones over my head, listening to playlists church-goers would criticize. As the color of the ocean blurred into the sky, it was hard to tell where the water stopped and where the sky began.

Surprisingly, my father had arranged for a limousine to transport me from the airport to the university. It was nothing more than a guilt trip—*literally*.

The sky was now shades of gray on the verge of a rainstorm. As we approached the tall iron gates of the school, the letter "D" was monogrammed front and center before they slowly opened, splitting the "D" in half. A tall brick wall wrapped around the entire campus. No way to escape once the gates closed. If it weren't for the security guard who was sent by Dolor's finest, I would have jumped out at the first opportunity, more than happy to leave my suitcase behind. Even my condoms. I could find my way around the United Kingdom, beg for food, sleep in alleyways. The thought of my dad receiving that call made me smile to myself. I would love to be a fly on the wall for that conversation.

The large German man sneered over at me as the idea crossed my mind, or at least I assumed he was German by the looks of him. He was tall with a shaved head, muscular build, square jaw, and light eyes. He didn't speak but looked like the kind of man vocal during a game of rugby. Did he know what I was planning? Inevitably, someone had to have attempted the great escape before. I could only imagine at least a dozen escape attempts, each one ending worse than the next.

I fell back into the black leather and averted my eyes from the silent German man and looked out the tinted window toward the castle before me.

The lawn was perfectly manicured with the lawnmower stripes still visible. Vines snaked vertically up the sides of the stone castle walls. A tall tower protruded on the left-hand side, and on the right sat a separate building wholly detached and made of concrete. Victorian windows covered the majority of the front of the castle with the addition of black bars across them.

No way out.

The limousine came to a stop, and a one-man welcoming committee greeted me as soon as the driver opened the door.

"Thank you, Stanley," the older gentleman said, greeting the Silent German as I exited the vehicle. "Hello, Ms. Jett, welcome to Dolor. I'm Dean Lynch. Now, follow me." Lynch didn't bother extending a hand for a formal shake, which filled me with relief. I followed behind him with my luggage in hand and my headphones around the back of my neck. We walked through the tall wooden double doors and a security checkpoint conveniently waited for me. Stanley took my suitcase and laid it across a revolving belt before it entered the scanner for the second time within the last twenty-four hours.

"Arms up," Stanley insisted with a wave of a stick. *He speaks.*

I raised my arms to my sides as my face found the ceiling. "Is this all really necessary?"

Stanley ran the detector down each side of my waist, and as soon as it met my hip, the beeper went off.

"Hand it over," Lynch said with a palm in the air. "Cell phones aren't permitted."

"You got to be kidding me. I can't even listen to my music?" *Screw talking to anyone.* I didn't care if I never spoke with my father or Diane again.

"I will need your earphones and any other valuables as well."

I unwrapped my headphones from around my neck and dropped them into his palm. "Would you like blood and a pap smear while you're at it?"

Lynch relaxed his shoulders. "That will come after our brief meeting."

My brows snapped together. I had been kidding, but he was serious.

After Dean Lynch collected the only items to keep me sane, I walked through the security checkpoint without any beeps. Lynch ushered me down the hall across the shiny white and gray swirled marbled floor.

I took in my surroundings as I followed close behind. Natural colored board and batten spread over the walls on each side of me. "We are two weeks into the new school year, so you're already behind. I understand this is your first year in a university?" Lynch asked as he quickly shuffled

16

ahead of me. He was skinny, breakable, and I hoped if he turned to his side, he would vanish into thin air.

"Yeah, that's right."

Lynch paused mid-stride, and I almost crashed into him. He turned at the waist, and instead of disappearing as I'd hoped, he peered down at me, his teeth crooked. "We use our manners here at Dolor." His face was white, and his eyes were cinnamon brown and hollow, acne scars covering his expression.

"Yes, sir," I whispered with a grin.

His lifeless eyes sliced into mine, but I held my ground. I'd lived with the same searing eyes for over nine years. Nothing could break me under pressure.

Lynch faced forward again and continued to walk down the empty hall at the same fast pace as before, but this time I kept a good five feet between the two of us.

Large portraits lined over the board and batten in a row. Each picture was framed in tarnished brass containing the same lifeless eyes as Lynch's. It seemed whoever walked through the doors would have the life sucked right out of them.

We turned a corner and entered an office. Lynch gestured for me to take a seat. Cherry wood bookshelves lined the entire wall behind his matching cherry wood desk, and a large window with a thick red velvet curtain took up most of the adjacent wall. His desk lacked clutter, aside from a single folder with my name printed on the tab. He took a seat, rolled under his desk, and opened the file.

"Your first year will be working toward your undergraduate degree, which is transferrable in the states. If you succeed the two years here at Dolor with appropriate grading, counseling, and group therapy requirements, *along with* good behavior, you will be discharged with a clear record." Lynch pulled a paper from the top and handed it to me. "Here is your schedule. You will meet with Dr. Conway twice a week, and you will start group therapy your second week after you have grown accustomed to our ways. Here is the Dolor handbook. I suggest you familiarize yourself with our code of conduct and dress code." The thick handbook was handed over to me. "Do you have any questions, Miss Jett?"

I shook my head despite the fact I had dazed off halfway through.

"Very well, then. Stanley will escort you to the nurse's station before showing you to your dorm." Lynch closed the folder and filed it into a drawer of the desk as I sat in a fog. "Miss Jett, if you miss a session, you will be forced to solitary confinement. If you cause any problems, you will be sent to solitary confinement. If you—"

An exaggerated sigh escaped me. "I understand. Solitary confinement."

"This is your only chance. If you cannot play nice, you will be forced to leave and be admitted into a mental institution per your judge's discretion. Do you want that?"

I stared, allowing the words to sink in when he pressed me with a glare. "No, sir."

Lynch nodded. "Stanley, she's all yours."

I followed Stanley to the nurse's station, the only sounds in the empty halls being the heels of my combat boots against the marble and a jingle of keys attached to Stanley's belt. I debated back and forth on whether or not to try to get Stanley on my good side with casual conversation and charm, but the moment I opened my mouth, we arrived.

The sizeable sterile room was blinding. All the walls were a crisp white under the fluorescent lights. Three hospital beds with the same fresh white bedding sat in a row, each having the option of enclosure by a thin white curtain. White machines covered in buttons stood against the walls, along with various wired baskets filled with different-sized blue gloves. The smell of hand sanitizer knocked my nose senseless.

"Do you need to use the loo before we get started?" a dark-skinned woman asked, coming from another door off to the side. Stanley had since left and closed the door behind him, but I was sure he wouldn't stray too far, possibly just outside the door waiting for me like a good watchdog.

"The loo?" I asked, turning back to face her. "Oh, that's right. You guys call it that here … no, I'm good."

"Let's get right to it, then. Drop your bottoms and knickers and lie back on the table. I'll wait behind the curtain until you're ready."

With pap smear, fingerprints, and blood work completed, I was violated in all ways possible. The nurse explained it was routine to check for sexually transmitted diseases, physical abnormalities, and disabilities as we went over my medical history. We talked about my birth control, which I no longer had control over. She would regulate it from this point forward.

Just as I had expected, Stanley greeted me right outside the door. We stepped up a flight of curved marble stairs with a black iron railing and walked down a corridor lined with the same board and batten before we turned a corner. "Classrooms are located on the third level. Living headquarters are stationed on the second. There is a map in your dorm." We made another left. "Here you have the community bathroom, and the mess hall is located straight ahead and to the right," he said, explaining with hand motions. "You will be staying in the fourth wing, sharing this bathroom with the third wing."

"Community bathroom? As in both genders sharing the same facilities?"

"We are gender neutral and don't discriminate. You will get used to it."

He paused to check for understanding from my part before he turned on his heel. Heavy steel doors lined the hall on each side. The floor was the same swirly gray marble, but the walls were now a cloud blue cement. We approached a door on the right as Stanley came to a stop. "No classes for you today. Get familiar with the handbook. Dinner is at five-thirty PM in the mess hall and curfew is eight-thirty PM. Doors will automatically lock at eight forty-five PM, sharp. If you need to use the loo during the night, there's a buzzer in your room. The guard on night shift will escort you."

Stanley grabbed the ring of keys from his belt and opened the door before entering. After thoroughly scanning the dorm, he welcomed me inside. "It will get better," he added, reading my body language accurately.

And the door slammed behind him as I stood in my new prison.

The walls of the room were gray-blue and cemented like the hall I'd just walked down. I hadn't been expecting this, though I really hadn't known what to expect. I suppose a white room with padded walls crossed my mind on the plane ride here. A twin bed without a headboard and a footboard sat against the left wall with a single gray sheet and pillow over a thin mattress, and an empty desk sat against the parallel wall with a single black metal chair. I approached the small window across the room to see a view of the back of the school behind the bars. Nothing but sparse woods and the brick wall in the distance.

My suitcase waited for me next to the door, but I didn't care to unpack. There wasn't a dresser, anyway, only a rolling cart under the bed. I sat on the bed and ran my fingers across the thin sheet. How many had slept in this room before me? A clock hung above the only door in the room that read 3:16 PM. I lay back on the bed, folded my hands behind my head, and stared at the ceiling as I thought back to what had put me in this hell-hole to begin with.

Me. I did this.

I'd caused multiple fights in school and landed myself in the principal's office more times than I'd attended a class. The day I'd lit Principle Tomson's car on fire was the day I was expelled and arrested. After hours of community service and therapy, I'd graduated with a perfect GPA under a home-school program. I'd hammered my own nail in the coffin when I drove Diane's BMW through the garage intentionally. My father negotiated with the judge and offered to send me here so I could pursue a college degree in lieu of being forced into the mental institution.

I was smart, but most sociopaths were. The judge wanted to make an example of me, but I knew better. No one ever did anything out of the goodness of their hearts. The only reason the judge agreed was to add

20

another success story to his resume at my father's expense. I suppose it was better than the mental institution.

I grabbed the handbook beside me and dangled it above my head before flipping it open to the first page when there was a rap at the door.

Ignoring it, I flipped over to the second page.

Another impatient knock.

My feet found the floor, and I cursed my way toward the door.

On the other side stood two individuals; a girl with medium-length curly black hair and a skinny blond-haired boy, a couple inches taller than the girl, with bright blue eyes and thin lips.

"See, Jake ... I told you someone came in here," the girl said to the boy, smacking him on the arm. She wore a black choker around her neck and a small, admirable mole to the side of her mouth.

"Not interested," I said and began to close the door.

The boy wedged his foot in the crack. "Not so fast."

I opened the door again and rested against it with my hand over my hip, waiting for the purpose of this intrusion.

"I'm Jake. This is Alicia."

"And let me guess, you're fucking gay as a two-dollar bill, and Alicia here feeds off that shit, both looking for another member of your pity party by showing the new girl around?"

Alicia and Jake exchanged glances before a laugh broke out between them.

My eyes rolled. "Well?"

"We don't see too many Americans come through these doors, but you're right,"—Jake giggled between breaths—"we could use someone like you in our *'pity party.'*"

I waved them both off. "Go suck a dick."

My comment didn't faze them. Jake leaned over with his hands on his knees, and his giggle grew loud and obnoxious. Alicia patted her friend's back as she came back from my comment. "I get it, you're a badass who hates the world," Alicia said, and I was sensing sarcasm in her tone, "but, if you're looking for a fun time tonight, find us at dinner."

21

Alicia and Jake turned away and proceeded to mock my accent down the hall. "'Go suck a dick,'" one of them said, shoving the other in the shoulder. Their laughs continued to echo through the wing before I slammed the door harder than I should have.

Lying on the bed once again, I pulled my cap over my face in an attempt to bring their annoying British accents to a stop as they bounced around in my brain.

By the time my eyes opened again, the clock read fifty minutes past five. *Crap*. I'd fallen asleep, and now I was twenty minutes late. With no time to change, I scurried out the door and wandered through the empty corridor, trying to remember Stanley's directions to the mess hall. I should have listened.

Then, there it was, the distant sounds of chatter growing louder and louder with each step I took forward.

A sea of white shirts and black pants flocked the mess hall. I kept my eyes in front of me as I walked through the middle between tables toward the non-existent food line to the back. The chatter calmed as a stillness replaced the madness. Whispers and questions about my presence danced in the air as I passed each table, but I still didn't bother to look at them.

An older lady in a hair net and sauce-splashed shirt approached the door to the buffet the same time as I did when she said, "Sorry, kitchen's closed. Maybe next time you'll be more conscious of your time." I opened my mouth to speak, but she interrupted me. "Oh, and … I would go back to your dorm to change if I were you."

And she closed the door in my face.

"Are you kidding me?" I shouted, hoping she could hear me on the other side of the door. The large mess hall fell silent, and when I turned back around, a hundred eyes were on me. "What?" I called out with my palms in the air.

Silence.

My eyes went wide for a reaction, but no one seemed to have a pair.

22

Everyone went back to their usual conversations, and I found an empty table beside the glass windows overlooking the front of the campus. Other than the gray day transforming to night, there wasn't much to look at. A man in a jumpsuit drove a golf-cart-looking vehicle over the lawn, picking up litter. On the other side of me was my new fellow student body. Placed randomly throughout the mess hall were round tables, and students grouped together at each table as smiles, chuckles, and a few sneers crossed over their faces. It was high school all over again.

I noticed Alicia and Jake glaring at me from across the room as they talked in each other's ears. There were four of them total at their table, and they didn't bother concealing the topic of their discussion. A guy sat on top of the table with his long legs propped over the seat of a chair as a girl with a toothpick frame, pale skin, and pixie black hair laid her head over the table beside him.

I could tell he was tall by the way his knees were bent as his elbows rested over them. A white shirt hung loose around his neck, black and white tattoos painted over each of his arms, and I could hardly make out the heavy rise and fall of his chest as he took in deep breaths. But I did notice. My attention made the journey to his face when our eyes met. A gray beanie covered his head, but dark strands poked out from underneath. His brows pressed together and then he—barely—nodded in my direction. When I didn't return his advance, he held his head up in his hands and brought his fingers to his mouth. Rings decorated each finger and a dimple appeared beside his hidden smile.

Breaking our connection, a small milk carton flew across the mess hall between us and my eyes followed it to a young boy who sat at the table across from me, smacking him right in the head. White liquid flew in all directions, ultimately soaking the young boy. The mess hall went up in a roar as the boy, who was just hit, jumped from his seat and threw himself back against the large window. A scream belted from his lungs and I pushed my chair back and stood to my feet.

Tattoo Guy hopped off the table and ran over to the boy. "What is wrong with you, Liam? You have a death wish?" His voice was loud yet controlled as he spoke to the group of laughing hyenas with his arms in the air.

Tattoo Guy crouched before the screaming kid. "Breathe, Zeke," he insisted, gripping the boy's arms. The young boy looked up at him. His face was turning from a deep red to a purple in a matter of seconds. "Deep breaths." Tattoo Guy showed him how by drawing in a deep breath of his own. He counted to three with his fingers in the air before exhaling, and the young boy watched him with the same amazement in his eyes like mine.

The young boy's screams dissolved and he was able to breathe again. Tattoo Guy glanced over at me, and I quickly turned away. "Let's get out of here, yeah?" He helped him up off the floor, and Zeke clung to his side as they walked out of the mess hall.

"America, did you think about our offer?" Jake asked as his posse surrounded my table.

I exhaled and retook my seat as Tattoo Guy and Zeke turned the corner out of sight and then answered, "I told you. Not interested."

"In case you change your mind, it starts at midnight," Alicia said.

These kids couldn't take a hint even if it punched them in the face.

The pixie-haired girl smacked Alicia over the head. "You can't be giving out these details to anyone, Alicia. You have to ask the group first. Have you even talked to Ollie?"

"She's cool. Trust me." Alicia continued, "If you're looking at your window, it's the fourth block to your left."

"And how do you suppose I get there?" I had no interest in going, but if there was a way out of my dorm without using my door, I had to know. Alicia discretely pointed up to the vent in the ceiling before the three of them turned and walked away.

THREE

"Exposing truths and stripping her lies all at once,
and just like that, panic and peace consume me."

OLIVER MASTERS

All night I tossed and turned over the thin, and incredibly stiff, mattress. Jet-lagged from the change in time zones, and having gotten too much sleep over the last twenty-four hours between the plane ride and my nap in the afternoon, trying to sleep was useless.

I'd managed to count every crack in the cement, every bolt in the steel door, and if I concentrated hard enough, I could see constellations in the swirls of the marble floor as the moon shone over it. A loud click, precisely at six in the morning, sounded when the doors automatically unlocked.

I was the first one in the community bathroom with a toothbrush, my new Dolor shirt, and skinny black jeans in hand. I wasn't allowed to bring shampoo, conditioner, or deodorant. Not even a razor. My father said everything would be provided for me.

The cement walls in the bathroom were painted white, and a row of six sinks were to my right. Tall mirrors lined the wall evenly, one above each sink. Across from the sinks were the shower stalls. Subway tile stretched across the back wall, and each stall was separated by cedar wood planks with a white curtain enclosure. Clean towels were stacked in the skinny shelves on both sides of the row of sinks, and basic toiletries were stuffed in baskets between the sinks—the same brand for men and women. Thankfully, the smell of coconut didn't make me gag.

I chose the farthest shower at the end and turned it on to wait for it to heat up. Even though I was fully clothed, I still felt naked and exposed without make-up on in the mirror. Impressing people had never been a goal of mine, and even though I never needed it, I still wore make-up because I knew it bothered Diane. I wore the heaviest of eyeliner, the boldest lip shade, and black on my nails for the simple fact it drove her crazy.

Staring at my reflection, I was just me, looking five years younger with the lightly sprinkled freckles under my eyes and across the bridge of my nose. Though, my eyes didn't lie. One look, and you could see the secrets, the pain, and the misery beneath the dull brown. My thick brows would usually distract others from the story my eyes held. No one ever took the time to look hard or close enough.

Take my father for example.

A presence entered the bathroom, triggering my attention to shift. Tattoo Guy shuffled toward me with clothes over his shoulder, wiping the corners of his eyes. Gray joggers hung low on his hips, and a plain black tee covered the rest of him as his wild brown hair lay flat on one side.

After he dropped his hand from his face and he noticed me, he stopped walking. His face held no expression as he stared at me from about five feet away. Then, a sleepy smile greeted me before his voice did. "Hi."

I returned a smile, but it was only because his was contagious—nothing more. "Hi."

But he still didn't move.

Once it dawned on me how long we were standing there for, I faced the mirror again and flipped on the faucet to brush my teeth. He drew nearer before he appeared in the mirror's reflection behind me, and leaned over to grab a towel off the shelf, careful to keep a distance, but also lingering longer than he should.

He switched the water on in the stall next to mine and hung his clothes and towel. When he turned back around, he approached the sink beside mine.

Our eyes met in the mirror's reflection. "Mia, right?"

It was in that moment I noticed his green eyes. They were beautiful. *Rare.* A color so distinguishable, but indescribable at the same time. It was the color of the reflection of palm trees across a shoreline when the sun was at its highest point in the day. The color was noon. It wasn't the deep blue shade of the ocean past the reflection of the tree line, or the white when the foam gathered in the sand, but the sweet spot in the middle. It was the perfect timing when three of God's creations collided: the sun, trees, and water.

It was breathtaking, even in the damn mirror.

"Yeah, that's right."

He turned his body to face me and leaned into the sink as he extended a hand, his eyes even more beautiful when they were looking into mine without barriers. "I'm Ollie."

His lovely eyes and formal etiquette caught me off guard. After darting my eyes between his face and his hand, I accepted his gesture. I hadn't shaken a hand in a long time. Was I even doing it right?

Ollie grinned.

He placed his toothbrush and a razor over the sink, and his face fell as he attempted to fix his thick and rebellious hair by running his fingers through. His hair wasn't long enough to cover his ears, but long enough to fall over his eyes if he didn't style it back. "Great first impression, yeah?" He followed up with a lazy laugh, but my attention was on the razor, and I eyed it as if it were a million dollars.

"How can I get one of those?"

Ollie looked down at the counter and back at me, a small wrinkle forming between his brows. "You haven't got a razor?" I shook my head, and he slid the razor in my direction as if we were dealing drugs. "You can have this one. It's fresh. I haven't used it."

"Thanks."

We shared a smile, and he dropped his head in acknowledgment before turning and disappearing behind the curtain.

The water didn't take long to heat up as I undressed behind my curtain before stepping under the showerhead. It wasn't hot, but warm enough to bear. I squeezed shampoo in the palm of my hand and massaged it into my scalp, taking my time and hoping Ollie would finish before my water turned cold. I wasn't good at small talk. It was awkward and pointless, and I avoided it at all costs.

His water cut off, and the sound of his curtain against the rod followed shortly after. "I would suggest hurrying if you want to avoid rush hour," he called out over the sound of my running water. His voice came deep and from the chest. He talked slowly, like each word he chose was carefully considered. I peeked my head through the small slit in the curtain just as his shirt fell over his tattooed stomach in the reflection of the mirror. "Only giving you a heads up."

Without a response from me, he left. Not even five minutes later, people trickled in as showers and faucets turned on around me, and a few comments were thrown around in the air.

Today was my first full day of classes and my first counseling session. I was not looking forward to either. My schedule consisted of four rotating courses. Mondays and Wednesdays were the same, with a one-on-one session to follow, and Tuesdays and Thursdays were the same with a group session to follow. Fridays were free days for extracurricular activities, in which I didn't plan on taking part.

I arrived here on a Wednesday, making today my first and last day of the week for classes before a three-day weekend. Even though today was supposed to be a group session, Dean Lynch left a sticky note over my schedule to remind me I would continue one-on-one sessions with Dr. Conway up until my second week here.

Since I wasn't allowed to have a blow dryer, I left my hair down and air-dried, and wore my combat boots over my black skinny jeans. I didn't despise the dress code. It could have been worse. The collared Dolor shirt wasn't too baggy, but not too fitted either as it laid nicely over my average-sized chest. I left the buttons undone.

The moment I walked into the mess hall, the smell of syrup and bacon made my stomach growl. I decided to sit at the same table as the day before, officially claiming it as mine. The atmosphere during breakfast was far different from last night's dinner. The morning sun peeked through gray clouds as its rays created spotlights through the window and into the large room. My new fellow peers stayed quiet, dragging their feet from the breakfast line toward their tables. Students slowly seeped in, the dread of the new day written all over their faces. Alicia, Jake, and their group of friends made their way to the same table they'd sat at the day before.

Jake waved me over from across the room, but I declined with a shake of my head. I didn't need friends, especially the tenacious kind. Humans annoyed me, and Jake would only drag out my days here. My only mission was to keep my head down and get through the next two years without complication. Having Jake believe we were friends would be a complication. Eventually, someone's petty feelings would get hurt because of my venomous tongue and reckless actions.

Ollie strolled in a few minutes later with his brown hair flipped into a lopsided wave and wearing a plain white tee around his tall and skinny build. Tattoos peeked from under his shirt, and his infectious smile lit the room as he entered. His dismissal of wearing the Dolor shirt had me intrigued. He seemed like the kind of guy to get away with shit like that.

Ollie walked in beside another guy a few inches shorter with midnight-black hair, longer at the top and buzzed around the sides. He had darker features and trimmed facial hair. Since I didn't plan on getting close enough to the group to learn their names, I'd decided to call him Midnight.

They both glanced over in my direction as Ollie talked in his ear.

The pixie-haired girl greeted Ollie with a kiss on the cheek, and he quickly glanced to me then back at her, and his posture changed. It could have been his girlfriend, but the way he reacted said otherwise.

My attention went back to my food. I took a bite of the bland pancakes as I stared at the screaming kid, Zeke, eating alone.

The people here, for the most part, stayed to their group or themselves. Loners scattered themselves throughout the mess hall, but you still had your group of sexually confused, your punks, thugs, jocks, mean girls, and handicapped—all most likely avoiding prison or a mental institution like me.

But then you had the crew Jake and Alicia were in. They were quite the mixture.

Ollie and Midnight took a seat at their table before Ollie found me across the room. He was interested. Humans were wired to stare at ones they were interested in.

I'd once read a study regarding the different levels of eye contact. *There are nine levels, by the way.* Ollie was on level three right now, which is the "glance and a half." Though, if he looked away then back at me a second time, he would be upgraded to a level four—"The double glance."

He looked away, and I held on a few more seconds.

He looked again, and—*boom*—level four, ladies and gents.

His gaze fixated on me, somehow holding all my attention now. *Level five.* Those fierce green eyes held a degree of gravity, weighing me down and lifting me off my feet at the same time. He grinned—*level six*—and I shook my head at his arrogance. *Am I smiling? Oh, Jesus, I'm smiling.*

Ollie raised a brow as his smile matched mine. His dimple deepened, and I managed to pull away from his hold to allow my smile to subside.

I needed to get laid—like yesterday.

The first block went by quickly. I had already taken college algebra during my senior year of high school, so now I was placed in trigonometry. Math was black and white, right or wrong. The answer was clear.

Next was the introduction to literature. I walked into the class, and I immediately saw Jake with wide eyes, slapping his hand over the empty desk beside him.

"Thank God," he whispered as I sat in the seat he'd saved for me since he hadn't left me much of a choice. "You made this class so much more interesting."

"That bad, huh?"

Jake nodded as he continued to tell me about the monotone professor and the number of papers we would have to write this semester. I hated English, literature, and everything else that went along with it, unable to understand why people would be intrigued by something that was entirely made up. How on earth was it essential for survival in the real world? Each story had a different meaning to different people, different interpretations, so there was never a precise answer.

After class, Jake quickly gathered his books together to keep up with my pace. I was almost out of the door—almost.

"Care if we walk together to the mess hall?" he asked, catching his breath.

"Only if you let me read you."

"Let you read me?" He panted.

"Yeah, it's a game I like to play."

Jake's face twisted with an amused and curious smile. "Alright, sure…yeah, read me."

Though I'd already figured him out, I took the time to study him up and down for dramatic effect. Jake straightened his posture and managed to grow another inch. I was only 5'3", and he couldn't have been more than four inches taller than me. "Alright, Jacob … goes by the name Jake because it makes you seem … less masculine …" He rolled his baby-blues before shifting his books to his other hand. Jake was in touch with his feminine side; you could see it in his stride. "You are a middle child surrounded by sisters—"

Jake opened his thin lips to speak, but I put up a finger to silence him.

I quickly added, "But you have an older brother who is the star athlete of the family, and whom everyone is compared to. So that would put you as the second youngest." Jake raised his eyebrows, and I knew from his expression I was on the right path. "You come from a religious family, and even though you are a poster child, always followed the rules, always did the right thing, your parents still sent you here to try and knock the gay out of you."

Jake shook his head in disbelief. "Bloody hell, you're good."

I dusted off my shoulder. "It's a talent. Though, what I don't understand, is why you agreed to come here. You're an adult. Your parents can't force you."

"You're right, they can't force me, but they sure as hell can bribe me."

During the rest of our short walk to the mess hall, I'd learned Jake had a boyfriend back home, whom he was caught in bed with by his father. He didn't even get to say goodbye before he was brought here. At first, the school turned Jake away, but since his father was a pastor of a church, they offered to help students with community service upon their release in negotiation to take Jake in.

Jake tried to convince me to sit with him during lunch, but I decided to keep to myself at my table.

After I finished eating, I pulled out my class schedule to see psychology was next—my favorite. I folded my arms over the table and laid my head down until the lunch bell rang.

My eyes wandered toward Jake's table. The pixie-haired girl had her head against Ollie's shoulder as he talked to Midnight. Alicia and Jake were laughing and pointing at a girl across the room who had trouble bringing her food to her mouth. Ollie caught wind of Jake and Alicia's amusement, turned behind him to see what they were laughing about, then slammed his fist against the table.

Since I couldn't hear a word they said, I instead pretended they were all part of a soap opera while making up commentary in my head.

Pixie-haired girl removed her head from Ollie's shoulder before curling into a ball next to him, and Ollie's gaze drifted in my direction. I quickly turned my head over my hands in the opposite direction to look out the window instead. The view wasn't any better, but I didn't like what his stare did to me. It pulled me in, and suddenly I was losing control.

I never lost control. Control was all I had.

The class was small in psychology, about ten students at most. Though there were plenty of desks available in the front, I chose one in the last row in the back. Again, I blamed it on my need to control the situation. I could see everyone in front of me, knew the location of my exit, and understood my surroundings.

The professor still wasn't in, and I took the time to analyze each student. The way they either slumped in their chairs, or sat tall and ready for class to begin, which ones had friends in the classroom, and which ones didn't. In the second row on the far right sat a girl with short blonde hair and small shoulders. She looked up from her desk and toward the door every ten seconds.

She was waiting for someone.

"Good afternoon, hello, good day," a gentleman rambled while bustling through the door. "Sorry I'm running a bit behind today, but if everyone could quickly get their textbooks and find the chapter regarding Maslow's Hierarchy of Emotional Needs, we will jump right in."

The teacher was a tiny fellow with gray wiry hair and patches of stubble surrounding his jawline. His glasses sat on the tip of his nose as he shuffled amongst his papers at his podium. He was a slob, with his shirt half tucked into khakis two sizes too big. From the looks of it, you could tell he was late often.

He glanced up from his desk, and his attention was immediately drawn to me in the back. "I'm Dr. Kippler. There are extra textbooks on the bookcase behind you if you need one." After I retook my seat, I flipped through the pages of the textbook when Dr. Kippler spoke up again. "Ah, nice of you to join us, Masters."

I lifted my gaze to see Ollie taking a seat at the front of the room in front of the girl with blonde hair, and then it made sense. She was waiting for Ollie. Her small shoulders relaxed and she tucked her short hair behind her ear.

"This time I will let it pass since I was late myself, but no more warnings," Dr. Kippler added, but I knew this was a regular thing for Dr. Kippler. He would never be on time.

Ollie nodded before turning his head to the blonde-haired girl who greeted him with a gentle hand over his shoulder.

But his attention quickly became mine the moment he spotted me in the back.

Three intense seconds passed with his eyes on mine before he mouthed, *"Hi."*

The blonde-haired girl turned to see what had robbed her of his attention. She narrowed her eyes, and I gave them both a small wave with my fingers.

Dr. Kippler cleared his throat, and both Ollie and blonde-haired girl snapped their heads back to the front. "Masters, what are the six human emotional needs?"

Ollie's posture relaxed as he stretched his long legs out in front of him. "Certainty, variety, significance, love, growth, and contribution," he replied without opening his textbook.

"And which ones are required for human survival?" Kippler tested him.

"Certainty, variety, significance, and … love."

I coughed out a laugh at the mention of the last one.

"Beg to differ … miss …," Kippler looked down at his desk. "Jett."

As I tapped my pencil on the edge of the desk, everyone turned around in their seats. "No, keep going. You guys are doing great," I said with a thumb in the air and a smile to match my sarcasm. I'd been in situations like this before, and it was a lose/lose battle. I had my beliefs about love, they had theirs, and I wasn't here to convince anyone otherwise.

"Becks, which one do you feel is most significant to your needs?"

The heat was taken off of me and was now on a red-headed freckled boy sitting in the front. He was a total fire-starter. He had the red hair to match.

"Significance."

My eyes rolled at my accuracy.

"I guess I want to be seen and heard," Becks added. *Yeah, with fire.*

"Gwen?" Kippler asked.

Gwen, also known as the blonde-haired girl behind Ollie, leaned closer to Ollie. "Certainty," she said. Ollie adjusted in his seat before she continued, "I want to feel safe and secure, I suppose. Especially in my relationships." The way she said it somehow made the air in the room thicker, stuffier.

"What about you, Masters? What is your most significant need?"

I was on the edge of my seat for this one, certain Ollie was going to say "Significance" as well. Since I'd been here, he'd managed to get more attention from girls than I'd received from Jake. He looked like the kind of guy to crave attention and the need to be desired by others as much as the next guy.

"Hard to say, Kipp. I want to say, out of my options, love, but love is hardly an emotion."

Wait. What?

"What do you mean?" Dr. Kippler asked.

"Emotions can change. They can go from one extreme to the next depending on various conditions, but love..."—he shook his head slightly—"love never waivers. It endures all other emotions. If it couldn't withstand, then it was never really love in the first place." Ollie let out a sigh. "Love is invariable, Kipp. Constant. Not an emotion."

I stared at the back of his head with my brows in the air.

Dr. Kippler scratched along his jawline in deep thought. "With that being said, what is a better term you would replace love with as an emotion?"

Ollie let out a small laugh. "You tell me."

The room went quiet again as Dr. Kippler looked around the room. "What about you, Jett? Which emotional need is most important to you?"

My head cocked in Dr. Kippler's direction now that the heat was back on me.

"Variety," I said sharply, not having to think at all about my answer.

"Care to explain?"

"Nope."

Dr. Kippler nodded at my honesty and brought his attention back to the class. "For those of you who are unfamiliar with variety, it's the motivation to seek change or a challenge outside of a normal routine. Unless Masters here would like to alter the pyramid once again?" he asked, looking to Ollie with a challenging grin. Chuckles spread throughout the class and Ollie shook his head before Dr. Kippler continued, "Very well. Your responses to my question could clarify the very reason why you're here in the first place." Kippler brought his hands together as he became proud of himself with his revelation.

After my last class of the day, I entered the office of Dr. Conway. The room was the same size as my dorm, and the sun cast enough light through the large window to brighten up the space. A leather couch rested against the wall, facing a desk with papers scattered across, and posters of positive quotes filled her pale blue walls.

Dr. Conway turned to face me from the chair with an authentic smile. "Mia, it's so nice to finally meet you." She stood with an extended hand. "Please take a seat."

As soon as she opened her mouth, I knew Dr. Conway was an American by her Boston accent. Her thick black hair framed her face and dropped just below her shoulders. "How was your trip here?"

"Long." My body sank into the leather as my eyes wandered around the room until they fell onto a poster of a kitten with the quote, *"Today I will not stress over things I can't control."*

What in the hell did a kitten have to be stressed about?

36

To my right sat a bookshelf filled with novels I'd never heard of, and a collection of self-help books.

"Yeah, I don't miss that flight," Dr. Conway said and let out a sigh. "Boston?"

"Born and raised. I came out to the UK during a sabbatical. Finding the love of my life here wasn't planned, but hey …"—she threw her palms in the air—"shit happens."

I spaced out after she said sabbatical, but continued to nod in interest. The term sabbatical reminded me of when my mom told me a story how she'd visited the UK during college as well for a short period of time. England must be a landing spot for college students abroad.

"So, tell me, why do you think you're here?" she asked.

"I'm here because my dad is in denial. The image of his only daughter graduating college and living out a normal life is the only reason why he refused to send me off to a mental institution."

"Do you belong in a mental institution?"

"I don't belong, period."

Dr. Conway tapped my file with her long fake nails as she crossed her legs. "I read your file, Mia. You suffer from Alexithymia and Emotional Detachment Disorder. You have already tried to commit suicide twice of which I'm aware, drove your stepmother's car through a garage, lit your principal's car on fire, and … this one's my favorite … showed up to your counselor's house dressed in a trench coat and heels portraying a hired prostitute?" She let out a small chuckle as she uncrossed her legs and rested her elbows over her knees. "I hope his wife was forgiving."

I shrugged, and the mood in the small room shifted along with her facial expression.

"If you don't mind me asking, why do you think you were unsuccessful with the suicide attempts?"

My head dipped back at her forwardness. "I would have been successful if my dad hadn't found me."

"Something tells me a part of you wanted your father to find you."

She was wrong. He was supposed to have been at work until five o'clock both days. "You're way off."

"No, I think I'm getting somewhere … Let me ask you something else. When was the last time you cried?"

She couldn't be serious. "I don't cry. You have to have feelings to cry."

"Did you cry when your mother died?"

No. "I don't talk about my mother."

Dr. Conway leaned back in her chair and folded her hands across her lap. "Your father noted you haven't always been this way. Something had to have happened in your childhood that was so awful, and your brain turned off a switch to protect itself. Medicine isn't going to help. It's only going to prolong your ability to turn it back on."

Silence.

"I'm going to speak with the dean and take you off your meds while you're here, but Mia, you have to turn the switch back on. You're the only one who has the power to do it."

"If someone would tell me what happened to me, it could help speed up this process," I said through a sigh.

"I wish it were that easy … but the only way for you to break through is if you remember on your own. Both go hand and hand."

I took my attention from out the window and faced her. "Do you know what happened to me?"

Dr. Conway took a moment to answer. Her big brown eyes looked past me like I'd seen my father's do so many times before. "From your father's point of view … yes, but it's never going to be enough." She stood and walked over to the bookshelf before plucking a novel and handing it to me. "Here is your first assignment."

"I don't read," I flatly said.

"From this point on, you do." She took a seat in her chair. "I will see you Monday. You need to be prepared to tell me what you think."

I looked down at the book titled *To Kill a Mockingbird*.

"That's it? I've been here for all of five minutes, and you want me to leave and read a stupid book?"

38

"I'll see you on Monday, Mia. Enjoy your weekend." Dr. Conway swiveled in her chair and turned her back to me. "Oh, and leave the door open on your way out for my next appointment."

The lady had no boundaries, unlike the other counselors I'd seen in the past.

I threw my stack of books across my desk when I reached my room and sprawled out over my bed. The clock above my door read 2:32 PM. Three hours left until dinner.

I stuffed the pillow over my face to block out the light, and not even two seconds later, there was a knock at my door. I opened it to find a man I'd never seen before with a satchel around his shoulder.

"You've got mail," he said, holding up an envelope. He had to be in his thirties. The wrinkles around his eyes deepened when he smiled, and his black hair fell over his dark hazel eyes.

"Dolor has a mailman?"

He shook his head. "Security guard, still in training. I do the dirty work."

He was cute, something I could work with. I fisted his shirt at his chest and pulled him into the room without thinking about the consequences. The mail in his hands dropped to the floor at our feet, and the door automatically closed behind us.

His eyes went wide. "I'm not allowe—"

"Oh, hush," I ordered and pushed him over my bed. I needed this. It was at the top of "Mia's Hierarchy of Needs," especially after the day I'd had. He just so happened to be at the right place and time.

I stripped off my clothes in seconds, and his eyes darted back and forth from me to the door, trying to decide which head to listen to. I pulled a condom from its box, the one I'd slipped into my suitcase, knowing it would eventually come in handy. "What's your name?"

A wicked smile grew across his face. "Oscar."

"This is your only chance, Oscar," I said, fanning the condom in the air as I stood naked before him. His lust-filled eyes gave up moral as he quickly undid his belt and pulled down his pants. His manhood sprung free, and I threw the condom over his stomach so he could put it on. "No talking, and don't you dare try to kiss me."

He nodded enthusiastically as he lay back against my bed. His abs flexed as he stroked the condom on in a matter of seconds.

I kneeled over him, straddling him as I gripped his length in one hand. He let out a moan as his eyes raked over my body. It didn't take long before he was inside me. I closed my eyes as I rocked against him, unable to watch what I was doing to him. His hands cupped my breasts and pinched my nipples as he cursed under his breath.

And at 2:36 PM, the trainee had already reached climax.

FOUR

"Moments don't go away,
they bury and become you."

OLIVER MASTERS

T ime stood still at Dolor. I'd officially been here a week, and everyone walked aimlessly from one class to the next in a fog as the seconds seemed like hours, myself included. I was sure boredom would be the death of me.

The only action—*and variety*—I got was from Oscar, the trainee, who came by on Tuesdays and Thursdays to drop off letters and useless cash my father sent me.

The only purpose of sex with Oscar was to pass the time and allow me to take control of my mundane schedule. I'd been called many names throughout high school. Slut. Whore. Floozy. You name it—I was called it. It never bothered me in the way it killed other girls' confidence, and it had almost destroyed Sarah's, my only so-called acquaintance in high school.

I tried to ignore it, but the crying only got worse in the bathroom stall behind me. Rolling my eyes, I nudged the stall door with my foot to see if it was locked, and it was.

After groaning, I called out, "Please, for the love of god, stop crying."

But she didn't.

"Open the damn door," I said, unsure of why I was irritated by it, only wanting it to stop.

The lock clicked, and weight carried the door open. Sitting over the toilet—pants up, thank god—was a chubby girl with blonde hair and big blue eyes. Her tear-soaked face was red. She looked silently up at me.

"What are you crying over?" I asked her.

She tried to catch a breath as her eyes and nose drained into her hands.

"I made a mistake." Her voice was shaky and words barely audible.

I leaned against the door, unsure if I had the energy to get involved. It wasn't sympathy I had for the girl. I honestly couldn't give two shits as to why she was crying, but I was bored and curious. "What did you do?"

She chewed her lip to stop the trembling. "I had sex with Trey Sullivan."

Air blew out of my nose as I let out a light chuckle. "And let me guess, he told everyone." She nodded as another tear fell, and I continued, "And Mallory and her whole posse let you have it? Slut shaming you?"

She nodded again.

"You screw around a lot?"

The girl narrowed her eyes as if my question was insulting.

"Hey, I like to fuck, too. I've been with Trey and his micro-dick. You can be honest with me."

Her shoulders relaxed, and her tears finally stopped. "I don't know why I do it … I guess I like the attention."

Exhaling, I fell back against the stall and crossed my arms. "Let me tell you something. The only person you need to worry about is yourself. If having sex with people makes you happy, and it makes you feel good, then who cares what other people think? That's the problem with people these days … Everyone wants to put others down because of their own insecurities. So, every time someone calls you a slut, what they're actually saying is, 'Man, I wish I was secure with my sexuality.' Anytime someone calls you a tramp, what they're really saying is, 'I'm fucking jealous I couldn't experience it myself.'"

The girl's eyes went wide, and her smile grew. "You really think so?"

"I know so. It's been proven single girls who have casual sex with multiple partners have higher self-worth and body image. Look it up if you don't believe me. They also have higher standards when they are ready to be in a relationship. I'm not saying go out there and sleep around as much as you can … All I'm saying is girls like Mallory and boys like Trey are the ones who are insecure." I shrugged. "No one has a right to insult something they can't understand, and tears shouldn't be wasted on misunderstandings."

The girl giggled, and I cringed. "You're unbelievable …" She smiled. "What's your name?"

"Mia."

"Sarah," she said as she pointed at herself. "I think we should be friends, Mia."

I forced a smile in return. "I don't do the whole 'friends' thing."

"What do you do, then?"

"Men with more to offer than a micro-penis, for starters …"

We both shared a laugh, and I would never admit it to anyone, but it was the only time I had been genuinely nice to someone.

Jake was the only one I couldn't seem to avoid since he couldn't take a hint. He was like an obnoxious dog looking for a bone, and I could only take him in small doses. He wasn't half bad, but that didn't mean I was going to keep in touch with him after Dolor. Every day, he begged me to join his friends for their midnight rendezvous, and every day I declined.

Until tonight.

I got the impression he would continue to harass me until I agreed. Plus, boredom was eating me alive from the inside out, and I supposed going would be better than reading the book Dr. Conway had given to me last week.

Doors automatically locked on time. Stanley completed his nightly security routine. Midnight came around, and I paced my small dorm room in my flannel pajama shorts and a plain white tee, talking myself out of it at the last minute. Who was I kidding? Shit like this had my name written all over it. My head fell back to see a vent big enough to fit a body through, but I had no idea how I was supposed to reach it.

The desk wasn't heavy. I moved my bed to the center of the room and somehow managed to lift my desk on top of it before climbing up. Standing over my makeshift mountain, I pushed up the vent to find the bolts already loose. *I swear, if there is a dead body up here, I will have both of Jake's heads—one in each hand.*

The distinct sound of Jake's giggle echoed through the maze in the ceiling. After crawling four blocks to my left, I reached the opening to where the party was going on, and poked my head in to see Alicia's curly hair below.

Alicia pointed up when she noticed me. "No way!" She moved out of the way. "Someone help her?"

Ollie appeared under the vent, wearing a black tee, sweatpants, and a smile reaching his exceptional green eyes. "Come on down, love," he called out, and I pushed my feet through the hole. "I have you." His fingers wrapped around my ankles before his hands slid up my hips and continued to pull me down until my feet reached the ground. His hands lingered around my waist, reluctant to break the connection.

"It's about time," he whispered as he scanned my face, then took my hand and held it high above my head. "Mia, everyone."

"Mia!" The group repeated in a cheer, and Ollie looked down at me as our arms dropped between us. His mouth quirked up to the side. "Welcome to my humble abode."

My eyes fell on Jake who sat on the floor wearing a red onesie and a content smile.

Yes, a fucking onesie—with candy canes, I might add.

Ollie's room had barely any furniture. No desk, no chair, no bed frame. Only a mattress on the floor and his clothes in a pile tucked away in a corner beside the mattress. How the hell was I supposed to get out of here?

"You already know Jake and Alicia. This here is Bria," Ollie introduced with his hand extended toward the pixie-haired girl sitting on the floor. "And this is my mate, Isaac." Ollie patted Midnight's chest beside him, the same guy I'd seen him talking to in the mess hall.

44

Isaac was without a shirt, showing off his naturally tanned and toned muscles and carrying a kind of swagger I'd seen before, and I knew immediately we could have some harmless fun together.

Ollie's green eyes fell back on me. "Have a seat. Tell us your story."

Everyone else settled back in their spots, either on the mattress or on the floor as I took a seat next to Ollie on the floor over the blanket.

"I'd rather not." All my opening up was saved for Dr. Conway and group therapy. At least they were licensed, unlike the peers sitting before me who couldn't be older than twenty-one. They had their own problems, their own judgments, and their own opinions. All these kids wanted was something else to keep their minds off their own complicated life.

"We're all screw-ups here, Mia. Give us something to talk about," Bria begged, unknowingly proving my point.

"Anger issues? Lawbreaker? Psychotic?" Isaac rambled off.

Five pairs of anxious eyes were on me.

"I killed my mom," I somewhat lied, and a stillness took over the room as the crew shot glances back and forth.

"Shit," Ollie breathed, reaching into his pocket.

Isaac held out the palm of his hand. "Pay up, Masters."

My eyes went wide as I watched the exchange of currency. "You're kidding. You guys made a bet? Getting me here was all a game to you?"

"Relax, darling," Isaac said as he pocketed his winnings. "Don't take it personal."

The group broke out into conversation as I sat in discomfort. For one, I would not peg any of them to belong in a place like this. Jake was a push-over, you could tell by the way he leaned on Alicia for social support. And I admit Alicia was cool. She didn't take the snickers from Bria and called her out on her shit. Alicia was beautiful. Her skin was smooth and dark, her eyes were the color of a hazelnut, and thick black ringlets framed her oval face. But the icing on the cake was the precious mole on her cheek. *If only I were into girls …*

Bria, on the other hand, portrayed herself as the sexy one with her cropped shirt and no bra. I was not judging. Whatever made her feel good about herself. She sought after the small moments when she would adjust her positioning, her head darting between Isaac and Ollie, taking notice in the way they looked at her, or if they looked over at her at all. She had a nice body, small perky breasts, and a long curvy torso. But as soon as she opened her mouth, her crooked teeth and annoying voice ruined her image.

Isaac *did* notice Bria's subtle movements. It was interesting how each time she leaned back and her shirt would rise higher, he leaned back and itched the tip of his nose with his thumb and finger, thinking it would hide his thoughts.

Ollie's entire body was pointing toward me now and I wondered if it was to avoid Bria's body language or because he was into me. It could have easily swung either way.

I never said I was a mind reader.

Even though I disliked humans, and tried to avoid conversations, I was brilliant at reading people's body language. Their motives. My father refused to watch movies with me because I could always call out who the killer was or predict the ending, but in situations like this, I had the upper hand. After many years of studying human behavior, there were no surprises. Actions of men were expected, the reactions of women just as predictable.

Take the trainee, Oscar, for instance. I knew the moment I opened the door he would submit himself to me—the way his eyes dilated as he leaned into the doorframe. It was typical. But he hadn't believed my advancements until I'd undressed before him. He could have said no, he could have walked away, but he wouldn't have.

Ollie pulled a bottle of vodka from his pile of things, and everyone's face lit up. "Now for the real fun." He waved the bottle from side to side and returned to sit beside me.

"Seriously? But how were you able to get the liquor in?" Perhaps Ollie had connections.

A twisted smile appeared over Ollie's face as he winked at me. He ran his empty hand up his forehead and through his thick brown mess on his head. "Someone ready for a good time, yeah?"

Alcohol and I never mixed well. People normally succumbed to the pleasure of alcohol drowning their emotions, but it had the opposite effect on me. With alcohol in my veins, I tended to feel things, want things. After taking a sip, I passed the bottle to Jake beside me as the clear liquid sizzled down my throat and burned in my chest.

The bottle continued to be passed along within our disheveled circle.

"We only have one rule," Alicia said to me from across the circle once the bottle reached her.

"Yeah? What's that?"

"No hurt feelings. Whatever happens in this room, stays in this room," Jake answered.

No feelings? *Perfect.*

I nodded in agreement, relieved I wasn't in a room with a bunch of little bitches.

After about an hour of banter back and forth, and everyone taking their fair share of vodka, I was finally able to enjoy a buzz for the first time in what it seemed like forever. I never needed a high—or a low—but it did help awkward situations such as this. I only hoped after the side effects of the buzz wore off, the paralysis of my feelings wouldn't hit me ten times harder like it had in the past.

Living without emotions was easy; it was the coming out of an induced emotional state that was hard—like an addict trying to get sober. Alcohol and drugs made me feel, and if I wasn't careful, tonight could get bad.

Low music filled the room from somewhere, and I looked down in Ollie's lap to see an older model iPhone. I didn't bother asking questions, and honestly, I didn't care to know the answers. He could wheel out a popcorn machine, and I wouldn't be surprised at this point. As long as he shared with me, and made my time here a little enjoyable.

Bria was feeling a vibe and stood to her feet. Her hips swayed back and forth as she lifted her arms above her head. The bottoms of her breasts peeked from under her cropped shirt. She sucked in her lips and scanned the room to see if the boys were paying attention to her. Following her gaze, I caught Isaac watching as he gnawed at his bottom lip from the edge of the mattress. Glancing to my right, Ollie's eyes met mine when the corners of his lips turned up.

The temperature was rising. One room, too many people, and that dimple.

"Come on, Mia," Bria begged with the come-hither finger. "Come dance with me."

Waving my hand in front of me, I said, "No, I don't dance." The only dancing I did was alone in my room.

Ollie tilted his head in my direction and raised a brow. "What are you afraid of?"

"I'm not afraid of anything. I just don't dance."

Isaac stood and joined Bria. Her body rubbed up against his pelvis to an electronica song as his reckless hands gripped her sides.

"I thought you and Bria were together," I said casually, looking over to Ollie. I knew this wasn't the case, but I was curious to see everyone's reaction to the idea.

Jake and Alicia spit out a laugh as Ollie shook his head.

"No, definitely not," Ollie said through an incredulous chuckle.

"There are no relationships at Dolor," Jake added.

Alicia's smile quickly dissolved and she turned her attention toward Bria and Isaac dancing.

"Really? Relationships aren't allowed?"

Jake leaned in. "Oh, there's no rules against it … but trust me when I say, you don't want to be in one."

"And why is that?" I didn't like people telling me what I could and couldn't do, even if a relationship was at the bottom of my list.

Alicia, Jake, and Ollie exchanged glances until Ollie faced me again. "A long story for another day."

"So, where you from?" Alicia quickly changed the subject just as Bria lifted her arms and wrapped them around Isaac's neck. Her cropped shirt raised higher, nipples almost showing. Isaac dragged his hand up her side to her breast and grabbed a handful, caressing beneath the thin fabric.

As I winced, Bria moaned while her eyes stayed on Ollie, but Ollie was oblivious as he scrolled through the music on the phone.

After a few seconds of the groping, Bria turned around and kissed Isaac. Not an innocent kiss, either. This was a tongue-dueling, spit-swapping, manic kiss, and I'd forgotten Alicia's question altogether.

"I ... eh ..." I snapped my head away from the two who were locking lips and back to Alicia. "P.A."

"P.A.?"

"Pennsylvania." I took another swig of vodka as Jake stood. He made his way toward Isaac and Bria with his bottom lip between his teeth.

All three of them danced. Well, I wouldn't use the term "dance." I didn't even know what term to use to explain what they were doing. They looked like three mammals in Antarctica fighting for warmth.

Alicia and I went back and forth with irrelevant questions to pass the time, and finally, the perfect amount of drunk hit, and I was feeling good, but not good enough to participate in the friction of the three starved animals.

Somehow our conversation went from twenty-one questions to laughing about Stanley, the security guard. Ollie sat with his long legs out in front of him and ankles crossed, leaning on his hands behind him and listening intently. The weight of his gaze stayed on me as I turned my attention back to the entertainment of Isaac, Jake, and a sweating Bria dancing.

"Come on, Ollie. There's room for you in here, too," Bria whined. Ollie shook his head, and Bria made a pouty face. "For once in your life, have a little fun."

"What are you afraid of, Ollie?" I asked mockingly as I bumped him in the shoulder with mine.

A nervous smile rose, and his adorable dimple appeared. "That." He nudged his head Bria's direction. "I'm afraid of whatever that is and what it will eventually turn into. That's not my cuppa tea."

Bria pulled Jake's face down to hers and they kissed. My eyes almost popped out of their sockets. "I thought he was gay," I whispered over to Alicia.

Ollie looked over to the mammals for the second time tonight. "He is," he stated simply.

What in the hell did I walk—or drop—into?

Alicia lifted her shoulders in a half shrug before she stood to join the other three, leaving me alone on the floor with Ollie.

"What about you?" Ollie asked.

"What about me?"

"Are you the type of girl to have fun or the kind who sits back and watches everyone enjoying themselves?"

"I don't know … neither … both." I sighed. "I usually don't drink, so I suppose drinking is my way of letting loose tonight."

Ollie smiled and leaned over on one elbow. "Why don't you drink?"

"Because I like being in control, and I don't want to end up doing things like that…" I pointed over to Bria making out with Isaac. "I don't kiss people. I've slept around but kissed only a few—fewer times than I can count on one hand. The act is too personal."

Ollie raised a brow. "You're trying to tell me kissing is more personal than sex?"

"Yes, both psychologists and scientists can prove kissing is more intimate than sex."

Ollie tried to control his lips, but small laughs blew through them.

"Laugh all you want, but it's true. You ever saw *Pretty Woman*?" Ollie shook his head as he recovered from his smile. "It's about a prostitute who meets a man. They have sex but agree not to kiss. But eventually they do, and once the kiss happens, everything changes."

"You're full of it," he said to me. "Sounds to me you haven't met the right one to prove you otherwise." He raised a challenging brow.

I glanced back at the other four dancing, lost in music and alcohol swimming in their veins, and decided I was done being boring. I brought myself to my knees and knelt in front of Ollie. He lifted himself back on his palms, supporting his upper half, and his expression changed.

"What are you doing?" he asked.

"Don't worry. I don't want to kiss you … I want to prove something." A sudden rush of adrenaline hit me all at once.

Ollie's mouth parted slightly before he nodded. He cleared his throat. "Alright."

Straddling his lap, I faced him and he lifted off his hands and leaned forward. He placed his hands over my lower back and dragged me closer to him. Our faces were now only inches away from each other. I tried to avoid eye contact. I hadn't thought this through. What *was* I thinking? Why was I doing this again? My mouth opened to say something, but nothing came out as everything else around us blurred.

Then my eyes helplessly met his, and a sudden calmness swept over me. He held my gaze as he crossed over an invisible barrier to whatever was hiding inside me. My mouth moved, and I didn't recognize my own words. "Your desire to look into my eyes right now is far greater than the thought of sex, even though you just touched me and pulled me across your lap." My fingers found his warm arms, and he closed his eyes momentarily at the sudden touch. "At this point, you don't want sex. You want something far greater, something deeper. All you want is to feel close to me. You want to take in my scent, take in my breath—"

"How do you know what I want?" Ollie asked, his voice cracking. He was still. Unmoving. His arms rested over my thighs, and his hands hadn't moved from their spot on my back.

"Because I'm sitting on top of you, and you're scared to move. I'm surprised you were capable of speaking, since you hardly could get through that sentence."

Ollie's lip twitched, but his eyes remained locked on mine.

I continued, "You've dropped your guard already because I can see it in your eyes. But you're still afraid I won't accept you because I hear the worry in your breathing. Yet, you haven't turned away because you have already accepted all of me, and the anticipation of knowing it's mutual is worth every torturous second."

Ollie's eyes fell from mine to my mouth. He wet his lips. My heart pounded. His fingers inched below the back of my shirt until they found my bare skin. I sucked in a breath as he exhaled. His fingers grazed their way up my back until his palms rested over my sides. It felt right when it shouldn't—it shouldn't have felt like anything. He dropped his forehead to mine and his chest rose and fell unevenly. "And I can't kiss you?" His minted whisper over my lips sent a shiver across my skin.

I shook my head against his and he closed his eyes. "Normally, kissing would increase an attachment among both parties. It's the only sexual act that allows both people to equally penetrate and be penetrated with the same, incredibly sensitive body parts—which is the lips. The lips have the thinnest layer of skin on the body, along with the tongue. If you truly want to be connected to someone, mind, body, and soul, then kissing would accomplish that. Not sex."

There were only two sounds: my pulse and his erratic breathing.

"We can't kiss, Ollie. Now that we both know we have chemistry, if we took it further with kissing, you would fall for me." I shrugged. "It's science."

My breath staggered as his green eyes sparked with vulnerability I hadn't seen in him before. The transformation of his sincerity caused the ice block in my chest to pound against my ribcage. The sounds in the room grew distant as I struggled to maintain my point in all this. I could smell the mint from the gum in his mouth and tried to find words.

Anything, Mia. Say anything.

"Do you believe me now?" I whispered.

Ollie swallowed. Ollie licked his lips. Ollie nodded. And I attempted to get up from his lap when Ollie stopped me.

"Don't," he stated or pleaded—I couldn't quite tell. "It's my turn now." His eyes searched mine. "I don't understand your need to have to over analyze a situation, or turn to science to justify the way you look at me from across the mess hall—and trust me, I notice—but sometimes you have to let go and allow moments to happen the way they are meant to."

"Meant to?" My mouth went dry, and I was surprised my voice didn't shake under his intensity.

"Yes, moments like this are meant to happen, and you are fighting against it. Look what this alone is doing to us. Could you imagine what our kiss would be like?" He brought his thumb to my bottom lip and grazed his fingerprint across the surface. One simple touch and my entire body was caving. "Mia, after everything you said, give me a clear indication as to why I shouldn't at least try."

"Because …" *I'm losing control.* "Because I have rules."

His brows dipped and he pulled his head back. "Rules? You have more rules?"

"Yes, my 'don't let a boy fall for me' rule. It's a dangerous position for you to be in and it's for your own good." I stood from his lap, taking the music player along with me.

In an attempt to calm my nerves from what had just happened, I fell across the mattress on my stomach and looked through his music. The alcohol managed to bring a moment of relapse, and I had to stay away from the liquor for the rest of the night. I only felt when I was under the influence, and I hated the feeling. The feeling of my arms being tied behind my back with a dozen rifles pointed at me while stranded on a deserted field. A defenseless target, waiting for an open fire which could destroy me in a matter of seconds. Only this wouldn't kill me. At least not in the way I wanted it to.

My gaze slid down to Ollie on the floor, who was now lying on his back, facing the ceiling. He met my gaze and let out an exhale. "Why do I feel like you just took something from me?" His tone was low and controlled.

"You're drunk. It will pass eventually." I was sure of it, but he closed his eyes and shook his head in denial. Bringing my attention back to the playlist in front of me, I changed the music to the only song seeming to fit the moment. I pressed play on "Feel for Me" by an artist named Foy

Vance, which I didn't recognize. A beautiful acoustic guitar drifted from the small speaker, and the others groaned at the loss of their encouragement to dance, but I didn't care.

The others eventually died down as they all sprawled out over the floor. Their conversations became white noise in the background, and I lay on my stomach, resting my head over my folded hands, looking down at Ollie on the floor. His green eyes kept me steady as I relaxed under my tipsy spell, falling into a trance.

"Good choice in song," he said as we fixed on one another. "Science is wrong, you know."

"Science is never wrong."

He turned on his side to face me and held his head in the palm of his hand. "There are notions more powerful that even science can't grasp," he said, and I had no idea what he meant. My brain wasn't working correctly.

Ollie folded his arms under his head and stayed silent afterward. I couldn't break away from the steadiness of his green eyes as the room swayed around us. Distant laughter and chatter stayed behind Foy Vance's beautiful raspy voice. His lyrics poured from the speaker as if they were intended for my ears. Ollie's allure kept me locked, or Foy's—I couldn't quite tell anymore. "The coincidence …" I sighed out loud.

"What's the coincidence, love?" Ollie asked as the song changed.

"You, me, Foy, the vodka, Dolor, this country … all of it." I didn't even understand my own words as they were leaving my mouth. I wasn't making any sense, and I attempted to lift my head, but gravity was unforgiving.

"Is there a science to back up your coincidence?" Ollie's tone was honest, but the grin across his face said otherwise.

"Science and coincidences are unrelated."

FIVE

"I'm bulletproof,
yet she's slowly
penetrating every
part of me."

OLIVER MASTERS

eaving Ollie's dorm was far more complicated than entering. I wondered why he didn't have any furniture for us to climb onto to get out, but they configured a system: climbing on top of one another, then the first person pulling the next through the hole.

Right after six in the morning, I reached the bathroom and turned on the water in the last stall. Only a minute passed before the water got to its warmest level and I stepped in and closed the curtain. I'd timed it perfectly. Ollie always left before I arrived, and I'd managed to avoid the morning rush. As long as I reached the bathroom at 6:10 AM and left no later than 6:25 AM.

Before I had a chance to rinse out all the shampoo, my curtain flew open with an angry Bria on the other side.

"*Shit.* You scared me," I said, wiping water from my eyes. Bria crossed her arms over her chest and pressed her brows together. "What do you want, Bria?"

"You need to leave Ollie alone."

Rolling my eyes, I continued to rinse the rest of the shampoo out of my hair.

"I'm serious, *America.* Find your own play-thing. Ollie and Isaac are with me."

"I thought what happens in the dorm, stays in the dorm." Bria thought she could make me uncomfortable by confronting me in such a vulnerable state. Little did she know, I happened to be more comfortable naked than clothed, and Bria didn't budge as she continued to stare me down. "You're an idiot." I grabbed my towel from the hook and wrapped it around my body before pushing past her.

"Excuse me?" She followed me to the mirror as I pulled the toothpaste from the basket.

"It's the reactance theory. You discourage someone from doing something, their freedom threatened, and they will be even more motivated to regain control by doing the exact opposite," I popped the toothbrush in my mouth and turned to face her. "Because the forbidden fruit tastes *so* much sweeter."

She shifted onto her other leg and straightened her posture. Her short black hair was flat and not sticking up in the back like it usually did. She was the dark version of Tinker Bell, but instead of sprinkling fairy dust, she discharged ammo.

"You were better off not saying anything at all," I added.

"Just … stay away from him."

I spat a mouthful of toothpaste before pointing my toothbrush at her. "You presented me with a challenge, Bria, and the best part is … I have nothing to lose."

Bria and I stood eye to eye for what seemed like minutes before she finally turned on her heel and left. I loathed drama, but I enjoyed making girls squirm just as much. I had no interest in Ollie. Hell, I had no interest in anyone. But seeing her unravel the way she had at the thought of losing one of her "play-things" was an excellent way to start my morning.

The inability to feel for someone always prevented me from having anything more.

I'd tried faking it once, only to see how far the relationship could go, and if anything would develop, but nothing. Love was nothing more than a myth, something produced by major corporations to increase profit. According to *dictionary.com*, the verb definition of love means to love someone and be affectionate. The definition of affectionate means to love. Case in point.

Proving my theory once in a high school project, I surveyed fifty people on what love meant to them. Fifty different people, fifty different answers. No one could give me a clear explanation, and what happened when something couldn't be proven? The results were inconclusive.

I believed in chemistry and comfort. You felt comfort and ease around someone, so you didn't mind being around them all the time—hence, my father and Diane. My father found some sort of comfort in Diane, more than being alone, so he married her. Chemistry attracts two people together, comfort makes them stay. Simple explanation. What *dictionary.com* should have said was:

love (*verb*)

/ləv/

the perfect combination of chemistry and comfort

I sat at my usual table during breakfast and played with my wet eggs as the crew from last night made their way into the mess hall toward their table. Jake waved me over, but I turned away. I've had enough of them over the last twenty-four hours.

Soon after, Ollie pulled out a chair and took a seat before finding me across the room. In a matter of seconds, he managed to remind me of our moment from last night, and I bit the inside of my cheek to fight off the tightness in my chest. He offered me a sleepy, lopsided smile, and I averted my eyes.

Chemistry was the damn devil.

The bell rang. I stood in a hurry, grabbed my tray, and left the mess hall before anyone else, walking at a much faster pace than I should have been this early in the morning. The last thing I wanted was for Jake to catch up to me, or anyone else from last night. As soon as I turned the corner down the left wing, a hand reached out, grabbed my arm, and pulled me from the corridor and into an empty room.

Face to face with familiar green eyes, I backed against the wall. The room was dark aside from a hint of the morning sun's rays coming through the window. Ollie leaned over me and rested each palm against the wall beside me. The smell of mint became a passenger between us as he licked his lips. His gum switched from one side of his mouth to the other before my eyes lifted to his. "I can't stop thinking about last night," he admitted. "This morning I woke up sober, and still feel a part of me is missing."

I opened my mouth, and when nothing came out, I closed it again. Ollie was breathing hard. I was breathing hard. His chest rose and fell with every breath. I couldn't break away from his stare.

"You said it would pass, but it didn't. And then in the mess hall, you can't even look at me … but I want to be seen by you, Mia." His eyes scanned my face. "I really like it."

"You like being looked at?" *Finally, words.* I was able to speak.

He raised a brow. "It does feed my narcissism, but it's different with you." He lifted a hand off the wall. "Even though you claim this to be so dangerous."

I straightened my posture when he took a step back. "You have no idea what you're getting yourself into."

His face was unreadable, and with my books clutched to my chest, I pushed passed him and walked out the door. He remembered every detail of last night—the confessing of my rules and the dangers of crossing the line—then had the nerve to use it against me. He was playing with fire, and in the end, he would get burned.

58

As I walked into Latin, I had come to the conclusion they were all crazy. People like Bria and Ollie walked around with rules they couldn't live up to, like "no hurt feelings," and I should have known better. Whatever happened in Ollie's dorm would never stay in Ollie's dorm, but at least I was the one who couldn't get hurt. I had decided to have my fun with them, and when everything came crashing down, it would be me laughing in the end.

I took a seat beside Liam. He was a year younger than me, and a complete asshole, but I enjoyed every second of it. With blond hair pulled back into a man bun, and full lips, I could see why the girls surrounded him. He was like me in a lot of ways. Perhaps the reason I stuck to him on Tuesdays and Thursdays.

We walked together to lunch, but I refused to sit with him and his friends. His group was something my old self would typically be drawn to, and a part of me did want to change. I kept telling myself I didn't care whether or not I ended up in a mental institution, but I knew somewhere deep down, I didn't want to go there, and if I fell into the arms of Liam's group, I would never make it out of here alive.

"What are your plans tomorrow?" Liam asked as we stood in the lunch line.

"I don't know … homework, I guess. What else is there to do on Fridays?"

Liam put his arm around my shoulder and turned me toward the students in the mess hall. He pointed over to the jocks, all of them with muscles bulging from their Dolor shirts and punching each other in the shoulder. "Every Friday, they have a game of football in the yard." He turned my attention to the group of girls at the table beside them. Gwen was the only one I knew by name. She flipped her short blonde hair as she talked into another girl's ear. Liam continued, "The girls sit off to the side and watch as they bat their pretty eyes." His fingers landed on a table seating six thugs. "Poker in the courtyard, 10 quid buy-in." And, finally, he pointed toward Ollie. Ollie clenched his jaw as Liam leaned into my ear. "They take off to the woods and … no one really knows what the fuck they do. They're all rubbish."

"What about you?" I asked, turning my attention away from Ollie's tense position.

Liam smirked and pulled me to his side. "Meet us after breakfast in the morning and have a gander, yeah?"

His choice of words made me smile. "I'll think about it."

After eating the horrible cheese sandwich at my table, I pulled *To Kill a Mockingbird* from my stack of books and read, keeping my attention away from Ollie at all costs, and not giving in to his narcissistic behavior.

"Mia, you're late," Dr. Conway stated and flicked her eyes over to the clock on the wall behind the couch.

After taking a seat on the sunken brown leather, I handed her the book. "I finished the book. It sucked. What was the point in wasting my time?"

Dr. Conway grabbed the book and placed it back in its rightful place on the bookshelf. "That was only a warm-up. Tell me why you didn't like it."

"You're kidding, right?" I leaned back into the leather and ran my fingers across the cracks in the arm of the couch. "You have a middle-class, middle-aged man who wants to teach his kids lessons in life, but then calls a rape victim a liar, and basically a slut. The author took advantage of the on-going racism in America to sell millions of copies, and give off the impression rape victims are asking for it and should be ignored. I can't believe they allow this shit in grade school."

Dr. Conway's brows lifted at my response. "Interesting … So, from all the characters, who do you think you could relate to the most?"

"This is ridiculous. What's my next assignment?" I turned out the window toward the front of the building where the gates were. The things I would have done to be on the other side of them right now and far away from here.

60

"You have a writing assignment." Dr. Conway swiveled in her chair and grabbed a pad of paper and handed it to me. "From this point on, I want you to spend at least twenty minutes a day free-writing. Write whatever comes to mind. I don't care what it's about. Put pen to paper, free your mind, and write."

"That's it for today, then?"

Dr. Conway gave me a hard look. She pressed her mouth together in a line, contemplating her next words carefully. I turned away from her and back at the window. The only sound in the room was the second hand on the clock clicking away and the air conditioning vent rattling.

"Whatever you have to say, just say it," I said through an exhale. "I can do this all day."

"I want to ask you a question, but I don't want you to answer. I want you to really think about it ..." She leaned back in her chair and folded her hands together over her crossed knees. "If today was the last day of your life, would you spend it differently?" My lips parted, but Dr. Conway held up a hand. "I don't want you to answer."

The funny thing was, I had no idea what I was about to say. Surely it couldn't have been some life-changing epiphany. More like a sarcastic remark. I didn't know if I would do anything differently today. I had my fuck appointment with two-humps-and-done Oscar. If I didn't wake up tomorrow, would I want my vagina's last moments to be with Sir Grunts-a-lot? Did I even really want to have sex with him at all?

Dr. Conway and her stupid question had me reeling. I grabbed my stack of books off the side table and gave her a curtsy. "Cheerio," I said in my best British accent before taking off.

After turning the corner of my wing toward my dorm, my eyes fell on Ollie who waited outside my door. My head rolled back at his presence. I had exactly five minutes before Oscar arrived.

"Is your narcissism running low? Need some more gawking to fuel it?" I asked with wide, ogling eyes and a smile.

Ollie's hand shot to his chest as if it were a blow to his ego, but he followed up with a crooked smile. "So, you and Liam friends now, yeah?"

"No, I don't need friends. I prefer solitude."

Ollie dropped his head and peered over at me with disbelieving eyes.

And there it was, the same incredulous look I'd seen in both his drunken and sober states. Even in disbelief, he was authentic. I liked that about Ollie. He was simple—easy. When I wore my venom on my sleeve, he wore his emotions. I never had a need to guess what kind of person he was or what he thought because he always came out and said it. He was not complicated, but this thing between us was.

"Then how do you expect to smile like you are right now all by yourself?" he asked.

Shit. I hadn't realized I was smiling. I pressed my lips together. "I'm not smiling," I mumbled through a controlled mouth.

Ollie threw his head back and ran a hand down his face. "I haven't got a chance with you, love. Tell me, when was the last time you actually laughed? Wait … do you even laugh?"

"Oh, is that the purpose of having a friend? You think you can make me laugh?"

"You and I could never be friends, Mia, but yes, I have a few jokes." Ollie leaned in. "But you can't tell anyone. It may ruin my cool reputation here."

I'm glad we were on the same page with the whole "friend" thing, but I couldn't help but think there was some hidden meaning behind the way he'd said it.

Shifting my heavy books to my other arm, I sighed. "Alright, let's hear them."

"I have you laughing, you let me inside?" he asked, taking the books from my arms. "I'll hold these in the meantime. No need to thank me …" His smile turned smug.

Resting my hand over my hip, I dropped my head to hide my smile from his fortitude. There no way he could succeed now I was prepared for it.

"Knock, knock," he said with a poker face, and I pressed my lips together.

A damn knock-knock joke? The determination on his face and his youthful antics could have ruined me alone. This was going to be much harder than I thought. "Who's there?"

"Tank."

"Tank who?"

"I told you no need to thank me, but you're welcome." He held up his empty palm with a wide smile.

My hand shot over my mouth to hide my grin, and I shook my head.

Ollie reached for my hand. "Did I see a smile under there?"

I took a step back. "You made me smile, but I haven't laughed."

"*Fuck.* Alright, one more."

I held up a finger to regain a straight face.

Ollie waited patiently, his eyes never leaving mine. "You good now?"

I nodded.

"Knock, knock."

"Who's there?

"Water."

I mimicked his accent, "Water who?" And the second it rolled off the tongue, I completely lost it as a loud laugh belted through my lips. My hands flew back over my mouth.

Ollie threw his palm in the air. "What was that? Your British accent?" He laughed between questions and brought two fingers to his eyes. "It was terrible … and you ruined it!"

I managed to catch my breath as I held up my hand. "Technically, I made myself laugh."

"As long as you're laughing." Ollie leaned back against the wall and propped his foot up with a daydream look in his eyes. "With a laugh like yours, you should always be doing it."

Oscar would be here any second, and for some reason, I didn't want to see him. Grabbing Ollie's hand, I surprised myself by saying, "Let's get out of here." I didn't want Oscar's hands all over me. What I wanted was to keep this smile for as long as possible. Dr. Conway's words replayed in my head. *"If today was your last day, would you spend it differently?"* And I supposed I would.

I led Ollie in the opposite direction toward his room. Once we were behind closed doors, I fell over his mattress as Ollie dropped my books on the floor against the wall.

"Isn't this dangerous?" he asked, standing tall. A dimple peeked beside his smile as he stood in the middle of his dorm room. He ran a hand through his hair before glancing around the room, unsure of what to do with himself.

"Extremely, but I can't be in my room for another second." I folded my arms behind my head and looked up to the ceiling. "My dorm is suffocating. Heck, this whole place is suffocating."

Ollie took a seat on the floor beside the bed, pulled his legs up, and rested his arms across his knees. "I see what you mean, but you have to look at the positives, or it will drive you crazy."

"Yeah, and what's the positives?" I asked, turning on my side to face the back of his head.

"If this place didn't exist, where would you be now?"

Where would I have been? What a loaded question. I could have been a runaway living off the streets in New York City. I could have been dead, buried six feet under and soon forgotten. I could have been in jail. But out of every scenario, I knew exactly where I would have been if this place didn't exist.

When I didn't answer right away, he turned around to face me. He stretched his long arm across the mattress in front of me, and after studying my face, he arched a brow.

"A mental institution," I said through a sigh.

"Right …"—another disbelieving expression—"because you killed your mum…"

Why couldn't anyone believe I had killed someone?

Narrowing my eyes, I teased him with my past. "Are you scared I'm going to hurt you, Ollie? You believe I'm capable?"

Ollie drew his fingers closer to my hand that was lying flat against the mattress between us. "Not in the way you're thinking," he said simply, but all I could focus on were his fingers not touching mine, and whether or not I wanted them to.

"Why are you here?" I asked, not really caring to know the answer. My need for distracting my mind from his distant hand weighed heavier.

"That's a conversation for another day."

"Let's have your notions decide then," I said, remembering his words from the night before. He believed in something stronger than science, and I couldn't judge him for it. Most people believed in that shit.

"What are you proposing?"

"We'll use music to decide the next ..." I glanced up at the same clock as mine above Ollie's door "... two hours. Where's your phone?"

Ollie reached under his mattress for the phone and handed it over to me.

"Think of it as a magic eight-ball. I push shuffle, and it'll answer our questions based on the lyrics." I looked over to him for a hint of understanding, and he rolled his head back but eventually agreed. "First question, why is Ollie here?"

Ollie nervously laughed as I pressed shuffle and a song I'd never heard before came through its speakers. The bright screen read it was "Lean on" by Major Lazer.

Glancing up from the bright screen, Ollie's mouth dropped open. "That's fucking weird," he breathed as he looked at the phone and back at me as if I'd done some kind of magic trick.

"Didn't have anyone to lean on?" I grinned.

He grabbed the phone out of my hand. "We're still not getting into it. My turn." He waited in thought while the chorus played for a second time and shook his head before he continued, "Oh, magic eight ... phone, should Mia get up and dance right now?" he asked into the phone and peeked over at me with a wayward smile.

Shuffle was pressed.

The intro to "Killing Me Softly with His Song" by The Fugees flowed, and Ollie's eyes widened as a smile crept across his face. "That's it … you have to get up, Mia. You can't turn down the Fugees, it's an unsaid law." He stood and pulled me off the mattress until both feet of mine were planted in the middle of the dorm room. My face flushed and Ollie, with a massive grin, fell back over the mattress. "Come on, love," Ollie teased, and held up his head in his hand. "The notions are saying you have to dance."

And finally, I did. My hips swayed to the smooth beat, lost in the rhythm. Adrenaline rushed through me as Ollie's eyes followed my body's flow. His eyes met mine as they burned with fever. "You're missing out," I said with a teasing conviction.

Ollie's eyes beamed back at me with a wild smile. "I can promise you I'm not."

Before the song came to an end, I grabbed the phone from his hand. "What is Ollie thinking right now?" And I pressed the almighty powerful shuffle button.

Kings of Leon's "Sex on Fire" played and I hunched over as a loud laugh came from inside me. Ollie's stuffed his face into a pillow and my laughter turned into the quiet kind as my vision turned cloudy.

"This whole thing has got to be rigged somehow," he said with flushed cheeks. He quickly jumped to his feet and towered over me while trying to grab the phone from my possession. My laughs only increased as he pinned me to his torso and wrestled the phone from my hand.

"Is your sex on fire, Ollie?" I asked through each breathless laugh.

He was able to secure the phone from me and fell back over the mattress as I sang the song with an air guitar and an invisible drum set. Around him I was free, stuck in a natural high as I whipped my hair and did stupid dance moves. Ollie watched me in awe, and I enjoyed the way I physically affected him. The dimple, the blushing, the glowing smile. It was all worth every embarrassing move as his eyes radiated in my direction.

"Should Mia leave or stay with me?" he hesitantly asked out loud and pressed the button.

An unfamiliar song played. He glanced up at me and waited for my reaction.

My laughing dissolved as I tried to recognize the tune. "What song is this?"

He smiled. "Wait for it."

I put my hands on my hips as I waited for a voice to come through, and when it did, I grabbed the phone from him and looked on the screen. It read, "Nice to Meet You Anyway," by Gavin DeGraw. *What the hell?* I tossed the phone over the mattress beside him and turned to leave since we were now following by the rules of my own game.

"Uh-uh. Where you going?" He wrapped his long arms around my waist, pulling me back. Shrieking, I fell on top of him and onto his small bed. "Gavin might think differently, but you're not leaving," he said through a laugh. Ollie rolled me over to his side, and when our eyes met, our laughter slowly faded.

We were so close, his staggering breath reached my lips. His fingers applied an eager amount of pressure to my side as his eyes wandered from my eyes to my mouth, and I had to concentrate on breathing to make sure I still was.

"Ollie ..." I breathed.

He trailed his fingers up my arms, and I couldn't seem to move. My body was under a spell of him. His warm hand left my arm and reached behind me for the phone still playing the Gavin DeGraw song.

Ollie turned his back and dangled the phone in front of him. His eyes darted over to me then back at the phone. "Should I kiss Mia?" he asked, then pressed shuffle.

I held my breath.

We can't kiss. I don't kiss.

It was a bad idea, but I couldn't seem to escape him. Did this mean I wanted to kiss him? I didn't know exactly what I was hoping for.

It seemed like forever had passed before a song played, but I knew it couldn't have been longer than a fraction of a second.

A beautiful acoustic melody from a guitar filled the dorm room. Another song I didn't recognize. The screen read it was "Rhythm Inside" by Calum Scott, and I couldn't understand what was happening.

Ollie closed his eyes, drew in a deep breath, and let it slowly go before he paused the song and tilted his head to face me. "Mia, this is fucking crazy. I really want to kiss you ..." His gaze moved back and forth between my eyes and my lips. "*Fuck, do I want to kiss you*, but I want you to listen to these words even more because I couldn't have said them better myself. Everything he says is how you make me feel when I'm around you."

I tried to swallow as he pressed play and placed the phone above our heads. He turned back on his side to face me. Calum's beautiful voice played in our ears, and Ollie moved the hair from my face and said, "Just listen."

And I did.

By the middle of the song, I had lost all sense of my past and future. The only thing in front of me was Ollie—my present, and I was surprised I still had a pulse because his eyes on me were breathtaking. It was as if they didn't belong anywhere else.

A mixture of panic and peace swept over me, and I couldn't make sense of it. My breath caught in my chest, and an undeniable pull brought my hands behind his head and into his brown hair. I nestled my face into his neck, and Ollie wrapped his long arms around my waist, pulling me close against him.

The coconut smell of his skin and his breath in my hair washed away the panic, and all that remained was the peace. It was the feeling of walking through the doors of your home after an extended vacation. The feeling of the bell ringing after the last class of the day, and the taste of ice-cold water on a hot day in July.

Peace.

Out of all the things that could have happened in his room, hugging him was never a possibility in my mind.

The lyrics said to show him what I was feeling, and for some unexplainable reason, I wanted to be close to him. Around Ollie, I actually had a feeling, and it overwhelmed me. I couldn't remember the last time I had hugged anyone. But I didn't want to hug anyone else. I wanted his arms around me, and to keep this satisfying feeling inside me for as long as possible.

He slowly, gently rubbed my back as he breathed into my neck, and we held on to each other as our legs intertwined—unsure of where he started, and I ended. Ollie didn't say another word, and neither one of us reached for the phone to ask another question. We lay in his bed as he cradled me and let the rest of the songs play out the way they were meant to.

SIX

"Beauty and pain
invade the same."

OLIVER MASTERS

The paradox of a hug was even though it was physically comforting, the healing properties to your mental state was just as powerful—if not more. For so long I had been under the impression I was so dead inside, I didn't need hugs. Though I lived with emotional detachment disorder, why did I so severely crave something so simple as a damn hug? And with my condition, why did it comfort me in the way it did?

Yes, I'd researched studies on human contact and the power of touch in my spare time, like I'd researched everything else under the moon. I'd wanted answers to everything—why people did the things they did— because I couldn't understand an action as simple as a hug, and even after all my research, I was still left confused. It wasn't until now, with Ollie's warm arms around me, his body pressed against mine, when I understood everything I had been reading. With Ollie, I'd found a safe place. I'd found refuge from the storm inside my head.

But as comforting as it felt, it was just as scary. And the fear slowly grew bigger and bigger, pulling Ollie's safety net out from under me with a force so much more powerful—the force of my past.

Instinctively, I pulled away and Ollie quickly searched my face. When he looked into my eyes—really looked—his face fell, and he slowly shook his head. "Where did you go?"

The air in my chest tightened as I knitted my brows together. "What do you mean? I'm right here." I understood him, though. A part of me was slipping.

He placed his hand over my cheek, and his warmth battled the gradually invading cold. "Your eyes ... Something's changed."

I pulled his hands away and rolled off the mattress until I got to my feet. "I have to go." Frantically, I searched the room as if I was about to leave something behind. *Oh, right, my books.* I picked up my books off the floor and took one last glance at Ollie. He lay confused over the mattress as if I'd pulled a chair out from under him. "I'll ... um ... I'll see you later."

Then, I walked out the door.

After dinner, I waited until right before curfew to head to the bathroom. Jake's squeals ricocheted from the opposite end of the bathroom as I ducked under and in between people to find an empty shower. He already had a new white tee on with his plaid pajama bottoms and Bart Simpson slippers covering his feet. With nowhere to run, I waved as the rest of his friends turned to see me.

Isaac was brushing his teeth in boxers with beer mugs all over them, and Alicia sat on the sink beside him, talking his ear off.

"It's always busy in here at night. When is the best time to come?" I asked as I set my things beside Alicia.

"In the morning," Bria said as she exited the shower stall fully dressed with a towel wrapped around her hair. "You have a better chance sharing a shower than finding your own this late at night."

Ollie strolled out of the shower beside Bria's with black boxer briefs clinging to his glistening skin. A collection of black tattoos painted along his chest and stomach as birds flew up his sides toward his back from a pair of hands. It was the first time I'd seen him this close without a shirt on, and the artwork hypnotized me.

Everything was black—the symbols on each bicep, the artwork scattering up his arms, and in the center of his torso, right below his chest, tree roots spiraled together into a silhouette of two people. He shook his head, and his hair sprayed water in all directions, knocking me out of his trance. When his eyes fell on mine, I lost the ability to move my feet as his lips parted. "Hi, love," I think he said, but my head felt submerged underwater.

"You coming through tonight, Mia, or what?" Isaac asked, pulling me from the tide.

I snapped my head to the side. "What's tonight?"

"We celebrate Thursday nights with something special," Bria whispered as her gaze roamed over the rest of them.

My gaze followed behind hers as everyone's faces lit up. Ollie dropped his head and turned away, and I wondered if he didn't want me to find out about it. "No, I'm good."

"Oh, c'mon, Mia. You can embrace us with your talents," Jake cut in. I narrowed my eyes at him and gave him a *shut-up* look. The last thing I needed was everyone requesting a read from me. I wasn't a circus act. What I had to say about the five of them would only hurt feelings, and once I opened my mouth, it was impossible to stop.

"What talents?" Ollie asked as he towel dried his hair.

"Nothing. Forget it." I disappeared behind the curtain and undressed, hoping the topic would cease.

"She wasn't fun, anyway. A waste of perfectly good vodka." Bria's whiney bitterness bounced off the tiles. "She doesn't deserve what we have in store tonight."

I saw right through her reverse psychology, but I couldn't understand why she wanted me there in the first place. She'd made it perfectly clear she didn't like me and didn't want me going after Isaac or Ollie.

"Still not coming, Bria," I shouted from under the water.

I did want to go—*shit*—but for some reason, I had to prove a point. I wasn't under Bria's influence like the rest of them, and although she couldn't control me, it did sound way better than staring at the ceiling in my room.

"Don't listen to her, Mia. Come and have a good time," Jake's voice boomed as the rest of them whispered to one another.

Rolling my head back under the water, I weighed my options. "I'll think about it," was all I could come up with at the moment.

Everyone had disappeared by the time I exited the shower, and I had one minute to get back to the dorm before the doors locked automatically for the night. After barreling down the hall, I made it safely behind my steel door with seconds to spare.

Jake, Isaac, and I sat around the blanket sprawled out on the floor in its usual place. Ollie sat on his mattress with his back against the wall, a touchy Bria beside him.

Alicia hadn't made it tonight, and it was even more awkward without her fearless mouth and spunky attitude to fill the void.

"What's so special about tonight?" I asked as the chatter disintegrated.

Ollie reached into the pocket of his sweatpants and pulled out a small plastic bag. Isaac sprang to his feet and crossed the small space to snatch it out of his hand. "No fucking way."

"Calm down, junkie. You think I'm feeding your roxie and oxy addiction? It's only mandy," Ollie said as Isaac examined the bag.

I lifted my head in Jake's direction. "What's mandy?"

"Ecstasy."

"Oh, we call it molly."

"Have you ever done it before?" Ollie asked from the mattress.

"Yeah. Once," I lied. Just because I was considered "no good" didn't mean I had a history with drugs, but confessing my lack of experience would only start another conversation I didn't want to have.

"Tonight's about to get weird," Isaac said, emptying the tablets into his hand. He was usually quiet, and this was the first time I'd seen him excited about anything. His dark brown eyes flicked over to me as he dropped a small pill into the palm of my hand.

Glancing over at Ollie, I popped the pill into my mouth and he slowly shook a disapproving head.

After the second tablet, it didn't take long for the effects to kick in. Jake's eyes went wide beside me. "Whoa," he said, or moaned—I couldn't tell anymore. "Mia, can I ask you a question? Actually, I'm not going to ask you … I'm just going to ask," Jake rambled, "should I go back to Jacob, or is Jake really a cooler name?"

"I like Jacob. I like Jake, too. But if you were to change your name, why not get something even cooler … like Cash, or Knox."

"Ooh, Knox. Call me Knox, yeah?"

"Okay, Knox. I'm going to try to stand up."

"Wait," Knox said, grabbing for my arm and stopping me. "What do you want me to call you?"

"You know, I never really thought about that." A laugh came from my lips as my favorite show popped into my head. "Crap-bag. Call me Crap-bag."

"Crap-bag?"

"Yeah, just think of a bag full of crap," I said, reciting the line through another spurt of laughter from the show *Friends*.

"*Crap*-bag. Crap-*bag*," Jake repeated as the whole room lit up around me.

All the colors were more defined. *Radiant.* Ollie's eyes burned into me from only a few feet away, but I swore it seemed like he was miles away

74

from me. Standing to my feet, I used the wall behind me for leverage before walking toward him and swiping the iPhone from the mattress. "We need a change in music. I need to dance." The screen was so bright, I had to pull the phone away for the words to make sense.

"Mia, you okay?" someone asked, and my eyes scanned the room to see where the haunting voice was coming from. "Mia?" Ollie looked up at me from the mattress. "You alright, love?"

"Never been better," I think I said, and pressed play on "Feel So Close" by Calvin Harris. The phone dropped from my hand as the room spun around me. The mattress beneath me was like a cloud, and I jumped in circles as a smile grew on my face. My entire being had a mind of its own as the chemicals took me over. I was feeling it: the music, the mandy, myself. Spinning in circles, my body felt like a feather floating in the air. *Drifting.*

Adrenaline coursed through my bloodstream and my smile became a permanent stain as my hands traveled up my waist and through my hair. Another pair of hands found my hips, and I turned to see Isaac wearing the same smile. He felt the same electricity as me, and this madness wasn't stopping anytime soon. The vibration influenced me, compelled me to let go and feel the music, and the music couldn't have been loud, but each pound of the bass beat harder, each stroke of a key more distinct.

Isaac pulled my back against him, and I peered down at Bria who watched us from Ollie's side. I had one of her men, and she couldn't claim them both in one night. Which one was more important to her?

The increasing tension in Ollie's green eyes was unmistakable as the music pounded in my ears and through my hips. My eyes closed, and Isaac spun me around from Ollie's glare and my fingers threaded through his dark hair before he dipped his head down.

Our lips had barely connected when a force pulled me away. I was lifted off the mattress and taken away, but I couldn't care about anything while floating on cloud nine. My head spun before Ollie's green eyes came into focus. I cocked my head. "Why did you do that?"

Ollie braced me against the wall and leaned into my ear. "You're fucked up right now. Isaac's bad news and I'm saving you from regret." I leaned over to look behind him and almost fell to the ground when Ollie caught me at the waist. "Mia. Look at me," he said with two fingers in front of his eyes. Distracted by the beautiful black ink running up and down his arms, I traced my fingers over the lines.

He tilted my chin until my eyes met his. His green bore into my brown. "There you are." He smiled and cupped my cheek, the touch of his thumb caressing my skin making me weak. "You're back."

I grabbed the back of his hand, keeping it on my face, afraid if I didn't, his hands would leave me. "What do you mean?"

"I can see a change in you sometimes. It's odd and hard to explain, but I know when you're with me, and I know when you're not. Not physically, but in here," Ollie said, bringing his free finger to my temple. "And in here." He moved his hand over my chest. His hand remained as each breath I took pressed against his palm. "Don't leave me this time, alright?"

"I want you to kiss me, Ollie."

What was I saying? Where was my filter?

Kiss me.

Ollie blinked a few times as he tried to push his smile away. "You don't know what you're saying."

"I want to know." I wasn't making sense, and I grew frustrated with myself, and with him for not giving me what I wanted. "Kiss me, Ollie … please," I begged.

No, I am not begging. God, please tell me I didn't just fucking beg.

Ollie shook his head. "No, you're not kissing anyone tonight."

Rejection.

For some reason, it hurt—more than it should have.

"Fine. Offer expired. I'm sure Isaac won't mind …" I ducked away from him and scanned the room. Isaac was dancing with Bria, and before I could take another step in any direction, Ollie grabbed my arm and pulled me back into his hold.

"Stop walking away from me, Mia." Pain filled his eyes, and his tongue wet his lips. He cupped my face again, and his forehead pressed to mine—undecided and struggling. "I can't handle it."

Then his mouth grabbed mine in desperate need.

Pressed back against the cold cement, our lips molded flawlessly together. He ran his thumb down my chin, and my lips parted for him before our tongues collided. An explosion of feelings went off in my heart as the rest of my skin tingled against his warmth. The taste of Ollie was the perfect mixture of mint and summer. *Ice and fire*. His lips became softer, as did our momentum. A gentle and slow rhythm of his tongue, of his hands, and his lips over mine could destroy me and put me back together simultaneously.

Ollie pulled away, affirmation flashing in his green eyes. "I am so fucked," he whispered as his eyes darted back and forth between mine and my mouth.

I bit down on my trembling lip, thinking the same damn thing.

Primal instinct took him over, and he picked me up off the floor and wrapped my legs around his torso. My back slammed against the wall again, and a source of electricity ran through us as I sank into his hold. His warm hands gripped my bottom as we both unraveled, becoming each other's oxygen. A dozen candles lit somewhere inside me, flickering against the wrath of Ollie Masters.

His fingers laced through mine and he pinned them above my head, the bass of the music persuading our cadence. My body became his, my lips became his, and the only thing keeping me steady was Ollie and everything he was blessing me with. His tongue ran up my neck and behind my ear before he whispered, "I was doomed from day one, Mia," He dropped his forehead to the wall beside my head as my arms draped over his shoulders. "*Fuck*. Why did you make me do that?"

"Please," I begged into his neck, unsure of what I was asking for exactly. Perhaps for Ollie to stop this torture and the way he made me feel, or possibly for him to keep going. He reached for the side of my face, his fingers tracing my swollen lips, and when his lips crashed against mine again, I was gone.

The fire stayed lit through a thunderstorm, and I wanted nothing more than to keep the feeling alive for as long as possible because once the chemicals left my body, I knew what would come next—a shadow of nothingness.

His dimple appeared as a smile stretched across his face. He brought me to solid ground and took my hands in his before pulling me off the wall. "You're dancing with me now," he said over the bass to a new song. I gripped his shirt at his sides, and he held my head in his hands as we danced in his dorm room. As far as I knew, it was only him and me. Green eyes filled my vision, as fire and ice spread over my tongue. My fingers moved through his hair, while he held up my weightless body. I only wanted Ollie. I only saw Ollie.

The beat of the song stayed with me as my cheeks went numb from my perpetual smile. The room around us blurred, but he was detailed. I wrapped my arms around him, and his minted breath brushed my neck as he became my ambition. Ollie had me reeling, or maybe it was the ecstasy. Either way, it felt incredible.

We were enveloped in one another—in another dimension, another time. Time itself stood still and sped in synchrony, and I couldn't get a handle on myself, but I grasped every second of it. I couldn't stop the pace, but I also couldn't keep going. I couldn't understand what was happening at all.

"Ollie …" My legs couldn't stand any longer as they buckled beneath me. He lowered me onto the mattress as his warm body hovered over mine. Slow hands ran over my bare stomach before gripping my hips as my hopeless being caved beneath him. His tongue traced my jaw before finding its way back to my mouth. My fingers landed on his waistband, and he pulled away.

"Not here," Ollie said as he shook his head between our kiss. "Not now, not like this."

Hours passed, and the music in the atmosphere changed along with it. I was back in Ollie's lap with my head resting into the curve of his neck. Weak and relaxed, the scent of coconut and Ollie bounced off his skin.

Ollie smelled like the ocean and marine breeze—fresh air and freedom.

"What the hell, Mia?" Bria asked as we all sat in a daze.

"It's *Crap-bag* now," Jake hissed, but then giggled at himself.

With no will to answer, I continued to trace Ollie's tattoos on his arm with my finger. Ollie dropped his head down into my neck. "I just got goosebumps," he whispered, and kissed my neck as his nose grazed my ear.

The feelings rushing through me intensified with every second near him. I knew who and what I was, but I was also aware of the way he made me feel, and I needed it. I craved it. My empty soul thirsted for something, and he quenched every gap—filled every piece.

"I don't want this to end," I whispered, the inevitable lurking behind his light. Ollie dropped his ear closer and ran his fingers through my hair, and I continued to ramble, "It's going to end. This will all go away when I wake up, but I don't want it to. I've never wanted it not to go away before." I couldn't shut up, my filter still nowhere to be found. This stupid ecstasy had me saying things I never thought I would say. My thoughts flowed straight from my subconscious and into the air around me.

Ollie moved his mouth to my ear. "I'm right here. I'm not going anywhere." His voice tickled my neck. His tone tickled my heart. His words tickled my soul. Ollie's lips brushed over my ear before trailing kisses below and down the tender parts of my neck. His fingers ran up the back of my head. My eyes closed, taking in every sensation, capturing it, and never wanting to forget.

Bria stood from across the room and waved her arms in the air. "Hello?"

"What, mood-killer?" Jake asked, then fell into another fit of giggles. Isaac laughed at Jake's contagious giggle, and Bria stood humorless.

"Sit down or go back to your dorm," Isaac said after catching his breath.

"No one is keeping you here," Ollie added. I picked my heavy head off his neck when he lowered his tone. "It's almost four in the morning. Everyone should go, anyway."

"So you can finish yourself off?" Isaac laughed.

"You're a dirty man," Ollie said, shaking his head.

I attempted to pull myself up from Ollie's lap when he reached for my hand.

"One more," he pleaded, looking up at me with that daydream look in his eyes. He tugged me back down into a pair of soft lips already aching for the taste of mine.

The sun woke me and my eyes blinked opened. The clock above the door said I had missed breakfast, but I couldn't care. I couldn't gather a single thought; my head was in a fog. When I tried to lift my arm, I couldn't. My eyelids grew heavy, and I drifted back to sleep.

There were a few knocks at my door throughout the day, but I couldn't move my body to answer any of them as I floated in and out of consciousness.

When I woke again, darkness surrounded me, and I didn't know what time or day it was. I tried to lift my head to look out the window. It was dark, and the moon shed a path of light across my floor, revealing a piece of paper. The note must have been slid under my door. I threw my legs over my bed and walked over to it.

"Making sure you're alive in there," it read with an 'O' at the bottom.
Ollie.

Memories of moments with him circled as my breathing grew shorter and shorter. A pain ached in my chest, and I reached for the door handle, but it was locked. I couldn't escape. A scream burned in my throat as I threw my fist at the door. No one was there to stop me as I beat the steel door, screaming until my lungs were completely depleted of oxygen.

My door suddenly buzzed open, and Stanley pulled me from my dorm by my arm and dragged me down the hall. My other hand clawed at his, trying to release myself from his grasp. His grip only tightened, and my head uncontrollably shook as I screamed out, "Let me go!" Stanley ignored me and continued to drag me down the hall. "What did you do to me?" I shouted, my fingers trying to grip the wall as we turned the corner. His silence only made me angrier as I fought against him and punched his shoulder.

"What happened?" the nurse asked as we came through the door. The light in the room was too bright, and I couldn't see anything. My free arm swung over my eyes to shield them as another scream left me. I felt a pinch in my arm before everything went dark again.

"She's experiencing an emotional collapse…it should be temporary…"

My lashes parted, and my eyes darted around the room to see Dr. Conway and Lynch speaking at the foot of my bed. It was bright. *Too damn bright*. I tried to cover my eyes, but my arm was constrained somehow.

"What's happening?" I asked as I tried to lift my head. My eyes couldn't adjust fast enough.

"No, darling. Just lie down," the nurse said before she took my vitals. Dr. Conway pulled a chair beside me and studied my face in silence.

"Answer me," I demanded.

"I believe you suffered a nervous breakdown, but I don't know what could have caused it. No one saw you at breakfast, lunch, or dinner on Friday. You were passed out in your room all day. What's the last thing you remember?"

Ollie immediately came to mind. I remembered his intense green eyes and the way his lips felt against mine. I remembered the mint, coconut, and the … *ecstasy*.

It was the ecstasy.

"I don't know," I lied.

"Something had to have triggered this. Something opened a door, and it was too much for your body to handle all at once."

The nurse took my temperature and I clenched my eyes shut as I tried to process what Dr. Conway was saying. "This all seems extreme for it to be something as ridiculous as a nervous breakdown."

"You'll be okay, this is normal." Dr. Conway turned to the nurse. "She's running a small fever, and her body is reacting. Keep her in here for one more day," Dr. Conway said before I drifted back to sleep.

SEVEN

"There's a fire within her,
golden embers in her eyes.
She burns into me so deep
that even breathing hurts."

OLIVER MASTERS

Time passed quickly as I fell in and out of sleep in the nurse's station. The last time I'd checked, it was Tuesday, when I was only supposed to be here for one more day. A steady fever idled days after the nurse said it should have been gone, and no one could understand what was wrong with me. Bringing up the ecstasy wasn't an option. I wasn't a snitch.

Jake's bright smile came from behind the white curtain.

"Hey, Mia," he said, empathy lacing his tone. He stood uncomfortably beside my bed with his arms full of books and snacks. He looked down, and pity struck his blue eyes.

"Don't look at me like that. I'm not dying, Jake. I only had a fever."

"A fever? Really, Mia? Everyone's talking and saying they heard you freak out in the middle of the night."

I groaned. "Great, so everyone's talking?"

"It doesn't matter, as long as you're okay." He adjusted the items in his hand before a bag of chips fell out, but he managed to catch it. "I brought your homework assignments and snuck some extra snacks from the vending machine. I didn't know if you had access to the good stuff in this ... sterile environment." Jake glanced around at the surroundings. "It feels like I walked through heaven's gates with all the white."

I squinted up at him. "I know. It's blinding."

Jake placed the stack of books on the side table and built a mountain of snacks over the top. He glanced over at me and brought his hand to the back of his head. "So, Ollie's waiting outside ... can he come in?"

The way he said "so" made it seem *so* casual yet afraid to touch a nerve. "Why is Ollie here?"

"Oh, I don't know, Mia. Perhaps he wants to check on you?" He rolled his eyes. "Believe it or not, you do have people who care about you."

Throwing my head back into the pillow, I faced the ceiling. "Fine, send him on in. Why don't you bring Bria and Isaac while you're at it?"

Jake made sense. He had a purpose for being here, bringing over my homework assignments, and, well, because he was Jake. But Ollie had no reason to come unless it was to find out if I had told the nurse anything I shouldn't have. I raked my fingers through my hair and wiped the corners of my eyes before Ollie stepped in from behind the curtain.

My chest constricted from his presence and his green eyes penetrated my empty soul, knocking on every door, reminding me it was never the ecstasy—or had my fever never left me?

He paused to take in my condition and surroundings.

"You look like shit," he said through a sarcastic smile and dragged a chair beside my bed.

I exhaled. "Thanks." At least this wasn't as awkward as I'd thought it would be. Maybe we could put the whole night behind us. He grinned as he fell back in the chair and crossed his ankle over his other thigh. His black jeans hugged him and his usual white non-Dolor tee fell past his waistband. "What are you doing here, Ollie?"

He arched a brow while his other arm fell across the arm of the chair. "Checking on you, love. What happened? Are you okay?"

"I'm fine and don't worry. I didn't say anything about the...you know..."

A small grin formed. "You think that's what I'm worried about?"

If I were him, I would have been worried about that. It could have gotten him, and everyone else, sent to solitary confinement in the best-case scenario. "I don't know ... what else would you be worried about?"

The expression across his face was nothing like mine. "You, Mia. I'm worried about *you*," he said as if I should have known this already. But the only thing I knew was the direction it was going.

"No, don't do that," I muttered and waved my hand in the air.

He quickly uncrossed his leg and leaned into his elbows. "Do what, Mia?"

"Don't take what happened as a sign we are in some relationship now. We were doped up." I laughed lightly. "It was a mistake."

He hung his head between his shoulders and slowly shook it from side to side.

Three seconds passed before he glanced back up at me, and something changed in his eyes. Half the hope was sucked out, and the only half remaining was mixed with confusion. "For the record, *you* were doped up. I wasn't. I did what I did because I wanted to. Dammit, Mia, what I wanted was to wait until you weren't fucked up, but you didn't give me much of a choice."

"You didn't ... take any?"

"No, I don't do that shit. I'll drink now and then, but there's a line I'm not willing to cross."

"Now I can see why," I said as I looked down at myself. From an outsider's perspective, I was sure I looked pathetic—ridiculous, even. Bria, Isaac, and Jake weren't here after taking the drug. It was only me in this hospital bed hooked up to a monitor, the one who couldn't hang, and who everyone else would make jokes about for the rest of the semester—or even worse, the rest of my time here.

Ollie reached for my hand, and I froze as his thumb stroked mine. "I'm sorry ... I didn't mean for this to happen." He paused and turned his head for a moment as if he was contemplating words he would later regret. "But what happened between us wasn't a mistake, and you know it. Frankly, I'm confused because you said it yourself. You said you didn't want the feeling to go away." He said the words regardless.

Shut it down, Mia. I pulled my hand from under his. "No, I don't think you understand. I have absolutely no interest in you. You were there, right place, right time I suppose. It could have easily been Isaac." I shrugged.

A heavy silence built between us, and if there was ever a time I wished the nurse needed to check my vitals, it was now.

Ollie stood to his feet and glanced around the room as he rested his hands over his hipbones. I could almost see the thoughts repeating in his head as if they were white bubbles hovering over him like storm clouds. Was he going to blow up? Was he in denial? Was he self-destructing before my eyes? Had he already fallen for me after one stupid, drug-induced kiss?

But he didn't take the drug ...

"I know you didn't kill your mum," he said to me. "Why are you really here?"

My heart rate on the monitor steadily increased as I lost myself in his question. It was the last thing I had expected him to ask, and the one question I didn't have an answer to.

"I'm tired." I turned away from him to lie on my opposite side. Maybe I was unfriendly—cold, even—but it was the only way to stop while he was ahead.

"No,"—he puffed before a doubtful laugh followed—"you're not *tired*, you're impossible." The sound of the curtain against the rod was the only proof of him leaving, and suddenly the room felt empty.

This was my fault. I'd let him chase me, but I'd been fucked up, and there was no possible way he could understand the truth. No one ever did. They believed it was a front, a charade, like I was doing this to myself.

I pulled the white sheet over my head to block out the fluorescent light. This was precisely the reason why I never kissed anyone. In the end, it was the boy who would develop feelings and get hurt in the end.

That evening, I was discharged after going twenty-four hours without a fever which ultimately screwed me on Oscar-Tuesday. I needed Oscar to smother this fire Ollie built inside me.

To avoid Jake's pity glare, and Ollie's assumptions, I skipped dinner as a precaution and showered instead.

Choosing comfort, I wore a pair of cotton shorts, a tank top, and a camo sweatshirt. My hair stayed up in a messy bun, and I glanced over my desk at the pile of homework and the blank pad of paper Dr. Conway had given me.

The decision was simple.

The blank space stared back at me as I tapped ink dots over the paper. Dr. Conway's words replayed in my head. *"Free your mind and write."* And so, I did. With a clear mind and pen to paper, my fingers took off as if they had a mind of their own.

A knock at my door pulled me from a trance, and I looked up at the clock to see a full hour had passed. My chair squeaked as I pushed away from my desk to answer it.

"She's alive!" Jake exclaimed as soon as I opened the door. He took a step forward with arms extended, but I withdrew behind the door out of habit. "Sorry. I know I can be a bit much and sometimes forget boundaries exist," he said after dropping his hands to his sides without a hug.

"It's fine." I forced a smile, waiting for the purpose of this visit.

Jake looked down the hall and back at me. "I would love it if you made it tonight." He held his palm in the air. "No mandy tonight. Promise. Only a good time with mates and booze. What do you say?" The force behind the flutter of Jake's lashes almost had me flown across the room and pinned to the cement wall.

"I don't get it, what it is it about me that makes you all so persistent to be my friend? I'm an asshole."

"You may be right, but it's exactly the reason why I'm so fond of you. You're an asshole, but not in the Bria way. There's no motive. No reason for it. More like in a cool way. I find it refreshing. The only thing Bria ever cares about is making sure all eyes are on her. You just don't care if anyone sees you or not. It's quite intriguing."

My hand found my hip as I leaned into the door. "I'm a cool asshole?"

A crooked smile appeared across his thin lips. "A *very* cool asshole."

"Alright, fine ... but don't mistake this as an agreement to go every night, and I'm not sitting at your table in the mess hall, either. I can only handle you all in small doses."

Jake shrugged a shoulder as his head slanted into it. "I'll take what I can get."

After Jake left, I returned to my desk to rip off the page-long written paper, folded it, and put it away so I couldn't read what I wrote. I didn't want to be confronted with whatever was truly occupying my mind. It was between my subconscious and my subconscious.

After the security guard checked the corridor, and a few assignments were completed, I built my mountain an hour after midnight. I'd changed my mind a few times during the last hour but decided I may as well keep everyone on my good side to have access to the only semi-fun here at Dolor.

Chatter echoed through the walls of the vent as I crawled closer to Ollie's. Everyone was already there, and Ollie was lying on his mattress with his hands clasped behind his head with his eyes closed. Taking in the moment, I appreciated his beauty. Telling him off the way I had was bitter, but I had done worse in the past.

Though there was something about Ollie I couldn't quite swallow.

"Ollie?" He opened his eyes and saw me over him with my head poked through the vent. He parted his mouth as his face drew a blank. He blinked a few times, but no words came from him. "Should I not have come?"

He quickly got to his feet and held up his arms. "No, of course. You're just the last person I expected to see on top of me ..." He let out a laugh as he waved me down. "I meant, you're the last person I expected to see. Period. Not on top of me."

Ollie pulled me down, and everyone greeted me as I immediately took a seat against the wall beside Jake. Jake gripped my shoulder and passed over a bottle of whiskey. "Thank you, Crap-bag,"—Jake smiled—"for coming."

Alicia cleared her throat, and I glanced over as she held a finger in the air. "Okay, Mia. Since you dropped in, it's your turn. Strip or dare?"

I downed as much of the whiskey my throat could stand, and Ollie fell back over his mattress without his eyes leaving mine. "Strip," I said once the burn subsided. I passed the bottle to Alicia and pulled off my hoodie, revealing a white tank top underneath. With the heat in the room, it was bound to come off sooner or later, and I wasn't in the mood to play childish games.

"If she keeps avoiding dares, we'll have her naked by the end of the night." Isaac snickered, looking over at Ollie. Ollie clenched his jaw, and the tension turned up a few more notches. "Relax, Masters. I'm kidding. Mia, go ahead and choose someone."

I glanced around the room. "How far can we go with this?"

"There are no rules; you either strip or complete the dare," Bria said.

"Okay, looks like Ollie could use some fun while he's over there by himself. Strip or dare?" I asked, looking over at Ollie, who sat by himself on the mattress against the wall.

He gritted his teeth before saying, "Dare."

A devious smile grew across my lips. "Touch yourself, Ollie. I want to see you make yourself come." There was no way he would go through with it.

Jake threw himself into a full-body laugh, almost falling over while everyone turned to look at Ollie. His brows snapped together. "You can't be serious."

"Yeah, like Ollie would ever do that." Jake giggled.

Flashing him a challenging smile, I said, "There are two types of people in this world, Ollie. Those who don't complete their dares, and those who do. Just slip that hand underneath those boxers of yours so I can see you lose yourself."

Ollie's mouth parted and his face flushed. Green eyes bored into mine. "I'm going to need some help," he admitted.

I raised my palms in the air. "Sorry, not part of the rules. It's what you get for being a cranky ass."

Ollie leaned back against the wall and pulled his legs up at the knees. "This is your dare, love … for your viewing pleasure only. You have to come sit in front of me and watch." He returned the same defying smile as if I had asked for this. Which I had. *Hand to forehead.*

"He's got a point, Mia. You didn't say for everyone to see, you said so you can see him 'lose himself,'" Alicia teased. "Next time, you'll learn to be more specific."

Now all eyes were on me as I took another sip of the whiskey, proving what kind of person I was. Wanting to kick myself the entire way, I stood and walked over.

Ollie leaned forward, grabbed my hand, and pulled me between his long legs, blocking everyone's view of him. Conversation picked up between the others like what was about to happen was no big deal, and I sat on my legs, trying to control my breathing. Ollie's brilliant eyes flicked to his friends behind me, then back to me as he relaxed against the wall. His hand disappeared beneath his black boxer briefs, and I closed my eyes.

"No, look at me. This is what you wanted. You wanted to see me lose myself," Ollie whispered, and I looked up to see the taunt in his eyes. The thought of his fingers wrapped around the length of him caused my core to pound to its own pulse, and I sucked in a sharp breath as a flare sparked

90

between my legs. His hand moved slowly inside his pants as his whispers continued. "You're only making this easy for me."

His bulge grew as the silhouette of his manhood pressed against his sweatpants. His shirt rose, revealing his happy trail and deep lines pointing to places I wanted to touch. His black ink crawled along the muscles in his lower abdomen as they flexed, and the veins in his forearm became visible. My breath hitched as he continued to stroke the length of him, his rhythm slow, torturous, and I imagined what it would be like to be with him. Ollie's other hand found my wrist, and his fingers danced along my skin. "Talk to me, Mia," he pleaded, his eyes and words mixed with lust and need.

I rested my hand on his thigh while the other found the wall beside his head as I leaned over him. His head fell into my neck as he deeply inhaled. "I wish I could be the one to make you feel as good as you feel right now, but I,"—I nudged my mouth closer to his ear—"I would make you feel so much better."

His free hand grazed my bare thigh, and I clamped my legs together to ease the current building between my thighs. His vulnerability had me falling, and his breathing got shorter and shorter as he pressed his lips against my neck.

"You have no idea what you're doing to me right now," I whispered, my mind saying things freely without my consent, and I couldn't think of a single dirty word. Ollie was beautiful. Everything about this was beautiful. He moved his hand from my thigh to the back of my neck and dropped his forehead to mine in desperation as he continued to caress himself beneath his pants.

Ollie's hand picked up speed and gasps fell from his lips, landing over mine. The taste of the mint in his breath coursed through me like a hit of menthol. I ran my fingers along his cheek and across his bottom lip. Tilting his head slightly, I partially quenched my need by trailing my lips along his sharp jawline.

Breathtakingly beautiful.

After kissing the tender spot below his ear, his eyes screwed shut and he gripped my hair as his breathing turned jagged.

Ollie's head fell back against the wall, chest heaving. "Holy hell ..." he breathed as his lashes flitted open. "That was the best time I've ever had with myself." A low chuckle came from him as his eyes blinked back to reality. "Mia?"

"Mmhmm?" Any coherent word had been sucked right out of me.

"Can you grab me a shirt?"

As hard as I tried, I couldn't force my smile away. Reaching over to the floor, I found a plain white tee in his pile of clothes beside the mattress and handed it to him.

"Okay, so that was boring for the rest of us," Bria moaned, and I hesitantly took my seat back in the circle. If I were honest with myself, I wished no one else was here—only Ollie and me.

"Go ahead, Ollie, your turn," Jake said and threw the bottle of whiskey in front of him over the mattress.

"I got nothing, mate." Ollie brought the bottle to his lips, then swallowed as he focused his eyes on me. "I'm still high from whatever the hell just happened."

His bluntness made me blush and weak and dizzy.

"I'll steal his, then," Jake said. "Alicia, I dare you to kiss Bria."

Alicia shrugged and crawled her way on her knees to Bria, and they met each other in the middle. Bria didn't hold back as she pressed her tongue between Alicia's lips before molding her mouth over hers. "Yeah!" Jake exclaimed with a fist in the air.

After their kiss finished, Bria peered over to Ollie and wiped the back of her hand over her mouth. "Go ahead, Alicia. Your turn," Bria said.

"Has everyone kissed everyone here?" I asked.

"Mostly everyone," Jake answered.

I wondered if Ollie had kissed Bria and Alicia. I wondered if he had kissed them the way he had kissed me. Most of all, I wondered why I was wondering about him in the first place. "I'm curious, who's the best kisser?" I needed to get my mind off the torment in my head.

"Hmm ... I don't know, but it's not a bad idea," Alicia said, and I could see the wheels turning in her head. "We should find out."

"Oh, no. I was only wondering. I don't kiss people," I said, shaking my head.

"You kissed Ollie," Alicia pointed out.

Shit. "It was the ecstasy."

"Let's get you drunk, then. Everyone else is down, right?" Isaac asked, and everyone nodded, except for Ollie. "Come on, Ollie. Don't be selfish with your new kissing buddy."

"Since Mia and Ollie are the only two who haven't kissed everyone, I say they go around the room and then we will all give our final results," Bria said with her palms together in excitement, but all I could focus on was the fact Ollie hadn't kissed everyone. Why was Ollie the only one who hadn't kissed everyone?

"Absolutely not," Ollie said as soon as I began to speak.

"No, really, guys ... I don't kiss people. Last time was a fluke." There was no way I was kissing Bria's crooked teeth and Jake's thin lips. I didn't mind Alicia. She was hot and straight and couldn't develop feelings for me.

Alicia clapped her hands together. "Mia, I dare you to kiss Isaac, then."

Ollie's low voice interjected, "She just said—"

"Precisely my point. She doesn't kiss people. It's the perfect dare for her. She can either start kissing or strip off another article of clothing. Simmer down, Ollie. You already had your fair share."

My head jerked from Ollie over to Alicia as a taunting grin slowly grew over her face. This was what happened when I stupidly opened up to people. I pulled my white tank over my head and was left in only my black bra and sweatpants. "I told you ... I don't kiss people."

When I'd kissed Ollie, I was under the influence, and until I had a buzz going, I would continue to take off clothes. "You guys want to come at me with nonsense, and I'll come back ten times harder." I narrowed my eyes in Bria's direction. "I dare you to lick Jake's butthole."

Isaac and Ollie's mouth dropped open before a cackle belted and Jake's eyes went wide.

"That's disgusting," Bria hissed and took off her shirt in defeat. "I dare you to kiss Jake," she countered with poison in her tone.

Walking over to Ollie, I grabbed the bottle from his hands. After chugging a couple of gulps, I wiped my mouth and handed the bottle back to him before withdrawing my sweatpants, leaving myself in only my bra and black panties. My eyes fell over Alicia as she shifted in her spot. "Alicia—"

"I choose strip," Alicia snapped before I could finish, and pulled her shirt over her head. "I don't even want to know what the dare was going to be."

Isaac and Ollie stayed quiet as Jake whined, utterly offended by Bria and my way of using him as a weapon.

"Mia, I dare you to kiss Ollie," Alicia said with a smile. Everyone's eyes grew wide when I reached for the clasp of my bra. They could strip me bare; I still wasn't kissing anyone.

Before I had a chance to pull it over my shoulders and down my arms, Ollie jumped from the mattress and took a step in front of me, pulling me behind him. "*Fuck*. Leave the girl alone," Ollie shouted.

A laugh escaped me as I stood behind Ollie. My bra already fell to the floor. The heat from the whiskey hit me, and I didn't care anymore. Ollie turned to face me, continuing to block me from everyone else's view. His mouth parted as his eyes roamed freely over my breasts, as if they were claiming me, and I could feel his stare penetrating my skin. The glowing buzz of the fever ran from my chest, up my neck, and to my cheeks. "Dammit, Mia," he muttered.

As I tried stepping to the side, he took a step also, moving along with me as if he was shielding me from a predator.

Ollie reached over his head and pulled the shirt off his back.

"What are you doing? It's fine. I don't care …" I said as he fit his shirt over my head. He seemed frustrated as I pushed my arms through the holes. The hem of the shirt hit me mid-thigh, and when I lifted my eyes to meet his, he dipped down and crashed his lips to mine.

A whisper of a moan escaped from me as his force sent me back against the cement. He wouldn't touch me; instead, his palms hit the wall on both sides of me, caging me in. The only link to each other was our lips, interlaced in dire need.

Ollie pulled back slightly and brushed his parted mouth against mine, testing me—teasing me. I wanted more, and he knew this, but he wanted me to come back for it.

Caving, I reached behind his head and took him. Ollie smiled before our tongues collided, spinning me into a rapture, whirling me into a heaven of him. His warm body melted against mine as his tender lips marked their territory. The gentle sucking only left me wanting more. I gripped his hair, pulling him closer, tasting him. *Ice and fire.* Nothing was ever enough. A familiar light ignited, and I held on to it a moment longer than I should have, before I pushed him away.

I kept him at arm's length. "Why?"

Our breathing was erratic.

A mix of defeat and determination washed over his features. "Because I'm selfish," he whispered and wet his already glistening lips, "and I don't want anyone else to see any part of you."

I was jealous of how freely Ollie spoke. I was jealous of the way he had no barriers to hide behind. He wasn't afraid of anything—rejection, feelings, or the way I was going to destroy him. He wasn't scared at all.

"Remember, you're doing this to yourself." I'd warned him too many times. Now, this was his doing. Not mine. My only problem was having to live in his aftermath.

As I stepped away, he wrapped his fingers around my wrist to prevent me from taking another step. He tilted his head to face me. "You're in denial." I jerked out of his grasp and found my seat back in the circle. All eyes were on Ollie as he stood in silence with his fingers gripping his hipbones, breathing still reeling from our kiss. "What?"

"Nothing …" everyone said in unison, averting their gaze and darting their eyes around the room. Ollie fell back onto the mattress and reached for the bottle of whiskey off the floor. He took a long, hard sip as the conversation went back to normal.

The game came to an abrupt end afterward, and the atmosphere died down along with it. Time passed, and Isaac passed out at the end of the mattress. Bria inched her way closer and closer toward Ollie as he finished off the bottle by himself.

His last comment about me being in denial replayed in my head. I wasn't in denial. What could I have been in denial about? Making myself very clear, I'd told him I had no interest in him. I couldn't feel. My feelings were all a reaction to the buzz. It would pass. He thought he could come to my rescue with a shirt and a kiss, but I didn't need saving.

"What did you do to Ollie?" Jake giggled in my ear. The whiskey in Jake's breath and his inability to whisper both told me he was toasted.

Ollie slumped against the wall, rambling things I couldn't make out. He could hardly keep his eyes open as Bria tugged on his hair.

"Watch this," Jake whisper-shouted, pointing in Ollie and Bria's direction. Glancing back over, Bria swung a leg over Ollie's lap and my stomach jumped into my throat. He tried pushing her away, but she continued circling her hips over him. "Three … two … one …" Jake counted down, and suddenly Bria forced her lips against Ollie's. "Like clockwork," he added, and slowly shook his head.

My stomach lodged in my throat was now doing backflips. "Do they do this when Ollie's not … when he's not drunk?"

Alicia joined in on the conversation. "You have to understand something. Ollie doesn't mess around. He's not the type."

"What do you mean?" I couldn't take my eyes away from Bria's back as her fingers moved across Ollie's bare chest—across the chest of the boy who made me feel things I was still trying to understand. My insides twisted as Ollie placed his hands over her arms to pull himself away. No one seemed to care, and with each passing second, the pit in my stomach grew bigger and bigger.

96

"Ollie provides the fun, but he doesn't participate. He never gets in on it," Alicia whispered. "The only time Bria can try to have a chance, is when he's tore up."

"Bloody hell, she's right." Jake chuckled. "You're the only one Ollie has willingly kissed, let alone jerked off in front of."

"So, none of you ever hooked up with him? Not even a kiss?" I asked, and I wasn't sure why I cared so much in the first place. All I wanted to do was get Bria off him, her hands off him, her lips off him. Ice frosted over my skin in a cold sweat as my eyes burned a hole to the back of her head. *Ice and fire.* This was different, though. *Rage.*

A blue and red twisted rage.

Alicia and Jake both shook their heads. "He refuses every time."

My brows snapped together. "Not even Bria?"

"There's rumors, but he hasn't since I've been here," she said. "She's way more into Ollie than he will ever be into her."

Jake interjected, "Yeah, Bria normally goes for Isaac by the end of the night. She'll screw him in front of everyone, but I suppose since he's passed out first, Ollie was next on her list."

"This is sick in so many ways, even for me." My attention stayed on Bria, watching her like a hawk. Suddenly, Bria stood and shimmied off her shorts and panties in one swoop, and my rage turned into a silent mania, slithering through the fire in my veins.

"What do you mean *even for you?*" Alicia asked, utterly oblivious to what was happening in front of us, or completely discarding it altogether like it was normal.

"I'm all about sex and a good time, but this is rape! You can't tell me Ollie knows what he's doing right now," I shouted, pointing in Ollie's direction. Bria sat back down over Ollie's lap.

Alicia looked over to Jake. "Yeah, but is it our place?"

"Hell yeah, it's our place." The mania influenced my legs as I stood to my feet. A few strides later, I peered over Bria as she gripped his length. Like glass, the frost shattered and all was left was the painful fire inside me.

"Mia, I don't think that's such a good idea," Jake called out, but I didn't listen.

Gripping Bria by her dumb short hair, I dragged her off and away from Ollie. "What's wrong with you?" I shouted as she clawed at my hand.

Bria struggled to her feet as her words slurred together. "Get the fuck off me!"

As I threw Bria against the wall, Jake and Alicia stumbled to their own feet. My fist clenched at my sides and I looked back at Ollie who remained oblivious to what was going on around him. He slumped over against the wall to his side before I turned my attention to Bria. "He's not a toy you can play with whenever the hell you want …" My eyes darted around the room, and everyone glared at me in a shocking silence, except for Isaac.

Isaac was still passed out in the bed.

Bria's face turned red as she slid down the wall until her bottom hit the floor. She wouldn't dare come after me. Shaking my head, I returned to Ollie's side and fixed the waistband of his boxers and sweatpants, then lifted his head off the wall. "Ollie, you have to wake up," I said, holding his head in my hands. Ollie struggled to open his eyes. "Why did you do this? Why did you put yourself in this situation?" It broke something inside me to see him so fragile and defenseless. "Ollie, open your eyes for me."

Ollie's lashes fluttered open, and his beautiful green eyes were bloodshot and broken.

"Mia." He exhaled. "I'm sorry."

And his eyes closed again.

As I guided his head over the pillow, everyone exited the dorm through the vent. Staying by his side, I wasn't going to leave the room until Bria was far away from him.

I understood sex. Hell, I understood drunken sex. I could accept messing around, experimenting with genders, and living in the moment, but nothing about this was okay. No one should be allowed to violate someone who didn't have the right mind to say "no."

I wondered how many times this had happened. How many times Bria, or anyone else here, had touched him in ways he didn't want to be touched. How many times he had he gotten so drunk, where he was oblivious to whose hands were on him and whose lips were on his. If I hadn't been here, how far would this have gone?

My adrenaline soared through the roof as I paced the dorm room cleaning because I couldn't sit still, and I had lost my chance of leaving already. Isaac was still passed out, hanging off the end of the mattress. Maybe when, or if, he woke, we could help each other out of here.

Eventually, my nerves calmed, and I took a seat on the floor beside the mattress. My eyes grew heavy as I fought to keep them open. Even though my fingers ached to scratch Ollie's back and swipe my hand through his hair, I was afraid to touch him. He lay on his side as he rested his hand under his head beneath the pillow. I admired his slightly parted lips, soft pink and perfectly made, and the small freckle off to the side of his mouth. What was it about him that made me do these crazy things?

EIGHT

"Leaving her breathless
in my aftertaste
is the worst way to leave.
The best is to stay,
but she isn't ready
for me yet."

OLIVER MASTERS

made it in time to my first group therapy session on Thursday and found an empty seat in the circle. Unfortunately, the whole crew was present, amongst other students I'd seen in passing. Everyone greeted me with a small smile but stayed quiet for the most part. Group therapy had to be the place where Isaac, Jake, Alicia, Bria, and Ollie had been brought together.

Chairs faced each other in a circle in the dark room, and in a corner lay a dusty piano under a lit floor lamp. The piano stared back at me, taunting me. My fingers itched to feel the cold keys, and my ears ringed, begging to hear the music my fingers could produce with each stroke.

"A musical genius," my mother used to call me, but I hadn't played since before she passed. It was bizarre, of all the places, a piano was in this room. My gaze touched over the black and white details, and I wondered if the F-chord still caused my pulse to skip.

"Mia Jett?" a man announced from the circle, breaking my attention away from the piano. I didn't know he was the counselor. He could have easily passed as one of the students with his young features. Not a single wrinkle or imperfection marked his dark and creamy face.

I nodded, and he continued, "Please, introduce yourself."

"It sounds like you just did. Why don't you tell me your name?" There was movement throughout the circle as if I had stepped over an invisible line.

"You can call me Arty," the counselor said, my comment not taking him by surprise one bit. "Tell us why you're here. This is a safe environment, I can assure you." There was no notepad in his lap, no pen in his hand. Arty only wanted to listen.

Ollie's green eyes fixed on me as his elbows rested over his knees. I hadn't spoken to him, or any of them, since the Bria incident. Trying to meet his gaze, I wondered if the brokenness remained in his eyes. Ollie had to have known what had happened to him. Even in my worst drunken spells, I always remembered.

Though, I couldn't remember what had made me *this* way.

Life was ironic like that.

Ollie blinked his eyes away from me. He did remember, but he wanted me to forget.

"I tried killing myself"—a small laugh pressed through mid-sentence— "a couple of times now. Not because I hate myself or my life, but because I can't hate. In fact, I don't feel anything at all." Ollie shifted in his seat before bringing his fingers under his chin, so I continued, "I thought maybe, just maybe, at the very last minute, I could flip a switch on a mental breaker, and care enough to stop myself ... but that never happened. My father found me, both times, and if it weren't for him coming home early, I wouldn't be here."

101

My focus stayed on Ollie as I let out the truth. "I'm incapable of feeling or showing emotion—completely detached. Dr. Conway listed several disorders I can't recall at the moment, but all in all, I might as well be dead. I'm incurable and a lost cause."

The room became quiet. If you listened closely, you could hear the distinct sound of a tab breaking open on a Coca-Cola can all the way in Texas. And if you closed your eyes, you could hear the small sigh of relief after the first sip. That's how quiet it was.

"Thank you, Mia," Arty said, bringing me back into the room without a drink.

"She can't be serious." Ollie laughed in disbelief as he snapped his head in Arty's direction. "And you're buying that tosh, yeah?"

"Safe environment, Oliver," Arty insisted with an eye-nudge. "Mia here"—he gestured toward me—"is disassociated from her emotions, and if she can't break through her roadblocks, there may come a time when it's too late."

Ollie turned his head back to me. His eyes squinted as if they were trying to see past the lies, stripping me down to my truth. But the truth was already right in front of him; he just couldn't accept it. His knee bounced under his elbow as I stayed calm, though I couldn't understand why he was so physically affected.

Bria let out a laugh. "So, let me get this straight. She's here because she doesn't care about other people? Doesn't sound like that was the case the other night ..."

Thanks for pointing that out, Bria.

Defending actions with words could only get one so far because mouths weren't created to be used as weapons, and not all battles were meant to be fought. But I also wasn't going to allow her words to plant ideas in other people's heads—in Ollie's head.

Leaning back into my chair, I crossed my arms over my chest and turned the tables around. "Enough about me, Arty. Why don't I learn more about the group? Let's start with Bria."

Bria crossed her legs and arms simultaneously, mimicking my actions, drawing her sword, preparing for battle. After Arty's nod of approval, her annoying voice echoed in the dark room. "What do you want to know?"

"Hold on, let me guess." I brought two fingers to my chin. "Fights in school, petty theft crimes, a bad crowd had you under their influence ... You're a people pleaser. You just don't know how to say no, or take no for an answer."

"Yeah!" Jake blurted and clapped his hands together. Arty held up a palm to calm the room buzzing from my comment. "I told you she had some talents," Jake whispered to Ollie, shoving him in the arm.

"You don't know shit!" Bria stood, her pale and delicate features flushed as she pointed a finger at me. I sat with a smirk as her appearance transformed before my eyes.

"Alright, let's settle down," Arty said as he raised both hands in the air, his soothing baritone voice louder than the chatter amongst the group. Bria eventually listened before Arty continued, "Isaac, you've been quiet. Why don't you clue us in on what just happened?"

Bria blew out a puff from her cheeks, and I raised a brow as I waited for Isaac to answer. Isaac sat beside Arty; his eyes darted to Ollie, then back at me. "It's a way for Mia to manipulate her surroundings. From the looks of it, she has sociopath tendencies. She gets off on this shit." *Tell me something I don't already know.*

Seconds and a couple of gasps passed and Arty glanced over to me. "You see right there"—Arty shot his palm in my direction—"nothing. Bria would have left with such a remark, but because Mia is so disconnected, nothing can break her."

Because I was already broken.

"Can Mia be affectionate?" Ollie asked, catching everyone, including myself, off guard.

Arty peered over to me, expecting me to answer the question for him.

"Only under the influence," I said. "But even so, it will never be real. I was only motivated by lust and a high. Once the side effects wear off, I'll be back to this: incapable of loving or maintaining any form of personal attachment." I pointed to myself and mouthed, *"Lost cause,"* as Ollie squinted.

Gunpowder flowed from my heart, up my throat, and lingered on my tongue. It tasted like pain and shame. "All of it meant nothing." Each word shaped like a bullet. And the moment the words left me, a slow burning ache returned in my chest. Quickly, I swallowed the bitterness and swiped my sweaty palm down the side of my jeans.

The air around me weighed heavy, stifling, and Ollie leaned over. He rested his elbows over his knee as he dropped his hands from his chin. "I don't believe you," he said to me from across the circle, his words slow, his tone low and direct.

I managed to shrug despite the sudden turmoil stirring inside me while he moved his head slightly from side to side.

"So, Mia is a sociopath?" Jake asked, breaking up the tension.

I scanned the circle, and everyone was either staring at me, staring at Ollie, or looking to Arty, hanging on his silence.

"She checks every box associated with the term, but do I think she is one?" Arty's eyes met mine, and I waited for his answer like everyone else. "No, I don't. She hasn't always been this way."

And I couldn't remember being any other way. He had no right to say those things. Saying I haven't always been this way allowed me to believe there was a small inkling of hope hiding somewhere, and hope was disappointing. Hope was a thin string hanging over my head as I fell into the darkness. I couldn't see it and I couldn't feel it, so pretending it wasn't there was for the best.

He had no right for me to hear it.

Ignoring hope, I dropped my chin and kept my eyes on the marble tile while everyone went around the room talking about their progress and setbacks.

I'd learned that Isaac had been dependent on pain killers, and had a past of doing whatever was necessary to fill that addiction. Alicia had been in and out of foster care most of her life, and found a family with a bad crowd, though there was a spark of hope in her eyes, and I wondered if

104

Dolor was the reason behind it. She mentioned wanting to pursue a nursing degree after she left here.

"Ollie, how have you been since last Tuesday? Have you found something to keep your mood stable?" Arty asked. I lifted my head, and Ollie had been in the same position the entire time, leaned over with his elbows digging into his knees. His right knee bounced nervously and he applied more pressure to try to control it.

Ollie closed his hands together in front of him as he cocked his head in Arty's direction. "Good question, Arty. Yeah, I mean, I've been okay since Tuesday. No outbursts."

"Oh, good. Have you found comfort in something?"

"You can say that." Ollie's eyes fell back on me as his bouncing knee suddenly calmed.

"Very well. Hopefully, this one will stick this time."

"I'm certain of it," Ollie said slowly, as if each word was meant for me.

At dinner, I ran my fork through my corn, dividing it up into two sections. The number of corn was uneven, so I popped one in my mouth.

"We need to talk," Ollie stated flatly as he approached my table. Maybe if I pretended he wasn't standing beside me, peering down with a hand to the back of his head, he would go away.

Steering my attention back to my tray, I stabbed another kernel with my fork. Ollie rolled his head back and drew in a deep breath before walking behind me, lifting my books off the chair beside me, and taking a seat. He set the books on the table.

My eyes were on the corn; his eyes were on me. I knew because they were heavy and light all at once. When I still didn't acknowledge him, he turned my knees until they settled between his and my whole body moved along until I faced him. "Stop acting like a child, Mia."

I dropped my fork over my tray. "I'm not. I just don't want to talk."

"Is that the reason why you're here? Because you're emotionally detached?" he asked, and when I didn't answer him, he continued, "I don't believe that. You may have everyone else fooled, but I don't believe it for one second." I turned my head away, but Ollie wrapped his fingers around my chin and forced me to face him.

As soon as my eyes met his, something occurred to him.

"You're scared …" He shook his head and softened his voice. "What are you scared of? What happened to you?"

I wish I knew. "Nothing happened to me. This is how I am." I jerked my face from his hold, and he ran his hand up his forehead and through the front of his wave.

"No. Since you've been here, you haven't defended anyone, but the moment I can't help myself, you come to my rescue. And your eyes, Mia." He grabbed my hand brought it close to him over his lap. "They light up when you see me, and every chance you had to kiss someone else, you refused or made up poor excuses. But you kiss me, and you fucking love it. Admit it, Mia, you do have feelings, and it scares the hell out of you."

Damn right I had feelings. I felt cornered—forced to confront the same harsh questions I'd been struggling to find the answers to. There was no study or Wiki Forum to give me explanations as to why an emotionally detached girl of ten years could start experiencing moments of weakness. And even if it was somewhere in the cyber world, even if someone had been through this before, I had no access to find out.

Somehow, he was the only one to get under my skin, and I needed to prove him wrong. I needed to prove to myself this was all in my damn head. My gaze darted around the mess hall until they landed on Liam, and I suddenly knew what I needed to do.

"Where are you going?" Ollie asked as I stood from the chair.

He made every cell erupt inside me, and there was only one way to stop it.

My feet marched to Liam, who stood in front of his usual table, and before he could get a word out, I reached around his neck and pressed my lips against his. Ollie and Liam despised one another, and out of everyone in this mess hall, Liam was the answer to get Ollie off my back.

Liam's hand found my waist as he pinned me against him and massaged his tongue against mine. The fire was gone, and the mess hall went up in a roar.

When I pulled away from Liam, I turned back to my table.

Ollie was gone.

Finally.

"What in the bloody hell was that for?" Liam asked with a lopsided grin, and the girls surrounding his table narrowed their eyes at me. Liam didn't deserve an explanation, so I turned and walked away. The only person who deserved any amount of words was Ollie, and I had just proved he didn't mean anything to me.

Jake, Alicia, and Isaac stared at me with disapproving looks as I exited the mess hall. I'd tried to warn them about me. They'd all found out the truth during group therapy, but no one had believed me. This was Ollie's fault, not mine. I'd told him my rules. He'd known what he was getting himself into. He should have known better.

As soon as I opened the door to my dorm room, I paused under the door frame. Ollie sat over the edge of my bed with his elbows over his knees. His head hung between his shoulders, and I could tell his hair had been gripped numerous times on the way from the mess hall to here.

After closing the door behind me, I took a few steps toward the desk and leaned into it. "I warned you."

Ollie lifted his head. "What the fuck was that back there? Was that your way of proving something to yourself?" His voice was thick but without malice, and there was a mixture of pain and sickness in his eyes.

"No, that was my way of proving something to you."

Ollie stood from the mattress and walked toward me. "You want to prove something to me, yeah?" He brought his palm to my cheek, and my head involuntarily sunk into his hold. "Prove this alone doesn't mean more to you than your ego."

His thumb stroked my cheek, and I closed my eyes against his warmth. "Nothing," I cracked in a lie.

"What about this?" Ollie lifted my chin and grazed his lips across mine, and I remembered the taste of him. I sucked in a breath. "We're both sober right now, and nothing is stopping you from pulling away from me, but you can't." His long fingers reached behind my neck as the mint rolled off his tongue. "Mia, I'm going to kiss you now, and when I'm done, I promise I'll leave, but—"

And I shut him up with my mouth against his.

As soon as our lips met, we caught fire, and a sort of frenzy took us over. His tongue danced along my lips before slipping inside, injecting me with life. I was sober, but he became my drug, my dose of medicine wrapped up in one tall and beautiful, tattooed pill. His other hand found my face as he pushed his torso against me, and the desk slammed against the wall. Each swipe of his tongue was more sensual, every catch of the lips was more determined, and every touch of his fingers satisfied every need I hurt for.

He became my oxygen, stealing my breath only to return it. My lifeline. And just when I thought the pieces of me were finally coming back together, he pulled away to leave me breathless. Ollie pressed his forehead to mine, struggling with his promise to leave on his ruined lips. The tempo in his breathing steadied, and I shut my eyes as he kissed my forehead.

"Don't ever kiss another before my eyes again," he stated before his hands left me.

The sound of the door closing caused me to flinch, and when I opened my eyes again, he was gone.

NINE

"To everyone,
she's seen as nothing.
With everything I have,
she is quite the someone."

OLIVER MASTERS

t was harder to breathe at Dolor. Everywhere I turned, I was being forced to talk about shit—*feelings and emotions*. People talked about me as if I weren't standing right there. They told me what was wrong with me, who I was, my symptoms, my disorders, what went through my mind as if they knew me. I wanted to scream nothing was wrong with me. They'd poked and poked and poked, and when I'd thought they couldn't poke any longer, Ollie had shown up and kissed me like *that*.

Pacing my dorm room, my lips beat like a drum to its own pulse in his absence. At one point within the last five minutes, I'd believed he was the actual devil. Surrounded by indestructible walls, only Satan could punch through and lure me in the way Ollie did.

Frustrated with my irrational thinking, I shook my head. Ollie clouded my judgment, and I couldn't think straight. A slow rising pressure built, and with each step I felt myself gradually losing it. He'd kissed me, and before leaving, he'd somehow managed to pick up my scattered pieces, stuff them in his pocket, and take them with him.

Before Ollie, I didn't have pieces. He'd built them, broken them, and stolen them.

Pulling on my hair, nothing took away the suffering brewing inside my chest. And when the pulling didn't work, I threw my fist into the concrete wall.

Instant regret.

"Mother fucker!" I cursed at the top of my lungs as my body crumbled to the ground. My chest burned, unable to find a single breath afterward. Thoughts even stopped as I curled into a fetal position with my fist clutched to my chest. My door swung open and a cool rush of air brushed past my already frozen body. Voices echoed throughout my room, but I couldn't focus long enough to understand what they said. Low moans came from somewhere. Was it me? Was I moaning?

My heart was in my fist as it pounded at an irregular pace.

My vision was stunned. I could no longer blink.

"Alicia, go get the nurse!" someone shouted. "Oh my god … Alicia!"

My eyes fixed on the gray cement wall I had punched moments before, and I couldn't find the will to move them in either direction. Voices came in and out of focus like a long-distance call.

"Don't move her. She's in shock. Everyone back up." It was my dark angel in all white—the nurse.

When I came to, a thin gray sheet lay over me. A cast covered my hand, and Dr. Conway sat in my desk chair, reading over papers in her lap. Her high and thick black hair framed her ivory skin. She belonged in the movie *My Big Fat Greek Wedding*. I wanted to smile at the thought of her spraying my fist with Windex, but I couldn't.

She brought her long red nails to her lips as a wide yawn broke out.

"What happened?" I asked, and she looked up from her paper.

She removed the stack of papers from her lap and placed them over my desk before crossing her legs. "You broke your hand." A light sigh blew from her dark red lips. "And tell me, Mia, what on earth did the wall ever do to you?"

I rolled my eyes at her attempt at humor.

"You can't resort to violence. If you have one more incident, we will have to remove all your furniture from your room, and if you harm yourself again, we'll have to place you in solitary confinement. Now, why did you punch the wall?" She raised a brow.

Her eyes were tired, and I could tell she had been waiting a while for me to wake.

I drew in a deep breath. "A guy kissed me," I said through an exhale.

Dr. Conway pressed her lips together.

"It's not funny."

She threw her hand in the air. "Hey, I didn't say anything."

"You didn't have to."

She turned her head to see out the window in order to hide the smile I caught regardless. She so badly wanted to laugh, and it took her a moment to reel herself back into the conversation as a psychologist. "I'm not concerned about the broken hand or the fact you punched a wall. I'm more concerned about the state of shock you went into afterward. Can I ask you something personal?"

"No." It was an automatic response, a response much easier to say than "yes." Others would disagree. Others would find "yes" was much easier because you wouldn't have to disappoint anyone. I didn't envy those types of people.

Dr. Conway glanced up at the clock above my door. "It's almost nine. I have to head home." She picked up her stack of papers from the desk and gathered to her feet. "In the meantime, I want you to think back at what's inducing this anger. What's the common denominator sending you into a rage both times? There you will have your answer."

Dr. Conway dropped her chin and left. She left me alone with a million more thoughts and unanswered questions I didn't have before my fist met the wall.

I thought Fridays would be my favorite, considering there were no classes, but they grew to be my least. During breakfast, I wrote lyrics to songs I couldn't listen to over my cast in a sharpie next to my tray of uneaten food. Since I'd arrived, I'd lost five pounds—like I needed to lose any more weight.

From the table in front of me, Screaming Kid stared at his tray, waiting for something magical to happen, as if it were a cocoon on the verge of becoming a butterfly.

Most didn't know this, but a butterfly spent the majority of their life in the caterpillar and cocoon stages. The caterpillar stage was the most dangerous and life-threatening. Then, if they could make it past the caterpillar stage, they had to hide in a defenseless cocoon for up to two weeks to only turn into something beautiful for a short amount of time.

What stage was I in? Was I the damned caterpillar or was I hiding in a cocoon? Would I ever turn into a butterfly, or would the storm take me away before I learned the truth?

Ollie was already a butterfly—*beautiful and strong*.

While I was damned, he was divine.

Zeke must have felt the weight of my stare and glanced up to see me. The longer we looked at each other, the more I noticed the deep agony embedded in his sad brown eyes. He'd never spoken a word. The only sound coming from him were shrieks.

And even in silence, his eyes were screaming.

I stood, walked over, and took a seat across from him. "What's your name?"

His facial expression froze as he stared back at me.

112

"I think your name is Zeke, and since you probably won't tell me otherwise, it's what I'll call you." *Better than Screaming Kid.* Leaning back in the chair, I dropped my right-handed cast over the table. Zeke's attention went to my cast. "I punched a wall. It was stupid. And yes, I regret it."

Zeke snapped his eyes back to mine, and his brown curly hair bounced off his forehead.

"Truth is, up until I arrived here, I hadn't been able to feel anything … but you want to know a secret?" I leaned in and pointed my eyes in Ollie's direction. "That stupid guy over there kissed me—*three* times now, and it does something to me I can't explain. So, I took it out on the wall." I fell back against the chair as Zeke looked over to Ollie and back at me. "Damn, it feels good to get that off my chest."

The corner of his lip turned up slightly. He'd understood every word.

"You're a good listener, unlike everyone else here. We should do this more often."

A shadow cast over us. My attention followed the source to see Liam hovering over our table. "What are you doing?" he asked, darting his glare between Zeke and me.

"What does it look like? I'm talking to my new friend, Zeke, here." I shot a smile over to Zeke, and he flinched under Liam's shadow.

Liam chuckled as he pulled his blond hair back into a bun. "Whatever floats your boat, Jett. Let's get out of here. I know a place."

Liam stuffed his hands into his pocket and arched an impatient brow.

Past Liam, Ollie watched us from his table in the middle of the mess hall. Reminders of last night sent heat through my bloodstream and across the surface of my skin. *Don't ever kiss another before my eyes again*, he had said to me moments before I'd broken my hand. Ollie didn't know I don't like to be manipulated, and the way his eyes were controlling me made me only want to defy him.

"Yeah, okay." I stood and turned back to Zeke. "Dinner, same place?" Zeke didn't move. "I'll take that as a yes."

Liam and I walked out of the mess hall and down the corridor side by side. The unknown of what I was walking toward kept my feet in front of me, but the memory of Ollie's eyes on me consumed my thoughts. Ollie's gaze wanted to pull me away from Liam, but curiosity kept me moving forward. A constant push and pull.

"Where are we going?" I asked as we turned a corner.

Two girls passed by us, both shooting daggers in our direction as they whispered between one another.

"Hey, Liam," one practically sang.

Liam only gave them a small nod before he leaned his head into my hair. "Can't ruin the surprise. You know, I've been thinking about your bold move to kiss me yesterday. Most girls aren't as aggressive."

Liam and Ollie were the same height, but the way Ollie leaned into me affected me differently.

A short laugh pressed out from my lips. "Don't flatter yourself. I used you, and I'm not sorry about it."

Liam looked down at me with hooded blue eyes. "Me neither." He had a one-tracked mind and wanted to pick up where we'd left off the day before.

We turned another corner, and after walking clear across Dolor, we approached a large black door with "dark room" etched into the plaque beside the door on the wall.

"What is this place?" I asked Liam as he opened the door.

He placed his hand on the small of my back as he guided me in before him. "It's a dark room for photography. No one comes in here anymore."

Trays lay evenly across a table in the back as old photos hung from the scalloped string from the ceiling. Machines, looking like they belonged in a science lab, took up most of the space, and I turned to Liam to see a dicey smile. His hungry eyes glowed in the dark red lighting of the small and stifling room.

"I enjoyed our kiss yesterday." Liam took a step forward. He gripped my waist as he leaned down.

"No." I held up a hand to his face. "If we're doing what I think we're doing, then no kissing."

Liam nodded excitedly as his eyes went wild. "Deal."

114

His cold hands dipped beneath my shirt, and my muscles stiffened at the touch. *What was wrong with me?* I'd done this so many times before. "Arms up," he demanded, and I silently obliged. He lifted my shirt over my head, and there were no words or will inside me to stop him as he pulled his bottom lip between his teeth.

Stupor robbing me of my intelligence, I reached behind my back and unlatched my bra. Liam's eyes went weak at the sight of my breasts before he cupped them in his hands. Guys like Liam needed this. You would think they were confident, secure, but they were anything but. Guys like Liam had the endless need to feel they were wanted and accepted.

"Fuck, you're so sexy," he said, and when he leaned in, I pulled away. "Sorry, I forgot. No kissing. Won't happen again."

I unbuttoned his jeans as he undid mine, trying to get the deed done and over with as soon as possible. He wouldn't be able to get me off. It was a never-ending battle with me and countless partners. Reaching an orgasm with anyone was like my success of suicide—an utter and complete failure. (There's a sentence I never thought I'd admit). Perhaps you had to have feelings to get to that point, and if that was the case, I'd been cursed all along.

Liam pulled a condom from his back pocket before pushing his jeans and boxers down to his thighs. His eyes remained on my breasts as he ripped the foil packet between his teeth, then slipped the condom on, turned me around, and tried entering me to find I was dry.

"You're going to have to help me out," I said, wondering his limits. There were three kinds of men in this world. The type who would use lubricant, the type who used their fingers, and then there was my favorite kind—the kind who were more willing and eager to please me before their own needs by going down on me, which were few and far between.

Liam pushed me forward over the table and spread my legs with his knee before his fingers stroked my sex.

Rookie mistake.

My eyes closed to see tattoos, green eyes, and an alluring smile when finally, my body reacted. "You're so wet," Liam whispered as he pressed his finger inside me. My eyes stayed shut as moments with Ollie clouded every thought, taking me away from what was actually happening. I had to get past this.

Liam gripped my hips as he thrusted inside from behind. He moaned as his body relaxed against me, but shortly after, a need for more of me propelled him into madness. "You feel so good," he grunted, and I ignored each comment he made thereafter. I'd heard them all before. *You feel so good. You're so tight. You're so sexy.* None of the comments ever did anything for me. I wanted silence.

Liam liked it hard and fast and grunted with each pump as I pretended to enjoy it for his sake. It was better for the both of us. The sooner he got off, the sooner this would be over, and after about four minutes of mental misery, it was.

He pulled out and rested his hands over the table as guilt immediately invaded me. "That was good, yeah?" His breath struggled to catch up. I pushed off the table and gathered my clothes from around us. "Hey, where you off to in such a hurry?"

I grabbed my bra off the floor and put it on as my eyes searched for my shirt in the dark. "I need to get some coursework done." *Shower. I need to shower.*

"You're such a bloke, Mia. Usually, I'm the one bolting after situations like this. Kind of hurts my feelings."

I pulled the shirt over my head. "You'll survive." And I left him alone in the dark room with his pants still pulled down to his thighs.

If I had a dollar for every time I'd put myself in those situations—*okay, maybe not a dollar, more like a hundred-dollar bill*—then I would have been rich. Sex didn't mean anything to me, but for some reason, sex with Liam conceived a guilt only growing larger with each step back to my dorm.

With a new pair of shorts and a random shirt in hand, I reached the shower, and the shame and remorse of what I'd done completely took me over. I cursed at myself under the running warm water as it attempted to wash away my crime, but no matter how long I stayed under the faucet, the guilt of my sin would not dissipate.

When I exited the shower, I trashed my panties, the only evidence left of the mistake with Liam. *Never again.*

"I did something stupid." I shook my head as if it could erase what had happened, and glanced back up at Zeke, who stared back with a blank face. "I had sex with Liam."

Zeke's young features didn't change, so I continued, "Before, I only put myself in those situations thinking it would switch me back to normal, and even afterward when it didn't work, it still didn't bother me. But now I'm bothered. *Shit.* I don't know what I'm trying to say. You understand what I'm trying to say?" Though there were more muscles in the human face than in the rest of the body, Zeke hadn't moved a single one of them.

I twisted my neck to look behind me, and saw Liam observing me from across the room. He pulled his stupid lip between his teeth, and my stomach twisted into knots as I forced down bile threatening to come up. "Dear Lord, what was I thinking? Here"—I pushed my dinner tray in front of Zeke—"I lost my appetite. You can have my cookie if you want."

Zeke stared at me from across the table, unmoving.

"Why are men so predictable? For once, can someone surprise me? Like you, for instance." I leaned back in the chair. "Yes, you don't talk, and I know no matter what I say, you'll sit there and stare at me with those big brown eyes of yours. That much is predictable." I let out a small laugh. "But I still have no idea what's going through your head right now, and I like that about you."

After folding my arms over the table, I laid my head down and found Ollie through the chaos. Ollie tilted his head until his eyes met mine. "Is it strange I pretended he was Ollie the whole time to get through it? I wonder what it would be like with Ollie, but we can never. He will be the one to destroy me, Zeke. I can feel it with him. I still can't believe he kissed me in my room, then had the audacity to walk right out afterward. *That* I wasn't expecting. Do you think he's waiting for me to talk to him about it?"

I lifted my head to see Zeke eating my cookie, and I flashed him a lopsided grin. "Whoa, take it easy there, slugger. With all this movement, you might break something."

TEN

"Don't waste ink on girls who are oblivious to their beauty.
Write about the ones who know, but choose to ignore it."

OLIVER MASTERS

The next morning, I found a paper slipped under my door. It read, *skip breakfast & meet me in room 23 @ 8.* The handwriting was in script with no indication as to who it was from. It was fifteen minutes 'til, and it only took me half a second to decide my need to know who it was from trumped the option of ignoring it. I grabbed my weekend clothes consisting of shorts, Converse shoes, a plain gray tee with a deep V-neck, and a hoodie. My entire wardrobe consisted of whites, grays, and blacks, without a pop of color. Everything went with everything.

After my shower, I left my hair down to air dry. The ends hit just above my chest and had already grown half an inch since I'd been here. It looked darker than usual, but then again, I hadn't been under the sun in over a month. I'd forgotten what the sun felt like against my skin, and wondered when I would feel it again—if this place didn't kill me first. Any opportunity we had to go outside, the sun was either hidden behind gray clouds, or it was raining.

Room twenty-three was on the first floor. My shoes made no sound against the marble stairs as I stepped down, praying it wasn't Liam waiting for me. After a sharp right-hand turn down a long hallway, my stride slowed when I spotted Ollie leaning against the wall with his foot propped, waiting for me at the end with a brown bag and two cups in hand.

Involuntarily, my body paused to take in the sight of him—and to breathe as if I couldn't seem to do it all at once.

When his eyes met mine, a sleepy but charming smile appeared. The sun's rays streamed through the windows as if the sun waited on his damn smile, and he dropped his head to hide his satisfaction. He styled his thick hair into its usual backward wave, and small pieces stuck out over his ears. He looked back up at me with a striking grin, and my pace picked up to get to him already—to get to the boy who'd made me punch a damn cement wall because, well, for once, I was ready to admit he'd gotten to me. And I'd never seen it coming.

"You're late," he said as I approached, and he handed over a drink. "I understand you Americans prefer coffee over tea. I hope it's how you like it." By immediately taking a sip, I was able to both calm my nerves and conceal my smile. The coffee melted in my mouth and a small moan escaped my throat, and he flashed me a grin. "I honestly didn't think you'd show."

"Me neither." Behind him was a tall wooden door arched into a half circle at the top. It looked misplaced, as if it didn't belong. Everything else was like me, cold and without personality. But the door was warm and filled with history and character. "What's this?"

Ollie took a side step and pointed to the sign reading *LIBRARY room 23.* "Come on, we're just eating here, but this place is really cool. I think you'll like it."

The door creaked open as I stepped inside, and it wasn't anything like I had expected. A small unattended desk stood in the middle of the floor, holding up a computer monitor belonging in the early '90s. Papers and

120

books scattered across the old wooden desk, and I turned to Ollie behind me.

"No one is here on Saturday mornings. We have the whole place to ourselves." He walked past me and behind the desk, where the room split into several options to walk through, and said, "Come on, follow me."

Ollie led me down an aisle not nearly wide enough for two people to stand side by side. Each row was narrow and stacked from floor to ceiling with books. The library had a sweet but musky smell like chocolate mixed with paper.

Ollie made a sharp left, which opened up another ten different possibilities to turn. Each row was narrower than the last, but Ollie swiftly moved as if he knew where to go. Unable to tell my left from my right, or up from down, corridors and passageways split in all directions, interwoven to create a dream world surrounded by literature. Books stacked every inch, and my eyes darted around as Ollie led me through the web until we finally reached our destination.

A hidden small round nook spiraled in color-coordinated books to the ceiling. Spotlights bounced off the circular walls and onto the floor, and I looked up to see a skylight. Ollie took a seat on the floor and patted the space beside him for me to sit before he opened the bag.

"Where did you get all this?" I asked when he handed me a croissant.

He took a sip of his drink and closed his eyes as if he'd been waiting to get to his spot to enjoy something as simple as the first sip. His eyes didn't open again until he swallowed it down, but when they did, he caught me in awe of him. "It's the little things, Mia." We shared a smile before he finally answered my original question. "I can't tell you all my secrets. Plus, if I told you, you wouldn't need me anymore."

My teeth sunk into the croissant, and it was the perfect amount of crispy flakiness on the outside and buttery fluff on the inside. "You bring me croissants every Saturday, and I'll gladly bear your children."

Ollie turned his head to face me and the lump in his throat moved. "I'm holding you to that." He grinned to lighten the seriousness in his tone, and I quickly averted my eyes from his to our surroundings.

"It's like a maze in here, though. How do you not get lost?"

He swallowed the food in his mouth before saying, "Oh, I do. One time it took me an hour to find the entrance, but no matter how long or far I stray, I always find my way back. I'm usually here every Saturday morning. Eating in the mess hall every day with the same people can get old after a while. You have to break it up to keep your sanity." He pulled his knees up and rested his arms over them. "Again … the little things."

After popping the rest of the croissant into my mouth, I took a sip of my coffee and stood to my feet. Ollie looked up at me with an open mouth and curious eyes. "And where do you think you're running off to?"

"We're going to play a game," I said, and a smile crept along his lips. "You find me first, and I'll give you an answer—"

"An answer to what?"

"Whatever one question you want to ask me, but"—I held up a finger—"if I can get to you first, you have to tell me why you're here."

He dropped the last piece of his donut in his mouth, and with a mouthful, he said, "Alright, let's do this." He dusted off his hands and stood.

Slowly, I backed away from him. "You stay here, count to sixty while I try to get lost."

Ollie took a step forward and I took another step back.

An assertive smirk played on his lips. "Don't leave this library, Mia. If I spend hours searching for you like a fool to find out you left …"

I rested my hands on my hips and returned the same smile. "What are you going to do?"

Ollie's gaze dropped to the floor as he shook his head lightly, hiding his smile. He ran his hand through his hair as he turned his back to me. "I'm not counting out loud, love. You better get going." He placed his palms against the circular book case and leaned over.

I watched him, admiring the way his shoulder blades moved beneath his shirt; then my eyes skimmed down his torso and landed on his cute butt.

"I know you're checking me out." He laughed.

122

My cheeks warmed and I took off in the opposite direction, trying to lose myself in the maze. After about a minute passed, my voice danced across the bindings of numerous books as I slowed to a walk through a passageway and down another aisle, "Come find me, Ollie."

I continued in front of me, hoping I'd reach a dead end, but I didn't. Every angle, every aisle had me more turned around than before, and after ten minutes passed, I found myself in the Romance section, plucking books off the shelf and analyzing their covers.

Each cover looked similar in a lot of ways. Either a man and woman holding hands, or hugging, or kissing, all showing affection toward one another, but it was all a lie. I didn't see it in their eyes or smiles because none of it was real. False advertisement. Book covers should only reveal the title, author, and short description. They say you shouldn't judge a book by its cover, but everyone always did.

A pair of hands brushed the surface of my arms, and the warmth of Ollie's body behind me made me smile. "Looks like I get to ask you a question." His breath heated my neck.

Fingertips traveled down the lengths of my arms until they found mine. The only sound was the beating in my ears, and I fought to keep my body from sinking into him.

Ollie had to have felt the same force because it was him who surrendered the distance between us, pressing his body against mine from behind. He moved my hair off my shoulder to the other side.

"One question." I managed to gather the two words as his struggling breath entangled in my hair.

"This isn't fair. There is so much I want to know." He laced his fingers into mine as he dipped his head down to my ear. "I want to know how you like your coffee, and what your favorite song is. I want to know what annoys you, and the worst thing you've ever done. I want to know your greatest fear, and whether or not you talk in your sleep. If you prefer chocolate over vanilla, and if you cried watching *The Notebook* ... if you've ever seen *The Notebook*, or like movies at all. What gives you the greatest high, and what can take all the pain away ..." Ollie drew in a deep breath, and at the same time, my heart skipped in my chest. "But what I need to know is … are you willing to open yourself up to me so I can find out?"

"Is that your question?" I stammered, lost in all his words.

"Yes." He exhaled. "That's my final question."

Turning to face him, his eyes filled with hope and wonder, but his absent smile expected the inescapable truth. We both knew there wasn't anything inside me to open up, an empty shell. So, what exactly did I have to lose?

And, so, it was there, in the middle of the romance section of the maze-like library at Dolor University outside of Guildford in the United Kingdom where I decided I was willing to show him I was nothing more than a hollow soul. "I will only disappoint you."

"I doubt it."

"And I'm difficult," I warned.

"Good." Ollie grinned. "I wasn't expecting anything less, Mia. I'm only asking you to knock down a wall. Not even a wall—fuck, carve me out a door. I only want to know you." He grabbed my hand, and a calmness washed over me.

I didn't have the tools to destroy a wall, let alone carve out a door. The barriers had endured ten years. Tough and sturdy and placed for a reason. Each one had a purpose, and even though I'd forgotten why they stood there in the first place, I was scared what would happen if I started carving out holes. The walls became my friends—they were safe. But I nodded, anyway, because the small glimmer of hope in his eyes spread like an infection.

"And to clarify, no, I've never seen *The Notebook*, and I don't plan on it, either."

Ollie threw his head back and a raspy laugh echoed in our maze.

A laugh I had quickly grown to adore.

We lost track of time as we lay across the floor with our heads side by side and our feet in opposite directions, staring up at the tower of books as if they were stars. The multi-colored binders scattered in no particular pattern.

124

If I concentrated hard enough, I could make out different shapes. If I stared long enough without blinking, it looked as if the colors slowly moved. All I had to do was close my eyes for three seconds, and when I opened them again, my palette refreshed under a new set of eyes.

"What is on your mind this very moment?" Ollie asked as he pulled a hand behind his head.

I smiled. "All the words floating around in this room. It's crazy to think we're lying here in a library, surrounded by stories that have gone through people's heads first. This aisle alone is completely made up of characters and worlds that have been thought of first, and now exist." I lifted my hand above our heads and gestured around us in amazement. "All around us are moments of death, tragedy, first kisses, last kisses, moments of weakness, intimacy, and tears cried … and I can't help but think I will never be able to know or possibly understand any of those feelings."

"You've never cried?"

"I'm sure I cried when I was a little girl, but I don't remember what it felt like." I turned on my side to face him as he stared up at the ceiling. "What about you?"

"You're asking if I have cried? What kind of question is that?" he asked with hilarity in his tone. His eyes slid to mine, and I nodded in all seriousness. "I'm known to shed tears, but only on Mondays and Wednesdays."

I shoved him playfully in the shoulder. "Ollie, be real. Tell me about it. How does it feel?"

"Alright, alright. No need to get physical." Ollie turned on his side to face me and held up his head in the palm of his hand. "There are two types of crying," he said, then paused. He pressed out a laugh as he brought his fingers to his eyes. "Wow, shit's about to get real right now, yeah?"

He regained composure and looked back at me. "Okay, so there's the kind from pain, not necessarily physical pain because there's that, too, and as much as everyone says they're the same, it's not. So, I'll go over the worst, which is emotional pain. It starts right here"—he pointed to my

125

lungs—"and suddenly you can't breathe, like a blow to the stomach, and whatever source brought this on stole all the air around you. Panic sets in…"

His fingers inched from my lungs to my chest, and I wondered if he felt the beating beneath his fingers. "An ache forms in your heart so intense, you'd rather suffer a hundred deaths than to last one more second of agony. Your heart pumps and you feel the burn as it struggles because pieces that once belonged are now missing."

Ollie moved my hair behind my ear before gently pressing his fingers over my temple. "And when you think it couldn't get any worse, your head is pounding now, deprived of oxygen and the appropriate amount of blood flow. Nothing and everything is flooding through your mind all at once. And right as the thunder rolls in your head, the lightning crashes behind your eyes. Electricity, stinging and begging to be released, and the best thing to do is stop fighting it. If you hold back tears, Mia, the pain builds up in your heart, and your heart is only so forgiving for so long."

Ollie rested his palm over the side of my face. I opened my mouth to say something, but no words formed. I wanted to ask him if he'd ever felt like that before, but he had if he remembered it all so vividly. So vividly, it couldn't have been only once he'd experienced that kind of emotional pain. How many times had his tall and strong man been broken down to only be pieced back together to go through the same torment all over again? Did I care enough to find out?

"The beautiful kind is when you don't even realize it's happening," he continued to say. "You're not fighting it because your soul is finally at peace with what is happening, and that's when you know …"

"Know what?" I blurted as I hung on to his every beautiful word.

Ollie grinned. "You felt something so powerful, you can no longer be without it."

We spent the rest of the morning talking and playing in the library, stuck in the fever of us. We ran through the history section, each stride crossing decades of battles, wars, and freedom fought for. Ollie tackled me in the children's section and carried me over his shoulder through crime and thriller. I escaped his grasp in mystery, but he caught up in romance as our smiles gradually faded. The mood between us changed along with the genre, as he took a step closer—our feet walking through traitorous waters, and our hearts playing with fire. I pushed off him and ran, and when I looked behind me, Ollie smiled before chasing after me once again.

And up until we had to leave for lunch, I had forgotten we were in Dolor at all.

"Will you come by tonight?" Ollie asked before we reached the mess hall.

I lifted my cast in the air. "Even if I wanted to, I couldn't make it up the vent with a broken hand."

"That's right. And tell me … why did you punch the wall?"

"Because you kissed me," I said with a single shrug.

He reached for the bridge of his nose as a cackle escaped from his throat. "Sorry, you"—he paused both his stride and sentence to double over and let out another laugh, and when he pulled himself back up, he inhaled deeply and straightened his face—"you punched a wall because I kissed you?"

"It's not funny, son of a bitch hurt …"

Ollie threw his head back as he clapped his hands together. "I'm not laughing because you got hurt, but the way you said it so nonchalantly … damn …" He let out an exhale, and his smile faded as he draped his arm around me, pulling me close to his side. His green eyes transformed as if a lightbulb had gone off in his head, and he slowed his pace. "You know what this means, don't you?"

"What?"

Ollie's lip turned up in the corner. "You'll see."

ELEVEN

"All at once, she's a monster and a masterpiece,
worthy of someone to both quiet the dark side
and light the colors of her soul on fire."

OLIVER MASTERS

A loud thunderstorm woke me Sunday morning as the downfall beat against my window. The rain sang its song over Dolor in the most soothing tempo in the dark sky. Nothing but gray skies hovered in the distance as I looked passed the brick wall surrounding the campus, and over the rolling hills. Nothing indicated the weather would lift for the rest of the day. The sun planned on taking the day off, allowing the rain to shine like it usually did in this city.

After my morning shower, which turned into a workout on its own with my cast, I pulled on my comfy gray sweatpants and a white tee, brushed my teeth, and threw my hair into a sloppy bundle over my head because it was one of those days. It was Rain's day.

Zeke had finished eating by the time I reached the mess hall, and Jake's entire crew was absent. They must have partied hard last night, and lost themselves in a dream through the morning.

Taking my seat across from Zeke, I pulled the hoodie over my head. Each time it was Rain's day, the building dropped ten degrees.

"Good morning, Zeke."

Zeke's wild eyes darted around before picking at his plate. The large floor-to-ceiling windows took up one whole side of the mess hall next to our table as the rain came down hard, beating like a loud drum. Zeke's hand shook as he held his fork.

"It's fine. You're safe."

My attempt at reassurance didn't seem to appease him, so I brought my attention back to my food. "I had a croissant yesterday, sure as hell better than this crap," I muttered, picking at the eggs. I took a mouthful and forced it down—starving—but anything was better than nothing. I was beginning to think the British didn't believe in seasoning because the food here was entirely too bland—probably also the reason why everyone in the UK was skinny, and everyone in America was overweight.

"So, yesterday, Ollie and I went to the library. Have you been?"

Zeke flinched under the clap of thunder with panic in his brown eyes. If I continued talking to him, maybe it would take his mind off the thunderstorm. "It's like a maze. You could get lost in that place. Books everywhere, stacked in piles over the floor all the way to the ceiling. It was a-maze-ing." I chuckled at my crack at a pun before looking back up to Zeke. "Oh, come on. That was funny."

Thunder erupted close by as lightning hit, sending the mess hall into complete darkness. Zeke let out a shriek, and I scurried to his side without thinking. I crouched down beside him, unsure of what to do—if I should reach out to touch him, or if I should speak. It was dark, and I could hardly make out his face.

"It's okay. Breathe, Zeke, just breathe. It's me. It's Mia. I'm not going to let anything hurt you," I said over his cries.

Zeke's scream died down as I continued talking him through it, waiting for the lights to turn back on, or the generators to kick in.

About two minutes into the darkness, the lights slowly flickered on when an announcement played over the intercom. *"This is Dean Lynch. Please report back to your dorms until the storm passes. I repeat, go back to your dorms and wait until further instruction."*

"Okay, Zeke, I'm going to take you back to your room, but you have to show me where it is." I helped him out of the chair. Based on Zeke's physique, he couldn't have been older than sixteen.

We walked close together as he led the way and people shoved past us in the halls. Doors opened and closed, party invitations in specific room numbers tossed in the air, and laughing and insults paraded the halls. Zeke paused from time to time to freeze in place.

Zeke's room was the same size as mine but seemed smaller with the amount of furniture stuffed in the small space. He had padded walls, and a television and DVD player sat on top of a dresser against the wall where my desk stood. In the corner was a small table and chair for one. Beside the table was a mini fridge. "You have it made in here, Zeke."

Zeke went straight to his bed and curled into a ball before I waved goodbye and closed his door behind me.

After reaching my dorm, I found another note passed under my door. It read, *"Breakfast in my room, knock two times —O."* A smile formed, and each time it did, it became easier and easier to smile in his name. This smile was different from others. It wasn't the kind of smile I had to fake, which was my go-to smile. This smile wasn't pressured like when someone told a horrible joke. This smile wasn't forced, like the times people said, "Smile, Mia. Things could be worse." No, this was Ollie's smile; habitual, distinctive, and easy.

I walked the four rooms down to Ollie's and knocked two times as instructed.

"Who's there?"

"Mia."

"Mia who?" Ollie asked, amused, from the other side of the door.

Shaking my head, my Ollie-smile reached my eyes. "Mia-come-in already?"

The door opened and a half-asleep Ollie stood on the other side with a lazy smile. I couldn't help but wonder if it was his "Mia-smile," or if he had one at all. His hair was a mess, and he wore sweatpants with a loose black tee.

"We're going to have to work on your knock-knock jokes, love." His two emerald eyes sparkled as he reached for my good hand and pulled me in.

His room was cleaner than I'd ever seen. There were pillows—*actual pillows*—and blankets over his mattress. "Did you not have a party last night?"

"I did, but I kicked everyone out early. Here, I got your glazed croissant," Ollie said, handing me over a bag, "but I couldn't get the coffee. That's only on Saturdays."

Wasting no time, I reached into the bag for the donut and sank my teeth into its glory. "Oh, you are incredible," I hummed with a mouthful.

Ollie climbed over the mattress and melted into a heap of pillows against the wall. "What are your plans for the day?" he asked as I fell over the mattress beside him.

"We're on lockdown, so I guess nothing. I'm supposed to be in my dorm right now."

"No, you're good. Stanley won't do a security check because of a storm."

After finishing my donut, I sucked the glaze off my fingers as impulsive moans were liberated from inside. Ollie's eyes lit up as I savored each finger. "Do you always moan when you eat? Because you're sort of turning me on."

I elbowed him playfully in the shoulder, and he fell back, pretending to be wounded.

"I'm told I make more noise when I eat than during sex, so yeah … as long as the food's good, I can't help it."

"I like it," he whispered, and another clash of thunder echoed in the room as the wind whistled against the window, "but I don't want to hear about your sex life."

"Jealous?"

Ollie shook his head. "Crestfallen."

"I don't know what that means."

"Gutted"—he wrapped his arms around my waist and dragged me back against him—"discouraged"—he moved the hair from my neck—"crushed"—he grazed his nose across the skin below my ear—"Shall I keep going, Mia?"

All I could think about were his hands on me and his breath on my neck.

Yes, keep going, Ollie.

"I understand."

Stupid, stupid mouth of mine.

Ollie released me from his hold and lay flat on his back behind me. It took all the strength I had to not climb on top of him. "So, how are we going to keep ourselves occupied?" I asked, wondering what was going through his mind, but then I remembered what Jake and Alicia had said. Their words replayed over and over. *"Ollie doesn't mess around. He's not the type."*

Ollie turned over onto his side and lifted his head into his hand. "Okay, before you say anything—"

I fell to my side, facing him. "Why does the beginning of that sentence scare me?"

"Before you say anything more …" Ollie reached under his pillow. "You said you were willing to open up to me, knock down a wall …"

"Cut out a door," I corrected with a finger in the air. "Don't push your luck, Masters."

Ollie laughed. "Alright, 'cut out a door.'" He pulled a book out and handed it over.

132

I dangled it above my head. "*The Notebook*? The movie was based on a book?" A groan left me and I handed the book back. "No, I don't read."

"First of all, I'm going to read to you … and second, I saw you in the mess hall with *To Kill a Mockingbird*. Do you pretend to read to attract guys like me?"

"It was an assignment from Dr. Conway. I don't read for pleasure."

"Then it's a good thing you won't be the one reading." He lay back against the pillow and opened the book, then looked up at me with a crinkle between his brows. "Something's missing," he muttered, and slipped his arm beneath me, dragging me closer to his side. My face fell into his neck as a giggle escaped. "Ah, much better. Now, quiet, Mia. I need to read." Ollie kissed the top of my head as the rest of me melted beside him.

He flipped past the acknowledgments to the first chapter titled "Miracle."

The moment the first sentence fell from his lips, I shifted my attention from the black ink inside the book to him, taking in the way his lips moved as his eyes danced along the page, flitting from one end to the other. His angelic voice remained steady as he ran his fingers lightly through my hair with one hand and held the battered book in the other. Ollie was captivating, and I was afraid if I turned away, even for a split second, I'd miss a beat—miss a word from his lips, miss a blink of his thick lashes as he lost himself in the world the author had created. *Absolutely breathtaking.*

We stayed like that for hours, him reading, and me listening to his every word, every syllable as it rolled off his tongue. Enchanted by the words of Nicholas Sparks, but only because they were spoken with his sound of grace. It wasn't only Ollie's accent making the story come to life; it was the way he enunciated each word with a slow elegance.

I buried my cold feet between his legs, craving his warmth, and Ollie paused for a moment to press his lips to the side of my head before returning to the page. The rain picked up at one point, then slowly faded as it played of its own accord against the window. My lids grew heavy, and I fought against them, but eventually, Ollie's poetic voice got the best of me.

It was Dean Lynch over the intercom who woke me, and my eyes opened to see Ollie's chest slowly rise and fall with the open book sprawled across it. I tilted my head from his chest to see his face, and he silently slept with his mouth slightly parted, and I smiled to myself.

A part of me wanted to stay beside him and pretend time didn't exist, but the rational side of me knew I couldn't hold on to this moment forever. Carefully, I moved out from his hold, making sure not to disturb him.

Ollie's hand sprang to grab my arm, and pulled me back on top of him without opening his eyes. I buried my face into the crook of his neck and giggled.

"Let me live in this moment for a bit longer," he whispered.

Breathing in his skin, the mixture of coconut and sandalwood created a weak marine breeze. Turning to his side, the open book fell between us and his arms tightened around me. "It's safe to say, you don't talk in your sleep." His eyes were still closed. It was a possibility if he opened them, a reality check would pour over us like the rain outside.

But only if he opened his eyes.

"That's a relief." *Stay strong, Ollie, for both of our sakes.*

Ollie opened his eyes, folded up the book, and stuck it under his pillow.

"Best nap ever," he confessed, and moved the hair from my face. His hand lingered around my cheek and he traced his thumb over my bottom lip. "You haven't got a clue how bad I want to kiss you right now, but I'm trying not to be selfish … for the sake of your wellbeing and all." A small smile tugged on his lips.

It was torture for us both. I could see it on his face, him falling for me. My reflection stared back through his green eyes, and for a split second, I saw myself the way he saw me, and I was beautiful. I'd warned him. I'd told him before we kissed not to fall for me, but it appeared the heart had a mind of its own and these things you couldn't control.

And now it was me without the control.

I inched my lips closer to his, and Ollie took in a sharp breath.

"Mia ..." He closed his eyes and slowly shook his head as if it were too much.

"I'm letting the moment happen the way it's meant to. Whatever you're doing to me, I can't stop it." I brushed my lips against his soft ones as I spoke, which wasn't satisfying my need for him. "Most of my time with you is either spent fighting some internal conflict or trying to comprehend what's happening to me. I don't even talk like this, Ollie. Why am I even telling you this? What have you done to me?" I smiled despite my frustration.

He pressed his forehead to mine as his breathing staggered. The refreshing mint in his breath sent shivers up my arms. "I'm utterly gobsmacked. I have no words right now. That is what *you* do to *me*."

Caving, my traitorous lips crashed with Ollie's, and the rest of my body betrayed me. My disloyal hand was in his hair as my unfaithful breath became his. Every part of me abandoned me, and I could do nothing about it. I belonged to him.

His lips parted in dire demand and as soon as his warm tongue flicked against mine, a moan freed itself between us. I didn't know if it had come from him or myself, but I didn't care. Yesterday's flames picked up in a frenzy as his warm hands found my bare skin at my sides, warming me in more ways than one.

Ollie pulled away and wet his lips. "I hope ... no, I'm *praying* you're not toying with me right now," he said breathlessly. "Mia, tell me you're not fucking with me."

Shaking my head, I couldn't grasp what he was saying. Here I was, telling him exactly what had been on my mind moments ago, more than I had ever admitted to anyone. "I don't know what you want me to say." I searched the question written on his face. "Look me in the eyes, and you tell me if I'm playing with you, Ollie." Honestly, I didn't know what he'd find. Truth, possibly?

Ollie rested his hand on my face and moved my hair to look into my eyes. I held my breath in anticipation, waiting for what would come of it. There was nothing there. There couldn't be. But once his green eyes stared into mine, it quenched his doubt.

His lips surrendered once again, and this time there was no holding back from either one of us. He pulled me on top of him, and I removed my sweatshirt between moments without his lips on mine. His taste, his smell, his warmth—it all left me intoxicated.

Ollie's mouth moved slow over mine, savoring every intricate detail of me. Unhurried, he appreciated us like a work of art. His long fingers gripped my hips, and I raked my fingers through his hair as I sucked gently on his neck and behind his ear.

"Mia, we can't," Ollie breathed.

My nose grazed the length of his neck. "We can't what?"

He flipped me over on my back, so he was now on top of me and settled between my legs. His hard arousal pressed into me as he said, "We can't go any further."

"Your body says otherwise …"

He hung his head for a moment, and when his eyes returned to mine, his cheeks flushed as he smiled. "Around you, my body tends to have a mind of its own."

"Then what's the problem?"

Ollie deeply inhaled while he stroked my forehead with his thumb. "The problem is, I'm not just a guy, and you're not just a girl, so the last thing we should do is treat this as such."

"I'm still not following." He wasn't just a guy. He was *the* guy capable of seeing me in a way no one else had. But I was just a girl, and suddenly I realized I would never be or give him what he needed.

"As much as our bodies would disagree, we're not ready." Ollie fell over to the side of me, and a chill replaced his warmth. "I'm not a quick fuck, Mia. Either you're all in with me, or you're not, and you're not ready for that, and you're not ready for what this school could do to us."

Rejection.

Looking around the room, I was convinced there was a hidden camera. No one had ever turned me down for sex. What did Ollie mean "all in"? What did he mean "what this school could do to us"? Instead of entertaining him, I found my sweatshirt and pulled it over my head as I gradually came apart at the seams. What in God's name was he doing to me?

Ollie ran his hand over his face before adjusting himself in his pants. "Talk to me. What's wrong?"

"Nothing, I'm fine." I leaned over him and pressed my lips to his forehead. And suddenly, I understood his mentioning of the stinging electricity behind my eyes. The lightning crashed, but I forced it away.

Around Ollie, I didn't feel like myself at all. He made me weak, exposed, and defenseless; he was no good for me, and it was all because I had carved him out a damn door. It was dangerous.

And here I was, kissing his forehead like a sucker.

My hands stilled over the doorknob, and before I opened it, I turned one last time to see Ollie with his hands over his face and through his hair, and I shook my head and left.

The mess hall was crowded more than usual that evening, and I assumed it was because it wasn't only Ollie and I who had skipped lunch. The storm had circled Dolor, and the worst of it had come back around for a second time. Zeke's knuckles turned white as he gripped the seat and bobbed his head in all directions. I attempted to talk to him through the rain whipping against the window beside us. After offering to switch tables, it seemed to anger him even more as he shook his head violently.

"Zeke, it's okay. It can't touch you," I assured him, but in a flash of lightning, a branch from a nearby tree slammed against the window, causing Zeke to fall out of his chair and scurry against an adjacent wall. He belted an ear-piercing shriek, and I pushed out of my chair and ran around the table to sit by his side.

Pinning his head against my chest, I stroked his curly brown hair as the scream dissolved, but he remained trembling in my arms. I was unsure of what had come over me, or why I felt the need to comfort him, but Zeke reminded me of someone and I had this compulsion to protect him.

I hummed a familiar tune as my fingers ran through his sweaty mop over his head, clutching him tight. Many eyes peered over at us, and the only sound was the bass of the thunder. Jake and Alicia's jaws went slack mid-chew, Bria raised an annoying black brow, and Ollie dropped his fork as awe stuck his green eyes, but I ignored their judgments and continued to calm the storm inside Zeke, humming a tune as he slowly relaxed in my arms.

The hum and the brush of my hand against his forehead were all too familiar. A door that had been locked for far too long opened, flooding memories of my mother. She used to do this to me.

In the middle of the night, my mother would wake me from a night terror. She held me close against her chest, wiping the sweaty strands sticking to my face as she whispered things like, *"This is all my fault, I'm so sorry,"* before humming me back into contentment. She smelled like a cigarette soaked in perfume, and I found it comforting because it was the smell of my mother.

As the memory coursed through me, my hand shook, and my hums were no longer soothing but now breaking. And a hot panic consumed me as if I absorbed Zeke's terror. A fog of fury washed over me, and I pulled away from Zeke. Using the wall behind me for support, I stumbled to my feet. All eyes were fixed on Zeke and me.

I gritted my teeth, my palms sweaty, and I rushed out of the mess hall in a panic over what would come next. The memories of my mother's smell, her sounds, the touch of her hand only tore open an old wound, ripping it deeper and wider with each long stride to the community bathroom.

I gripped the edge of the sink as my chest heaved, begging for a fix. The girl in the mirror crumbled before my eyes, and I despised her. She was weak and broken. I locked her away with the memories of her mother,

138

and suddenly, there she was, staring back at me with truth in her eyes, and I shook my head, resisting what she had to say.

My throat burned as a scream belted, and my cast crashed between the girl's eyes, destroying her and sending shards of glass all around me. The basket from the sink flew across the bathroom before slamming against the wall—trial sized bottles spilled down the tile. I gripped my hair when the door to the bathroom flew open.

Ollie paused under the door frame with wide and worried eyes. My cast rested over my lungs as I paced the bathroom, hyperventilating. Ollie took a step forward.

"Get away from me!" I screamed. My voice cracked, but it wasn't the only thing breaking before him.

"No," he calmly said and took another step toward me with his palms in the air.

I tore a curtain from its rod and threw it toward him as a threat. Ollie didn't flinch.

I only saw red. Even though I never felt before, it was all I was doing now. I felt, and it fucking hurt. I wanted it to go away. The only thing I could do was hurt myself. Take the pain in my chest and lungs and transfer it somewhere else. Focus on a different kind of pain. Throwing my left hand into another mirror, the glass cut me, but I was numb to the physical pain. It didn't work. Nothing would work. Memories still ransacked me, the night terrors, the …

I couldn't remember.

I couldn't go back far enough to remember.

"Mia," Ollie whispered, reminding me he was still there, watching me self-destruct before his eyes.

"Get away from me, Ollie!"

Ollie stepped over the white curtain and broken glass. "No, Mia."

I launched at him, and he wrapped his arms around mine and pulled me into a shower stall, pinning me against his chest. During the struggle, he flipped the shower on, and cold water drenched us as I thrashed in his arms. "It hurts," I cried out, but no tears would fall. He pinned my arms tight against my chest, and his back slammed against the tile before dragging me down to the floor under the biting cold of the shower head. I begged for relief from my past as I withered away in his anchored hold. "Make it stop!"

My screams turned into a chattering of my teeth.

My hot rage was smothered with frostbite, and our bodies shook forcefully under our drenched clothes as Ollie's tight grip held on for the both of us.

TWELVE

"The inescapable truth is, we are destined for this.
No matter your resistance, our hearts are relentless.
Each time we drift, we'll only collide once more
over and over again in inescapable truth:
you and I belong together."

OLIVER MASTERS

Solitary confinement wasn't as bad as Dean Lynch had threatened it to be. He should have used forty-eight hours of being stuck in a classroom with Dr. Kippler as punishment. I didn't mind solitude. I preferred it.

All in all, my two days in solitary were more like a vacation. A security guard brought me breakfast, lunch, and dinner. Each time the tall and skinny dark man passed by my door, I attempted conversation, mainly using him as the person on the opposite end of my knock-knock jokes, but he didn't find it the least bit funny.

Being locked in the room only temporarily repaired the scar that was ripped open, and even though I managed to stitch it back up and subside my anger spells, the ghost of the memory still lingered.

It had been over ten years since I'd thought about my night terrors. I couldn't remember why I'd had them to begin with, or why my mother had thought it was her fault, but I could no longer care to put the pieces together. The paralysis set back in, the walls rebuilt strong and sturdy, and solitary confinement was just what I needed to feel like my normal self again. Dr. Conway tried to push me to talk about what had happened, but there was nothing to talk about.

Everything had happened so quickly. Ollie had insisted it was him who had destroyed the bathroom as Stanley yanked me from his arms. Other security guards had been called in to control Ollie as threats against him ricocheted off the tiled walls. Bullets had fired from their mouths in all directions as I'd stood with my hands behind my back, shivering against the wall near the door. I couldn't comprehend their threats, but it was enough to compel a belligerent Ollie to a standstill with defeat in his eyes as Stanley took me away.

Ollie had made multiple attempts to speak to me when I returned to my regular schedule on Wednesday, but I'd brushed him away after thanking him for my vacation over the last two days. If it hadn't been for the weekend with Ollie, my mind wouldn't have been so fucked up. I wouldn't have cared enough to go to Zeke's side, which resulted in the memory of my mother. A memory I physically and mentally wasn't prepared to face. I couldn't blame Zeke for what had happened; he hadn't known what he was doing, but Ollie sure had.

Ollie had known exactly what he was doing.

But I'd found peace with it all.

I was back to Mia.

Many confused my disorder with depression or anxiety, but it was far different. To be depressed, you had to feel hopeless or sadness. I felt neither and nothing—a black hole. My defenses surrounded me as I continued to fall through the emptiness. Ollie's door I'd carved had led me to believe there was an escape hatch, and a part of me had drifted to his door and held on by a finger. I'd felt, then. I'd felt the pain of what holding on did to me. It had started in my heart. The color of red had slowly replaced the black darkness from the inside out. The burning in my chest, the dozen candles flickering, its wax dripping through my veins, and I'd remembered why I'd shut it all out in the first place. It had taken the forty-eight hours to slowly rebuild those walls back up without the damn escape hatch this time before jumping off the ledge.

Now, I was falling once again through the hole surrounded by my new fences in total peace.

I arrived at group therapy early and found my seat. As others trickled through the double doors of the large, useless room, I turned my attention over to my cast, using a Sharpie to scribble music notes across the white bandages of a tune stuck in my head—the things I would do for my headphones this very moment. Music had always been my excuse to avoid conversation, my reason to escape an uncomfortable situation. I would put my headphones over my ears, and everyone seemed to leave me alone. *Ta-da. Magic.*

Someone cleared their throat.

I glanced up from my cast to find Arty's wide white eyeballs peering over in my direction. After snapping the Sharpie closed, I twirled it between my fingers. Ollie sat across from me like last time, and he looked different—tired, even. His hair wasn't in its normal perfected wave, but instead hidden under a gray beanie.

Jake snuck a small wave to feel out my current mood.

I flashed my fake smile.

It was the only one I had left.

"We're going to do something a little different today," Arty said, passing sheets of paper and pens around the circle. "I want each of you to write down two truths and one lie. We will take turns going around the room, guessing which one is the lie. And please, let's keep this PG-thirteen."

As I stared at the blank paper, I continued to twirl my Sharpie in my good hand—well, better hand. Fresh cuts extended from one end of my knuckles to the other, leaving new scars from my manic episode.

You could tell who was finished by the way they fell back and relaxed in their chairs, small sighs breaking the silence. After five minutes, I still hadn't written a single letter.

"Okay, time's up. I'll start it off," Arty said and glanced down at his paper. "I'm originally from Egypt, I have six brothers and sisters, and when I was a boy, I wanted to be an astronaut."

Him having six brothers and sisters was the lie. Many factors from the way his tone changed when he said it, the fact it was the most boring of the three, and the exact number he used put up a big waving-in-the-air flag.

The group called out him being from Egypt was the lie, but I stayed quiet.

"Actually, I have nine brothers and sisters," Arty said with a smile. "Okay, Isaac, let's hear yours, and we will continue clockwise."

Isaac shifted in his seat before he listed off his three sentences, and as the truths and lies continued around the circle, disbelieving remarks followed shortly behind.

Ollie straightened his posture when it was his turn. The battle in his eyes was evident as he looked down at his paper. He crumbled the sheet in his fist and stuffed it into his front pocket before saying, "I have died and come back to life, I've given up a life, and I've saved a life."

Silence.

A cough.

Then the comments came.

"Ollie hasn't given up a life. He wouldn't even kill the earwig crawling up his arm." Bria let out a giggle. "Remember, Jake? How he lifted it off with the leaf and brought it over to the tree?" Another laugh.

Ollie's attention remained on the floor before him. He stuffed his hands deep into his pockets. The fact he used the term "given up" told a silent story of his past only he knew. "He hasn't saved a life," I said so low, I was surprised anyone heard me.

"Mia, why do you say that?" Arty asked.

"I just know."

Arty looked over to Ollie, and Ollie nodded. "She's right."

Jake's two truths and a lie stayed light-hearted, making sure everyone knew he was gay.

When my turn came, I glanced down at my blank paper and leaned back in my chair as my mind spoke for me. "I can play any song on the piano, I don't eat meat ... and ..."—*both Arty and Ollie are going to hate me*— "I had sex with Liam last Friday."

Gasps and laughs immediately followed, and I lifted my head from my blank paper to Ollie, whose hands were now out of his pockets and over his chin. His elbow bounced over his nervous knee.

"PG-thirteen, Mia," Arty reminded me, and I shrugged my shoulders.

"There's no way she slept with Liam. I was with him all day," a blonde-haired girl from Liam's table said.

"I've seen her eat meat. It's got to be the piano," Jake insisted.

"I agree. A girl like her can't play the piano," Bria added.

The blonde-haired girl stood and pointed over to the piano in the room, her face red and tears threatening to fall. "Prove it. There's a piano right there, and I need you to prove to me this isn't true."

I had no idea she felt this strongly for Liam. She wasn't the target of my attack. My whole point was to show Ollie I wasn't who he thought I was.

"I'm in a cast," I reminded them with my arm in the air.

"Told you she couldn't play," Bria scoffed to blondie.

Instantly, I stood and walked over to the piano before taking a seat. My battered hand lightly ran over the keys, not pressing hard enough to make a sound, but touching enough to familiarize myself with its coolness, its flow, its size. Playing was going to be difficult in a cast. I glanced up to see Blondie's arms crossed over her chest, Bria with a smirk, and the ounce of hope left in Ollie's eyes I was about to strip away.

After over a decade, the wait was over as my fingers danced along the keys to an acoustic version of Demi Lovato's "Sorry not Sorry." I didn't know what had come over me, but suddenly, I was humming the tune, and the hum turned into a song, and then I was singing the chorus as the room went up in a roar. My eyes closed as I lost myself in the music I made, forgetting how good it all felt. My voice seemed foreign but still the same as my eight-year-old self. More mature, more powerful, but still held the natural gravelly sound I had perfected at a young age.

After the last key lingered in the air, I let out an exhale and glanced over the piano. Ollie hung his head between his shoulders as he slowly shook it back and forth while the rest of the room cheered. I retook my seat and the circle's chatter died down, but Ollie stood and walked out without a single word in his wake.

Did he deserve that? No.

Despite my returned numbing state he had previously stolen from me, Ollie was everything I wasn't. He was light in the darkest moments, he was belief when no one else could see, and he was the indication of hope as walls etched with doubt caved around him. But I embodied truth, and the truth was—I could never change. And if I'd let him continue down this path, he would have eventually suffocated under my truth as he attempted to free a cursed soul.

Believe it or not, Ollie, I did that for you.

After group therapy was dismissed, Arty kept me behind to talk about what happened and made me promise never to act out again. Of course, I obliged, telling him whatever he wanted to hear. *No, sir.* Nod. *Yes, sir.* Nod. And out the door I went.

My pace slowed before I reached the corner of my wing. My stomach drifted, my mouth went dry, my breath caught, and I instantly knew. It always happened whenever I sensed Ollie near. My body deceived me when my mind couldn't. Leaning against the wall beside my door was the boy whose heart I had ripped out moments before.

It was still beating in the palm of my hand.

"It's best you stay away from me," I insisted as I drew nearer. Ollie looked up from the floor and removed his hands from his pockets. His beanie was pulled down lower over his forehead, and red rings circled his eyes. "And you look like shit," I added, knocking him while he was already down.

"Why are you doing this?" he asked, following me into my room.

"Oh." I dropped my books over my desk and turned to face him. "You mean me fucking Liam? I figured it's only fair for you to know what kind of person I am. Liam is not even half of what I've done." It was best for him to know everything.

He folded his fingers together over the top of his beanie as he looked into my cold and distant features. "For once in your life, Mia, can you stop pushing me away and be honest with yourself for five minutes?" he asked, and I paused mid-pace, "I know what kind of person you are, and this isn't you," Ollie dropped his hands and took a step toward me, "I know you feel something with me because if you didn't, you wouldn't have punched a bloody wall. I see it in your eyes, Mia."

"Stop! I don't feel!" I shouted and took a step away from him before pacing the room again. "Whatever you think is happening is all in your head."

Suddenly, Ollie picked me up at the waist and set me on top of my desk, gripping the edges as his frustrated eyes searched mine. "You're a fucking liar."

He looked down and grabbed my hand from my lap, wrapping his fingers around my wrist. "Your pulse is racing, Mia, and I know what it's like because mine does the same damn thing when I'm around you. And when I look into your eyes, I can see my Mia is in there. The girl who pretends not to care, but her heart is relentless. The girl who kisses me unapologetically, watches me read, laughs into my neck, and has a genuine fucking smile when I'm beside her. My Mia."

I forgot what had happened altogether. I forgot what had put us here, in this position. I forgot why Ollie was upset and only wanted to see him smile again. But he took advantage of my faltered mind and continued.

147

"Distance isn't good for us. Only two days in confinement and I already lost you, but you will come back because you always do with me." He dropped his head before wiping his face against his sleeve. "*Fuck*. I don't care what you did. You weren't right before the weekend, but I know you're right with me. You have to break through, and it's going to hurt, and it's going to be painful, but you have to because I'm fucking selfish and I want you." He shook his head. "No, I *need* you."

Ollie brought his hands to my face. His nose grazed mine as he breathed me in. "I need you to feel for me, and once you do, I need you to stay."

And then my lips were on his as I silenced him and he stole my breath all at once. He was my weakness and my strength—the life and the death of me. He gave and took with each caress of his tongue, unwilling to ease up as the desire between us only heightened. "I'm so sorry, Ollie," I whispered between moments of mourning without his lips on mine. He shook his head and stole my breath once again. His mouth grasped mine as if it were the lighthouse in the middle of a storm. His eyes shut tighter while he kissed me more firmly, his tongue's gentle rhythm sending his hips deeper between my legs. And when my hand fell over the waistband of his jeans, he pulled away.

"Please don't do this to me …" He breathed heavily. "I don't have the strength anymore."

"Have me." My words quickly rolled off my tongue.

Ollie only shook his head.

I wrapped my fingers around his chin and forced him to see me like he had done to me so many times before. "Right now, I'm yours. I never wanted anyone else, Ollie. I have only and always wanted you. I'm all in; whatever's left of me, is in with you. Please, don't reject me again. I can't handle it."

It only took Ollie a few beats to battle it out with himself. He slammed his palms over the desk before pushing off it. I held my breath. *Don't you dare leave me like this,* I wanted to say. But my words were caught, lost somewhere between my brain and tongue.

He walked toward the door.

Paralyzed, my non-existent heart was already breaking, mourning the loss of this moment that would never happen.

Everything had stopped. My breathing. My brain. The pumping of my heart. Ollie.

The sound of my door locking echoed.

My heart thumped.

He turned to face me.

My heart thumped.

His powerless eyes filled with lifetimes of longing—longing for me.

My heart thumped.

And Ollie withdrew his white tee, exposing tattoos along his ribcage, chest, and lean abs. In two long strides, he stood before me again, picking me up off the desk effortlessly and laying me across the mattress. He slowly pinned my hands above me as he covered my mouth with his.

I could breathe again.

"I'm not going to fuck you, Mia," he said slowly, his nose grazing mine as the mint bounced off his mouth. Before I had a chance to question him, his tongue slipped between my lips and our impatient kiss spiraled. We were on fire as a familiar spark went off inside me. My lips trembled against his as his fingers traveled down to the button on my jeans. Ollie had the ability to break me, and I knew it the moment my eyes fell on him.

He hesitantly pulled away and stood over me with one knee between my legs and his other foot planted on the floor. "Are you on birth control?"

I nodded. "And I never have sex without a condom … I have a box in my suitcase."

Ollie looked over to my suitcase and back at me. "You always use a condom? Not even one slip-up?"

I nodded and shook my head, unable to contain the buzz of him. "Never slipped."

"Then I'm not making love to you with a fucking condom on." An ache and adoration mixed in his eyes, and his voice held a promise. "It's all or nothing, Mia."

"Okay," I whispered, and lifted my shirt over my head, dropping it to the floor beside me.

His eyes praised me before his lips did, and his warm hands reached behind me to unlatch my bra, freeing my breasts. Ollie guided my arms above my head before his fingers inched their way down the length of them, past my breast and at my sides. My nipples hardened instantly under his warmth. Gasping, my body buckled under his wet lips as they trailed along my collarbone and down the middle of my chest.

Ollie took his time, and his nose brushed my stomach as his lips left impressions over my skin. My impatient hips moved beneath him as he undid my button and zipper.

"The feeling you have right now—I need you to hold on to it for as long as possible. Do you understand what I'm saying to you?"

"I think so," I breathed.

Ollie paused and dropped his hands on each side of me. "The moment you start slipping away, and you don't feel anything anymore, I can see the change in your eyes. They turn hollow. All I'm asking is for you to stay with me for as long as you can. When you notice your damn switch turning back on, remember this moment. Remember me and the way I make you feel, alright?"

"Yes, Ollie," I said eagerly.

He removed my boots and peeled off my jeans as I lay there in anticipation, watching him adore every inch of me. Soft lips trailed along my hipbone and over my panties. He rested his chin over my lower stomach and looked up to me. His two emerald gems sparkled, asking for consent in silence.

I nodded, and his mouth moved to my inner thigh and my insides illuminated. He bent my knees and ran his fingertips down the backs of my thighs. Hooking the strings of my panties, he stripped them off with ease.

Ollie pulled my knees apart, and his hands massaged the insides of my thighs as his eyes fell over my sex, then my stomach, then my breasts, and then my face, taking in all of me.

I was already his and whatever he wanted.

His slave. His savior. His anchor.

"You are so beautiful," he whispered from his throat.

I shook my head. "No talking."

His eyes drifted up and down before they met mine again. "I don't think you understand, love. I'm talking, and I'm saying you are fucking beautiful." His gaze roamed down to my sex again before he drowned in weakness. "All of you." Before I could detest his verbal abuse, Ollie lowered his head. The heat of his breath landed on me before his warm, wet tongue stroked my center from bottom to top.

Oh, my god …

My head fell back and my hips instantly reacted against his fever. He pulled away only to spread me wide before his mouth consumed me entirely. I screwed my eyes shut, broken moans escaping me, and my fists found his hair as a wave built up inside me, his skillful tongue sweeping me into another dimension. He pushed my thighs wider as his green eyes soaked me in with each precise strike.

Ollie swiped across my heat once more before his lips covered my knot of nerves, sucking tenderly, and the tingle in my core flared, spreading an electric forest fire.

It was happening. Ollie pressed his finger against my entrance, making slow circles to the same tempo as his torturous tongue. My hips moved against the feelings I'd never felt before. A storm inside sent waves crashing over and over on top of the inferno. *The fire and ice.*

Then he dipped his finger inside, and I ignited all over again. Each steady graze of his graceful finger went deeper and deeper, catering to every need, touching places that desired him. I bit my lip to stifle a cry as my legs shook under his grasp.

"Ollie," I urged in a whimper. I couldn't hold on any longer, or I couldn't hold on again. I couldn't distinguish between where one ended, and another began. My orgasms all blurred together. He pulled away from me too soon and quickly ripped off his jeans and boxers without taking his eyes off me.

Then he was stripped bare, standing before me as if he was offering himself to me, giving me a piece of him he knew he could never take back.

He was beautiful.

He crawled up my pining body until his mouth met mine, his lips more tender and sensuous with each kiss. He kissed me slowly again and again as his rock-hard arousal pressed against my wetness.

He held our kiss as he eased himself inside, inch by inch, driving me to whimpers as he filled me. Our once-intense kiss weakened at the feeling of our connection, and his head fell into the curve of my neck. "Holy hell…Mia…I need a second…" he breathlessly said, and whatever remaining walls I had shattered into a million pieces, the flood gates opened, and Ollie and I were bound together by something more profound than the both of us could have imagined. I gripped his silky, thick hair to bring him back to me, and when his mouth covered mine again, we were gone.

"Mia, look at me," he demanded as his gentle thumb swept across my glistening forehead. My eyelids parted to meet green trusting eyes as he pumped into me again and again and again. The only thing keeping him up was his elbow digging into the mattress beside me, but even his elbow trembled.

He ran his thumb across my bottom lip before he kissed me again. The perfect length of him stroked me, and I felt every sensation, *every thrust*, as he slid against my walls. Every flexed muscle of his moved beneath my wild fingers.

His free hand moved to my breast, to my waist, to my …

He made slow, gentle circles over my clit, sending me over the edge as his elbow kept the tremor in my leg steady. I swiped his hair off his sweaty forehead as his pumps grew closer together, making me moan. I dug my nails into the muscles of his back as a surge accelerated, and my name fell from his lips in a plea. "Mia … I'm about to … Let go, and come with

152

me." He gripped my bottom as he took me deeper, touching places needing him with a slow, nerve-detonating grind.

Suddenly, every blood vessel, every molecule inside me burst, sending a thousand stars into a midnight sky behind my eyes as I reached a peak of pure euphoria. My legs clenched around Ollie's waist as my entire body tensed in hysteria. The pleasure motivated my cries before Ollie silenced me with his lips, swallowing my testimony away as he chased the same holy feeling.

THIRTEEN

"Some search
their entire lives
for this single moment.
Don't blink, my love.
We're finally here."

OLIVER MASTERS

L ife consists of tiny moments. Moments that define you,
moments that shape you, moments that lead you down a path of
reflection, self-discovery, and purpose. These heartbeats of
moments are collections of who you are and who you are meant to be—
little moments. And we only remember the ones that have impacted our
souls.

Until now, I had genuinely believed my soul had left me a long time
ago. I would never forget this moment that made me realize it had never
really been gone, only locked away behind trauma, lies, and utter denial.
I'd stomped on my past, forcing it into obscurity. If I believed it had never

happened, it hadn't. I'd hid behind my denial for so long, my past became nonexistent.

My reflection burned in his emotion-filled eyes as his inked and sweaty body trembled to hold himself up after his release. In this pivotal moment, he subconsciously reminded me my soul was still there, begging for redemption as he silently pleaded for reciprocation—pleading for me to remember. To confront the demons of my past, and the same trauma I never could as a child. It would be then, and only then, he could have me completely. He knew this. I knew this. After all, with him was where my soul belonged.

But I handled the situation the only way I knew how.

I rejected it.

Because no matter how deep our connection was, and no matter the strength of our bond, nothing would ever be enough. No one could break the already broken. My mind and heart existed on two different playing fields. My worthless heart was the slave while my mind was the master.

Fear was the biggest culprit, lurking in the shadows outside the walls that rebuilt in a matter of seconds. It was Guilt who took over my senses, and it was Anger who controlled my body and drove out my soul. While my barriers were down, it was these three demons that haunted me whenever I was alone. And eventually, I would be alone again. It was inevitable.

So, up the walls went like clockwork. My subconscious was my shield, having complete control. I tried to hold on—with every fiber of my being—to the rapture we had created together, but the master of my heart ultimately won. The rage formed by my three demons took over, drowning out any remaining chance of my heart staying with him.

Ollie noticed the shift in my eyes immediately.

"No, Mia." He shook his head. "*Fuck.* Stay with me." He cupped my face in his hands, but I pushed him off me. My rage escalated, and it was too late. My feet found the floor as I searched for my clothes.

"Bloody hell, slow down and come here," Ollie whisper-shouted as he brought the sheet around him and sat over the edge of the bed, confusion clear across his face. Ignoring him, I slipped my jeans back on and threw a random shirt over my head. Unable to sit still, I paced the dorm, my head shaking the moment away.

"Please, you have to talk to me," Ollie pressed as he got into his pants. I glanced over at him, and despair struck in his green eyes.

My feet took long steps toward him, and I pushed him once in the chest. "What the hell was that?" I hit him again. He became my anger. He became my muse. He became everything hiding inside me, and he was the one to bring it all out—and I hated him. With a passion, I hated him. My arms flung at him as I screamed out. "What did you do to me?!"

Ollie gripped my flailing arms and turned me around to pin my back against his long torso. "I fucking hate you!" I screamed, and Ollie placed his hand over my mouth to silence me.

"I'll be your punching bag if it's what you need," he choked out. "Whatever it will take to get you past this."

I jerked my head from his hand and turned to face him. "Get past this? Am I a game to you? A conquest?"

His eyes glossed over—*hazy*. He shook his head as tears gathered at the corners, threatening to fall. "God, no, Mia. I care about you, alright? More than I've ever cared for anyone or anything."

"You need to leave. Now." I reached my breaking point, and Ollie reached his.

"No, I'm not going anywhere until you tell me what you're feeling."

"Right now, I feel … I feel …" I searched inside me, and there was absolutely nothing. "I told you I don't feel, Ollie. What the hell do you want from me?"

Ollie took a step back and whispered, "You, Mia. I just want you." He studied my face for a moment as his tears held on by a thread. All it would take was one blink of his eyes, and they would roll down his cheeks.

There was so much he wanted to say, but I was already gone, and Ollie was defeated.

He let my arms go, took in a deep breath, and glanced around the room until he located his shirt. "You hate me. It's a feeling, and I'll take it for now, but we have something, Mia. I don't know what it is yet, but it's real, and it's rare, and I'm not letting it go. You can deny it and push it down as much as you want, but we're both here for a reason, and until you start realizing what's going on, I'll be the one to show you." He paused and slipped his shirt over his head. "I'll continue to fight for as long as it takes."

I glanced up at Ollie in silence as his lively eyes searched mine one last time, but there was no going back to him. He closed his eyes, let out a breath, then turned and walked out the door.

Inevitable.

Life with Ollie was like a broken record.

Numb. Ollie. The walls fell. Feelings. Memories. Anger. Without Ollie. Walls rebuilt. Numb. Repeat.

A tedious cycle no one had prepared me for on the flight to the United Kingdom. I had thought my barriers were invincible—not susceptible to a beautiful creature walking an offbeat path filled with unrealistic notions.

Eventually, the side effects of Ollie Masters would wear off, but all I needed to do was keep my distance from him. As long as he stayed away, I would stay numb.

It was six in the morning. Since there were no classes on Fridays, I planned on everyone else sleeping in, and the bathroom would be empty.

And I was right.

I reached into the stall to start the water, then stared blindly at myself in the mirror and noticed a few changes. My eyebrows had always been thick, but without the ability to pluck them, they looked even fuller. I was growing to like my freckles. Maybe once I left this place, I wouldn't cover them up any longer.

"I'm starting to think you are avoiding us," a high-pitched voice said, breaking me away from myself. Bria strolled toward me with her clothes pinned to her chest.

"Your thoughts are correct." I stepped into the shower and undressed, but her questions didn't stop.

"You didn't make it to Ollie's last night. Did something happen?" she asked as the sound of her shower turned on beside me.

"Nope."

"Eh, it was boring, anyway. Ollie was in a mood, and no one wants to be around Ollie when he's in a mood," she called out over the sound of the water. "Why don't you hang out with us today? After breakfast, we're heading out to the woods."

"No, thanks."

My curtain opened with an annoyed Bria on the other side. She raised her finger at me. "I don't understand you. You'd rather be cooped up in that dorm of yours, yeah? I'm trying to be nice, and if this is about Ollie..."

I rolled my eyes as a laugh blew from my lips. "It's not, trust me. I don't want anything to do with Ollie. He's all yours."

Ollie would never belong to anyone aside from me. I knew this, and he knew this. Even my damn demons knew this. It was the reason they were running around scared as shit this very moment, trying to erase the damage he had done yesterday.

"Well, Ollie doesn't want to go, anyway, and we need one more person—"

"Ollie won't be there?" Distraction was what I needed, and if Ollie wasn't going to be around, I didn't mind using Bria and her friends as my diversion from him.

Confusion crossed her face. "No?"

"Okay, I'll go."

A pleased smile flashed across her face before she closed my curtain, and I relaxed under the water while enjoying the rest of my shower in blissful silence.

Sitting at my old table during breakfast, Zeke stared at me from one table down. Each time I took a bite of my food, he blinked, but the rest of his facial expression maintained transfixed. There was so much I wanted

158

to tell him, and I couldn't understand why I needed to pour everything out to the mute. Another bite and Zeke's gaze burned a hole in me. Sighing, I said, "Alright, Zeke. You win."

After lifting my tray, I walked one table down to sit across from him. "Better?"

Zeke didn't move, but a small grunt came from somewhere inside him.

"Okay, I won't do that again. I'll always sit with you. No matter what."

As I told Zeke what had happened, the weight of Ollie's eyes drifted through me, comforting me like a warm blanket. I turned my head slightly to my left to legitimize the peace washing over me. And there he was, his beanie flopped over his head as his hair stuck out from beneath in all directions. He held my gaze, trying to see which Mia he had today. Was it *his* Mia—the one he'd gone on about before we made love?

I didn't know myself, but he always knew.

All he had to do was look into my eyes.

"Mia, you coming?" Bria asked from across the room, disrupting my thoughts.

Ollie stood, his eyes darting from Bria and back to me. He said something to her I couldn't quite make out.

"We needed another person," Bria replied to him with a shrug.

Leaving Zeke behind, I walked toward their table. "Need me for what?"

"Power," Isaac said. "It's better with at least five players."

My brows rose. "Power?"

"I'll explain on the way." Bria stood with the rest of them. "Have fun in your dorm, *Ollie*."

"No, I'm coming," Ollie muttered under his breath.

His agreement to join should have been my cue to back out, but before I could, Bria already had me by the arm, dragging me toward the double doors.

Fresh air hit my face, and I hadn't realized how much I'd missed it. Coming to a standstill, I lifted my face to the sun, appreciating the way it felt against my skin. The slight smell of tree bark and freshly cut grass mixed in the gust of cold wind as it brushed through my hair, making the hairs on my arms stand. Even with the sun shining behind my closed lids, it didn't help the sixty-something-degree temperature. When I opened my eyes, the rest of the group was already ten feet ahead, but Ollie stood beside me, mesmerized.

"Okay, so, we all write down an action, and we'll use … Ollie's beanie to place the actions. You have to perform that action, and the rest of us will judge based on a number one through three. No one can know the action until it's complete. By the end of the game, whoever wins has the power, and they get to be in charge for a full hour. You have to do whatever they say," Bria explained as we reached the woods.

"That's the stupidest game I've ever heard," I sighed.

"You can either play with us or have fun playing football over there with those wankers," Bria said, pointing back to the kids kicking the ball around.

I let out a moan. "Fine."

We walked through the sparsely scattered wooded forest until we reached the end of the lot, and sat in a sloppy circle near the tall brick wall. I sandwiched myself between Jake and Isaac while Ollie sat across from me with Bria to his left and Alicia to his right. He pulled his knees up and rested his long arms across them.

Tall trees hovered over us, and I looked up to see the sun above, coming through the branches. The brisk wind blew the weakest leaves off the branches as they fell around us.

I focused on one leaf, watching it wobble back and forth against the force of the wind until it dropped between Ollie and Alicia in its final resting place.

Alicia ripped a paper into six parts before passing a piece around. "No screwing around this time. I can't lose because I refused sex with Jake," Alicia said.

"Yeah, that was harsh," Jake whined.

"You guys have sex in this game?"

"Not today, apparently," Bria muttered.

"Actions have to be specific. If another person is needed, make sure to write their name," Isaac explained. "What's the level of nudity?"

"Knickers," Ollie insisted.

"Full nudity," I countered.

Bria put her hands together and agreed, "Full nudity it is," then snatched Ollie's beanie off his head, and his thick brown mess bounced free.

Ollie ran his hand up his forehead and through his hair, but refused to look in my direction. When the pen was passed down to me, I wrote out an action, folded up my paper, and placed it in Ollie's beanie in the center. "Who's keeping score?"

Alicia held up a paper and pen. "I got it."

Jake went first and withdrew an action from the hat. He giggled as his eyes scanned the words across the paper while his face flushed. "Alright, alright." Jake stood and took in a deep breath as I watched him from below. He brought his hands over his face and shook his head, and when he dropped them to his side, a broad smile appeared. He laughed as his body moved to a beat only he could hear in his head.

And then he sang as his torso rolled in what I could only describe as Jake's attempt at sexy dancing. The first verse of Ginuwine's "Pony" came from his lips as he stripped his shirt and dropped it over my face. His fingers landed on his pants, and Alicia stifled a laugh with her hand over her mouth. Isaac covered his eyes and turned his head away from the view of Jake's strip number.

"Someone help me out here," Jake interjected between lyrics.

My fingers snapped, and I belted out the second verse with him.

Ollie shot his head in my direction, and Alicia squealed, "Ah, she's brilliant!"

Alicia and Bria joined in on the chorus as Jake tried lifting Alicia off the ground. Alicia waved him away through uncontrollable laughter, and Jake turned to me with his palms and shoulders in the air.

After gathering to my feet, I danced and sang the chorus while Jake continued to strip.

Ollie sat amused with a bona fide smile and nirvana in his eyes. He wet his lips while flashes of our moments together sent a rush of heat through me. Everyone else around us laughed or sang, but Ollie mouthed *"I want you"* as he leaned back on his hands.

I shook my head. He made me feel so right—it was so wrong.

"Okay, okay … striptease. Now let's score," Alicia said as Jake and I sat back down, "Mia?"

"Three," I said before everyone else rambled off their scores.

It was my turn, and I reached for an action in the hat. It read, *'Give the person to your left goosebumps whichever way you wish.'* Grinning, I crouched behind Isaac, and Ollie shifted in place and narrowed his eyes.

My hair fell over Isaac's shoulder as I leaned over him. Keeping my eyes on Ollie's, I traced my tongue up the length of Isaac's neck until my lips fell over the tender spot behind his ear—the spot I knew drove Ollie insane. Ollie clenched his jaw as my lips touched Isaac's skin with delicacy. My fingertips traced the length of his arm, and I whispered sweet nothings in Isaac's ear.

"Shit, Mia," Isaac breathed. I looked from Ollie down to Isaacs' arm as goosebumps and the hairs on his arm raised.

Ollie averted his gaze.

"Goosebumps? Really, Alicia? Every time …" Bria scoffed as I settled back in my place between Jake and Isaac.

"Five. I give her a five," Isaac said with enthusiasm.

"The score goes up to three," Bria reminded him.

"I still give her a five."

"Three it is."

The rest of the group rambled off scores, and when it got to Ollie, he refused to score.

It was Isaac's turn, and he had everyone stand up in a circle. After blindfolding him and spinning him around three times as he directed, I took a step back. Isaac put his arms out in front of him, and no one had any idea what the goal of this was. Isaac took a step toward Alicia and found her face. Alicia froze as Isaac dipped his head down and planted a single peck across her nose, completely missing her mouth.

A mortified expression crossed Alicia's face as Isaac pulled off his blindfold. "Sorry, darling." He laughed.

"Oh, come on, you could have done better than that." I laughed. "One for me."

"Wish he chose you?" Bria asked.

My eyes rolled at her nonsense. She was next, and with only three people left, I hoped she was the one who got my action. After everyone said their scores, Bria reached into the hat and pulled out a piece of paper. Her eyes went wide as she read it before snapping her head in Ollie's direction.

Mission complete.

"In front of everyone?" she repeated as she read the last part out loud.

"W-w-whoa, you can't say anything," Jake reminded her.

Bria stood and reached her hand down to Ollie. "Come on. You're a part of this one."

Ollie looked back at the group, and I pressed my lips together to avoid laughing.

"Whoever this was will be ruined," Ollie said as Bria pushed him against a tree. She dropped to her knees and reached for his waistband.

My heart went haywire in my chest, and though this had been my idea to begin with, regret filled me without notice. His top button came undone, his zipper was pulled down, and Ollie lifted his face to the sky. Inside, I was screaming. *Why did I do this to myself?*

Then Ollie pushed her hands away. "No, I can't." He took the paper out of Bria's hand and read it. "I'm not bloody doing that, are you mad?"

"You're turning down a blow job with no strings attached?" Bria asked, surprised.

"Yes, that's exactly what I'm doing," Ollie said with his hands in the air. "I can't...not with you."

Bria stood as her hands flew to her hips. "Excuse me? What do you mean not with me?"

"Just forget it," he muttered under his breath, and walked away from her and back to the group. "Now, who did that?"

Jake was in tears from laughing so hard, and I was still recovering from the fact I had tested my feelings for Ollie without realizing it, and I didn't like the outcome.

Ollie bent down and snatched a paper from the hat and read it. "I need someone to count mentally for one minute." Bria sat back down, the rejection stinging her a million times over as Ollie walked over to me. "Come with me," he said and held out his hand.

Taking his hand, Ollie helped me to my feet and I glanced around at the others while he led me over to the brick wall. He positioned me against it, and I glanced past him to the group behind him, all having no idea what was about to happen.

"Keep your eyes on me," Ollie said before turning over to Jake. "One minute, mate."

Ollie drew in a deep breath as he took a step closer. A lump made of concrete formed in my throat as he came within inches of my face. "I don't know what you're trying to do, love, but I can promise you it won't work. If you hadn't already noticed, you had me from day one ..."

Ollie exhaled and placed a palm against the wall beside me. Leaning into my ear, he said, "Mia, I only want you ... I want to be found by you across the room, I want your lips on mine whenever I want, and I want to feel myself inside you. *I need it.* You and everyone else your entire life has told you that you're incapable of feeling, but you're all wrong. What happened in your room, that was real—a feeling so strong, you flipped out because you haven't felt like that before, and I promise you will never feel that again with anyone else. I'm not going to save you, Mia. I don't want to be the one. I'm going to show you how to save yourself."

"Twenty seconds," Jake called out.

Ollie brought his attention back to me. "Now this paper in my hand says I can't touch you, and I'm not supposed to have you speak, but I have to hear it from you. And be frank with me, Mia, do you feel for me?"

My palms began to sweat and my mouth went dry as his green eyes searched mine. "I know you're in there," he whispered as the mint from the gum in his mouth brushed my trembling lips, and I wasn't sure if it was a reaction to Ollie or the biting cold. All I was sure of was I needed his warmth.

I dropped my chin in a small nod and met his eyes again. A boyish smile reached his eyes and a single finger rested under my chin as he leaned in a little closer. "Say it, Mia."

"Time's up, Ollie," Jake announced.

Ollie turned around. "Ah, fuck off, mate," he called out, and while he was distracted, I stole the paper from his hand and read it to myself. "*Give Jake a hand-job OR finger Bria for one minute.*"

He snatched the paper from my hand and stuffed it into the pocket of his joggers. "It's between you and me." He returned his palm to the brick and leaned back in. "Now, I'm dying right now. Answer me."

"Yes," I said, voice cracking. "I feel for you, I always have. And no matter how hard I try not to"—I shrugged—"it won't go away. It's always there."

Ollie's lips twitched. "You can stop fighting now, Mia."

My heels lifted off the ground, and without an afterthought, my mouth found his. I felt his smile against my lips before they molded with mine, and I slipped my tongue inside, craving the taste of him. Ollie's body relaxed against me as he held my head in his hand, and took my bottom lip between his teeth.

"Ollie, it's over!" someone shouted, but Ollie reached one hand behind them and flicked them off without parting from me. A giggle escaped between us.

"You. Me. Tonight. Your room," he whispered, and took my hand and lifted me off the wall. His words bounced around in my head the whole way back to the circle. He refused to keep his distance after and pulled me over to his spot between his legs. Everyone's eyes darted around, but neither one of us could care as he kissed my neck and kept me warm inside his arms, where I should have been all along—my safety net.

"Think it's your birthday, mate?" Jake teased, looking over at Ollie and me.

"Every day is a present," Ollie replied with a lift in his tone.

Alicia leaned over and whispered in Ollie's ear, "You're walking a dangerous line. You need to be careful."

Ollie nodded and brought his attention back to me and ran his palms up and down my arms.

"What was that all about?" I asked, looking up at him.

Ollie dipped his head down. "We'll talk about it later, love." And he kissed my temple.

Out of anyone who could have said something, Alicia was the last person I expected. It took a lot for me to admit to him my feelings for him openly. I had confessed it before to Zeke, but because Zeke didn't talk, I never really treated him as a real human being—more like a part of my subconscious. I had been afraid until now to openly say it. But after seeing the look in his eyes, the one that said, *trust me and I will never let you fall alone*, without having to utter a word at all, my words came out effortlessly.

Perhaps he was right, and he would be the one to help me save me from myself.

"Mia?"

"Yeah?" I asked, snapping my head to the source.

"How about a score, yeah?" Alicia asked.

I dropped my head back to look at Ollie. "Eh, I'll give him a one."

Everyone laughed, including Ollie as Alicia tallied up the scores before she dug her hand into the beanie. "Okay, my turn."

Alicia withdrew her action and read it, her eyes darting around the circle. "Mia and Isaac, you're on here. Stand up," she said.

Ollie's fingers tensed against my arms as Isaac and I exchanged glances. We got to our feet and walked outside the circle in front of Alicia. "You're my life-sized Barbies for the next minute, and you have to do whatever I say," she whispered to us.

166

Pursing my lips together, I stood before Isaac, trying refrain from an awkward laugh.

"This one's mine," Jake bragged from the circle.

Ollie shook his head. "Yeah, thanks for that, man."

Alicia started her roleplay game, using Isaac and me as her pawns. "Oh, Ken. Please take your shirt off, I want to feel your body against mine," Alicia said in the most authentic British versioned Barbie voice, and Isaac obliged. He removed his shirt as everyone in the group let out a laugh, except for Ollie. Ollie wasn't the least bit amused.

"I want to feel your body," Alicia hinted again at me.

"Oh, right," I mumbled and brought my hands to Isaacs abs.

"Yeah, Barbie. That feels nice. Why don't I help you out of your shirt," Alicia said in a deep man voice. Isaac took a step toward me and helped me out of my shirt, and it dropped to the ground as we waited for our next instruction.

"Kiss me, Ken. I want to feel your hands on my boobs, and your tongue down my throat," Alicia said through a laugh, and I looked over at Ollie with wide eyes.

"No, she doesn't kiss, Alicia. You know that," Ollie said, drawing the line.

As I remembered the sickness on Ollie's face when I'd kissed Liam, my legs wobbled. It had been right before Ollie kissed me sober and I punched a wall. *"Don't ever kiss another before my eyes again,"* he said in my dorm room before he left.

"She kissed you, didn't she?" Alicia asked.

Ollie scrambled as his attention went from me and back to Alicia. "Yeah, but that's different ..."

"Different?" Alicia turned to face me. "Mia?"

Talk about being stuck between a rock and a hard place. I darted my head between both of them as my mind raced, trying to do the right thing for once. I'd hurt Ollie too many times to count, and I couldn't bear to see the pained look in his eyes again.

Ollie got to me. He got to me in so many ways, on so many levels. Even though Ollie couldn't accept the way I was, he was the only one who fought for me, which was more than I deserved.

I picked my shirt up off the ground and pulled it over my head before taking off through the woods.

That's right—I ran.

It was the only option that made the most sense at the time. I darted through the woods, past the green lawn, and back through the double doors of Dolor.

FOURTEEN

"This girl is my heaven.
With lips of an angel,
the sweet taste of mercy lingers.
She has halos in her eyes,
and my heart beats to the sound of her wings."

OLIVER MASTERS

We were halfway through the broken record, and I felt like an idiot. Did they see what Ollie could do to me? Were they pushing our buttons on purpose to see me lash out again? Were my public displays of affection and feelings a joke, when it had been so entirely hard to get to this point? A wall came up as anger brewed, but I fought through it, keeping Ollie's words rolling as the record got stuck on this specific song.

"Stop!" he called out, but I shook my head as I turned the corner. "Dammit, Mia. Slow down," he shouted before I reached the bathroom, and I wished it were a private bathroom where I could lock the door behind me.

After turning on the faucet, I splashed cool water over my face, washing away the last ten minutes. When I opened my eyes, Ollie stood beside me, chest heaving as he tried to catch his breath.

"I couldn't go through with it, Ollie. I couldn't do it to you …"

Ollie stayed silent as he flipped the water on and washed his hands, studying my face in the reflection of the mirror. *Say something.* He ripped the paper towel from the roll, taking his time drying his hands as a smile rose, and I shook my head at his audacity. *Say anything.* He crumbled up the paper into a ball before throwing it in the trashcan, and turned toward me.

"Why did you take off running?" Ollie asked as he adjusted his gray joggers around his hips. He pulled down the bottom hem of his white tee and took a few steps to stand behind me so we were both standing in the same mirror.

"I don't know," I said, and Ollie wrapped his arms around my waist. My tense body relaxed in his hold as I continued. "It seemed like the right thing to do at the time."

He held my gaze in the mirror, his green eyes glued to my brown ones as if once they separated, he would lose me.

"Would you look at us together." He nudged his head toward the mirror as he grinned. Two pairs of eyes stared back in the reflection. One pair was mine. The other was his—a vibrant soul, bright enough to compensate for my lack thereof. He was beautiful. I wondered what he saw.

"Right there … you see your eyes?" He asked. "Usually your color is so dark, it's hard to tell when your pupil ends, and your iris begins. Most of the time, this hollow void dominates you, but look at your eyes now." I honed in on my eyes in the mirror. They were an amber color I'd never seen before. "The glow … it's your soul shining through. Your eyes brighten when we're together, and that is how I know …"

"Know what?"

170

Ollie smiled and pulled me closer against him. He lowered his head to my ear. "I bring out that light in you. You do feel for me, and I never needed to hear you say it, Mia. All these times I asked you, it was for you to hear it for yourself. It's only when we're apart when we're broken like two jagged pieces—we belong together. I can see it in your eyes, and now you can see it, too. But you've always known, haven't you? You never needed proof."

Wordless, I lost myself in this new shade of color he'd shown me. He was able to have this effect on me. There was no logic or science behind it, but the proof was in front of me this whole time. A part of me did always know there was something about him. My enslaved heart knew before my mind could comprehend—the reason I could never shut him out entirely, no matter how hard I tried. It was because he was already a part of me. All along, we'd been connected. My light illuminated in his presence because his soul was the one mine had been promised to.

It was him.

It was Ollie.

"I once asked you to open yourself up to me, to carve me out a door," his warm breath traced along my neck as he spoke and I had a hard time standing still, "but I need you to let me in entirely. I need all of you, Mia." I tried to swallow as he pressed against my back. "Why do you continue to pull me in only to push me away?"

My head spun. My ears rang. My Ollie-level raised to complete overdose. He wanted me—all of me. Every broken piece of my body, my heart, and new-found soul, all pierced with glitter made of pain. A hassle to shake away because they were tiny fragments embedded into the deepest parts of me. "Because you scare the hell out of me."

His gaze left the mirror and peered down at me. "Why?"

"When you're beside me, you make me feel alive, and when you're gone, the small fire you built inside me is left burning, reminding me of the way I felt with you. And it's not good when I feel, Ollie, because when I start to feel, the pain seeps through the cracks, and it hurts." I drew in a breath. "I can't stop it; my brain automatically shuts it off, the feelings, the emotions, the pain, you … all of it. It has become a subconscious habit for so many years. A defense mechanism."

Ollie's hands disappeared under my white shirt and grazed my bare skin. "Is our fire burning now?"

I sucked in a breath and nodded. "But what happens when it burns out?"

He pressed his lips together in a grin. "This is us we're talking about. That will never happen." He unbuttoned my jeans and lowered my zipper. "I'm not going anywhere, Mia."

His hand reached over my panties and his long fingers pressed against me. My head rolled back into his chest as my legs went weak. His tongue trailed up my neck as he lightly sucked the sensitive skin, and his skilled fingers kneaded places longing for his touch. "I'll always fight for you, no matter how many times your habit takes you over, do you hear me?"

My grip around the sink's edge tightened as I gave up posture. "Yes," I whimpered.

He parted my legs with his other hand while his erection pressed hard against my backside through his thin joggers. He moved my panties to the side, and his finger stroked up my heat again. Making circles over my knot, he held my gaze in the reflection as the same fever from my sex traveled up my neck. A soft pink glow lit my cheeks as I lost myself in his green eyes. "You are so goddamn breathtaking," he whispered to me.

The fire inside me set ablaze and I bit down on my lip to control it.

"Fuck," he breathed and withdrew his hand only to pull me into a shower stall and pin me against the tile. His lips found mine and my legs went slack from his torture. "You need to stand on your own, love," and he dropped to his knees before me, dragged my jeans and panties down to my ankles, and spread my legs, "and this time, stay with me."

He skimmed a lone finger down my core before dipping inside me, and my breathing shuddered all over again. Through each embrace of his supple finger, Ollie lowered his mouth until his lips pressed against my abdomen and my hip. My legs buckled and my arms felt heavy as I tried to keep myself together, and I quivered on the edge of exploding.

"Mia," he breathed from below, and my eyes blinked open as the rest of me broke apart. "You're my everything. You're my heaven."

"And you're my hell," I replied, cupping his face in my palms and pulling him to his feet. My impatient mouth found his before he could stand all the way, but once he did, I kicked off my jeans and panties from one leg and dragged his joggers and boxer briefs down in a need-filled rush of him to be inside me already.

Ollie stripped off his shirt before ripping off mine, then unclasped my bra impatiently. "I need to feel you against me," he said unapologetically, and picked me up at the backs of my thighs. I wrapped my legs around his hips and our chests crashed together.

He sank inside me, filling me to the brink, and his forehead fell to mine as his eyes screwed shut. Seconds passed for Ollie to regain himself, and for me to overcome the initial shock of him inside me all over again. I held on to the back of his head as he tried to catch his breath. "Fuck, Mia, it's all too much."

"Open your eyes," I begged with his head in my hands. "Look at me."

Ollie wet his lips and opened his eyes. "Mia, I …" he began to say, but I silenced him with a kiss. My back slammed into the tile, his tongue flicked across mine, and he pumped in and out of me at the most incredible flow, hitting all the right notes, knowing the connection we both needed until we came undone in perfect sync.

I'd never expected to get swept up in his hurricane and have feelings for him—but I did. It had been in the cards all along. Ollie and I were an unforeseen omen. A force of nature.

Stanley pulled me aside as soon as I walked into the mess hall for dinner. He mentioned the dean wanted to see me before he left for the night and insisted I bring my dinner because I wouldn't be back in time.

The dinner tray shook in my hands as I followed behind Stanley through the corridor, down the stairs, and toward Lynch's office. The food would be cold by the time I got there, but I didn't care. This sudden meeting with the dean had my thoughts straying to every possible worst-case scenario. I wouldn't have the stomach to eat regardless.

"Mia, yes, have a seat," Lynch said. "Thank you, Stanley." I turned to see Stanley nod and close the door behind him. Setting my tray down on the desk, I took a seat in the same chair from my first day here. It seemed so long ago, but it had only been a month. The room dimmed as the sun set outside, sending shades of orange and red through the half-opened window.

"You may eat," Lynch said.

Silence.

"How have you been doing, Miss Jett?"

I grabbed my fork and moved the macaroni around. "Well, I suppose." I relaxed a little. His voice didn't indicate trouble. Maybe this was only a talk—a conversation to check to see how I've been coping.

"Having some headway with your therapy sessions?"

"Yes, sir," I lied—well, partly. I'd gained headway with my Ollie therapy.

"I called you in here because … in the first month so far you've spent a weekend in the nurse's station, broken your hand, destroyed a bathroom, and visited solitary confinement. I'm not sure this place is suitable for your havoc, Miss Jett, and I cannot put other's lives in jeopardy."

The abandonment was apparent across his face. He was removing me from the program, and the voice in my head said things like, "*Good, get me out of here,*" and "*Finally, please … ship me back to the States,*" and "*I don't care.*" But the pounding in my ears, the cold sweat building across my skin, and the stinging behind my eyes reminded me of my body's betrayal. The truth was, I was scared to wake up in a life without Ollie. I was terrified of my mental habit to push his existence, and our moments together, down, and pretend like none of it had ever happened because I knew from experience it was the only way I knew how to cope.

No. I needed to stay with Ollie.

All the air in my lungs had been replaced with water as I slowly drowned inside. A fog blurred my vision, and I shook my head. "What ... what are you saying?" My voice ruptured.

Lynch dropped his chin and folded his hands over his desk. "You're being transferred to Building B, Mia ..." He let out an exhale. "You're being transferred to our psychiatric division."

An extended moment of silence induced Lynch to shuffle around his desk and type a few strokes across his keyboard. If I opened my mouth, I would regret the things I would say. If I lashed out, he might have me leave the campus entirely. Biting my tongue, I crossed my arms and dug my nails into my elbows to prevent myself from doing something I ordinarily would do. A victim and a monster, fighting a war inside my head.

"Stanley will take you back to your dorm to pack your things. They will be expecting you." He stood from his chair and leaned over his desk. "Mia, this is your last chance. One screw-up, you'll be forced to leave permanently."

Stanley stood outside my dorm room as I shoved my belongings into my suitcase. "You won't be seeing those items for a long time. They will be processed and placed in the basement," Stanley mumbled. "They'll give you new clothes and a toothbrush on the other side."

The moment I closed and zipped my suitcase, I felt myself slipping. Shaking my head, I focused on Ollie's green eyes, his words, his smile, anything to keep me from tripping over the edge into darkness. I wanted to throw my suitcase into the wall. I wanted to throw my casted fist into the cement, *again*. I wanted to escape my body and shake myself because I was slipping. I could never feel it before, but now it was unmistakable. It was happening; one by one, my mind turned out the lights in a home with a dozen rooms, getting darker and darker by the minute.

"Ready?" Stanley asked, and I turned away from my old prison before I made my way to the next.

The dinner rush moved sluggishly down the hall, retreating to their dorms. Standing beside Stanley, I waited as he did a once-over of my room before closing and locking the door. With my suitcase in hand, Stanley and I turned toward the crowd.

And then my eyes settled on Ollie. His raspy laugh echoed through the hall with Jake and Isaac at his side, coming in my direction. I closed my eyes as I buried his laugh into my memory, afraid I would never hear it again.

Jake noticed me first, and stopped suddenly. Ollie followed Jake's gaze as his pace slowed. Ollie's eyes darted between me, Stanley, and the suitcase in my hand when the color drained from his face. He slowly shook his head as he clenched his jaw.

"Let's go, Mia," I think Stanley said, but I couldn't move as Ollie detonated before my eyes.

Ollie took off in a sprint toward us and, in a matter of seconds, had Stanley shoved against the wall. "Where are you taking her? What's going on?" Ollie demanded, desperate questions flying through the thick air.

"Back off, Masters. You don't want to do this," Stanley said, pushing Ollie's hands away.

Ollie's face was pale. His once beautiful green eyes now strung out as he pushed Stanley again in the chest. "Where the fuck are you taking her!" he shouted, his face only inches away from Stanley. I'd never seen this side of Ollie before, but it was a look so familiar and a place I had been many times before. It was myself in him.

Anger mixed with fear—the perfect concoction to eradicate even the strongest.

"I'm warning you to back off," Stanley said calmly but sternly as he reached for the radio latched to his belt.

Ollie turned to me and searched my face as Isaac pulled him in the opposite direction. "Let her go, mate! It's over! You got to let her go," Isaac repeated, but this only infuriated Ollie more.

With tunnel vision, Ollie shoved Isaac off him, his force sending Isaac across the marble, and pushed passed Stanley, clearing everything in his path between him and me. He held my head and studied my face. "Talk to me, are you okay? Where are they taking you?" Ollie asked, urgency in his eyes, but his voice cracked through each word. "Answer me, Mia."

"Psych ward." I shook my head in his hands. "I'm not coming back, Ollie ... I'm so sorry."

Ollie's eyes glossed over right before Stanley ripped him away from me and slammed him against the wall. A pain entered my chest as I stood frozen. All I could do was watch Ollie crumble before my eyes, and I couldn't comprehend what was happening. My mind slowly shut down as my heart pounded hard against my ribcage. The ringing in my ears competed against the loud thumping in my head.

Stanley attempted to zip-tie Ollie's wrist behind his back as Ollie struggled against him, but Stanley was stronger. He slammed Ollie once more against the wall, this time applying the pressure of his forearm to the back of Ollie's head, pressing his face against the cold cement. Stanley whispered inaudible comments in Ollie's ear, triggering Ollie to stop struggling.

Ollie turned his head to face me with water in his eyes and red in his cheeks. His green eyes grew more beautiful when everything else had failed him. *He needed me.*

My feet moved toward Ollie, and he jerked against Stanley.

"No, Mia. Stay back," Ollie pleaded, then winced when Stanley twisted his arms back, finally getting him into the zip-ties. My head darted between the two of them, feeling completely powerless as I took another step forward. "Jake, get her back!" Ollie shouted, and Jake pulled me away in seconds, keeping me farther than arm's length—farther than I ever wanted to be.

Ollie pressed his forehead to the cement for a moment before turning to face me again. Tears fell from his bloodshot eyes and over his lips as my hands shook at my sides. "Mia, listen to me. You have to stay with me even when I'm gone, you hear me? Don't let it burn out. Promise me," he begged, but I couldn't form any words. My body weakened in Jake's hold and Ollie's eyes screwed shut as more tears fell before he opened them again. "Dammit, Mia. Promise me!"

Before the last light went out in my mind, I was able to speak.

"I promise."

FIFTEEN

"And if one day I
don't recognize you,
I'll love you anyway."

OLIVER MASTERS

When I'd shown up to Dolor, I had been sure of two things. First being the fact I would do whatever I could to get kicked out to spite my father, and second ... I needed to find someone to fuck in the meantime. Needless to say, I'd accomplished both.

My brown hair blew violently in the night wind while Stanley and I walked across the green lawn to building B—also known as the "Looney Bin." Stanley stayed quiet and composed, keeping his eyes fixed in front of him. But I could tell by his stance he was ready to pounce if I made the hasty decision to take off into a sprint through the woods, and because of how much weaker I'd become between the lack of physical exercise and my unhealthy eating habits, I wouldn't doubt his ability to catch up to me.

As we reached the entrance, he pressed a button on the black intercom beside the steel door and rambled off some words my head was not mentally prepared to comprehend before the door buzzed open. Stanley walked in behind me and handed off a clipboard to another security guard through the opening of a glass divider. The security guard, with a shaved head and bags under his eyes, looked over the clipboard before buzzing another door open.

We walked through the second set of doors and Stanley advised me to wait for the nurse to arrive. He handed my suitcase to the security guard, and I wondered if I'd ever get to wear my Dolor shirt again. I stood at the entrance of a long hallway, which I was sure led straight to hell. The walls on both sides were lined with white doors, and the fluorescent lights flickered as a buzzing sound sizzled through its eeriness.

A lady in white scrubs approached me and handed me a clean stack of gray clothes. "Follow me," was all she said. I turned back to Stanley, and he lowered his head in a single nod. Would this be the last time I would ever see Silent Stanley as well?

I followed the small woman down the poorly lit hallway before she made a sharp right-hand turn. Another corridor branched off, darker than the previous hall. Low moans and cries from the rooms we passed sent shivers up my neck and down my spine. Scared to speak, I quietly shuffled close behind her as if she could protect me. The constant feeling of a presence behind us kept my head turning behind me and over my shoulder.

We approached one of the white doors. The lady walked in after me as we entered a small white bathroom, nothing like the community bathroom back in the main building. This one wasn't nearly as clean. Water dripped from a spot rotting in the corner of the ceiling as she turned on the faucet in one of the three stalls. Dark red stained the cracks in the tile. *Is that blood? Holy shit, it is blood.* My head snapped in her direction as if she heard what I was thinking.

"Undress. You need to remove all jewelry, articles of clothing, and any hair accessories," she explained without looking me in the eye. "You'll shower before I show you to your room."

I did as I was told, afraid if I didn't listen, she might grow horns or sharp fangs before ripping the flesh off my bones with my blood spraying against the same tile, joining the others.

The water was cold. The temperature only brought back memories of Ollie and me holding each other on the floor of the stall in the community bathroom. He'd hugged me so tightly that night under the water, it had managed to wash away my relapse. He'd been my only antidote in a time I was against myself. He'd always been my cure, but I'd been too far gone to see it before.

The only item in the shower was a bottle of soap, which smelled like baby powder. I used it in my hair and over my body before rinsing off and stepping out. The lady kept her eyes on a book in her lap as I dressed.

The gray drawstring pants hung low on my waist, clearly a size too big, but everything would be huge. I had no meat on my bones anymore. I pulled the plain gray t-shirt over my head, and then the plain gray sweatshirt. It was much colder in building B than in the main building, and the sweatshirt made sense.

The quiet, tiny lady had a young face, but gray painted the part in her hair. She kept her dialogue to a minimum, only speaking to give me instruction, and never looked me in the eye. Much like me, she detached herself from those around her. But her reasoning was different. Only here, she became this cold and removed person. If she grew an attachment, it made her job more difficult. I wondered at what point she had changed to this. Was there someone she'd grown to like? Had something happened to said person? Did she know I wasn't going to make it out of here alive? Was that said person's blood on the bathroom tile?

She walked me to my room. A stiff mattress lay over plywood, with no other furniture in the room. No pillow, no sheet, only a mattress. Not even a window in the wall. *Only a fucking mattress.*

I curled into a fetal position over the blue mattress, wanting and willing to cry, but no tears would come out. So instead, I stayed still—lost in my own head, wondering what Ollie was doing, if he was enjoying the company of liquor and Bria during his midnight rendezvous, or forced in solitary confinement after the incident in the hallway. Was he thinking about me?

Ollie had cried. I had seen my dad cry before too, but it hadn't affected me in the way Ollie's tears had. Seeing him cry before me had only intensified the pain in my chest. Like someone had taken a dagger and pierced my heart, then twisted it. It hurt, and I knew if Jake hadn't pulled me away, I would've done anything to make sure he knew he wasn't alone. To wipe his tears and hold on to him the same way he became my angel in my darkest hours. Ollie had cried, and now he was alone. Or was he?

Either way, there was nothing I could do about it.

I was unable to measure time as it passed. The door opened numerous times with the small lady on the other end offering me food, but I declined. It was hard to say how long I'd stayed in this fetal position, staring at the blank wall in front of me. There was no sun, there was no moon, and there was no clock above the door—only white padded walls, and this fucking mattress. The irony in all this was, it was how I'd expected it to be before stepping foot out of the limousine on the first day I'd arrived. The psych ward was how I'd imagined it.

Not emerald eyes, inked skin, and a beautiful soul.

I'd never imagined Ollie.

I'd never seen him coming.

My stomach eventually stopped growling as I drifted in and out of a somber state. My body trembled as the pain grew thicker and deeper in my chest. I promised I would keep the fire burning inside me, but it was difficult without having him close. My body fought as my mind slowly lost balance. Determined to see his face, I clenched my eyes shut and imagined his lips moving as he read to me. The pain inside my chest set ablaze as I remembered the way he kissed me, the way he laughed. *Dear God ... his laugh.*

It was a genuine laugh—one he threw his whole body into. His hands always went immediately to his face as his mouth shot wide open and his eyes would turn into slits. Sometimes his fingers would reach his eyes, sometimes he would bend over to his knees, but my favorite kind was when he would slap his hands together, and the cackle came from his throat.

And the way he made love to me.

The way he made me feel alive.

The way he made me *feel*—period.

A low whimper vibrated within me, and I pulled my knees closer to my chest. Nothing would make the pain subside. A slowly rising panic dominated, and my whimpers turned into screams.

I screamed until my voice broke and there was no air left in my lungs. Turning to the fucking mattress, I beat the bed before turning against myself, pulling at my hair and clawing at my arms. A mania took over as I beat my cast against the cement wall until it cracked open. I ripped it off and threw it across the room. *Hysteria.* All I wanted was out of this room. All I wanted was to fucking remember. Why couldn't I remember? Why was I doing this to myself?

The door swung open, and I launched at whoever was in my path, but I wasn't prepared to be out cold before I managed to lay a hand on them.

My conscious woke before anything else. I reached for my dry throat, but I was unable to move my hands. When I opened my eyes, Dr. Conway stood over me, reading from a paper in her hand. A blanket of relief washed over me at the sight of her.

"Oh good, you're awake," she said with a grin. "I was worried they gave you too much."

"How long?" I asked. My throat felt like it had been sliced open with a knife.

Dr. Conway sat beside me, and I scanned the unfamiliar room.

"You were in psych ward for six days," she said, and I closed my eyes at the time that had passed—six days without Ollie. "Your system is running on fumes. You can't keep starving yourself. We had to constrain you and bring you to the hospital to get you on fluids."

The hospital? "I-I can't go back there," I said, shaking my head. "Please, I'll be good, just bring me back to the main campus. I'll behave," I begged.

"I'm sorry, Mia. It doesn't work like that." She patted my leg. "But, I am curious…your writing assignment, it was brought to me along with your books and paperwork. Have you read it?"

My writing assignment? She was bringing up my writing assignment *now*? As much as I wanted to go off on her, I shook my head. *She's on my side*, I had to remind myself.

"You remember everything, Mia, or at least your subconscious does. Whatever the trigger has been for you, I need you to latch on to it. Hold on to that feeling and dive as deep as you can go. Once discharged, I'll meet with you back at the psych ward to see how you're doing."

"You're leaving?" I asked desperately. My cuffs clashed against the railing as I tried to reach out to her. "Please, you can't go …" She was my comfort when Ollie couldn't be. My throat burned, my head felt heavy, and all I wanted was for her to stay.

But she stood and ran her palm up my forehead and through my hair before turning to leave. The way she laid her warm hand over my forehead brought flashes of Ollie forward, and how I used to find comfort in that single touch, but it now only haunted me.

My mother used to do that, too, but it was before …

Before.

I grasped on to that single word as the door to my hospital room creaked open and Dr. Conway exited.

That sound.

No …

I shook my head rapidly, attempting to push it back down.

But I had been depleted of all strength. Memories of my past cascaded as a dam finally busted open. The pressure of the water was too much for my barriers to handle, and they collapsed around me.

I remembered everything. *Every sickening thing.* The beeping on the monitor beside me rang in my ears. My eyes darted around as I searched for air. Nothing could escape my mouth as I tried calling out for Dr. Conway. She continued to walk down the hall behind the glass dividing us. I pulled the cuffs against the hospital bed, fighting against the memories.

"Stay with me, Mia," Ollie's words rang over and over in my head. And suddenly, everything went calm. My lungs found air again, my heart rate went back to a steady rhythm, but I remembered everything.

I remembered the way my door had creaked open when he'd come into my room at night, allowing a sliver of light through the darkness. It had been the fear of the sound keeping me up as I'd prayed to God that once, just once, the sound wouldn't come. But every night the sound still came. I'd thought maybe if I pretended I was asleep the creak wouldn't happen, but it always did—for an entire year, and God had never saved me.

I remembered his hot breath on the side of my face as he'd lean over to see if my eyes were open. My body would tense as I'd stay as still as possible, afraid to move a single muscle. The smell of beer and an ashtray would hit me like a drunken tornado. I'd shut my eyes tight as I prayed for my mother to wake. Maybe, I'd thought, she would sense something was wrong with her daughter, and feel the need to come to check on me—a mother's sixth sense. But my mother had never saved me.

I remembered the sound of his belt coming off before he'd climb in next to me. The mattress would slump to one side, and I'd clutch my blanket to avoid rolling closer to him. His callused and overworked hands would violate me in ways I couldn't understand at eight years old. I'd pray my father would show up with his pistol, but my father had never saved me.

Every night like clockwork, but I'd still prayed.

And even as he'd raped me, I'd prayed it would somehow kill me.

But not even death had saved me.

I'd spent three hundred and ninety-four days crying myself to sleep, knowing no one would come and save me from my uncle's abuse and torment. It had been me. I'd had to save myself. And on the three hundred and ninety-fifth day, when the door had creaked open, and I'd tensed under the hot breath against my cheek, and his fingers had slipped under my nightgown, I'd reached under my pillow to grab my father's pistol I'd stolen earlier in the afternoon, and shot him in the head.

I remembered how much effort had gone into pulling the trigger, but I'd used everything I had—all my pent-up anger and shame. I remembered the way my uncle's surprised dark eyes had grown wide seconds before, and I remembered the calmness thereafter.

He can never touch me again.

July 27th, 1999 was the day I killed him, and the day I stopped crying. A mental switch flipped the second I pulled the trigger, and my brain went on autopilot, protecting me from the trauma. My childhood, my innocence, all of it stolen from me since the first night.

I couldn't even shed a tear when my mother took her own life. She surrendered to the guilt for not protecting me from her brother, and I was already numb to it all.

I remembered when my father had found me staring at her corpse in the bedroom after he'd returned home from a business trip. He'd cried over her dead body. The blood was already dry. I remembered the way he'd looked at me as if I'd shot her myself—like I was a monster. *"What have you done?"* he had asked me. *"What's wrong with you?"* But I'd stood stiff, watching and waiting to see if her eyes would open—waiting to hear her voice again. Understanding death, I'd known none of it would come. But I'd still waited and watched, and I hadn't known why.

They'd found the letter she wrote on the nightstand next to her glass of pink wine, and even though it was another piece of evidence proving I hadn't pulled the trigger myself, I may as well have. My father never looked at me the same way, though it couldn't hurt me.

Nothing could.

I was already gone.

It wasn't until junior high when he'd realized I was different from other kids. It was around the same time Diane had shown up in his life when she'd pointed out everything that wasn't "normal" about me. He'd explained what I'd been through, but she'd accepted it all as excuses. She'd make comments here and there when she thought I wasn't listening, but I'd heard everything, and it had never bothered me because *I was already gone.* He'd done his fatherly duty and sent me to counseling, a psychiatrist, many doctors, but nothing had ever gotten through to me because *I was already gone.*

My need to rebel was to get under their skin. I wasn't angry. I wasn't sad. I was only tired of my dad and Diane regularly sending me here and there as if it would have made a difference. They'd bounced me around, handing me off so they wouldn't have to deal with me.

They wanted me gone.

Memories came flooding back times a hundred, but all I felt was the calm of the storm. The rage inside drifted throughout, but it was a different kind of anger. The calm kind, if there was such a thing. Ollie's voice inside my head reminded me to stay with him, and I did. I wouldn't allow my havoc to blow out the flame.

Even in his death, I refused to allow my uncle take one more thing away from me.

SIXTEEN

"If the universe has forbid us,
let's give them something to write about."

OLIVER MASTERS

L ater that evening, I was discharged from the hospital. A security
guard I'd never seen before escorted me back to Dolor. The old
man, with a wrinkled face and large nose, chatted the entire hour-
long drive back, and I found myself missing Stanley's silence. The old man
asked a question, then answered it himself, not allowing me a word in
edgewise. Not that I would have bothered to speak, but I would have liked
to have had the option.

The sun descended in the sky as day turned to night, and by the time
we reached the psych ward, starless black devoured the fiery sunset. The
small lady sent me through the same routine I went through the first day
I'd arrived, first removing my clothes before stepping under the shower.
Afterward, I dressed in the gray drawstring pants, a gray shirt, and a gray
sweatshirt. I rung out as much water from my hair as I could, and once I

reached my room, I curled up over the stiff mattress and closed my eyes before drifting to sleep.

Dr. Conway said she would come to see me at the psych ward upon my return, but she never showed. It was morning when the tiny lady forced me out of my dorm and into the common area among others. I hadn't seen anyone aside from the doctors since I'd been here, only heard their cries at night.

"Dr. Conway said to get you out of your room and make you sure you eat," the tiny lady said before she turned and left me at an empty table.

A heavy-set man with a cart appeared. He didn't ask questions as he set the tray down in front of me before taking off. The cart squeaked until it came to a stop at the next table. Looking down at my food, there was a bowl of what looked to be oatmeal and two slices of burnt bacon.

"It's porridge," a voice said. I glanced up as a girl took a seat in front of me. She swept her straight brown hair behind her and shook her overgrown bangs from her narrow face. "I'm Maddie."

Crystal blue eyes dressed with the infamous "Looney Bin" bags stared at me for a reply.

"I'm not much in a talking mood." I sighed.

"Lucky for me, I like to talk ..." Maddie trailed off, and I wanted to slam my face into the porridge. How was this for payback. Now I knew how Zeke had felt with me. " ... so, I have been here ever since. You're American, ya? I've been to America once before. To Florida, actually. My mum and dad brought us to Disney World. It wasn't as I hoped tho—"

I shot my palm into the air, slicing the thick Irish accent. "Please stop talking."

Maddie pursed her lips together. "Take the puss off ya face, I'm only codding ya! I wanted to see how long you would go before ya cut me off."

I glanced over to Detached Tiny Lady who watched me from across the room, probably making sure I ate. Maddie turned her head to see what had caught my eye. "Ya, she's a brutal one. If ya don't eat, they'll hold you down and force feed ya."

"You're joking."

"Ah, I wish." Maddie leaned back in the chair and fixed her sweatshirt. "You see that girl right over there with the blonde pony?" She nudged her head.

Turning slightly behind me, I saw a girl about the same age as me. Her hair was pulled back so tight, I wondered if she aged ten years once she released her hair tie—instant Facelift.

"Just yesterday they strapped her to her chair and fed her like a chiseler. It was a holy show." Maddie let out a chuckle, and the thought alone made me bring the spoon to my mouth.

"There ya go. All you need is five bites, and Dr. L will leave ya be." Maddie smiled, and I flashed her a tight-lipped grin with a mouthful of porridge in return. "Ya play cards?"

I shook my head.

"After you eat, I'll teach you."

As I counted down each bite, I wondered if Maddie was a secret informant hired by Dr. L to get the crazies to eat. She seemed annoyingly normal, and I wondered what she had to do to end up here. Every person who passed our table stopped for a quick conversation with Maddie, and she smiled back up at them as I ate.

After my last disgusting bite, I pushed the tray away from me as Maddie pulled a deck of cards from under the table. Had she been holding them this entire time?

"What's the craic on campus? I haven't been there since the summer."

Great, Maddie liked drama. "I'm sure nothing has changed."

Maddie shuffled the cards flawlessly like a professional. "Liam still a dick-wad?"

I laughed. "Liam is harmless."

"Sounds like ya know from experience," she said with amusement in her tone.

Rolling my eyes, I relaxed in the chair. "Liam is predictable. It's people like you who you have to watch out for."

Maddie slowed her shuffling pace, and there was a small lift in the corner of her mouth. Anyone else would've missed the slight curve, but I didn't, and a part of me knew I was correct about her. She was trouble.

"You and Liam together or something?" she asked.

"Nope."

"You with anyone on that side?"

"Nope."

"What group you attached to over there?"

What was this, twenty-one questions? My patience was thin. "What's it to you? If there's something you want to ask me, stop beating around the bush and ask me already."

Maddie slammed the deck of cards on the table and leaned in. Her tone was harsh but controlled. "I'm only trying to get to know ya, pet. Nothing more. Now don't cause a scene." She scanned the room before retreating back into her seat and reshuffling the cards. "Me fella is on that side. He's waiting for me to come back."

Remembering what Jake, Alicia, and Ollie had told me, I said, "I thought there were no relationships at Dolor."

"Ours is a secret."

"It's not a secret if you're telling people about it, now is it?"

She chuckled. "Ya have a point there."

Her mood swings made me dizzy, so I didn't bother answering any more of her ridiculous questions. After one round of poker, which she won, of course, everyone took off for recreation as I retreated to my room.

Later, I ate lunch in my room to avoid Maddie, and by the time dinner rolled around, Dr. L dragged me out again to the common area. Maddie eyed me from afar as I tried figuring her out. She was tall, thin, and with a pretty face—I would guess five-foot-eight. She sat poised as her bangs dropped slightly below her eyebrows. Every few minutes, she shook her head to move them from her eyes as she shuffled the deck nervously.

Everything about her stance, the way she spoke, and her facial expressions screamed confidence, but irony filled her blue eyes.

"These meds are for you," Dr. L said, handing me over a small cup containing two pills.

"No, I'm not supposed to be on meds. I'm not taking anything until I talk to Dr. Conway."

"Alright, so be it. I'll give you one more day. But if Dr. Conway doesn't show, you'll be forced to take your meds. It's in your paperwork, Mia."

Even though it was in my paperwork, Dr. Conway had taken me off all medication since my first office visit with her. It had to be in her notes. Where the hell was she? I couldn't go back to the way I was. "Has anyone tried reaching out to her?"

"I'll make a phone call." Dr. L sighed before leaving.

"They're serious about those meds, ya?" Maddie asked as she pulled out the chair in front of me. "Pretend to take them like I do."

"How do you pretend?"

"It takes practice, but ya have to hold them in your throat … then when she leaves, cough them back up." Maddie shrugged. "Or ya can hide them between your gum and upper lip if you can't."

"You do that every time?"

"Sure do. I am how God made me. We're all normal. It's the pills making you not the full shilling."

I partly agreed with her, partially disagreed. Sure, God had made us, but was it with a blank slate or with our lives already planned out? Because it was what happened to us that changed us, molding us into who we'd actually become. Nature vs. nurture bullshit. I hadn't been born emotionally detached. I'd become this way because of what my uncle had put me through. But then I thought about actual psychopaths. The ones raised in decent homes and loving families. Had they been born that way, or had a moment in their life happened to trigger it? Did they ever have the same chance? Were we all born with the same amount of light in our hearts?

"Penny for ya thoughts?" Maddie asked.

"Ha. My thoughts would put you in debt."

Maddie giggled as her overgrown bangs swayed from side to side. "You're funny. I like ya, Mia."

Wonderful. Maddie knew my name.

After dinner and the shower routine, Dr. L led me back to my empty room and closed the door behind her before I curled over the plastic mattress. The room was freezing and I pulled my arms into my sweatshirt, then pulled my knees up inside, hugging myself as I shivered in a ball.

For a split second, I wished I was numb again because having all these feelings without a reason to have them was torment. Easily, I could get by here with my Emotional Detachment Disorder—with my walls. Free of heartache. Free of pain. Free of my past, which I now remembered.

But I had made a promise to Ollie, and I clung to my promise because it was my only attachment left to him.

It was the sound of my name that woke me. My eyes parted to see Ollie kneeling beside my bed with a finger held to his lips.

Great. I had gone mad.

I blinked a few times as his fingers brushed my forehead and ran over the top of my hair.

"Ollie?" *Please be real.*

A small grin appeared over his face. "Hi, love."

In an instant, I sprang to my knees and swung my arms around his neck, breathing in his scent. He was real, and he was here. Running my fingers through his brown messy hair, I kissed his neck and cheek and lips. He wrapped his long arms around my waist as he dropped his head into my neck. "But how?"

"I told you I have connections," he said and pulled away to see me. "You don't belong here, Mia." He looked around before his eyes met mine again. "Are you okay? Why were you in the hospital? What happened?"

All the questions seemed irrelevant at this point, and I brought my hand to Ollie's face. He closed his eyes under my touch. He was so beautiful. My thumb grazed his bottom lip as his jaw relaxed. I had no chemicals in my body, nothing to influence or persuade me to feel for him. I just simply did. Our flame flickered, reminding me it was still there. As long as I had Ollie, it would continue to burn.

Softly, I pressed my lips to his and kneeled over the mattress. Ollie's mouth was tender, his tongue soothing as he kissed away every doubt I'd had since I'd arrived at the Looney Bin.

"Oh god, I missed you, Mia," he whispered with his forehead to mine. I slipped my hands under his shirt and over his warm and familiar skin. Ollie captured my lips with his momentarily before hesitantly pulling away again. "I came to make sure you were alright. Please, talk to me, Mia. Tell me what happened."

Fighting the urge to tell him everything, I chewed on my lip. "I don't want to waste our time with the hard stuff. I'll tell you everything later. I need this"—I kissed his lips—"I need you" I kissed his lips again. "The thought of you is the only thing I've been holding on to through this."

Ollie raised his brows at my confession. He'd never heard me say anything like that, because I never had. It was new to the both of us.

A small smile tugged on his lips, and then he gave in, surrendering himself to me. He wanted it, too. He tried to be the gentleman I knew he was, but the need for our physical connection was stronger.

Clothes came off quickly, one by one between breaths and tongues colliding before he melted over me. His warmth enveloped me immediately, and the bitterness from the Looney Bin vanished. It was only us. He moved the hair from my face and found my eyes. "I'm sorry." He exhaled.

I shook my head and pulled my brows together. "What are you apologizing for?"

He dropped his head for a moment before looking back at me. "You told me not to fall, but I've fallen so fucking hard …" He wet his lips and scanned my face before his eyes returned to mine. "I'm so in love with you, Mia."

Each word hit me like a clash of thunder, and I swallowed the stinging sensation behind my eyes as I looked into his. I'd never seen the look of love before, but it was staring right back at me. It wasn't so much about how his eyes were transfixed on me, a firm grasp on my heart, his soul anchoring to mine, but how they made me feel.

And suddenly, I wasn't falling anymore.

I was flying.

Ollie wasn't expecting anything in return. Instead, he lowered his head, and his kiss was its own testimony. The calm in his lips, the slow caress of his tongue against mine, and the way it was so powerful yet tame transformed a heart of gray back to color. Ollie had that power—*together*, we had that power.

"I don't know how much time we have, but I'm going to appreciate every second," he said after he left my lips and moved to the end of the mattress. He brought my leg over his shoulder, and my bare body shivered without his warmth.

Starting from my knee, he ran a trail of kisses up my leg to my inner thigh as he watched me shudder.

"You're no one's property, but I can't stand the thought of you being with anyone else. Do you understand what I'm saying?" A flash of insecurity set in his eyes. "It's no one else, only you and I?"

Nodding, I sucked in a breath. "You and I. Always."

And then his mouth was on my sex as his hands gripped my bottom. I leaned my hips into him, and suddenly, his tongue drove through my entrance, twirling and stroking. I searched for anything to grip, but there was no sheet over the mattress and no pillow to grab as I barely held on. I cried out, and Ollie shot a hand over my mouth to stifle it as he continued to do things, sending me into a whirlwind of ecstasy.

He crawled back up my torso and replaced his hand with his lips as I moved beneath him, begging to feel him inside me already as my body shook for release. He ran his hand down my center before dipping a finger inside me, and pressed in and out of me unhurriedly.

"Ollie," I pleaded, every cell walking a tightrope over a sea of pure pleasure.

"Not yet, my love … patience." He silenced me once more with a kiss. The combination of the kneading of his thumb and the pumping finger was earth-shattering, and when I fell through the cracks, Ollie brought me back every time.

He wrapped his arm under me and lifted me off the mattress to straddle him. Taking the length of him in my hand, I filled myself with his arousal slowly, just how he liked it. His eyes closed as his mouth made a perfect silent O.

Seeing his beautiful features react from the feeling of our connection magnified every other sensation. I dragged my nails through his messy hair as I took him deeper. Hands roamed everywhere, from my breasts, to my hair, and behind my back. A cold sweat built up between us as his teeth scraped along my jawline. He gripped my thighs to steady my shaking legs as the blessings of my name fell from his lips in gasps. I rolled my hips against him while my clit slid across his pelvis, sending me closer and closer to climax.

It only took one more thrust, one more "I love you, Mia," one more graze of his tongue against mine before I cried out through our kiss. Ollie chased my orgasm with his. His muscles flexed as he gripped my hips, keeping me pinned against him with him deep inside.

Our chests rose and fell in unison as my head dropped into the curve of his neck. He wrapped his long arms around me, pulling me close as our heavy breathing gradually went back to normal. He ran his hand over my hair before lifting my chin to kiss him, and it was in that moment hot water spilled from the corner of my eye, and the taste of salt seeped onto our lips.

Ollie pulled me away and searched my face. "Mia, you're crying," he said through an exhale, and kissed a tear below the corner of my eye before it had a chance to fall. "Bloody hell, you love me." Relief set in his eyes.

"But, I don't believe in love," I whispered.

"Then believe in me." Ollie grinned. "Believe in us."

Unfortunately, the cold air got us back into our clothes, and we lay over the mattress, entangled in one another. I didn't tell Ollie how I had remembered my past. I couldn't find the strength to tell him the truth—what had happened to me and what I was capable of doing. The worst possible case was if he'd look at me differently. The same way my father had looked at me. But this would be worse. Much, much worse.

I traced over the tattoos on his arms as he described each one to me.

"And the scissors?" I asked, dancing my fingers across his forearm. The intricate details from the handle of the scissors to the sharp tip looked perfectly curated.

"That was a cover-up tattoo."

"What did you cover up?" I tried to look past the newer ink to make out the older behind it, but the artist was brilliant. You couldn't even tell.

"I had a crest to represent brotherhood," Ollie said with a distant depth of pain in his voice. "I got it with my brother when I was fourteen. It was stupid."

Noticing the reluctance across his face, I placed my hand in his and gave it a squeeze.

"When I was younger, I looked up to him as a baby brother should, you know? I was blind growing up, saw the good in everyone, but I was naïve. And as I got older, I only got more confused by the actions of others and why people did the things they did. I couldn't get a grasp on why there was so much evil in the world. And one day, I woke up and saw my brother for who he truly was. So, I got the scissors as a reminder I'd cut him out of my life completely. He's like a vampire, slowly sucking the life out of me, taking everything I have. I hung on to him for so long because, well, he's my brother, and wish he would change. That maybe I could be a good influence for him."

Ollie only paused to control his breathing. He ran his fingers through my hair and behind my ear. "We were … we didn't have a good upbringing. Not saying others didn't have it worse, but every day I did whatever I could to make sure my mum and brother were taken care of. A huge burden for someone like me. I carried both of their weight for so long with nothing in return. But never once did I expect anything. And as I got older, instead of me carrying him on my shoulders, he only dragged me down with him. He took advantage of me."

My heart broke for him. Each word fell from his mouth like it was skimming over the surface of a pond that was frozen over, afraid if once the ice broke, he would drown. "You know you can tell me, Ollie. You never have to hide from me. I'll never think differently of you. You know that, don't you?" I kissed the palm of his hand.

Ollie drew in a deep breath and nodded.

"Then talk to me. It's your turn to let me in."

"It was bad, Mia," he choked out. "For years I watched my mum give herself away. She was a prostitute and kept my brother and me locked in a closet while she fucked some real low-lifes. I covered my ears as my brother watched. He was fucking sick, still is. Got off on it. He's ten years older than me, and after he left home, she poisoned me a couple of times. Twice I died, drowned in my own vomit, but then I guess she changed her mind and brought me back. She said she loved me and was sorry. I'm very different from my brother—we don't have the same father, and she said I reminded her of the man she despised. She just didn't know how to handle me."

I exhaled a shaky breath. This man lying beside me had been rejected his whole life, and he still walked around with a smile on his face. I'd never noticed the pain of his past until now. It was never inside him—he never allowed it to dim his light. More than ever, I wished someone had created the perfect words I could say to comfort him because I couldn't think of a single one that seemed fitting.

"It wasn't until I found out he was the one who took over the prostitution ring my mum was a part of when I cut him off entirely. Then, as if things couldn't get any worse, he beat my mum's punter so bad for not paying, he's now on life support and pinned the whole thing on me. He had a false alibi, and my history with EI didn't help either. Now I'm here, and if I can't make it here, I'll go to prison. He faded out of the business and has been following me around ever since, making my life a living hell."

Ollie never belonged here. "What's EI?"

"Emotional Intensity. Basically, I feel too much, while you feel nothing." Ollie dropped his head to see my reaction. "It's as if this world is playing a cruel joke on us." He laughed softly. "But I can't help but know we belong together." He moved his fingers up and down my arm. "And I refuse to take the medication. I don't like the way I feel while I'm on it. It completely neutralizes me, makes me feel like I'm nothing."

"They prescribed you medication?" Ollie didn't need medication. How could feeling too much ever be considered a disorder?

"Yeah, they put me on it when I first got here over the summer. It was the worst. You would have certainly hated me, but something told me to stop accepting the meds, and I did. The transition was horrible. The dean had me in solitary confinement for weeks before classes started."

"I wish I could feel things like you, Ollie. It's a gift. There's nothing wrong with you. I can't imagine how you would be on medication. I guess you would be like how I was, and I don't want that for you. Sometimes I believe you're so good, not even this world deserves you—*I* don't deserve you."

"Are you kidding? I've been waiting all my life for you," He smiled. "With you, I have to fucking pinch myself constantly because there's no way I'm this lucky. When I first saw you in the mess hall, I kept staring, waiting for you to disappear." He laughed lightly. "You are real, yeah? You aren't some figment of my imagination. You're a real girl who feels for me?" He closed one eye, and he couldn't force his beautifully stupid smile away.

I shoved him in the shoulder. "It's terrifying, though. I'm so afraid that, at any moment, my mental switch will flip again and there won't be anything I can do about it."

He picked up my hand from between us and brought it back to his face. "Embrace it, Mia. Every moment, no matter how long it lasts, it's all worth it, yeah?"

I nodded.

"Let me do all the worrying. You only focus on living in the moments we do have. If you ever get lost, I'll always find you."

Ollie pulled me closer, and I rested my head over his chest. He ran his fingers through my locks as I thought about everything he'd gone through. Even after his past, Ollie refused to shut off his breaker or take medication. He still wanted to feel.

He always wanted to love, he just never had anyone to love him back.

"What's the first thing you're going to do when you get out of here?" he asked.

"Put my toes in the water. What about you?"

"Find you … then take you to the ocean." He couldn't see, but I was smiling. "I want a life with you, Mia. I've never wanted anything more. Do you think we can survive the next two years? Think we'll be able to make it?"

I sighed. "God, I hope so."

There was a sudden skip in his breathing. "I can't lose you," he whispered.

"You won't."

The rising of his chest and the beating of his heart soothed me as my eyelids grew heavy.

"I have to leave soon," he hesitantly said.

"Wait until I fall asleep. I can't watch you walk out the door."

"I should have brought *The Notebook*." He laughed lightly.

"I'm serious, Ollie."

"I know, I know …" He leaned down and pressed his lips against the top of my head. "Do me a favor, go to recreation tomorrow. There's a fenced-in area out back, and I'll be waiting for you on the other side."

"Okay," I breathed, my eyelids closing again as I began to drift.

"And Mia?"

"Mmhmm?"

"Stay with me, even when I'm gone."

"Promise."

SEVENTEEN

"We were meant to be together,
but this lifetime wasn't meant for us."

OLIVER MASTERS

"BREAKFAST!" someone yelled and pounded on my door, managing to wake me the following morning. My eyes opened to find Ollie gone, his presence replaced with an ache in my chest. It had been six days before I was able to see him, and waiting another six days wasn't possible. Another pound at the door brought me to my feet.

"Dr. Conway insists you eat your breakfast," the man said, holding a tray out to me as he stood beside a cart. "Otherwise, I wouldn't have made the extra effort."

"When's recreation?" I asked, disregarding everything he'd said.

"Recreation will be inside today after breakfast. It's pouring rain."

My eyes dropped to the floor and I closed the door without taking the tray. I turned to scan the room behind me, looking for any evidence of

Ollie. Unfortunately, there was nothing of him left in here. Not even his smell on a pillow or sheet because there was none—only the fucking mattress.

Dr. Conway finally showed up not too long after, bringing nagging along with her. "You need to eat, Mia. You can't keep doing this." She sat in a black folding chair, clearly uncomfortable as she balanced her clipboard over her lap. We were in a small office somewhere in the psych ward, and a small window displayed it was raining.

I fell back into the plastic-covered couch. "I remember," I whispered as I stared out at the weather keeping me away from Ollie. "I remember everything."

Dr. Conway arched a brow as she moved the clipboard over to the table beside her before scooting the chair closer to me. She dressed casually, wearing jeans, flats, and a plain blue shirt, but her black hair was teased high and unmoving from all the hairspray, and her makeup was heavy. She was the typical Greek from Boston, and neither the United Kingdom, nor Dolor, had taken that away from her.

"What do you remember?" Her tone was calm and steady.

"Don't do that. Don't go all doctor on me." I shook my head.

"Fine, you want me to be real?" She stood and took a seat next to me on the couch. "I'm livid. I've been working with you for a whole month, and the moment you go to a psych ward, *then* you remember …" She slapped her thighs. "Talk about a blow to the stomach. I may as well quit my job."

I pressed my brows together the same time she pursed her lips, and we both burst into a full fit of laughter. I laughed to the point no sound could escape, and tears fell from the corners of my eyes, but eventually, the laughter faded, and those once happy tears turned into the ugly ones.

"Oh, Mia, come here." Dr. Conway pulled me into her chest, her large breasts swallowing me whole, though it was comforting in a way. She held me tight as tears fell freely and I gasped for breath.

"I'm so angry," I cried out, my words muffled by her shirt. "Why didn't anyone help me? Why didn't anyone hear me? Why couldn't anyone care enough to save me?" Each question brought out more cries into her hair, more tears longing to fall, and more built-up confessions escaping as she held me close. "I was locked away in my own personal prison. *Me*! I did that! Clawing and punching to feel again, but no one fucking heard me!" I pulled away from her. "Do you have any idea how that feels? To silently be trapped?" I lowered my head into my hands, gasping for more air.

"Mia, look at me," Dr. Conway insisted. I lifted my head to see her sad and forgiving eyes before she continued, "You are so strong. You're a fighter—"

"No, I'm not a fighter. I'm weak. If I was strong, I wouldn't have pushed my past away and flipped the damn switch. I would have fought through it."

"You were eight years old, Mia. Cut yourself some slack. Not everyone can shut it out, but you did. At eight years old at that. Could you imagine if you hadn't, having to deal at such a young age? You're much older now, and you have the strength to heal, and Mia, it's time. You have to let it all out. You have to start talking about your experience. You can't keep it all inside any longer."

"But it hurts … it hurts so bad."

"And I promise you, after you get through the pain, there is a light at the end of all this."

She pulled my head back into her chest and ran her palm up my forehead. "I think it's time for you to return to the main campus. What do you think?"

The following two weeks were the slowest two weeks of my life; too many emotions kept me up at night, thinking of all the horrible things I had done over the last ten years. Regret kept water in my eyes as I thought back at all the people I'd hurt. The way I'd hurt myself. My head bounced from pointing blame to everyone else, back to feeling remorse for what I'd caused, back to blaming it on the world. I was a casualty of the war in my head, and this had all started with the actions of my uncle.

204

I tried to remember what I'd been like before him—before the first night he'd come into my room. What my favorite color was, what I liked to eat, and most of all, my favorite song to play on the piano. But that girl no longer existed; she'd been destroyed the night her uncle stole her innocence, but her death had been a slow and painful one. At least that little girl had the audacity to give him a quick and painless death. He hadn't deserved a death so gracious.

Then my irrational thoughts traveled to what I could have possibly done to ask for it. Had I given my uncle any indication I wanted it? Was I Mayella in *To Kill a Mockingbird*, and would Ollie see me the same way Atticus saw Mayella? I sighed to myself at the similarity. All along, Dr. Conway had put me through stupid assignments, but only in an effort to remind me.

Clever, Dr. Conway.

Maddie always took the opportunity to talk to me during dinner. We played poker every breakfast and twenty-one every dinner. Each time she brought up the main campus, I changed the subject.

"Dr. Conway is discharging me from here," I said to her. Maddie continued to play with the deck in her hand as I studied the expression on her face. Not a damn change. She was good.

"So, you're leaving Dolor for good, then?" she asked.

"No, I'm going back to the main campus."

Maddie slid two cards across the table in front of me. "I've never met Dr. Conway, but it sounds like she really likes you, ya?"

"Yeah, we've grown close since I arrived."

"Maybe I can request her."

"She normally doesn't work over here on this side, so I doubt it." *Why was I getting territorial with Dr. Conway?* "Hit me."

Maddie flipped over a ten of hearts, and I threw my head back and groaned.

"You lose, as always. You have the worst bloody luck," she said through a laugh.

I smiled at her choice of words. "No, trust me. I'm the luckiest girl in the world."

Because I have Ollie.

Monday morning, I was discharged from the Looney Bin and processed back into the system on the main campus. It had been two and a half weeks since I'd seen Ollie. Every night, I waited for him to come back, but he never showed. Terrified, I wondered if he'd gotten caught because of me. Did they have him in solitary confinement or had they forced him off campus? Was he in prison? Too many thoughts ran through my head, and all I needed was to see him and make sure he was okay.

First, I suffered through another meeting with Dean Lynch, but this time with Dr. Conway by my side. She explained my breakthrough, and I sat quietly beside her as she went over the next steps in the healing process.

"She needs to be back to seeing me twice a week, and involved in group therapy again," Dr. Conway insisted. "She needs to interact with her friends, get back into a regular routine. Mia has been living in isolation long enough."

Dean Lynch agreed, but with conditions.

Dr. Conway, Dean Lynch, and I exited the office to find Oscar waiting outside with my suitcase in hand. He wore an official security guard uniform with his black hair gelled back and a small smirk over his smug face. Flashes of our sex-fests from the beginning of the school year swam around in my brain.

"Where's Stanley?" I asked, glancing over to Dr. Conway. My stomach twisted at the reminder of my indecency.

Dr. Conway opened her mouth, but Dean Lynch interjected, "Stanley is no longer with us. However, Oscar has been in training for four months now and is familiar with our commitment. He's more than capable of taking care of you."

206

Oscar's smirk grew into a devilish smile, full of white pearly teeth. "As the Dean said, I'll take great care of you, Mia."

If the Dean weren't standing right beside me, I would have punched the smile off his face, but instead, I gave a single nod before he escorted me back to my room.

The halls were empty since everyone was in class, and when I entered my dorm, I was surprised to find the room had changed. White padding covered my walls, and my bed was stripped down to a mattress on the floor with a clean stack of clothes lying on top. No desk to climb on to get to Ollie. The door closed behind me, causing me to flinch.

I turned at the waist as Oscar propped my suitcase against the wall. He untucked his shirt and began undoing his belt. My mouth went dry, but I still managed to speak. "What do you think you're doing?"

"What do *you* think I'm doing?" The belt was gone, and he unclasped the button on his slacks. "I'm going to fuck your brains out."

Shit. "No, Oscar. That's over. I'm not that person anymore."

Oscar's face fell, but a disbelief in his eyes rose. "People don't change, Mia. You know you want it. Stop teasing me." He took a step forward, and I backed away.

"You need to leave," I choked out through a constricted throat.

Instead of obeying, he took steps toward me until I was flush against the wall. "Let's get one thing straight—I take what I want."

This wasn't anything like the Oscar I thought I knew. Perhaps I never noticed it because I willingly gave myself to him.

Stunning both Oscar and myself, I raised my hand and struck his cheek. He brought his hand to his face and cocked his head. There was a look of confusion flashing in his eyes, but his confusion quickly transformed into a fury. He grabbed my wrists and slammed them against the padded wall. "You're lucky you have what I need, but if you so much as hit me or disobey me again, I'll drag your ass straight to the dean's office."

My eyes went wide. My body went numb. "What do you want from me?" I knew. *God, I knew.* I just didn't want to believe it. *Powerless.*

All over again, powerless.

Oscar's taunting smile grew. "Today, I only want to touch you, darling." My jeans were yanked down to my knees. My body went rigid. "Only a little touching." He pressed his hand over my panties and slid his hand back and forth. "I have a problem, Mia," he admitted. I wanted to scream, but I couldn't find my voice—again, silently trapped. "Once you give it to me, you can't take it back. You belong to me now."

His fingers stayed over my panties as he continued to rub. "See, not so bad, right?" My throat tightened more, and I clenched my eyes closed. Frozen, I couldn't even move my head in any direction. All I could do was stand against the wall as my past and his threats choked me.

"No one is going to believe you, you know. I've read your file. I know how fucked up you are … using sex as a weapon to get what you want, spreading your legs for strangers, getting caught fucking your previous doctor." He chuckled and tightened his grip around both wrists as a tear ran down my cheek. "You'll just be a girl crying wolf."

He released my wrist and pushed off the wall. "I'll see you around, darling."

The door slammed behind him as I slid down the padded wall until my bottom hit the floor. I dropped my head into my hands as I let every tear fall, each one for each mistake I'd ever made. It hadn't crossed my mind I would ever get to the point enough to care again, and now that point was here, facing all my mistakes, all my wrongs. It all came back to haunt me.

His hands had been on me, and I tasted bile in my throat as my mouth watered. *The bathroom*. After pulling up my pants, I rushed down the empty hall to the community bathroom and collapsed in front of the toilet just in time to throw up.

I was different now, but still all the same. This situation was different, but still all the same. I was the same weak girl, and this world was just as cruel as before. If I told Ollie, he would do something to get himself kicked out. I couldn't tell Ollie and risk anything happening to him. Oscar was right; because of my past, no one aside from Ollie would believe me, anyway. Eventually, Oscar would go away because he couldn't do this forever—or maybe I was in denial.

If I hadn't been through the abuse before, this would have taken a bigger toll on me. But because I'd been down this road, I had the tools to push it away and pretend it hadn't happened. Instead of going to the mess hall for lunch, I took a shower instead, helping to erase the memory of Oscar's hands on me.

I met with Dr. Conway that afternoon at our usual appointment time. Being back in the main building was strange. Everything seemed to have kept moving along without me. I was no one important. The world kept turning on its cruel axis.

Dr. Conway didn't hide her agitation when I told her I'd skipped lunch, and ordered us take-out so she could babysit to make sure I ate. The full hour with her, eating fast food and talking about her stories from her college days, took a weight off my shoulders. For a full hour, I didn't think about Oscar.

"So, how do you like the boys here?" she asked. "Anyone you've had your eye on?"

"W-w-whoa we're not at that point yet, *Doctor*," I teased.

She set her burger down and ran a napkin over her mouth. "So, there is someone." She smiled. "What's his name? Do I know him? Is it the same boy who kissed you before you punched the wall?"

I rolled my eyes. "The last thing I'm doing is telling you his name."

"Oh, my God, you really like this guy ..."

"Stop."

Dr. Conway's eyes grew wider. "Bloody hell, you've fallen in love with him."

"You've been here way too long." I laughed. "And no, you have to believe in love to fall."

She held a finger up at me as she swallowed her last bite. "If there's one thing I've learned over the years, you don't have to believe in love for it to exist because love is not something *you* choose—love chooses you.

And when love happens, you will know because there will be no other explanation."

An awkward silence fell over us as I stared at her, trying to blink her advice away.

Nope, it was still there—in the air—swallowing me whole and spitting me back out.

"Just think about it," she said with her palms in the air.

The thought of seeing Ollie kept me pacing my dorm room, all the while keeping an eye on the little hand as it slowly ticked by the second. I couldn't understand why I was so nervous to see him. He'd told me he was in love with me. His words belonged in movies and romance novels. I didn't deserve for those words to belong in my life, especially coming from him.

Ten more minutes, I told myself—only needed ten more minutes. No one knew I was back yet, and I'm sure everyone—maybe not Bria, but everyone else—would be happy to see me. But would they be glad to see the new Mia—the Mia who had feelings and shed tears? I was still trying to get to know my new self at the same time as sorting my past, sorting my feelings with Ollie, and sorting this torment with Oscar.

Sorting.

Filling my lungs, I opened my door and walked out into the hallway. When I approached the mess hall, I paused under the archway to scan the room, but Ollie was nowhere in sight.

"Mia?!" A shriek bounced and I immediately knew it was Jake. He stood from his table with wide eyes and his mouth agape. In no time, his arms were around me. "You're back!"

After he pulled away, he walked me over to the table as warm smiles greeted me from the rest of them.

"Was it as bad as everyone says it is?" Isaac asked.

"No, not really. Honestly, I was unconscious the majority of the time, so I don't remember too much …" I trailed off as I scanned the room again impatiently.

"He's not here," Alicia said. "He hasn't eaten with us since you left."

"It's fucking strange. I've never seen Ollie like this before," Isaac added.

Bria sat in silence as she kept her eyes on the table before her.

"I'm going to go find him. I'll see you guys later."

My hands shook as I approached Ollie's door, and I ran them down the front of my pants before waving them in the air to shake out my nerves. I knocked twice over his door, and his beautiful raspy voice came from the other end.

"Who's there?"

His voice resurrected my Ollie-smile.

"Water," I said, this time in my American accent.

Seconds passed, and I imagined seeing his lips turn up into his contagious smile.

"Water who?"

"Water you doing, love? Let me in …" I laughed.

The door opened, and Ollie stood in his black jeans, loose white tee, and a lopsided grin. His hair poked out from under his beanie as he leaned against the open door. "I'm dreaming, yeah?" His body relaxed at the sight of me. "Because if I am, don't you dare wake me up." I closed the gap between us and reached for his hand before lacing my fingers in his. Ollie's eyes closed as a slow exhale left his lips. "I was lost without you."

He pulled my hand around his waist and wrapped his long arms over me, pinning me to his chest. And we stood like that for a while, holding each other in an affectionate silence, unwilling to let each other go. Burying my face into his chest, I knew Ollie had been the one to show me how to save myself.

He pressed his lips against my forehead before his chin rested over the top of my head. "I'm so sorry. I tried to get to you, but I couldn't, and I don't know what to do, Mia. Please, tell me this means you're back …"

"I am, and it's going to be different now."

He dipped his head back to see my face. "What do you mean?"

"I didn't say anything before because I wasn't sure myself, but Ollie, I remember everything that happened to me. But most importantly, I can feel, and it's going to stay. I'm *staying*. All you asked was for me to believe in us, and I do. That belief turned into something beautiful, and now I understand." My voice broke as my eyes watered. "I'm staying because with you I have a home, Ollie, it's in here." I rested my palm against his chest.

A single tear fell from his eye before he wiped his face on the sleeve of his shirt. "Emotional intensity …" he reminded me through a mutter as if crying in front of me would make me look at him differently.

I reached for his face and fixed his glossy eyes in front of me. "You should never be ashamed, Ollie, never in front of me. Your heart is beautiful. You're beautiful." He nodded as another tear fell and I stood on my toes to press my mouth against his salty lips.

His kiss in return was more firm and urgent, and his lashes were wet against mine as he pulled me away from the door and over the mattress on the floor.

We lay over his bed as he stroked my hair. "No one can know about us, Mia."

"Why? Does this have to do with the whole Dolor's anti-relationship clause?" Ollie didn't laugh when I expected him to, which alerted me to sit up. My eyes searched his. "What happened?"

Ollie sat up with me and leaned his back against the wall, us side by side. "A lot of people here aren't like Jake, you, or myself. When they see people happy in a relationship, it fuels them to do whatever they can to destroy it. They want to bring everyone down to their level. Basically, if they can't have it, no one can."

"I'm still not following the severity of this …"

"There's a history, but I'll tell you about the most recent: Thomas and Livy. Their relationship started at the beginning of school a year ago, much like we did. They were quickly in a close, committed relationship, despite the damn curse that came along with being in relationships here. They thought it was all nonsense. Until students fucked with them, spreading rumors, starting drama, doing little things to break them up. When that didn't work, the people here brought it to the next level. It got so bad, Livy, who was Alicia's best friend, was gang raped in her dorm and—"

My hand moved over my mouth. "Oh, my god."

"It gets worse. She ended up getting pregnant. Thomas went ballistic. He already had anger issues to begin with, but between the rape and the pregnancy, it sent him over the edge. He killed one of the guys who raped her and was sent away after. I believe he's now in prison."

"But what about Livy?"

"After Tommy's dismissal, she couldn't go on anymore. They found her in her room over the summer—" he paused and drew in an unsteady breath. "She killed herself, Mia."

"No ..."

"Yes. Two lives destroyed because of a relationship. It's sick." Ollie grabbed my hand from my thigh and brought it into his lap. "The moment you walked through the mess hall, I knew I was fucking doomed. And, Christ, when we first kissed ..." he shook his head. "I can't go back to a time before you, Mia. We can never not be together."

Grabbing his hand from his lap, I dropped my head over his shoulder. "We can't. We won't."

Ollie released a breath and kissed the top of my head. "So, we have two options. We can either say 'to hell with everyone' and it will always be us against them until we leave this place, or we can keep us hidden— no one knowing. Both will be equally hard for me, and I wish things were different. But they're not. I'm okay with whatever you choose. All that matters is you and I, alright?"

First, our disorders tried keeping us apart, and now it would be Dolor. I was sure of Ollie. I was sure what we had was strong, but sometimes the easiest decision isn't always the right one. "We have to stay undercover." The risk wasn't worth it.

Ollie exhaled. "Come here," he said, picking me up and planting me over his lap. "Then we can't tell anyone about us ..." he sighed.

"I know."

"I can't show you affection when I want to ..."

"I know."

"I'm going to fuck this up because I can't help myself ..."

"Yeah, I know."

Ollie grinned.

Dinner was cumbersome with Ollie being so far away after spending weeks without him. He said he doesn't fuck, but the way his eyes were on me, told me differently. He sent me a wink, and my head did the stupid shake like always when I didn't know what else to do.

He mouthed words even a porn director would not approve of, and my mouth dropped open. Ollie laughed silently, and I rolled my eyes with a stupefied smile.

"Eat," I mouthed back, and he took the entire spoon into his mouth before licking it clean. My head fell in my hands, and I had to turn away. "Zeke, remind me to kick his ass later," I said as Zeke watched us with amusement.

Minutes passed, and Ollie slid in the chair beside me. He pressed his forehead to the side of my head and mine leaned into it like a reflex. "How do we say goodbye if I can't kiss you?" His breath in my ear, the graze of his nose, and the closeness of his body all violated rules from our conversation earlier.

"Easy. We don't say goodbye."

Ollie pulled away and the frown lines between his eyes deepened. "I can't leave a room without thanking you for your presence, Mia."

214

I grinned from ear to ear. "Well I have a hard time watching you walk away from me, so I suppose that makes us even."

"I don't want *even*. I want a solution," He growled and turned his whole body to face me. His eyes looked past me out the window as he licked his lips, in deep thought. The beanie had disappeared since I came back, and I wondered if it symbolized his mood. Every time he'd worn the beanie, it was only while he was upset, as if it hid him from the world or blanketed his worries.

"Alright, I have an idea." His eyes met mine and a smile emerged from his gleaming lips. "You know how I always ask you to close your eyes?" I nodded. "When one of us has to part from the other, I'll tell you to close your eyes. We imagine we're kissing—and in your mind, I'm a fucking fantastic kisser, by the way—but we don't say goodbye, and you count to ten before you open your eyes again so you won't have to watch me walk away."

The way his eyes lit up, I couldn't say how ridiculous it sounded. "Okay."

Ollie squeezed my thigh. "Close your eyes, Mia."

EIGHTEEN

"How do you do it, my love?
My haven is in your heart and
my shelter is in your arms.
When your eyes find mine,
they give me refuge from the storm.
Did you know I'm homesick without you?"

OLIVER MASTERS

ater that night, Ollie reached for my good hand to pull me up through the vent to go back to his room. I couldn't wait for my hand to heal completely. Two more weeks.

"You ready?" Ollie asked as he propped himself up on his hands and knees in the vent. His hair was in chaos since he'd showered earlier; not an ounce of grease held it down. He wore his gray joggers and a black tee, but his perfect white smile was the best look on him.

I sat up, and he crawled over me until my back met the foundation. "I have to steal moments where I can," he whispered, and after patiently waiting to be alone together, two pairs of longing lips touched in urgency from holding back for too long.

His mouth moved eagerly, seizing his moments and giving me life. His tongue brushed mine greedily, yet savored the taste of me as he rushed then slowed his speed, unable to make a decision. He was fierce and calm concurrently. He tugged my bottom lip, sucked and kissed before crashing his tongue to mine once more as quiet moans came from his throat.

Ice and fire. Winter and summer. Ollie and Mia.

He brushed his nose against mine, and across my cheek until he found my neck.

"Okay, I think we're ready now." I giggled as he breathed into my hair.

"No. I don't want to go back. Let's hang out in your room. *Fuck*, I'll stay right here all night. Who cares about them, anyway."

Not me. Well, Jake had grown on me. "If we don't show, they'll know something is up."

Ollie groaned into my neck before raising himself by his arms. "Our first night back together of not being together …" He hung his head before picking it back up to face me. "I know it will be really hard, but you have to keep your hands off me. And don't tempt me, my love. I struggle to hold myself together around you as is."

This made me laugh and blush all at once. "Oh, yeah?"

Ollie smiled. "Yeah, and if I come on strong, you have to push me away. You have to. You're stronger than me." I knew he was serious, but he couldn't force away his smile even if he wanted to. "Or, we can always get drunk and blame it on the alcohol."

He was happy—we were happy.

"This is the last night," Ollie informed the room after helping me down through the hole. "I can't have any of you showing up anymore."

"What? Why?" Bria complained, wearing her notorious crop top and booty shorts.

Ollie glanced over to me as I leaned back against the wall beside Jake and passed over the liquor bottle without taking a sip. Isaac, Bria, and Alicia all watched Ollie, awaiting a reply.

"Because it's not worth getting caught," Ollie stated clearly. I peered up at him as he rested his hands over his hipbones. His hair was in disarray, his smile still burned, and his natural sun-kissed skin glowed against his tattoos.

Bria lifted a curious brow. "But you never cared before."

"I had nothing to lose before," Ollie countered. He was growing impatient and becoming defensive. His smile was withering. *Don't let her get to you, Ollie.*

Bria rose to her feet and narrowed her eyes at him. "What do you have to lose now?"

Ollie ran his hand through his hair and grasped the ends. The tension in the room was undeniable. "Everything."

When Ollie spoke, which was rare amongst others, he had the ability to silence the world around him. Not because he wanted people to listen, but because people wanted to hear. His voice was smooth, his tone deliberate, and each word delicately considered. It was music—no, it was poetry. Yes, each time Ollie opened his mouth, he silenced the world with poetry.

"Fine, then tonight we're going big. You're drinking, Ollie," Bria said, walking over to him with the liquor bottle in hand. "You too, Mia. None of that skipping shit."

"Bottoms up," Isaac added amongst Bria's influence, speaking up for the first time since I'd arrived.

Ollie glanced down at me as I sat pinned against his wall and I raised my shoulders in a half-shrug. We were doomed either way; at least we could end the night making out and blame it on the alcohol like he'd suggested.

The music played in the background, liquor circulated between us and through us, and Jake and I couldn't restrain our laughter as Alicia awkwardly danced around a drunken Bria.

Bria's attention rested on Ollie, and from the look in her eyes, and Ollie's eyes on me, something told me she knew what was going on between Ollie and me. "Who's up for a game of strip or dare?" she asked with her hands in the air. "I'll start."

She shimmied out of her little shorts to reveal a black lace thong underneath. She had no boundaries. None. I had used to be bold, and I supposed a part of me was still daring in a way. I wasn't exactly sure anymore—stuck between the girl I once was and the girl I hoped to be. A girl who experienced feelings. Real feelings. A girl who cried and showed emotion. A girl who was inspired to love herself because a boy loved her.

"I'm not playing," Ollie said, and Bria marched over to him and raised him off the mattress by his arm.

"This is our last night, Ollie. You're playing." She dragged him across the room and tugged him down beside her on the floor. "Okay, since I stripped first … Ollie, strip or dare?"

Ollie withdrew his shirt and leaned back on his hands. The birds along his ribcage and up his back moved as his muscles flexed. It had been too long since we'd been intimate, and it took all the strength I had not to climb over his lap and have him right then and there. Ollie met my gaze and winked at me from across the circle. *"I want you,"* I mouthed to him like he'd done to me before. His cheeks flushed, and his smile resurfaced.

"Alicia, strip or dare?" Ollie asked with a lingering smile on his face.

"Dare."

"Change clothes with Jake."

Alicia and Jake swapped looks before they scanned each other up and down. Alicia only wore a tank top and little spandex shorts while Jake wore long sleeve flannel pajamas.

They both stood and tipped the mattress into a standing position as they undressed behind it, giggling. When Alicia and Jake stepped out, the rest of us fell into fits of laughter as Jake strutted toward me. My eyes immediately went to the bulge hanging from the tiny shorts. One giant testicle slipped out. My hand flew over my mouth.

Ollie's mouth shot open as a loud cackle emerged. He slapped his hands together before falling into Isaac's shoulder when his cackle went silent, and his body shook, fighting the tears. Isaac didn't know who to laugh at more: Jake or Ollie.

Ollie barely recovered as his eyes glossed over. "I guess the ball's in your court now, mate," he said through controlled lips, and then we all lost it.

Isaac fell onto his back, and Ollie brought his hands back over his face as he leaned forward, unable to control his laughter anymore.

Jake looked down and tried to stuff his testicle back into the shorts. "Whatever. Yes, alright? I have a testicular disorder, and you know what else? Bryan fucking loves it."

His confession only made things unfavorable for him. Ollie crawled on the floor, and the rest of us couldn't breathe with tears in our eyes.

Within the hour, Ollie refused a few dares by stripping, leaving himself in only his black boxer briefs. Alicia kissed Jake, Bria was still in her crop top and panties, and I was fully clothed with my t-shirt and shorts. I took three shots of liquor and performed my best Bria impersonation. Everyone was drunker than we should have allowed, including me. Perpetual smiles were plastered on everyone's faces, and the giggles flowed smoothly.

Bria whispered into Isaac's ear as they peered over at me, and I couldn't help but feel they were devising a plan.

"Alright, Bria. Strip or dare?" Isaac asked.

"Dare … a *proper* dare this time," she said and took a good long swig of the bottle.

"I dare you to touch yourself right here in the middle of the circle…"

My eyes widened, my smile died, and I glanced over at Ollie to see his reaction. Something like this had been bound to happen. It had only been a matter of time.

Ollie lifted off his hands and leaned over. "She's not fucking doing that, are you mad?" His gaze darted between Isaac, Bria, and me.

"Oh, yes I am, and I dare Ollie to watch me the entire time," Bria said before she crawled to the middle. The rise out of Ollie was what she wanted. My eyes rushed to see everyone else's reaction, but all eyes were on Bria as she lay on the floor, knees spread apart, her sex directly in front of Ollie.

"Come on, get off the floor. You're making a fool of yourself," Ollie said, still maintaining what little composure he had left.

Bria wiggled on the floor. "You either watch me or strip off your last article of clothing."

Ollie clenched his jaw and looked up at me.

"No, not at Mia. Look at me," Bria hissed before dipping her fingers into her panties.

"Oh, shit," Isaac breathed.

"Stop, Bria," Ollie pressed. "Your drunk, you don't know what you're doing, and Isaac—" he slapped his friend in the chest "—stop provoking her."

"I know exactly what I'm doing," Bria said. "I'll let you touch me, Ollie. Right here …" Bria continued to rub herself inside her panties. My stomach twisted into knots as I looked over at Ollie, but he tried to focus on everything else in the room besides Bria and what she was doing to herself.

"Is this what you wanted?" Ollie asked out loud as he stood and gathered his clothes. "Fuck you, and fuck you..." he said, pointing to Bria and Isaac. "I'm not playing."

"Calm down, mate. She asked me to," Isaac said in defense. "I only gave her what she wanted. You always have to ruin everyone else's good time."

Ollie fell over his mattress and shook his head.

What exactly was the goal behind her motives? Did she want to see Ollie's reaction? Did she really want Ollie to touch her? Who was I kidding? Of course, she did. She'd been trying to get with Ollie since before I had arrived.

I stayed beside Jake against the wall as the rest of them continued going over strip or dares. The whispers between Bria and Isaac continued, and eventually, all my dares turned physical, and my clothes started coming off.

"You guys have it out for Mia tonight, yeah?" Alicia said, noticing the tension in the room. Only in my bra and underwear, I swam in the pressure.

"Alright, Mia, last strip or dare. Don't worry. It's easy. You only have to kiss Isaac," Bria said casually.

How did I always find myself in these situations? I glanced over at Ollie, and he motioned me over with the come-hither finger and defeat in his eyes. I shook my head at him. We couldn't let them win. My eyes scanned the circle until they fell over Bria. She lifted her thin brow. "Well, what are you waiting for?"

"Mia," Ollie called out. I cocked my head back toward him. "Please," he urged with fear in his features.

I stood and walked to the mattress he was lounging on. Ollie gripped my waist and lifted me off the floor and placed me over his lap, facing him. "Is this a bad idea?" I asked as he brushed my hair back with one hand before cupping my neck.

"Probably." He grinned. His breath was a mix of liquor and mint. And then he kissed me, already giving up everything we'd discussed earlier about keeping us a secret.

"I knew it," Jake squealed. "They're like a thing!"

Ollie smiled against my lips before he pulled away. "No, we're not. Now leave us alone, would ya?" He returned his attention to me, grazing his lips and nose across mine, and everyone else picked up the conversation ten feet behind me. "They're drunk. They'll forget about this in the morning. Right now, it's only you and me. The only girl I want to touch is you, the only girl I want to kiss is you, and the only girl I want to be inside is you." A lazy, glowing smile appeared across his face.

"I think you're the one who's drunk, Masters," I said through a small laugh.

"Yes. Yes, I'm very drunk." Ollie looked over my shoulder, "And forgive me, but I need you right now, and no one is paying attention to us." His hand slid between my thighs before his fingertips brushed over my panties. "May I?"

Stunned, I turned my head to see the rest of the crew continuing the game, laughing, utterly blind to Ollie and me. My eyes met his hazy ones again. His lips glistened, and I sucked in a breath as his finger brushed my sex. Adrenaline pumped through my veins as heat touched my cheeks.

I nodded.

"You trust me, Mia?" he asked, all-knowing he had full control over me. Nodding, I was rendered speechless. He leaned forward and touched his liquor-soaked lips to mine. "Don't move, no matter what."

Instantly becoming high on him, I pulled my bottom lip between my teeth as Ollie slid down lower against the wall. His hands trailed up the inside of my thighs, grabbing, squeezing, and spreading my thighs apart. My foggy attention stayed on him as his eyes darted behind me, back to mine, then down to between my thighs.

My breathing faltered at the touch against my sex as he hooked a finger at the center of my panties and moved them to the side. "*Fuck*, I would do anything right now to taste you," he whispered, green eyes drowning in desire. His erection pressed against his sweatpants beneath me, and Ollie reached for a blanket off the floor and pulled it around us for more privacy.

He gripped my bottom more firmly in one hand as his fingers slid up and down my heat, causing all my senses to disable. My hips involuntarily rolled against his hand, and then he suddenly stopped.

"I told you not to move, and I'm just getting started. Do you want me to stop, Mia?" Ollie whispered slowly, torturously. The only word I needed to say caught in my throat. I shook my head, answering him in ways my mouth couldn't.

Ollie's smile returned. He bent his knees behind me and ordered me off my bottom so I balanced on my knees. "I need more access," he explained. His tight and inked torso lay between my legs, and Ollie spread me with two fingers before leading me back down over his warm skin above his boxers. He grabbed my hips and guided me, sliding me up and down against his pelvis, the sensation of his warm skin against me causing me to whimper.

"You have to stay quiet, my love," Ollie's voice shook in a whisper as my legs grew weak. His palm descended and covered me again, rubbing against my clit, then sliding back, and his finger pumped inside me. My hold around his shoulders tightened as a low moan sounded from me. The room spun as I trained my focus on his face, afraid if I turned away from the only thing holding me together, I would move or cry out, and he would stop again. His flow was moving steadily. The room dimmed. The silence buzzed. A tornado touched down, spinning me, spiraling me into his rapture. I was getting closer.

His eyes fixed on mine as his hands continued the heavenly spur. "Come here and kiss me," he said through short breaths of his own, knowing the point I was reaching.

My mouth collided with his and he swallowed my cries. My legs trembled as he leaned forward and pressed his forearm over my thigh, trying to control it for me. His assault slowed its pace, showing gentle attention to the only parts to lead me to the top and over the edge. His warm, intoxicating tongue flicked against mine, until I reached falsetto.

The height of my orgasm took away my ability to kiss him any longer as my lips turned to mush. I dropped my head into his neck. "Jesus, Ollie…"

He slowly removed his finger from inside me, and when I looked up, his finger slid out of his mouth between his lips, tasting me with a grin.

And all over again, I was ready for round two.

"You okay?" he asked, fixing my panties.

I shook my head. "I want you inside me, like right now," I admitted, satisfied and in utter need all at once. With Ollie, no amount of pleasure and time will ever be enough. In constant craves, I needed our physical connection like a drug addict.

"Trust me, I want you, too. Though not in front of them. I *am* a gentleman," he whispered into my ear. "I shouldn't have even done that with them here." He kissed my forehead. "I respect what we have, alright? But sometimes I lose control at the same time."

I understood, but I didn't have the same restraint as him. Determination seeped through my veins, and my hand slipping under the blanket and over his boxer briefs. His arousal was rock hard, willing, and waiting.

Ollie closed his eyes. "Mia …" his voice cracked in a warning, but he didn't push me away. His shaft sprung through the opening of his boxers, and I wrapped my fingers around the length of him. The muscles in his stomach flexed as he moved against my taunting strokes.

"Mia …" he breathed again.

"You lay there and be a complete gentleman, Ollie—" I climbed over his longing body "—and let me be bad for you."

Ollie's brows rose before his gaze slid around the room. Bria, Isaac, Jake, and Alicia were laughing and chatting. In a moment of his distraction, I rubbed his length against my already soaked sex, making him just as wet and easy for my stroke.

"Oh … fuck, Mia. You're going to make me want to have you right here and now," Ollie panted. He brought his hands over his face, running them up and through his hair.

"That's the point."

Ollie looked past me at the others again, then back at me. "This in no way means you mean anything less to me."

"I know, Ollie," I stated, rubbing up against his hard, tight length again.

"*Fuck.* I respect what we have."

"I do, too."

"Promise you'll keep quiet?"

"Promise," I said as the anticipation pumped in my blood.

Ollie shook his head with a smile and reached over to grab the phone from off the floor to turn on a song, I assumed for the others to dance to, but the one he picked was nothing I'd expected. "Is this Miley Cyrus?" I asked, and let out a giggle.

"Oh, hush. I pushed shuffle, but this 'Adore' one's good." Then he raised the blanket higher over me. "How are we going to do this?" he asked with a crooked smile and adventure in his eyes. "You're making me feel like a bloody kid again. I love it."

"As I said, you just lay there. Don't move," I said mockingly.

Ollie's face flushed as his eyes glowed. He was still tipsy, beautiful, and boyish as if it were his first time.

Swiftly, I removed my panties off one leg before hovering over him. Grabbing the length of him, I fell all in with Ollie, my slick walls hugging him, taking him deeper until he filled and fulfilled me entirely. "Mia. You feel so … Christ …" He grabbed my thighs as his body jerked forward. "You feel fucking amazing."

"Don't move, Ollie," I teased, pushing him back against the wall. I brought my fingers to his lips, and his jaw relaxed. As I circled my hips against him, he dug his fingers into my thighs. The mood shifted from taunting and torturous to what always came of our bond—a connection so pure, all the angels in heaven would be jealous.

Gently rocking against him, my mouth met his as I settled his head between my arms. His lips brushed my cheek, down my neck and over my shoulder, trailing his wet lips across the surface of a body created for him. It was all we both needed, a slow and heavenly grind.

Everything else faded, and it was only Ollie and me. Even in our drunken, spontaneous moment with the others only feet away, Ollie made me feel like we were the only two people in the universe. He grabbed the back of my head, pressing our lips fiercely together to suffocate his moans, and my fingers held on to his hair tightly. "Mia, I'm—"

I nodded before his mouth crashed to mine again. His entire body flexed as he pinned me against him, holding our kiss until the holy feeling passed.

Knowing I was the one to bring him pleasure—to cause his breathing to shudder and his body to tense before melting into a perfect bliss—gave me every reason to adore him that much more. He dropped his head into my shoulder as I ran my fingers through his hair.

This beautiful creature loved me, and I would never understand it.

After a few adjustments, he pulled me over his chest and stroked my hair as we calmed our breathing. "Ollie?" I whispered.

"Yeah?" he asked with his fingers in my hair.

"How many people have you loved before me?"

He grinned. "None."

"How many have you slept with before me without a condom?"

"None."

I lifted my head off his chest. "Why?"

"I had my fair share, Mia. But I knew as soon as I saw you, I was looking at the one. A condom means a casual fuck to me, and you are anything but. I believe in what we have, and as long as you were on birth control, I wanted to give myself to you completely. No barriers, no fucking condom, just me. Something I'd never given any woman before you. There never will be anyone else, I'm certain of it ..." He ran his thumb down my bottom lip before resting his fingers under my chin, "I love you, Mia. I never told anyone that, ever. You have my entire heart, and you have the power to rip it out of my chest and obliterate it completely, but I have belief you won't."

It was a far better explanation than I could have asked for. Ollie had given me more than just himself. He'd lain it all on the line—his love, his feelings, his body—following a belief we were meant to be together. It was a beautiful thing, becoming entirely vulnerable to another human being who could potentially destroy you. But no doubts ever came from him. No hesitations. No questions.

"What are you two doing over there?" Isaac asked, and I'd forgotten we weren't the only two people in the room as Ollie's nose brushed mine.

"Mind your own, mate," Ollie called out.

"Why are you glowing over there, Ollie?" Alicia teased. "You sure seem to be in a better mood all of a sudden."

Ollie let out a raspy yet nervous chuckle as he grabbed the closest pillow and chucked it behind me at them. "Shut up, would ya?" he said and leaned back against the wall, his cheeks flushed.

"Mia, why don't you come over here and take care of me next," Isaac suggested and followed with a laugh, but the mood shifted entirely.

Ollie gripped my waist and pulled me to the side before springing to his feet. Before I knew what was happening, Ollie had hoisted Isaac off the floor and pushed him against the wall at his chest. "You don't talk to her like that. Do you understand what I'm saying to you?" Isaac's face turned crimson and nodded against the wall before Ollie took a step back. "It's time for everyone to go."

Everyone was too startled to speak another word as they all helped each other up through the vent. Ollie took a seat at the edge of the mattress with his head in the palms of his hand. His knee bounced uncontrollably, and I crawled over and sat beside him.

After everyone left, I placed my hand over his back to calm him.

"I'm sorry, Mia. I didn't mean to, but I can't control myself. You're not a fucking knickknack. No one should ever objectify you. You deserve better …" he explained as he ran his hands through his hair.

"It's okay. I'm stronger than you think. I could care less about what those people think or say about me. Hell, I've done enough to myself to deserve it."

He cocked his head to face me. "No, don't do that …"

"Do what?"

"Don't justify other people's actions or comments because of your past. I don't care what you did. No one deserves to be treated that way. He needs to start respecting the girls here, especially you."

Climbing off the mattress, I got to my feet and stood before him. "Well, now we're in quite a pickle."

Ollie lifted his eyes to mine. "Why's that?"

"My exit plan just left."

NINETEEN

"Even the darkest parts of us
become beautiful when seen
through a different set of eyes."

OLIVER MASTERS

// If we get caught, the plan is I kidnapped you from your room and held you prisoner." Ollie walked in circles with his hands on his hips. "Don't stray from the plan, love." I pressed my lips together as I watched him pacing about the dorm. Worry caught in his features as he chewed his lip. "And if they interrogate us in separate rooms, which I know they will, just remember what I said. I'm the one who lifted you out of the room and kept you here. I've seen it on the telly so many times. They *will* separate—"

Ollie paused and glanced over at me, one hand still clinging to his hip bone and the other in the air. "Why are you laughing? This isn't funny."

My laughter doubled as I rolled back over the mattress. "We ... we will be fine!" I gasped out. Ollie only shook his head with an unconvinced grin.

Once calm, I continued, "They don't even do a security check in the morning. The doors will open at six, and I'll sneak back to my room before anyone notices. I've done it before."

Ollie raised a brow. "Oh, yeah? When was this?"

"The night Bria almost had her way with you. I sat right there while you slept until the automatic locks opened." I pointed to the spot beside the mattress.

Ollie dropped his arms to his sides, his voice soft. "You stayed with me all night?"

"I didn't touch you, Ollie. I wouldn't take advantage of you if you didn't have a choice. No one should," I said defensively. I couldn't believe me, a girl, was saying that to a boy.

"No, it's not that. It's just ... I can't believe you did that for me."

I lifted my shoulder in a casual shrug. Ollie's smile beamed as he walked toward the bed, leaned over, and kissed the top of my head. "You're incredible."

He sat over the edge of the mattress, thoughts still circling his mind. "Perhaps you're right ... I'll set the alarm on the mobile just in case."

"You sound so proper for someone who just fucked their girlfriend in front of four other people."

Ollie cocked his head back in my direction. "One, don't ever say I fucked you ... Two, it wasn't in front of everyone. You were covered, and they haven't got a clue and ... did you call yourself my girlfriend?"

It had rolled off my tongue so quickly, I hadn't even realized I said it. "Yeah, I guess I did, didn't I?"

"It sounds so ... downplayed, underrated for what you are to me. I don't like it."

"Friend a better term?"

Ollie picked up a pillow off the floor and chucked it at me. "Get out of here..."

"Partner?"

He shook his head. "No."

"Companion?"

He pulled his brows together. "You're not a bloody dog, Mia."

"I give up," I said, throwing my hands up.

Ollie crawled over me and attacked my neck with his lips. "We don't need a title. All we need is each other."

And he was right. What we shared shouldn't and couldn't be defined by a single word.

Tuesday morning should have been like any other Tuesday morning, but it wasn't. It was different, and not the bad different. With Ollie, it wasn't just comfortable. It was a delirious state of captivation. The whole time, it was Ollie. He was the drug I kept taking during my time here, and I would gladly overdose on him.

A foreign buzzing of an alarm woke me, and I quickly shuffled around to turn it off before it woke Ollie, who slept soundlessly beside me. After finally hitting snooze, I lay back down and stared at the ceiling with his legs still intertwined with mine and an unbidden smile on my face—exhausted, sleep deprived, but smiling.

"Why are you smiling, love?" Ollie whispered, his voice sleepy and tired.

Glancing over at him, I saw his eyes were still closed as he lay on his side, facing me. The room was still dark this early in the morning, but the moonlit morning sky cast a soft glow over him.

"How did you know I was smiling?"

"I can feel it."

Turning on my side to face him, I ran my thumb across his lashes. "Because I'm happy."

He exhaled before the corners of his lips turned up. He was the one who made me happy, and he knew it. His dimple said so.

"Open your eyes, Ollie."

"No."

"Why not?"

"If I open my eyes, it means you have to leave, and I'm not ready for you to go. When my eyes are closed, I get to pretend it's a Sunday morning and we have no place to be." A bigger smile grew, and his dimple deepened. "Go on, close your eyes …."

"Why?"

"Just close them …" His hand moved up my side and behind my back. "Are they closed?"

Letting out a light laugh, I closed my eyes. "Yes, Ollie. My eyes are closed."

"It's a Sunday morning, and I already made your coffee before sneaking back in bed with you. You smell it?"

"Mmhmm …"

"The whole day is ours, no work, no obligations … only you and I. The sun is coming up, Mia. You feel the warmth coming through our bay window and the darkness behind your eyelids slowly lifting? Do you feel it? The sun?"

The smile on my face was inescapable as I lost myself in his imagination. "Yes, Ollie. I can feel it."

"We can take your coffee to the water and finish watching the sunrise, or we can lay in this bed all day. I have a few books on the bookshelf I haven't read to you yet. Or, we can put on our trainers and walk along the boardwalk, hand in hand, because that's what we do in the summer on a Sunday morning. What would you like to do today?"

"Mmm … all of it."

"Good thing we have all day." He slowly exhaled. "Now, drink your coffee before it gets cold."

My eyes opened to see Ollie's still closed, lost in the world he'd created for us. And when he opened them, his smile returned. "One day, yeah?"

"One day." I wrapped my arm around his waist, and he brushed his nose against mine before kissing my forehead. "What do you want to do when you leave here?"

"You mean after I steal you and take you to the ocean?"

I smiled. "Yeah, like for a living?"

Ollie wet his lips, which I noticed he didn't only do before he wanted to kiss me but also was a habit when he was in deep thought. "I have three passions, Mia. One is literature, two is helping people and making a difference, and my third, and most important, is you. If I do get out of here, I want to start a non-profit charity."

"Really? Charity for what?"

"I have this idea of traveling the world and meeting people from all walks of life. Learn their stories, write them, turn the collection of short stories into poetry—into a work of art, a novel. Allow the world to see the beauty in all of us, even in the most devastating circumstances. This world needs to know what others are going through. You understand?" I nodded. His eyes glowed. "Sometimes even the darkest parts of us can become beautiful when seen through a different set of eyes."

"What will you do with your novel?"

His grin resembled the flicker in his eyes. "So, each year I'll make a new novel about people's lives, their struggles, their hopes, and defeats. Then give the profits back to those who truly need it." He shrugged like everything he'd just said was no big deal, but I was affected by his vision. "I never needed much, Mia. I hope you're not in it for the money." He laughed, and I wanted to kiss him for it. "Well, what do you think?"

"Ollie, I'm just sitting here, listening, and I want to experience it all with you. Watching your face light up when you talk about it …" I shook my head in amazement. "I want to be there. I want to be a part of it."

He grabbed my face, and his kiss was brief and delicate. "You just made me so fucking happy hearing you say that." He pulled me closer and wrapped his arms around me. "What have you always envisioned?"

"Honestly, I never thought of a tomorrow. I was dead until I met you. The only thing I was remotely interested in was studying people and why they did the things they did. I became obsessed with human behavior, psychology, how the brain works, all of it. I did so much research on my own because I couldn't understand people's actions or feelings. I tried to justify everything."

"Why does this not surprise me …" Ollie laughed lightly into my hair. "This reminds me, when did you truly feel connected with me? Was it the kiss or the first time we had sex, Miss kissing-is-more-intimate-than-sex?" He raised an eyebrow as his grin flashed like a beam, screaming, *"Told you so."*

I covered my face to hide my blushing, embarrassed Ollie remembered one of our first conversations. "There are notions so powerful even science can't grasp, Ollie."

He dropped his head back and brought his two fingers to his eyes as a laugh slipped out.

I'd never thought much about my future, what I wanted to do, or where I would end up. I'd never cared enough before. As a little girl, I'd dreamed of what typical little girls would dream of. One day becoming a ballerina, or a princess, or even a star playing and singing in Madison Square Garden in front of thousands of people. But those were illusions belonging only in dreams. None of it was real, and I'd quickly met reality when my uncle had shown me the difference. In real life, there was evil. In real life, parents couldn't protect you from everything, and most importantly, in real life, there was pain.

But Ollie was real. He had opened my eyes to what my future could look like, and I'd never wanted anything more than a life with him.

Weeks passed, and I found myself taking my courses seriously and staying away from trouble. During the week, we stayed apart in the public eye, only showing affection behind closed doors. And as more memories surfaced, panic attacks became a regular thing, but Ollie coached me through every one of them. He taught me how to release my anger through music, and we spent hours on the weekends in the vacant group therapy room.

I still hadn't told him about my past, afraid he would look at me differently. I only wanted to hold on to the way Ollie saw me for as long as I could. Would he see a used and worthless little girl? A murderer? An evil inside me like my father saw?

We were now into October. You couldn't see the change through the windows of the building; the skies were the same jaded gray. Though, the temperature slowly dropped inside the building. It was Thursday, and one of those days where my hair rebelled against me, my mind was mush, and I seemed to be five minutes behind all day. I hurried from my dorm to grab my gray hooded sweatshirt to group therapy.

Okay, it wasn't mine.

It was Ollie's hoodie.

I had a bad habit of stealing his clothes, but he wouldn't have it any other way.

All eyes were on me as I took my usual seat across from Ollie in the circle. He leaned back in the chair, wet his lips, and mouthed, *"You look beautiful."* And his infectious smile spread to my face.

"Today is the day," Arty said, interrupting Ollie and my unsaid conversation.

Everyone looked over at Arty with confusion. "What's today, boss?" Isaac asked.

"Mia is going to open up and tell us about what she went through as a child. We haven't heard from her yet. She's always quiet," Arty said.

The mention of my name suddenly made my heart beat at an uncontrollable pace. I wasn't ready. My stomach coiled as I glanced around the room. I didn't want to tell Ollie like this. Not in front of everyone. My eyes found my constant source of calmness and Ollie studied my reaction. "But … I'm not ready," I stuttered and shook my head.

"The only way you'll be able to start the healing process is if you talk about it openly. We're all on your team, Mia," Arty insisted. My mouth went dry. I tried to swallow, but I couldn't. Could I do this? Could I tell everyone what I'd done?

"You can't force her to do this," Ollie stated, coming to my rescue as always. He was afraid for me or afraid of me going into a rage right here in front of our counselor.

Arty looked over at me, ignoring Ollie's statement. "It's been a month since you've been back from psych with your memories. If you can't talk about it now, then I don't think group therapy is appropriate for you at this time. We've been patient, Mia, but it's not fair for you to take someone else's place in this session who is ready to heal."

The walls around me caved in as I darted my eyes between Ollie and Arty. My knee bounced under my hands as I ran my sweaty palms down my thighs. I clenched my fists as the anger stirred inside me, my nails digging into my palms. The hot rage was built along with the fear. I couldn't tell everyone. I was still that angry little girl ready to explode at any second.

Until Ollie's warm hands covered mine.

Opening my eyes, I saw his green ones staring back at me as he crouched in front of my lap. "Listen to me, Mia. If you're not ready, then don't. Who cares what Arty says."

I looked around the room, and everyone glared at us in shock. Whispers spread like wildfire throughout the circle, but Ollie grabbed my face to force me to see only him. "The fuck with everyone, they don't matter. If you want to tell your story, I'm right here. It will be only you and me. If not, I'll walk out of this room with you right now. We'll get into a lot of shit, but I'll do it. I told you, Mia, you're not alone in this."

The patience in Arty's face wore thin. The truth was, I knew if I ran out of this room, regardless if I asked Ollie not to follow me, he would. Ollie would get in trouble, and I couldn't risk it. The only option I had was telling my story, and afterward, Ollie would never look at me the same.

I glanced back and forth between Ollie and Arty. "I … can I have a minute?"

The impatience was evident, but Arty's training to be empathetic seemed to remind him as he responded, "Sure."

Ollie squeezed my hand, struggling to hold back in front of everyone. "It's okay. Go sit down," I said to Ollie, and he dropped his head.

Seconds passed, and he finally stood and took his seat in his chair.

Everyone observed me as I stood and paced outside the circle. The glaring didn't help and only made me more nervous. I walked over to the piano and strummed my fingers over the cold, shiny painted wood. My cast was finally off, and I took a seat and played. My nerves gradually dissipated with each note, each stroke of a key, allowing the song to take over me as my nerves finally calmed.

As the song finished, I dropped my hands from the keys and into my lap. They were no longer shaking. I glanced up to see Ollie watching me from the edge of his seat. He rested his chin in his hands.

This was it.

Ollie would never look at me this same way again.

I was sure of it.

"I was only eight years old," I said, and everyone's eyes were on me, "and from what I remember, I was a good girl. I never took more than I needed. I never lied, never stole. I never whined when I didn't get my way, and never hurt anyone. I had everything a girl could want. I had both a father and mother who loved me for who I was, which is more than I can say for some of you ..." My eyes met Jake's, instant pain in his eyes.

"But I was a naïve and sheltered girl. Bad things didn't happen in my world. They were only in Disney movies. Who knew a monster didn't have horns or sharp teeth? They don't, by the way. I learned the hard way. The monster who hurt me a long time ago paraded around as my uncle, and no one warned me your own family could hurt you in ways you never thought were possible.

"So, when he came into my room the first night, I thought the intentions behind it were different. I thought at first, he was coming to kiss me goodnight. Or maybe I had a nightmare, and he was coming to check on me. Hell, I didn't know. But what he did do never crossed my mind because I was only eight years old at the time and I didn't know any better. I thought family was supposed to love and take care of you.

"But every night, after my parents fell asleep, and all the lights were turned off, and the house was so quiet you could hear every little noise its old age made, is when the monster came. Every night for over a year, he raped me.

"The first night I thought I was being punished, like I'd done something to deserve it. Like my father whooped me with the paddle, this was my uncle's way of punishing me for dropping his beer the day before. Or maybe it was because I'd said something wrong at dinner time. I didn't know, and I couldn't understand. But each night after, he took a piece of me with him.

"For exactly three hundred and ninety-four nights I cried, and no one heard me. No one bothered to help me, and as each night passed, I slowly died inside until the point I was nothing. Every morning, the sunrise would remind me I was not physically dead when I wished so badly I was so I wouldn't have to suffer through another night."

I paused to take in a deep breath. Tears gathered at the corners of my eyes, and my vision blurred. I couldn't look up. The room was silent, and my hands shook again. I dug my nails against my flesh to ease the pain in my heart and the shuddering in my breathing. The wave of the rage built back up as the sound of the gun firing echoed in my brain. The look on my uncle's face flashed before my eyes and the tears finally fell.

"So, on the last night …" I wiped my tears with my trembling fingers "… I hid my father's gun under my pillow. And when the door creaked open, and he leaned over me to see if my eyes were open, and he crawled in the bed beside me, and his fingers went under my nightgown to take off my panties, I pulled out the gun, and I shot him."

I fought for air as I tried to get out the rest of the story. "I promised myself I would never cry again. I would never let anyone hurt me again. I never wanted to feel anything, ever, *again*. I didn't want to feel pain, hurt, betrayal, not even love because it was all a lie. I wanted all of it *gone!*"

Through my strained and watery eyes, I saw Ollie. He hid his face in his hands, so I continued, "I had used up everything I had. For over a year, I used up all the tears, hope, prayers meant for a lifetime, and the moment I pulled the trigger, my mental switch flipped.

"So, no. It was my uncle I killed, not my mom, but I might as well have shot her, too. She took her own life, and the worst part is, I remember looking down at her body, thinking, *'Good, you deserve it.'*"

I shook my head as the truth came from my lips and tears soaked my cheeks. "Why couldn't she see what he was doing to me? Why didn't she hear me crying out for her at night? Why didn't anyone care enough to save me? Most of all, why was it her who got the easy way out? Why did Death chose her when I'm the one who deserved it? Every night for over a year, I prayed his rape would somehow kill me, yet she was the one who was dead, and I stood over her body, not sad, but fucking jealous."

Ollie looked up from his hands with bloodshot eyes, and no one else was in the room anymore. No one bothered to interrupt me when I so badly needed someone to stop me from talking. My mouth kept going.

"Trapped in my own head for almost ten years, and on the outside, sure, I looked fine, but my subconscious was always there, screaming to come out and deal with this, and I kept pushing her down. And still, no one heard me.

"Ten years ago, my uncle stole everything from me. He stole my innocence, my childhood, my dreams, my ability to love, to be happy, my mother, or maybe this is all my fault because I wasn't strong enough. If I were strong enough, I could have fought him off. I could have had the courage to fight back. This was all my fault ..."

I broke piece by piece in front of everyone. Every thought exited my mouth, and no one had the nerve to shut me up. "My dad won't even look me in the eyes! He sees the same person I see when I look in the mirror: a waste. I'm the monster, and I was so afraid to tell you." I was shouting to Ollie now, and he bent over with his head in his hands as his shoulders shook. "I was so scared once you knew the truth, that I killed someone ... that I was capable of ending someone else's life and spent the rest of mine doing the only thing I was meant to do, which is to fuck, you would never look at me the same.

"Because my uncle screwed me in every way for over a year, then I killed him. His life flashed before my eyes, and I couldn't even feel bad about it. I'm the monster, Ollie!" As my testimony finally left me, I stood from the piano bench as my legs wobbled beneath me. "I don't even deserve to be looked at by you." I turned to Arty, who sat stunned. "Is this what you wanted, Arty? Does my story get you off?"

Arty stammered in shock at my long-winded confession. "Mia, that's not what this is …"

My eyes darted around, and the entire circle couldn't even look at me as they all turned their heads away. Then my eyes fell on Ollie. He pulled the neckline of his shirt over his eyes, still unable to see me.

"Just forget it," I shouted, and walked through the circle and out of the room.

My mind raced as my feet moved to their own accord in front of me. I found my way back to my dorm, and as soon as my door closed, I fell against my padded wall and sunk into a fetal position on the floor. I couldn't catch my breath as my chest ached for air. With no tears left to cry, my eyes burned for relief.

The door to my room swung open, and I looked up to see Ollie. He collapsed on his knees before me. "Mia … I'm so sorry," he cried. His chin trembled as he tried to hold it together. "I'm trying, I really am. I'm trying to be strong for you." I pulled his sweatshirt I was wearing over my head as I fought for air. My once dry and burning eyes found more tears as my nose ran into his hoodie. Hyperventilating, I pushed his hands away.

"Go … go away. You don't have to do this!" I choked out.

Ollie fought against me, and I soon surrendered as he pulled me close to his chest. My entire body went weak in his arms, and eventually, my breathing returned to normal as the rest of my tears drained. It felt like an hour had passed, but it could have easily been minutes in his arms.

"Look at me," Ollie insisted. "Look into my eyes and tell me I don't see you differently, because if you say otherwise, you're wrong."

His eyes—broken, green, and beautiful as ever—stared back at me as the rest of his face proved this was affecting him just as much as it had affected me. He held my wet face and continued, "I'll never look at you differently, Mia. I love all of you. *Fuck*. If you didn't kill that bastard, I would be swimming across the Atlantic right now to do it myself. You're not a monster. Do you hear me?"

I shook my head. I understood what he was saying, but I couldn't accept it. How could he not see me differently? "I am a monster, Ollie."

"No, love, far from it. You were a little girl who was put in an impossible situation, and having to deal with it all on your own for too long." He paused and wiped his face across his sleeve. "You got through it the only way you knew how, and now you have me. You never have to go through it alone. Ever. I'm right here, Mia. I'll never leave you. I'll always hear you. I promise you. It's going to be you and I, do you understand me?"

"I'm no longer the girl you fell in love with, Ollie. I'm broken now. I'm not strong anymore. I don't have my walls up, or my flip switched."

"How is the light supposed to shine through your walls, Mia?" He exhaled as another tear fell from his eye, and he looked up to the ceiling for composure or to find words. "You think that's why I fell in love with you, yeah? Because you were tough? I saw straight through your bullshit from the beginning. You could never hide from me. Yeah, you tried to push me away, but I saw the truth in you. Around me, you are different because it's us. And I fell in love with us."

TWENTY

"And if they knock you to your knees,
pull the rug out from under them."

OLIVER MASTERS

t was late October, with the holidays right around the corner. At Dolor, there was no going home for Christmas because they treated this as more of a prison sentence than a university. We hadn't celebrated the holidays at home, anyhow, until Diane came along.

My father had started dating her around Thanksgiving. He'd cooked an entire meal for the first time in years, only to hide how dysfunctional we were. It had all been a façade. Same when Christmas came around. I'd laughed at him as I'd stood on the stairs while he dragged the tree into the house under his arm. What I'd never realized, until now, was how he'd only wanted to share those holidays with someone who was excited for them. When it had been only us two, I'd never bothered to care.

"Your dad coming in for Christmas?" Jake asked as we waited in line for lunch. I reached over my tray for a banana and my shirt slid across a heap of ketchup.

"Shit," I moaned, looking down at Ollie's shirt I was wearing. Not only would the ketchup stain, but now I had to wear my own clothes. "That's a major negative. My dad doesn't do well on planes, anyway. I couldn't imagine him on a flight longer than two hours."

Blowing out a breath, I dipped my napkin in my water to try to blot the ketchup off, only to find it spreading into a larger stain. I growled as Jake rambled on about Parents Day.

"My mum and dad are coming, possibly my brother and sisters, too. You're more than welcome to join us for lunch off campus. I know Alicia's coming since hers won't be able to make it."

Giving up on the shirt, I moved up the lunch line. The possibility to leave this place for an entire day sounded too good to be true, but I genuinely didn't believe my father would make it, or if he even knew about it. Once a week, I had an opportunity to call him, but never did.

There was an awkwardness between Jake and me since I'd revealed my past in group therapy. People tip-toed around me like I was going to snap at any moment, scared I would lash out from a single word directed at me. Jake made an effort to keep our conversation light. I knew he had so much his nosy-self wanted to ask, but was afraid of how to go about it.

"Apple?" he asked

I slammed my tray down. "Stop, this Jake."

"Stop what?"

"Ever since I told the truth about my past, you've been different around me. I can't take it."

"Don't take your ketchup mishap out on me, woman. I'm not acting different. It's all in your head." He patted the top of my head with raised brows. "We can talk about Parents Day another time, but seriously … do you want an apple or no?" His smirk grew, and I took the apple from him and dropped it on my tray. "I think we're due for a get-together tonight. You need to take some edge off. What do you say?"

"No, Ollie won't have it, and you know it."

"Mia, Mia, Mia." Jake shook his head. "I'm talking about in my room."

I coughed out a laugh.

"What? I'm serious." Jake placed his juice on the tray.

"I'm down," Liam interjected, coming up behind me and bumping my shoulder with his. "It's been a while since we got together, Mia. What do you say we have some fun tonight, yeah?"

My gaze dashed back and forth from Liam to Jake, and Jake flattened his lips together in a thin hard line.

"So, you guys hang out all of a sudden? Since when did this start happening?"

"Since you and Ollie went off in your own 'Ollie and Mia world.' You guys coupled up, and now you're gayer than me."

I dipped my head back at his accusations. Completely true accusations, but still. "Not true. No one could be gayer than you, for starters, and Ollie and I are not together like that." We were, a thousand percent, but we still couldn't have anyone know.

"Here we go again, you making light of your relationship …." Jake trailed off.

"Wait, so you and Ollie aren't together?" Liam asked, confused.

"No. Definitely not together …" It pained me saying the words out loud.

"Then it's settled. You come to Jake's, then," Liam said, then grabbed my ass and whispered, "Make sure you're ready for me, darling."

I pushed him off me with my shoulder, and he quickly released me before turning and strolling away.

Ollie was in viewing distance in his normal seat. I looked over my shoulder to see him, eyes blazing, jaw ticking, and leaning over the table on the brink of pouncing. Returning my attention in front of me, I let out a drawn-out exhale and said to Jake, "I can't believe I ever had sex with Liam."

After lifting my tray, I walked away from Jake, irritated, and sat across from Zeke in my usual spot.

"I'm going to kill him," Ollie said, climbing into the seat next to me. I pressed my fork in the direction of Zeke who sat in a trance, eyes fixed in front of him. "Right ... hey, mate." Ollie flashed Zeke a smile before turning back to me. "He's dead, Mia. I can't stand this shit anymore. You think I fancy seeing you being groped right in front of me?"

"You know what will happen once everyone finds out." And it was true. Ollie had told me what happened last year between Thomas and Livy. Once everyone had found out they were together, the claws came out, and it was everyone's main agenda to tear them apart whichever way they could. Life at Dolor was pretty dull, for the most part, so anytime there was a hint of a challenge, people would take it and run with it, beat it to the ground until there was nothing left. No one here wanted to see the next person happy.

Ollie ran his palm up his forehead and through his hair. "Don't let him touch you again. You let it slip, he'll keep doing it. I'm trying hard to stay away, but if you don't do anything about it, I will."

There was a pause in the air between us, the kind where a conversation could go one of two ways. The pause sat there, teetering back and forth on the highest point of a mountain, and I noticed the debating across Ollie's face. "Shit. I'm sorry ... I sound like a fucking prick, yeah? I swear it's not me staking a claim on you, it's everything you've been thro—"

"Ollie." I grabbed his empty hand on his lap underneath the table and gave it a small squeeze. "It happened so fast, but there won't be a next time ..." I flashed him a small smile to try to ease his troubled mind.

But in truth, he was right.

Though Oscar had strangled me with threats, I still hadn't done anything about it, which only made that situation worse. Hearing Ollie say he would handle Liam only made me scared of him finding out how Oscar, the ex-trainee turned security guard, was tormenting me. Certain Ollie would do something to send himself to prison. I knew I was hiding the situation only to protect him.

"Jake is expecting me at his place tonight," I said, changing the subject. "Apparently, he's throwing parties now—one's that Liam attend. They cornered me, and I didn't know what else to say. Will you go with me?"

"Bloody hell." Ollie rolled his eyes. "You think I'm letting you walk into a den of hungry wolves? Of course, I'm going with you." Ollie's smile reappeared. He looked over at Zeke, who had his eyes glued to the tray in front of him before he turned back to me. "Close your eyes, love."

Every time Ollie asked me to close my eyes, my heart skipped against my ribcage. It was the little sacred moments in crowded rooms when he couldn't give me the affection he wanted but still tried to make it known how he felt before separating from me.

Shortly after I closed my eyes, I felt his long fingers trail up the side of my thigh before grabbing my hand from my lap, always breaking his own rule of no touching. He brought it to his lips and kissed the inside of my palm before returning my hand over my thigh. I counted to ten mentally, imagining Ollie kissing me goodbye the way he actually kissed because he was already a fantastic kisser, and I opened my eyes as soon as he turned the corner out of the mess hall.

After switching Ollie's stained shirt out for a fresh one, I strolled into the last class late and paused under the doorway at the view before me. In front of Ollie, in my chair, was Maddie. Ollie immediately averted his head from me, reluctant to meet my gaze.

"Take your seat, Miss Jett. This class doesn't revolve around you," the professor hissed. My feet moved in front of me toward an empty chair on the opposite end as my insides burned to a crisp.

During the entire hour, my focus was on Maddie. The way she shook her head to move her bangs out of her eyes. The way she turned in her seat to smile up at Ollie. The way she would prop her elbow on his desk behind her, a chance to get closer. I tapped my foot vigorously, impatiently waiting to be dismissed.

"See you all next week," the professor said, releasing us. Quick scenarios ran through my head. *Do I ignore all of this and run out of here? Do I confront Ollie? How does he know her? Does he even know her?*

Quickly gathering my things in my arms, I stood too fast, and all my belongings plummeted to the floor. "Shit," I grumbled and hunched down.

Ollie's black Chuck Taylors appeared in front of me before he bent down and searched my face. "You okay? You look pale." He reached for my cheek but dropped his hand before he made contact.

Shaking my head, I said, "I'm fine."

Ollie gathered my things for me and helped me off the ground, and there she was—Maddie—standing right behind Ollie with a faux surprised expression.

"Mia! Looks like I don't need to introduce ya to the fella I told ya about," she said sweetly, but toxins rode the wave of her voice. The boy she had told me about? I thought back to our conversations. The porridge. The cards. *The secret boyfriend.* My eyes raced back and forth between them as a sickness knotted in my stomach.

"You two know each other?" Ollie asked, surprised.

Maddie gently laid her fingers over his arm. "Mia and I were in the psych ward together."

Ollie honed in on my expression. He knew me. He knew what I was thinking. "Mia, no ..." He snapped his head to Maddie. "What did you tell her?"

"She told me enough," I said, taking my books from him and walking away before he could stop me.

My eyes blurred while I made my way back to my dorm. As I locked the door behind me, my mind sprinted a million miles a second. It had been Ollie all along. Ollie was her boyfriend. Maddie's boyfriend was Ollie. No matter which way I deciphered it, it still wasn't making sense. My breaths ran closer together as I paced my room, running my fingers through my hair. This couldn't be happening.

Then there was a knock at my door followed by Ollie's urgent tone. "Mia, open the door."

I stayed quiet.

"Mia, please …"

I shook my head violently as if he could see. The thought of his lips on hers. The thought of him inside her. It was all too much. My hand shot over my mouth to suffocate my cries as tears streamed down my face.

"Dammit, Mia. Please … let me in so I can explain." There was pain in his tone, but I wasn't a fool.

And eventually, Ollie left.

I curled up into a ball over the mattress and brought the sheet over my head, forcing my cries to put me to sleep. Sleep replaced Ollie as my new cure, because otherwise, the hot fury would only send my fist through something. And the only thing deserving to be on the opposite end of my fist was Ollie, but one more mistake and my ass would be on a one-way trip to the mental institution.

During dinner, Maddie sat next to Ollie with Jake, Alicia, Bria, and Isaac. She walked back into their lives as if she had never left.

"Funny thing about all this, Zeke, is I was supposed to be the sociopath." I glanced up at Zeke as he ate his spaghetti. "But I guess Karma's a bitch, right?" Pushing my tray off to the side, I lay across my hands and forced my focus in front of me, to Zeke. "Is this what jealousy feels like?" I sighed. "I must be mistaken because none of this is making sense. I'm jealous and overreacting. But what if I'm not, Zeke? What if this whole time he had a girlfriend and only used me as a distraction?" Zeke didn't move—as always. "But he said he's in love with me, so I must have it all wrong and Maddie's fucking with my head."

Zeke looked up at me. His small eyes dilated as he blinked a few times. I forced a smile over at him, almost wanting to reach out and put my hand over his. But I didn't. Zeke didn't like to be touched the majority of the time. I'd learned this the hard way.

248

The feeling of Ollie's warmth behind me and his breath against my ear stunned me. "Meet me in your dorm. Two minutes," he whispered.

"No, Ollie."

Ollie growled. "Dammit, Mia. If I mean anything to you, you'll come." He took a few steps away, paused, then turned back around. "Close your eyes, Mia."

But I didn't, and Ollie hung his head and walked back toward me. He planted his palms over the table and leaned in to capture my eyes with his in a plea. "Please, don't do this ..."

I closed my eyes and counted to ten because even though I was upset, I still couldn't watch him walk away from me.

After he was gone, I opened my eyes and groaned. "If I have to hear one *more* '*Dammit, Mia*' I think I will scream," I said to Zeke, each word increasing in volume, but Zeke sat there stunned by Ollie's swift presence. Ollie knew better. He should have acknowledged Zeke upon arrival. Groaning, I dropped my head in my hands for a moment before snapping my eyes at Zeke again. "Should I go? I should probably go. I need to hear him out, right?"

The door to my dorm closed behind me when I found Ollie standing in the middle of the room with his arms crossed over his chest. He unfolded his arms, took two steps forward, and grabbed my chin, tilting my face up to his. He let out an exhale. "Don't do this, Mia. We're stronger than this."

I pulled my head out of his grasp and took a step back. "Were you guys together?"

Ollie shook his head. "Whatever happened between her and me was before you."

"She told me you are her boyfriend, Ollie. *Are*. As in, currently."

"No, she isn't right, Mia. She's delusional. You have to believe I feel nothing for her. Never did, and never will. It's always you."

"Or are you juggling two girls? Telling them both to keep the relationship a secret in case the other one finds out? Because"—a laugh pressed through my throat—"that's fucking brilliant, Ollie. Well done."

A rush of emotions played across his face, and I instantly regretted every word. In my heart, I knew Ollie. He wasn't capable of it.

Injury pierced his eyes. "You really think that low of me, yeah? You think I would do something like that?"

Shaking my head, I instantly rambled my regret away. "No." I closed the gap between us and laced my fingers into his. "God, no, I didn't mean it. I don't know what's the matter with me, Ollie. I've never felt like this before. She told me she is your girlfriend. Then I see the two of you together. I feel sick about it. Explain this to me. Tell me what this is."

Ollie brought my hand to his chest, pinning them and steadying me. Steadying us. "Truth?"

I nodded.

Ollie drew in a deep breath. His chest moved under my hand. He exhaled. Impatience was eating me from the inside out. "It was just Maddie, Alicia, Isaac, and me here in the summer. She was around during a time when I was on my meds. She was a diversion to pass the time. She was into me, and I took advantage of it because I was a different person on my meds. I didn't have a care in the world—no fucking conscience. I was doped up to forget who I was. And the truth is ..." Ollie let out a breath as I held mine "... I played her. I knew how much she was into me, so I fucked her."

Ollie paused. I blinked three times. One for each word. *I. Fucked. Her.*

"Mia, say something," he pleaded.

I dropped my hands from his chest and sat at the edge of the mattress. My stomach tangled in nausea as the picture of them together played out in my head. It couldn't have been the same with them as it was with us. This was different. We were different. I had my past, and Ollie had his. I looked up to see him standing before me. "And what happened after you fucked her, Ollie?"

He crouched down in front of me and took my hands from my lap, rubbing his thumbs over mine. "Maddie was convinced it was more than it was. She started obsessing, stalking, causing chaos. One minute she would be fine, the next she would grab Alicia by the throat if I so much as looked in Alicia's direction. So then, after we cut her out of the group, I showed up to my dorm to find her lying naked in my bed, and I fucking lost it." Ollie's breath got shorter as his voice shook. "I grabbed her by the neck and threw her out before breaking anything I could get my hands on. Every piece of furniture." Ollie dropped his head for a moment before looking back up at me. "She caused so much turmoil in my life because of one bloody night."

He brought my palm to his mouth and pressed his lips to it, kissing any lingering doubts away before he continued. "Anyway, Conway took me off my meds, and Lynch had me in solitary for two fucking weeks. The transition was terrible. And when I got out, she was gone."

Ollie brought his hand to my cheek. "That's the truth. As much as I hate to admit the way I treated her, that's what happened, Mia."

And I believed him.

I let out an unsteady exhale and nodded.

Ollie fell to his knees and settled himself between my legs, laying his arms across my thighs. "She told me she's better now, been taking her meds, seeing Conway regularly. She told me she was sorry for what happened and she wanted to keep it in the past."

Dr. Conway? Medication? Visions of her pretending to take pills flooded. Our conversations flooded. "I don't trust her, Ollie."

Ollie maintained my gaze. "Do you trust me?"

"Yes." In all honesty, yes, I did and would trust him until he gave me a reason not to.

The air in Ollie's lungs blew out through his lips before he placed his hands over my head and ran them down the sides of my face. "You never have to worry, love. You have me completely." He pressed his forehead to mine. "You so fucking have me."

TWENTY-ONE

"She was my heaven,
I was her hell."

OLIVER MASTERS

//"Mia!" Jake squealed as my feet landed on the marble of Jake's dorm room. It took a circus act to get us here, but with the help of Isaac, we made it. Ollie's hand lingered around my waist as I observed my surroundings. It wasn't the posters or pictures on his walls that got my attention at first, or the fact he had an actual comforter over his bed, but it was who was in the dorm.

Maddie.

Wearing black yoga pants and a matching sports bra, Maddie smiled from ear to ear, laughing as she flocked to Isaac as soon as we arrived.

"Do you want to leave?" Ollie asked in my ear.

"No," I said, and he kissed the side of my head from behind me.

Liam, Alicia, Bria, and Gwen were also here. Gwen was the short blonde from psychology who used to sit behind Ollie.

"Do you want me to make you a drink?" Jake asked, pulling me away from Ollie and toward his dresser lined with cups, liquor, and mixers. I turned my head back to see Ollie now engaged in conversation with Alicia.

"How did you get all this?" I asked Jake, taking my focus back in front of me.

Jake put a hand on his hip as he leaned against it. "You know better than to ask questions." He giggled. "Here, I'll make you my secret recipe. It's delish."

He then shook, mixed, and poured before handing me a drink.

Reaching to take the drink from his hand, Ollie swooped in and grabbed it from him. "Thanks, mate, but I'll make her drink."

Jake snapped a finger in the air before turning to leave.

Ollie took a red cup from the dresser. "You can't be too careful." He broke the seal of a new bottle of vodka and poured a shot in a cup. "Just sip on this," he said and handed me the cup.

I raised a brow at him. "Paranoid?"

"Cautious." He winked at me, then made himself the same. We clinked our red cups together. Here was to a long night of staying away from the only person I wanted to be around, to Maddie's madness, and faking it.

Bria pushed her way through the small crowd and stopped before us. "Did you bring it?"

Ollie reached in his pocket, pulled out his phone, and flashed it in front of her. "Though, I'm keeping it in my possession … I'll start some music." Ollie stared at the screen while scrolling through the playlist. Bria whined, but the music quickly started, which changed her mood instantly.

Bria grabbed my hand and dragged me away, forcing me to dance. "No, Bria…" I moaned as she pulled me beside Alicia. I glanced back to see Ollie with a lopsided grin and his red cup in the air.

"You know, Mia, I think we got off on the wrong foot," Bria said as she held my arm in the air. "Can we start over?"

Bria seductively twisted her hips as I stood there awkwardly. "Where is this coming from?"

Bria stopped and leaned over in my ear. "Alicia told me about Maddie. I think we're better off in numbers."

"You have a point there." I took a sip of my drink when the song suddenly changed. It was The Fugees' "Killing me Softly with His Song."

"Yes!" Bria cheered, and I cocked my head in Ollie's direction, who shrugged his shoulders with a smile, showing all his perfectly white teeth. *"Have fun,"* he mouthed to me.

An unstoppable smile spread across my lips as I remembered the time in his dorm room. When the beat dropped, so did my guard. Sandwiched between Bria and Alicia, we all danced—rolling our hips, feeling the flow, and allowing myself to enjoy this night.

"Sing, Mia!" Alicia requested out loud over the music. And I did. Turning to face Ollie, I belted the lyrics as my body's rhythm continued. Ollie dipped his head back and squinted before a bigger smile played on his face. Jake joined in, singing and dancing with us until the song ended.

"Okay, I get it. I see why you dance," I said to Bria through panting as the song changed.

Bria nodded. "Now, come on. Let's get you a refill."

Bria, nice? Have I crossed over into an alternate universe? Maybe I'd never noticed it before because of the way I was, or perhaps it was because there was another girl who'd shown up in the mix. Either way, I couldn't complain.

Following her back to Jake's dresser, she pointed at the bottles. "What's your poison tonight?"

"Vodka, straight." I leaned into the dresser. This was my chance to make things right between us. "Bria, I'm sorry for whatever I may have caused before. It's not who I am anymore, and I have nothing against you."

Bria kept her eyes on pouring, making sure not to spill as she swayed. "As I said before, we got off on the wrong foot. We're good." The little bit of Bria-weight lifted from my chest. One bad taste bud in my mouth was gone, a million more to go. Bria handed me my cup. "Now, how am I supposed to get Maddie away from Isaac?"

Shaking my head, I let out a laugh. Same old Bria. "I think Isaac is smart enough to know not to get involved with her." Looking back at Bria, I caught a pain in her eyes as she watched the two of them together in the corner. Maddie danced up against Isaac as he stayed pinned to the wall. "Bria …" The look on her face was so familiar. "You like Isaac. As in *like*, like."

Bria snapped her head in my direction. "No, I don't."

Smiling, I said, "Yes, you do. It's written all over your face. You have a thing for him."

Bria groaned. "Help me, then. What do I do?"

I glanced back over at Maddie and Isaac. Girl-talk was all new to me. "March over there, pull him away, and kiss him."

Bria shook her head. "No, I can't kiss him."

"You *always* kiss him," I said, narrowing my eyes at her.

"But I didn't like him like this before. It's easier when you don't have feelings for the bloke."

She had a point. "You guys can play a game?"

"Ah, yes!" Bria grabbed my face and laid a peck over my lips before pulling my head away. "Mia, you're brilliant." I stood stunned as she marched away and announced a game of strip or dare to everyone.

Between the sudden hand on my back and the breath in my hair, I instantly knew who approached me from behind. "Did Bria just kiss you?" he asked amusedly into my ear. I nodded as Ollie's breath sent goosebumps across the surface of my skin.

"I hate staying away from you, love," he whispered again, and his fingertips dipped beneath the back of my shirt and grazed my bare skin. His warm touch pulled me like a magnetic force field. He pressed against me from behind. To hide my blushing, I brought my cup to my lips and took a sip.

"Are you two fucking now?" Liam asked. Ollie dropped his hand and took a step away from me, coldness replacing him.

"No, we're not *fucking*," Ollie scoffed from behind me.

"You really should," he said, holding up his cup. "Because, mate, let me tell you, her pussy …" Liam shook his head. "Unbelievable."

From the corner of my eye, I saw Ollie take quick strides toward Liam. My fingers sprang to his wrist, holding him back and steady, not having to speak a word because he knew.

Ollie looked down at me and back at Liam, who wore a smug smile. If we weren't at Dolor, I would gladly not keep Ollie back. But, we were at Dolor—observed and judged with our entire futures on the line. My past had already been stolen from me, and I wouldn't let anyone take away my future.

Ollie stood tall beside me as I dropped my hand from his wrist. "Never again," Ollie warned him before chugging the rest of his drink.

Liam nervously laughed as he turned and joined Bria, Maddie, and Isaac in the game of strip or dare.

"Ollie, you playing?" Maddie interjected as I took a sip from my cup.

Ollie pulled out a chair from under Jake's desk and took a seat. "No way in hell."

Alicia and Jake were in some deep, drunken conversation on the bed, and I stood alone. How was I going to turn this whole night around? My eyes strayed until they landed on Ollie's phone in his hand. Low tunes became background noise. "Wanna leave?" Ollie asked, staring up at me with his drink in the other hand.

"No, I think we should dance." I took a step toward him.

He dropped his chin to his chest, but when his eyes returned, so did his smile. "Mia, you know we can't dance together." His tone was hushed and raw.

I pulled his almost empty cup from his hand and set it over Jake's desk. "Just because we dance together, doesn't mean we are together."

Ollie leaned back in his chair and stretched out his legs. His green eyes roamed over my body as his dimple flashed beside his gorgeous grin. "You come any closer, and I won't be able to keep my hands off you."

I wedged myself between his knees and Ollie ran his hands up the back of my thighs. "I'm warning you. I'm intoxicated."

Leaning over him, I whispered, "Me too," and grabbed the phone off his lap. "Magic phone, should Ollie dance with me?" I asked then pressed shuffle. Ollie's smile stretched as his face flushed.

"Take You Higher - Club Mix" by Goodwill and Hook N Sling came on and I dropped the phone over his lap. "Well?"

Ollie ran his hands from my thighs to up my sides as he gradually stood to his feet and kicked the chair out of the way. I dropped my head back as a laugh eluded me. His smile became permanent as he twirled me around then dipped me backward. His eyes scanned the room before he lowered his head to kiss my neck. As I giggled, he pulled me up, and we danced to the beat of the song. Jake and Alicia joined us, jumping up and down together, but my focus stayed on Ollie. His breath in my hair, in my neck. His warm hands under my shirt, at my sides and back. He took me higher—away. Ollie always had that ability. With him, I wasn't a broken girl suffering a past. With him, I wasn't lost. I was found.

"You're amazing. You know that?" he whispered into my neck and wrapped his arms around my waist as he persuaded my hips back and forth. "You make me so incredibly happy, Mia." Then he turned me around, so his back was to everyone else. His fingers pulled the hem of my neckline while his fragile lips sent kisses over the surface of my shoulder and up my neck. Staying away was a constant struggle.

"Oh, fuck it," Ollie pronounced raw, caving, taking my face in his anchored hold. Alcohol influenced his lack of judgment as he melted his lips over mine. His tongue, eager and impatient for the taste of me, slipped through our cracks and damn near brought me to my knees.

"I can't hide us," Ollie panted, pain absorbing his eyes and voice. He backed me against a wall and took my face in his hands. "I can't do it anymore."

He wasn't hiding us now, but when liquor was involved, we had something to blame.

"You're not thinking straight right now." I brought my palms over the backs of his hands. "Do it for me. For us, okay?"

Ollie licked his lips and nodded. "Alright." He kissed me again. "You're right."

"You okay?"

When he didn't respond, I slipped my hand beneath his shirt and flattened it across his chest. The drumming of his heartbeat came through his tight skin. His erratic behavior was becoming more frequent, and anytime this happened, I had to talk him down. Remind him. Calm him. Bring my hand to his chest to show him I was with him, that I understood, but also to feel his fear slip away from him. To indulge myself in the process of the weight lifting off his shoulders.

The truth was, Ollie did feel too much. The majority of the time, it was beautiful. Other times, when he got so far into his head, his heart was his own worst enemy. Maybe it was Maddie's return, or Liam's crude comment, or the façade we regularly played messing with his head. Either way, we had to get through it.

Ollie pinned my hand against his chest and closed his eyes to let out an extended shaky breath. "Yeah, I'm okay." He opened his eyes and shook his head. "I'm sorry."

I lifted my shoulders in a half-shrug. "We're both screwed up, but you're my perfect rock bottom." I leaned closer to him. "And you want to know what's so great about being at rock bottom together?"

Ollie beamed. "What?"

"We can only go up from here," I said with my finger in the air.

"Oh yeah?" He wrapped his hands around my hips and lifted me high in the air. "Are you going to forget me or take me with you?"

"Ollie!" I laughed as everyone's eyes were on us. Half the room was laughing with me, and half the room was rolling their eyes, and as I was in the air, I noticed Maddie was down to only her panties, her boobs on display for everyone to see.

He lifted me higher. "I'm not putting you down until you answer me."

"Taking you," I squealed, hitting his shoulders. "I'm taking you!"

Satisfied, Ollie lowered me, sliding me down across his long torso until my feet were safely back on earth. "And I'll never let you fall," he said and pressed his forehead to mine.

"Oh, my god, you guys are too cute," Jake gushed out loud from behind Ollie. "If you won't ship each other, I will."

"Shit," Ollie whispered to me. "I forgot we weren't alone."

After sidestepping away from Ollie, I walked outside our bubble, bursting it, and returned to our frontage. "Ollie's only mad because I rejected his advances."

"Ouch." Ollie held his hand over his chest as he took a seat on the desk chair. "Low blow." Ollie leaned back in the chair, and his eyes went wide when they fell on Maddie. "No one wants to see that, Maddie. Cover up."

I took a seat on the floor between Bria and Jake's legs that hung over the mattress. Maddie leaned back on her hands, her perfect breasts sticking out in front of her like a news headline. "Nothing you haven't seen before."

"It was part of strip or dare," Isaac explained after taking a sip of his cup. "Want to know what else she has to do?" His lips turned up in the corners. "Go on, Maddie. You have to strip off your knickers or complete your dare."

Isaac and Liam high fived one another as Maddie stood to her feet. "Who did you say, Isaac?" she asked.

He pointed his cup in Ollie's direction. "Ollie."

Ollie raised his brows. "Ollie what?"

Maddie walked over to Ollie, and my insides turned. She paused before him. Bare-chested.

Ollie clenched his teeth. "What are you doing?"

"My dare," she said teasingly, then leaned over and tried to kiss him.

My eyes went wide as my heart beat hard against my chest. Ollie pushed Maddie away instantly and shook his head. "What is wrong with you?"

"Oh, come on, Ollie. Now the girl has to lose her thong ..." Liam announced through a smile.

Maddie turned around, her back facing Ollie, bent over, and dropped her thong as Liam and Isaac cheered. Ollie sprung to his feet, shaking his head. "You are all fucked up," he breathed.

"You need to drink more, mate," Isaac said, bringing his cup to his lips. "Maddie, make our boy another drink, yeah?"

On the verge of tears, I averted my gaze from Maddie and Ollie to keep myself somewhat together. Ollie had warned me about this. Maddie, who was now completely nude and had not one imperfection on her body, poured a drink into a cup before walking up to Ollie and handing it to him. "Drink up, buttercup."

Ollie sat back down in the chair and stared at me, his eyes apologizing.

"How about a lap dance for our boy?" Isaac said after taking another drink and pointing to Ollie.

"Stop," Ollie said, shaking his head. "This is not a fucking game to me." He gulped down his drink and threw the cup against the wall. I could see it in his face, his demeanor walking a dangerous line.

"Ollie, I dare you to have another drink and calm the fuck down," Liam barked. "We got beautiful naked ladies here more than willing to please you, so be fucking appreciative."

Liam turned, snaked his arm around Gwen's neck, who was also topless, and made out with her. It was all becoming clear to me what this party was, and Ollie dragged his hand through his hair while Maddie made Ollie another drink. He was already intoxicated, and it wouldn't be long before he was gone, and I had no choice but to hold in everything.

Ten minutes turned into an hour. Liam and Gwen were in the corner of the room, humping like two rabbits, while Bria and Isaac made out. I turned back to Ollie to see him leaning back in his chair with a cup in front of him, his eyes hooded, staring at me. Maddie danced within the circle naked while keeping Ollie's drink filled. "Come here, love," Ollie said, and Maddie walked up to him. Ollie shook his head. "No, not you." He pointed at me. "You. Come here. Now. Please." He made a pouty face.

I shook my head. Maddie, the party, Ollie, it was all too much for me to handle. Ollie sat his drink down on the desk, stood to his feet, and walked toward me before falling by my side and grabbing my hand.

"Come here," he said, pulling me on top of him and wrapping my legs around his waist. "This is where I belong." He smiled. "Right here with you."

We shared a smile as I raked my fingers through his brown hair. His cheeks were pink, and his smile was lazy. "What are you thinking about right now?" I asked him.

"Fuck …" he breathed. "How bad I want to kiss you."

"Are you drunk?"

Ollie shook his head. "Kiss me, Mia."

"No, Ollie." I traced the outline of his lips with my finger.

"For the love of God … kiss me."

I slowly shook my head again as he ran his hands down the skin on my back.

"Dammit, Mia …" he growled and dropped his head over my shoulder.

"So, what's the story with you two, anyway?" Maddie asked from behind me.

"With who?" I said, playing dumb, avoiding saying Ollie's name, or making light of what was happening—either reason equally acceptable. I slid off of Ollie's lap. He pulled up his legs as I rested between them, facing Maddie now.

Maddie narrowed her eyes. "There is a story … ya must be serious. Let me ask ya, Mia, did ya go after him before or after our talks in psych?"

Ollie's forehead landed on my shoulder. "Ignore her," he muttered, and he kissed my shoulder, and my neck, and behind my ear. Giggling, I leaned my head into him and lifted my shoulder because it tickled. Ollie smiled against my skin, and Maddie suddenly disappeared. Everyone disappeared. "Let's get out of here," he whispered.

"There is no story," Bria piped up. "Plus, you should learn to keep your pretty little nose out of other people's business."

Utterly surprised, my head slowly turned in Bria's direction. Bria sticking up for me? Had hell frozen over? When had she and Isaac stopped making out?

"Alright, Mia. How about a game of Twenty-one for old time's sake?" Maddie asked, reaching for the deck of cards she'd brought with her on top of Jake's desk. Banter spread around the room.

"No, not a good idea," Ollie said, his warm breath still against my neck.

A small laugh came from Maddie, sounding more like a sigh. "Calm down, Ollie. It's only a game." Maddie took the cards from the box and shuffled them in front of her. "Remember how to play?"

I shifted between Ollie's legs. "Well, yeah …"

"Main campus rules … each time ya lose, ya have to answer a question honestly. If ya don't answer, ya take a shot."

Maddie's taunting tone was like a hissing slimy snake, biting me. Everyone in the room knew I was a lightweight. Before Dolor, I hardly drank. Sophomore year, they gave me the nickname of "Gondo" because I was literally gone after *dos* drinks. Now I was face to face with my current enemy. I could either answer her questions or be gone.

Maddie slid two cards in front of me, then took two cards from the top of the deck and placed them before her. I had a ten and a Jack. Feeling the gravity of Ollie's tense position behind me, I said, "I'm staying."

She took another card from the top of the deck for herself. "Damn, busted." She collected the cards from the floor between us. "Fair play, Mia. Want to ask me a question?"

"Not particularly."

"Fine, I'll drink anyway." She waved over a liquor bottle from the dresser. Isaac reached up and grabbed it before passing it over. Maddie took a swig and placed two more cards in front of me from the top of the deck. Five and seven. "Hit me." The pressure rising, she flipped over a card. A queen. *Shit.*

Ollie leaned over and rested his chin on my shoulder. Maddie smiled. "Busted," she barked. "First question. Since I already know about ya and your problem from psych ward gossip. Why don't ya tell me about your personal life?"

"What's the question, Maddie?"

Her gaze slid to Ollie and back at me. "How many people have you slept with exactly?"

"I don't know."

"Oh, come on, Mia. If you can't keep track of the number, try throwing out a ballpark number. Ten? Fifty? A hundred?"

My blood seethed as my skin seared. "I honestly don't know."

She wrapped her fingers around the neck of the vodka before handing it over. "Drink up, slapper."

"Watch your mouth, Maddie," Ollie growled from behind me as Bria gasped. "She might not understand, but I'm not allowing it."

The vodka lit my throat on fire as the burn flowed down into my stomach, having no clue as to what Ollie was talking about.

Two cards were already in front of me—a nine and four.

"Hit it," Bria whispered.

"Stay," Ollie whispered.

"Stay," I said to Maddie.

She took her card from the pile. She won. She would have won anyway since the king would have put me over.

Maddie scooped up the cards, placing them over the discard pile. "What do you honestly think about each person in the room."

Sighing, I smoothed my attention across everyone. I never hid my feelings toward anyone. "Jake is annoying at first, but once you get to know him, he's a pretty good guy. Alicia is badass and gorgeous. Bria, I'm sorry, but you're a bitch when someone seems threatening to your targets"—I laughed—"but once the threat is gone, you become this completely different person." My attention moved on, and I pointed toward Isaac. "Horn-dog. And …" I pointed toward Liam, who was now watching with a topless Gwen by his side. "Horn-dog number two. And Gwen, I don't know you too well to say."

"And Ollie?"

My arm dropped into my lap. "Everyone knows Ollie is a sweetheart when he wants to be."

"I didn't ask what everyone else thinks. I asked what you think."

I turned behind me when my eyes met Ollie's. His fingers were over his mouth as always, believing it would somehow hide his thoughts. But truth always flared in his eyes. "Ollie's a beautiful person."

Maddie coughed up a laugh, pulling my attention from Ollie's smile. "Guess you don't know him as well as you think."

"Deal the cards."

She hit me with two more.

I lost.

Again.

"How many people have you had sex with—"

"You already asked me that."

"You didn't let me finish."

I slumped back against Ollie.

"How many people have you had sex with in this room?"

Leaning forward, I grabbed for the bottle in front of me and brought it to my lips.

Maddie sneered, placing two more cards in front of me. The alcohol was already warming me. "Hit me."

"Busted again," Maddie cheered. "Okay, Liam, Isaac, and Ollie. Who would you kill, have a one night stand with, and marry?"

I rolled my head back.

"Just answer the question, Mia," Ollie breathed.

With the bottle still in my hand, I took another gulp for courage. "Kill Liam, one night stand with Isaac, and marry Ollie."

"This is brilliant," she laughed.

"No." I wiped my lips with the back of my hand. "This is fucking tupid…" I groaned as the others chuckled around me. "Stupid," I said slowly, drawn out, showing everyone I wasn't as drunk as I actually was.

Two more cards slid in front of me, and I had to bend down to see. "Hit me."

"No, Mia," It was Ollie's voice. No matter what condition, I'd always recognize his smooth voice. He sounded so far away, yet so close to me.

"Busted." Maddie laughed. "Did you fuck Ollie?"

"No," I said, then laughed as soon as the words came out.

"Alright, she's had enough," Ollie said.

"One more." Maddie scoffed with cards already placed in front of me. Blinking numerous times, I couldn't make out the numbers or letters.

"Stay, Mia."

"Stay," I said, repeating whatever bone Ollie would throw.

"I win again. Guess the cards aren't in Mia's favor tonight."

Dropping my head into my hands, I missed but fixed myself quickly.

"When was the last time you had sex with Ollie, Mia?"

"What is it with all these questions about Ollie?" I shouted, attempting to stand to my feet.

"Answer or drink."

I laughed. "You want to know about Ollie and me?"

"Don't, Mia." It was Ollie in my ear as he pinned me to his back. "Don't say another word."

Maddie raised her brows. "Sounds like someone is ashamed of you, Mia."

"God, no … stop!" Ollie shouted and ran his hand through his hair.

I was already angry. And drunk. And those two didn't mix well. "What about you, huh? When was the last time you really took your meds, Maddie? Or tell me what you had to do to get to Dr. Conway."

Maddie stood to her feet as I crouched down and reached for the bottle. Shoving it into her chest, I said, "Want to answer or want to drink?" Hastily, I took a sip and brought it back to her chest. The adrenaline made me insane. The liquor made me slur. And Ollie took the bottle from my hand and set it over the dresser before standing in front of me.

He brought his hands to my face, and I latched on to his imploring green eyes. "Let's go, alright? She's done enough already." As I held on to his arms, he kissed my forehead. "Please."

"Exactly what I thought," Maddie stated.

Once we crawled back to Ollie's room, he laid me down over his mattress. "Ollie?"

"I'm right here," he said as he climbed in beside me.

"I think I'm going to puke."

Ollie immediately jumped from the mattress to across the room and grabbed a small trash can. He made it just in time as my body hurled over the side. My hair was instantly pulled back as Ollie crouched down beside me. The only thing coming up was pure vodka. My throat burned as the residue of the dry heaving brought tears to my eyes.

Bringing my hands to my forehead, I shook my head. "I'm so embarrassed."

Ollie moved the trashcan and let my hair fall before taking off his black shirt. "You think this is my first time seeing someone vomit, Mia?" He smiled and took my face in his hand, wiping my tears and my mouth.

"I'm embarrassed for reacting the way I did. I should have never let her get to me."

"I'm surprised you didn't yank her by the hair and drag her across the floor." He grinned. "You good now?" he asked, patting the trash can.

I nodded.

Ollie tossed his shirt across the room and climbed back over me. As he pulled the blankets around us, his scent and the covers both blanketed me. Calming. He intertwined his legs with mine and moved my hair off my neck before pressing his lips against my skin. "I can't keep pretending, Mia."

"Ollie …"

He pinned me to his torso. "No. What we have isn't meant to be a secret." He took my hand and brought it out in front of us before slipping one of his rings over my finger. "My promise to you, Mia. Whatever happens, it will never burn out, alright?"

Nodding, I laced my fingers into his and brought his hand close to my chest as Ollie burrowed his head into my neck.

I didn't know much about love, but one thing he had taught me was to embrace it. Seize it as soon as it touches you. Drown in the feeling when it penetrates your soul. With love so deep, and a tomorrow never promised, every second in its brilliance was precious.

These were our moments that would fade into memories, and no one could take them away from us.

TWENTY-TWO

"I knew it was forever
when I cherished our
conversations as much
as our love making."

OLIVER MASTERS

Twisting Ollie's ring around my pointer finger, I waited for him to stroll through those doors. Even though he'd put the ring over my ring finger, my thumb or pointer were the only two it didn't fall entirely off from. I ran my thumb over the scroll of the ring, feeling its edges, its swirls, taking in its silver beauty with black lines. Intricate details. He'd never told me where the ring was from, or what it meant to him, but the fact his promise to me was now tied to the ring was all I needed to never be without it.

It was a Wednesday, and our last day before Christmas break. The professors left for two long weeks on holiday—but our Christmas would be spent on Dolor grounds. We were punished, not them. But a Christmas with Ollie was a far cry from a punishment.

In psychology, I sat in the back. As soon as Ollie entered the room, his smile sent a warming circulation within me. His hair grew longer, crazier, piling over his head. The lopsided wave transformed into a tsunami, but it only meant more for me to hold on to. He took his seat before Dr. Kippler arrived.

Dr. Kippler, disheveled and sloppy as ever, apologized for his tardiness like every day before.

There was no class after lunch today, only my counseling session with Dr. Conway. I wanted to trust her, but after what had happened with Maddie, I couldn't bring myself to let my guard down again. Why would she make an exception for someone who isn't assigned to her?

None of it made sense to me.

Jealousy.

I was jealous and territorial over my counselor. It sounded ridiculous, I know. *"That sick feeling in your stomach, the knotted pit growing when you saw Maddie talking to me, or heard she got to Dr. C. That's jealousy, Mia. Jealousy will destroy you if you let it,"* Ollie had said to me.

Though I was considered an adult, the child who'd never gotten to live still resided within me. Having no experience with the multitude of emotions sweeping through me on a day-to-day basis had me questioning everything I thought I knew. All the research I'd done, now out the door.

When they were your own emotions, everything changed.

The halls were quiet as I quickly walked back to my dorm from Dr. Conway's office. I took the stairs two at a time, rushing to get into my sweats, rushing to get to Ollie. We were almost finished with *The Notebook*, and I would still agree to the fact I hated reading, but having him read to me had become my favorite part of my week—next to our sexcapades.

"Whoa, darling. Where you off to in such a hurry?" Oscar asked as soon as my foot came off the last step. His gelled hair was combed back as his dark eyes sliced into me, charring my bones to ashes.

"My dorm," I said flatly, pushing past him. I'd been trying to avoid him since my return from the Looney Bin, but each time our paths crossed, his perseverance had only strengthened with time.

He snatched me by the arm and pinned me against the wall. What I wanted to do was backhand him, knee him in the groin, or call out for help, but he had me by my past. He gripped those threats tightly around my neck every chance he had.

"I've seen this ring before. Where did you get this?" he asked, examining the ring on my hand. Jerking my hand from his hold, I took the ring off and slipped it into my pocket. *My most treasured item.* I had to keep it safe. "Mia, where did you get that?"

"It was a gift. A family heirloom," I lied, then ducked under his arm and attempted to take a step from his stifling space. He pressed his hand against my chest as he slammed me back against the wall.

"Oh, no you don't," he growled.

Trembling, I asked, "What do you want from me?" He became more confident, surer of himself and the hold he had over me.

"What you owe me." Oscar grinned as he drew closer. His hot breath against my cheek held me rigid. "Remember I own you, Mia. "His hand was between my legs, inching its way up. "I fucking own you, and there is nothing you can do about it." Then he cupped my sex. I turned my head, wanting to cry as he applied more pressure. A knot of fear lodged in my throat as the aching swelled in my eyes.

"Please stop," I begged. "Just stop this."

"You know what they say when a girl says no."

He didn't stop, only rubbed his fingers more forcefully over the fabric of my jeans and I shook my head violently. Oscar grabbed my chin. His cigarette breath coated my lips. "Stop fighting it, Mia. It's better that way." And then he let me go with a single step back. "I'll see you real soon, darling."

I ran the rest of the way back to my dorm. Clicking the lock behind me, I fell back against my door and slid down until my bottom hit the marble. If I told Ollie, he would do something to get himself kicked out.

If I told Dr. Conway, Oscar would only use my record against me and say it was all lies. He would say I had come onto him. Every time, Oscar reminded me of the repercussions, scaring me so I wouldn't run. And it worked.

A rap at my door caused me to wince. Crawling away from the door, I waited.

Another knock.

"Mia, it's me."

I jumped to my feet and unlocked the door. As soon as it opened, I flung myself around Ollie, wrapping my arms around his neck and digging my head into his chest. He stroked my hair with one hand while wrapping the other around my back as he held me tight. "Shit, Mia. What happened?"

I was only able to shake my head, so he walked me into my room and closed the door behind us. "We talked about this. You have to talk to me," he said, pulling my head off his chest and searching my face. "Please, this is fucking killing me ..."

"I can't, Ollie. I wish I could, but I can't. Not this." The tears fell rapidly. "I can't tell you and it's for your own good."

"You keep saying that, but it doesn't change the fact I can't do anything to fix this until you talk to me."

"Just read to me."

And after I changed into my sweatpants and pulled his hoodie over my head, he did.

He read chapter after chapter, threading his fingers down my hair and over my back. His comforting touch soothed me from the moment he was unaware of.

Forcing myself to focus on Noah and Allie's troubles, my thoughts were slowly stolen by Oscar. He invaded my reading time, my moments with Ollie, my brain.

If I allowed this to go on any further, it might bring me back to a place I had worked so hard to get out of. Was my mind capable of building a switch again, then flipping it? Would Oscar bring back my walls? I wasn't going to make the same mistake again. Telling someone was my only option. Dr. Conway was my only option. Either she wouldn't believe me, and I would be forced back to the psych ward permanently, or all the lights inside me would shut off again if Oscar went too far. Either way, I would be defeated.

But what if she did believe me?

In two weeks, she would return.

I only needed to get by for two more weeks.

"I know something Ollie doesn't know," Maddie sang as she approached me in the hall. Christmas was in six days, but Dolor didn't necessarily reek of holiday spirit. There was a small tree set up in the corner of the mess hall, but its lack of lights and ornaments made it look like a bad joke. It had been a donation—a pity donation by someone who only wanted to feel good about themselves during the holidays. Without classes to keep us occupied, and half the staff gone, the campus felt like a ghost town.

Tilting my head in Maddie's direction, I wondered if entertaining her childish games was even worth it. "Good for you, Maddie." Nope, not worth it. Maddie was never worth it.

"And I know something you don't know," she bit back.

Her comment stopped me in my tracks, and I crossed my arms over my chest, taking her in. The devilish smile on her face, the satisfaction in her eyes, her posture, it all screamed the fact she couldn't wait for whatever she had planned to come to a head. "Whatever you have to say, just say it."

Ollie appeared beside me and slung his arm around my shoulder. "Maddie starting her games again?" He looked down to me without so much as paying her a lick of attention.

"Trying to."

"Ah, she's reaching, love. Come on," he said into my ear and pulled me away from her toxic antics.

272

Maddie's voice bounced through the hall as we put more distance between her. "He will never forgive you for what you did!"

I jerked my head around right before Ollie opened the door to my room and pulled me inside. "Fuck her," he breathed as soon as the door closed. "Remember what I told you about jealousy? Well, she's jealous of you. Forget her."

"What do you think she meant by it, though?"

"Who the hell cares? She's like a little rat, crawling and scratching at whatever she can get her claws on." Ollie weaved his long fingers through his thick hair before cupping the back of his neck. "Let's not waste any more time on her. Christmas is in six days, and I was going to wait until then to give you this, but I'm like a kid when it comes to these things." Ollie dug his hand into his back pocket.

He groaned. "Shit. Hold on." He turned around while I sat at the edge of the bed and watched his shoulder blades move against his white shirt.

When he turned back around, he dangled a white origami rose from his finger by a ribbon attached. My eyes darted back and forth between the rose and his lopsided grin as I brought my hand to my mouth.

"You like it?" he asked, crouching down in front of me.

"Ollie …"

He took my hand from my mouth and laid it flat before placing the rose inside. "Truth is, I'd never cared much for Christmas. Most people don't know it's a busy season for prostitutes." He shrugged. "Growing up, I spent all day on Christmas in a bloody closet, and as I got older, the day only got worse. But with you, I want to experience everything. And when we leave here, together, we'll have a tree, lights, music. A proper Christmas. And this here is going to be the first ornament on our tree." He grinned. "If the paper survives."

I ran my fingers over the delicate edges. "Where did you … How did you learn to do this?"

"Zeke knows origami. I went to the library the other day and tore a page from one of my favorite books and Zeke taught me the rest."

Zeke. My heart swelled. Ollie kissed my forehead.

"I didn't know we were … I didn't get you anything," I quickly said, then let out a deep sigh. "I always hated Christmas, too."

But suddenly, I wanted to decorate a tree, play Christmas music on the piano for him, send out ridiculous Christmas cards from *Ollie & Mia*, and surprise him with gifts, wanting to experience all of it—with him.

Ollie removed the rose from my palm, stood, and set it carefully on my suitcase. "I already have you. What more can I ask for?" His eyes held the daydream look, and I knew what was coming next. "Well, if you really want to give me something…you, on top of me, naked, always works."

There it was, and when he talked like this, it was no underlying joke. He wanted me *now*. This very moment. No filter, always telling me what was on his mind.

Me. On top of him. Naked.

He tilted his head, spiked an eyebrow, and his eyes held on strong. My insides pulsed as the tingling sensation ignited. Leaning over, I wrapped my hands around his legs and pulled him toward me between my knees. Glancing up at him standing over me, I slipped my fingers into the waistband of his joggers.

"Mia …" he breathed. My name falling from his lips meant everything. It was a beg, a plea, a demand, a promise, a relief, a praise, a question, an answer, a longing, a desire.

It was everything, all in one breath.

"I want to give you something I've never given anyone." And it was true. Before, my egotistic needs were my only concern. Giving head was a purely selfless act, and I had been a self-centered, egotistical, bitch before Ollie.

Ollie grabbed my wrist and stopped me. "You never had your mouth around anyone?" He was surprised. I didn't blame him.

Staring up at him from the edge of the mattress, with his fingers wrapped around my wrist, I shook my head. "No."

He turned his head slightly as a dimple beamed from his cheek, and he ran his palm down his face and through his hair. When his eyes met mine again, his smile was everything. "I can't seem to wipe this stupid smile off my face."

"Why are you smiling?"

He sighed, still smiling, still in awe. "I haven't gone down on anyone either before you …" A laugh pushed through his lips.

My brows pulled together as I leaned back on my hands. "You never went down on anyone?"

Ollie shook his head. "Not until you."

"But you're so good at it."

"You make me good at it." He winked and released my wrist. "And if I could go back and take away every other first, I would … If I knew one day you'd come into my life, I would have waited."

"All those small steps were leading you to me, Ollie. If a stone was thrown in one of our paths, if one little thing had changed, would we have met at all?"

Ollie smiled. "Every second is a life-altering decision, but all routes lead to one destination. Weaknesses aren't strong enough to deter you from your fate—they never were. We're created with fault, Mia, and whether or not we made a different decision, all my paths would have still led me to you."

Shaking my head, I said, "How am I supposed to give you head if you keep me smiling. Now, stop. You're killing my gift-giving vibe." I returned my hands to his legs and looked back up at him. His expression was a mixture of adoration and lust, his eyes heavy with need, and his lips parted slightly in anticipation. "Take off your shirt, Ollie."

Ollie reached behind him and withdrew his shirt on command before dropping it to the floor. The lines peeking above his joggers deepened, and the ink on his torso stretched as his muscles flexed. He lowered his hand to my face and ran his thumb over my bottom lip. I kissed his fingertip, and Ollie closed his eyes. "You have no idea how fucking beautiful you are right now," he whispered, blinking his eyes open again. "Fuck, Mia. You're always so goddamn beautiful, but right now…" He shook his head in awe.

His hard-on pressed against the thin fabric of his joggers, starving for release. Pulling his pants and boxers down together, they slid over his arousal and down his thighs, and I kissed his lower abdomen. Ollie combed his fingers through my hair, keeping the locks away from my face as his eyes drowned in desire.

Grabbing the length of him, I ran my tongue up the bottom of his shaft before wrapping my lips around him. Ollie's eyes closed as every muscle in his face relaxed. My lips slid across the tight skin, each stroke taking him deeper. Ollie's head fell back as he moaned. "Holy … Christ, Mia …" He looked down again, and I held his gaze.

Sucking, my tongue slid across each vein, one hand at the back of his thigh and the other holding his length at the base. I learned which parts were more sensitive than others by his reactions—the way his fingers gripped my hair and the way he jolted against me. His tip hit the back of my throat, and I flicked my tongue against the sensitive part underneath.

Ollie tried pulling my head away, "Mia … I'm about to … fuck …" And I grabbed his backside, my mouth covering him, sucking, then taking him deeper once more and it was all he needed before he pulsed in my mouth. Every muscle in his beautiful body went rigid before relaxing against my hold.

Pulling away, I looked up at Ollie, who had a lazy smile on his face. He cupped my face and brought me to my feet and kissed me hard, eagerly. "You were …" He kissed me again. "That was … " He slammed his mouth to mine in desperation.

He kicked off his joggers and boxers, wrapped his arms around my waist, and spun me around before falling over the mattress, taking me on top of him. He gripped the back of my head as his lips never left mine, soft, sensual, and craving me. He dipped his other hand under my shirt and ran it across my bare skin.

Pulling away from our kiss, I straddled him and lifted my shirt over my head as he reached around me to unclasp my bra. He pulled the bra straps down each shoulder and arm, one by one, until he removed it altogether. His eyes radiated as he took in the sight of me. Thirsty for our connection, he wet his lips and grabbed the back of my head to lead my mouth back to his. His other hand maneuvered the buttons of my jeans before tugging them off entirely.

Once I was completely naked, he rolled me over to my side as we faced each other. He gripped the back of my thigh and pulled my leg over his. "I want to cherish right now. Let's lay here for a moment," he said as he trailed his fingers up my thigh, to my bottom, and pinned my sex against his. His arousal grew again against my wetness, and it was a blissful torment.

My fingers fell over his face as I etched his jawline, his chin, his lips, his freckle by his mouth as Ollie's fingertips ran up my curves, over my hips, dipping at my waist, then cupping my breast.

His lips grabbed mine tenderly before he slipped his tongue through, meeting mine with a slow cadence. His taste held the same fire and ice as the first time as we relished in this moment, admiring one another, taking in each other's allure. Hot tears gathered at the corners of my eyes before spilling in our beauty.

"Why are you crying, love?"

"It's because I know.

"What do you know?"

"I can no longer be without this ... without you," I said. Ollie grinned and pinned my chest against his as I continued, "Until I met you, I never thought about a tomorrow..." Another tear fell down my cheek, warm and comforting. "I know not today, or next year, but maybe when we get out of here, if you ask me to be with you forever, my answer will always be 'yes.' I wanted to tell you now because right now I realize I love you, Ollie, and I wanted you to be a part of this moment in knowing, too." I exhaled. "And somehow, I've loved you this whole time ... I just wasn't ready to accept it."

I'd never in a million years thought those words would ever fall from my lips. I had it bad for the boy who felt too much.

Ollie dipped his head back and raised a brow. "Mia Rose Jett, are you pre-proposing to me?" A boyish grin spread along his features as he scanned my face.

Lifting my shoulder in a half shrug, I only replied with the same smile.

"You know, I'm supposed to propose, right? I'll be damned if you take that away from me." He rolled over on top of me and settled between my legs. "You want to know when I knew?"

I nodded as he rocked his hips back and forth against me.

"I woke up one morning from a nasty hangover, made my way to the bathroom, and when I opened my eyes, there you were. Standing there, staring back at me, and I just knew."

I pushed against his shoulder playfully. "We'd never even talked yet."

"We didn't have to. I looked up, and this voice inside my head said, 'There she is, there's the girl I've been waiting for,' and you stared back at me with those bright light-brown eyes and I swear I almost fell to my knees right then. It took everything I had not to. In the mess hall, I thought you were an apparition, like a figment of my imagination, but the morning in the bathroom, you changed my whole world, and you had no clue." He brought himself on his elbows as my head rested between them, and ran his fingers up my forehead and through my hair.

His passionate kiss left promises of forever across my lips. He lowered himself, scraping his lips across my jaw, down my neck, and over my collarbone. He took my hard nipples between his lips, gently pulling them between his teeth before slipping further down my torso. My breath wavered when his hands reached the back of my thighs, gripping as his lips marked their territory across my stomach.

Lower.

Ollie trailed kisses along my hipbone and over my pelvis. He rested his head against my thigh, between my legs, and looked up at me, helplessly in love. He didn't have to speak the words; I knew.

His warm breath spread across my sex first, breathing on me and breathing me in. "I am embarrassingly obsessed with the taste of you," he confessed. "Utterly addicted." His words hit my insides, shooting rockets up the center. His warm tongue hit my entrance as he stroked through my groove before landing over my knot. "Infatuated," he breathed.

"Don't tease me, Ollie ... I can't ... handle it." Each word struggled to free.

Ollie grinned.

He reached for a pillow, folded it in half, and lifted my bottom over it. "Don't move," he demanded, and pushed my knees apart. "Keep these open. I want to see and taste all of you." Then, in one precise and demanding stroke up with his tongue, his mouth covered my clit. The vibrations in his light moans only added fuel to the manipulation of his tongue. Biting my lip raw, I gripped the mattress as Ollie held the rest of me together yet shattered me to pieces at the same time.

His two hands put pressure down the sides of my sex, spreading and massaging me simultaneously. My vision went hazy as every muscle in my body tightened against him. His supple finger dipped inside, grazing along the spot he knew would push me over the edge, then he sucked his forefinger off between his lips. "You taste so fucking good, Mia."

The heat from his comment ran to my cheeks as he smiled. And he drove his skillful tongue through me, flicking inside as his lips covered me, his thumb attending to my clit. It was all I needed to let go. I cried out as my climax pulsed against his mouth and his hands pinned me wide and still as he tasted my orgasm.

After landing three soft kisses over my sex, Ollie got on his knees and slowly eased his arousal inside me. His body curled over as his palms hit the mattress on each side of me. "My god, Mia ..." he breathed. "You're still pounding. I can feel you beating against me." He stilled inside me as he kissed my neck, his hands roaming across my chest and down my sides as I whimpered. "Fuck, I'm going to come from your on-going orgasm around me alone." He pulled my head between his arms and kissed my lips. "Did that feel good?"

"I'm ... still ..." I panted, unable to find words, so I nodded.

Ollie brushed his nose against mine. "You want me to stop?"

Pulling my trembling lip between my teeth, I shook my head.

Ollie smiled as he lifted himself back up on his knees. He watched himself slide out only to pump slowly back inside me. His skin tightened, every muscle flexing in his arms and abdomen, and he wet his lips before grinding into me once more. Every cell in my body was in a pleasured frenzy as my sight caved to his beauty.

Ollie cursed and praised my name in one word as my legs shook, trying to keep it together. Returning his eyes to mine, I only saw forever. He brought his thumb to his lips, sucked the tip, and rubbed it over my clit, repeating circular motions as he continued his torturous slow grind, grazing inside, attending to every sensation. He moved slowly at first, each thrust bringing us both closer. The battle between keeping the slow pace to outlast the pleasure and the need to arrive at the inevitable brink was written all over his desperate expression.

Ollie's chest crashed against my breasts as he fell over me. He grabbed my hand and laced his fingers with mine and brought it over my head to hold himself up. Each grind grew faster and needy. "Baby, I love you …" he said to me, then kissed me, his sweaty body slick over mine through each thrust. His love penetrated deep into my soul. I gripped his soaked hair and tasted the salt on his lips and the fire, ice, and me on his tongue as we both released ourselves into a monumental and earth-shattering orgasm—*together*.

A love like this couldn't exist in only one lifetime.

TWENTY-THREE

"I tuck myself in at night,
never afraid of what
comes behind closed eyes.
It's there,
inside the madness
of a wonderland,
where this dreamer
found a home;
a secret place
untouched by all,
visited by few,
and created by one."

OLIVER MASTERS

t was Christmas morning. The sun wasn't out yet, but the clock above my door read it was only 5:55 AM. Five minutes I had left before the automatic doors opened. In ten minutes, Ollie would already be completely naked in the shower like he always was at this time. The best thing about his early showering habits was no one else would be in there.

Grabbing my clothes for the day, which was nothing more than a black pair of jeans and one of Ollie's shirts reading "MAKE LOVE NOT WAR" across the front, I snuck across the hall toward the community bathroom. He would disagree, but I was beginning to think he was a hipster.

Once I reached the bathroom, thick steam barreled as running water sounded. The mirrors fogged up, and I quietly laid my stuff over the bathroom counter before opening the curtain.

Ollie jumped back. "Dammit, Mia …" He laughed and ran his fingers through his hair and down his face with a bright, sleepy smile.

"I wanted to be the first one to wish you a Merry Christmas," I said, closing the curtain behind me and taking in the amazing sight of him. His head almost reached the shower head as the water fell over his hair, off his lashes, down his lips, then through the lines of his inked, defined skin.

Ollie cupped my face, and even the water couldn't wash away his grin. "Merry Christmas, Mia," he said, then he kissed me hard. His mouth was freshly minted, and water from the shower ran across our lips. "I love you…" He kissed me again. "So much … but you asked for it." Then he wrapped his arms around me and dragged me under the streaming water, thoroughly soaking me. I shrieked as the warm water weighed down my clothes, and my shirt clung to my skin. I giggled as he leaned in and pressed his smiling lips back to mine.

Dolor didn't do anything special on Christmas morning for breakfast. It was the same wet eggs, and quite frankly, I would happily never eat another egg for as long as I lived.

"Merry Christmas, Zeke," I said as I pulled out the chair in front of him. Zeke only rolled his head around before taking another bite of his breakfast.

Ollie sat beside me. "Hey, mate. Merry Christmas."

Zeke smiled.

"Why do you get a smile and I don't?" I mumbled.

Ollie shoved a fork full of eggs in his mouth. "I've known Zeke longer than you."

"I've talked to Zeke more than you." Though it was always a one-sided conversation.

"Zeke taught me origami," he countered.

"Zeke knows all my secrets."

Ollie pulled his brows together and swallowed. "Everything?"

I nodded once. "*Everything*." I dragged the word out for emphasis.

"Is that so?" Ollie dropped his fork over his tray. "Guess I need to get the boy talking, then." Ollie waved his hand in front of Zeke to get his attention, then out of nowhere, made rapid movements with his hands. I snapped my head in Zeke's direction as he signed back, and this went on for a full minute.

A full minute.

Ollie brought his fingers to his eyes as a controlled laugh spilled from his pressed lips. He turned away for a moment before turning back in front of him and lifting his fork to take another bite of eggs with a grin.

My jaw dropped. My eyes went wide. *No.* "What was that?"

Ollie couldn't contain his smile as he tried to close his mouth while eating the eggs.

"Ollie!" I hit him in the leg. "He knows sign language?"

"Yup," he said after swallowing.

"And what did he say?" I wanted to hide under the table. I wanted to run out of here. I wanted to drive my face into the tray full of eggs.

Ollie's cheeks flushed as he fixed his eyes on Zeke. "The only way you could get through sex with Liam was to imagine it was me." He pressed his lips together harder. His dimple pierced his cheek.

"Oh, my God." I exhaled, bringing my hands over my face.

Ollie removed my hands and slid one over his lap. "Can't say I'm not flattered, love."

Every confession I'd ever told Zeke raced through my mind. Pointing a finger at him, I said, "We're not friends anymore."

Ollie rested my hand over his thigh before using his to communicate with Zeke again. With more movement from Zeke, more than I had seen since I had arrived, Ollie let out a raspy laugh and fist bumped him before returning to my hand under the table.

"What did he say now?" I asked, impatient. Eager. *Annoyed.*

Ollie quickly kissed my cheek as he bounced my hand over his knee. "Never trust a bromance, Mia. The bond Zeke and I share is lethal."

Heat rose to my cheeks as Ollie took another bite, the smile never leaving his face.

"Hey, you adorable two, Merry Christmas!" Jake said as he took a seat beside Zeke.

Zeke moaned, and Ollie quickly swallowed and waved him away. "No, you have to pull up a chair. You can't sit by him."

"My bad." Jake held up his hands in defense and turned around to grab a chair. He dragged it to the end of the table. "What are you guys doing today? We're free all day, no lockdown."

"Let's get outside," I suggested. It was a beautiful day, and it had been precisely a week since I'd felt the sun.

"Power?" Jake raised a brow. We hadn't played power since I ran off in the woods, and I never wanted to play another game again. It should be called "powerless" instead.

Ollie shook his head. "No. No more bloody games."

"How about football? American football? It's a tradition in the states to play or watch football on Christmas day. I'm sure there's a ball here somewhere."

Ollie squeezed my hand in approval as a smile reached his eyes.

We stood in the middle of the field, bundled up in hoodies. The brisk winter air blew fiercely as the sun did nothing to warm me. The tip of Ollie's nose was red as he blew hot air into his palms and rubbed them together before cupping my face. "Maybe this wasn't such a great idea. You're freezing."

Correction: he was freezing.

"I'm fine. I'm from Pennsylvania," I reminded him, used to snow and temperatures lower than this. "This isn't bad, and once you start some physical activity, you'll warm up."

Ollie raised his brow as his smile slowly grew.

"Not that kind of physical activity." I laughed and pushed him playfully in the shoulder.

Ollie caught my wrist and pulled me closer. "Kiss me," he commanded, "before everyone gets here." Relaxing against him, I stood on my toes as he dipped his head down to meet my lips. "Mmm ... I'm warming up already," he growled.

Breathing him in, I whispered through an exhale, "I love you, Ollie."

He moaned. "Say it again."

I kissed the sensitive spot below his ear because I knew what it did to him. "I love you."

Ollie hummed into my neck, and it was a beautiful sound. "I'll never tire of hearing you say those words." And he captured my mouth again.

"Found a ball!" Jake said, snapping Ollie and me away from each other instantly. "Seriously? You guys don't have to hide from me ..."

"What are you talking about?" I asked casually and shoved my hands into the front pocket of the hoodie. We weren't drinking. There was no excuse for us to be kissing in Jake's eyes. In my eyes, there were a thousand reasons why we should, starting with Ollie.

Jake caught the ball he threw to himself in the air before planting it between his hip and his arm. "You guys can trust me, you know. I would never keep whatever you guys seem to have apart. That right there is precious," he added, pointing back and forth between me and Ollie standing at least three feet apart.

"I appreciate it, mate," Ollie said to Jake, genuinely, then tipped his head in my direction. "I'm in love with her, you know ..." Ollie beamed. I beamed. Jake's eyes swelled as they slid back and forth between us. "Damn, it feels good to finally tell someone else," Ollie said and closed the gap between us again. "Now, don't go and throw a spanner in the works, alright?"

"I thought you guys were just doing the rumpy-pumpy." Jake smiled and shook his head in surprise. "This is brilliant. The two of you." He gushed with his hand over his chest. "Can I be in the wedding party?" He fired his arm high in the air. "Oh! I call maid of honor!"

Ollie laughed as he took his beanie off his head before stretching it over mine and down over my ears. His mouth covered mine once more as our fingers intertwined. "Alright, alright, Mia … now you're just rubbing it in." Jake threw the ball at Ollie's back, and Ollie released me before swiping the ball up from the grass and gesturing for Jake to *go long*.

Alicia and Bria finally showed up, followed by Isaac. The whole crew was finally here, and so was the sun, gradually moving higher above us. The skies were open, the wind was quieting, and I went through the basic rules of American football. "No tackle, we're playing touch. You have to touch with both hands," I reiterated. It was boys against girls. "Who's the better catcher?" I asked in our small huddle. Bria pointed to Alicia, and I figured. "Okay, I'm going to snap the ball, and you make a run for it."

"Snap the ball?" Alicia asked as she held a brow in the air.

"*Hike* the ball." I sighed. "Screw it, I'll just throw the ball to you, just make sure you're in the end zone."

"And where is this end zone, exactly?"

Huffing and wishing I was on the other team, I pointed between the two trees behind the anxious boys who stood with their arms crossed over their chests.

"Come on, ladies. We haven't got all day!" Ollie called out before warming his hands back up over his mouth.

"Ready?" I asked.

"No," Bria whined. "What am I supposed to do?"

"Distract Isaac and Ollie. You're already good at that."

Bria nodded with a wicked smile.

"Break!"

"Now we're having a break?" Alicia asked.

Holy shit. Groaning, I rolled my eyes. "No, it means I'm done talking. Now we can play."

286

After directing the girls with rapid finger gestures, I shouted, "Hike," and Alicia only stood there while Ollie took off toward me. "Run, Alicia!"

Alicia ran to the end zone with Isaac on her tail, and I threw the ball before Ollie got to me. Ollie spun around, both our eyes on the ball in the air, only one of us silently praying for her to catch it.

And surprisingly enough, she did.

My hands flew in the air as I shouted, "Touchdown!" followed up by a victory dance.

Alicia and Bria jumped up and down as Ollie turned around with an impressed smile on his face. "Nice throw, babe." Then his smile dissolved when something behind me caught his attention. "Mia, go back inside," he warned with an altered tone.

"What, why?" I attempted to turn around, but he gripped my shoulders.

"Go back inside, please."

"Room for two more?" a voice asked. Pulling my gaze from Ollie, I spun around. A sudden illness churned in my stomach, slowly devouring the rest of my insides when Maddie approached us with Oscar by her side.

"*Fuck*," Ollie groaned, but the only thing possessing me was Oscar's presence. I stumbled backward as his gaze scanned me up and down.

Maddie smirked as her gaze darted between Ollie and me. "I wanted to take a moment to introduce you. Ollie, this here is the guy Mia fucked..." Maddie cocked her head to Oscar. "How many times did you say? Was it once or twice?"

"Twice," Oscar said through a chuckle, making my insides crawl.

Ollie snapped his head, his gaze calling me, urging me. The weight behind it was unbearable, and I shamefully peered over at him to find him shaking his head. "No..." He turned back to Maddie. "Stop this shit, Maddie," he shouted at her. "Stop your fucking games!"

"And Mia," Maddie scoffed, taking my attention from Ollie and back on her. She held up a palm to Oscar. "This is Oscar ... Ollie's brother."

Instantly, all the oxygen abandoned my lungs—nothing—a wrecking ball to the stomach. Everything left me and bled across the lawn as I stood, fixed and in utter disbelief.

Ollie took a step in front of me, trying to meet my gaze, but I couldn't look at him. I couldn't face him. Heat radiated from his touch as he gripped my shoulders, leaning in front of my face, spewing words my brain couldn't decipher. All I felt was the steel knife lodged inside my chest. The burn. *The ache*. Probably the same knife that had just come from Ollie's chest.

"I didn't know." My words stumbled as everything else slipped from my grasp. "Ollie, this was before you."

"Stop talking, Mia. Don't say another word." The cold replaced his hands as he stepped away from me. "How could you do this to me?" Ollie asked Oscar, shoving him in the chest, "Anyone else! Why her?!"

"Just wanted to wish you a Merry Christmas, little brother." He laughed, the sound sick and masochistic and curdling the blood in my veins. "And for the record, the slut pulled me in first … I had my way with her *first*." He took a step toward Ollie and puffed out his chest. "You broke our number one rule, Oliver…"

My feet instantly broke out into a sprint across the field and into the woods. Leaves crunched beneath my combat boots as I ran. The wind smacked against my face, stealing the little breath I had left. With no direction in mind, I ran until my legs buckled beneath me, and I caught myself against a tree. The sickness brewing in my stomach came up into my throat, and I hunched over as I threw up. My body convulsed as my eyes strained until I was left dry heaving in the middle of the woods.

After staying in that position until there was nothing left inside me, I crouched down, unable to stand on my wobbling legs. The tears stopped, but only so my mind could focus on breathing as I gasped for oxygen.

A hand against my back told me it wasn't Oscar, but it also wasn't Ollie.

"Are you okay?"

It was Jake.

Shaking my head, I turned to face him as I held my hand against my chest.

Stay with me, Mia.

"I'm going to get help," Jake said in a panic, but I clutched on to him as I cried out for him not to.

"Panic attack. You have to talk to me," I panted, stumbling over to another tree and collapsing to the ground.

Jake took a seat beside me and ran his hand up my back. "Ollie kicked that security guard's arse, and you would think the security guard would have taken Ollie into custody afterward, but no. The bloke walks off, and I still don't even know what happened. One second I see you there, the next you're running across the field the moment Ollie launches at the bloke. I figured, well, Ollie looks like he has things under control, and I'm not helpful in a brawl, so now here I am."

Here Jake was.

Here I was.

"Do you want to talk about what happened?"

I shook my head. "I think I just really need to be alone, Jake." My voice faltered. I dropped my head into my trembling hands as my head pounded against them.

"Yeah, alright." Jake stood and brushed the back of his pants with his hands. "Know I'm here whenever you're ready to talk."

With that, Jake walked off.

Losing the struggle to fight back tears, I pulled my knees to my chest as the aching returned, sickness competing against it. Loving Ollie was the easy part. He made it so incredibly easy. It was everything else that was complicated. Flipping up the brim of Ollie's beanie, I dropped my head over my knees and clenched my eyes. Maybe if I drifted to sleep, I would wake up to reality. Oscar couldn't be Ollie's brother, and if he was, it only meant things between Ollie and me would never be the same.

I couldn't come back from this.

The wind swirled angrily as the cold grew bitter, biting my cheeks, stinging my fingertips. I wasn't sure if I'd fallen asleep, or how long I'd been sitting out here. The sun descended. My bones trembled, but I deserved to feel the burn. My throat was raw, but I deserved to feel the harshness. My stomach was in knots, but I deserved to feel the shame. I deserved everything happening to me because I didn't deserve him. My eyes could barely stay open. They stung as they fought against the cold wind.

His silhouette off in the distance arrested my swollen eyes. He walked toward me, every detail of his beauty coming into view the closer he drew near. He held two fingers at the bridge of his nose as he walked in my direction. Long, determined strides, but shoulders slumped inside his gray hoodie. His hood was pulled up over his head, and I tried to stand, but it was no use.

He crouched down in front of me and searched my eyes. His were bloodshot and broken—he'd been crying. Leaning over, he kissed the top of my head before grabbing my hands and helping me to my feet.

We walked back to Dolor, hand in hand.

He didn't say a word.

It was a curse and a blessing.

Through the doors, down the corridor, and up to Ollie's door, we stopped. My hand shook in his, not ready for the inescapable truth—we could never be the same, and he could never look at me the same. Not after being with his brother.

Once inside his room, Ollie took off his shoes. He withdrew his sweatshirt, and then his shirt. My heart struck against my ribcage like a trapped bull, watching him silently. He stood before me and wrapped his fingers around the bottom hem of my sweatshirt and pulled it over my head, my shirt following. He crouched down, untied each of my shoes before I kicked them off. Then he slid off my jeans.

His actions were bizarre, but if he didn't want to talk, he didn't. Perhaps this was his way of coping, and I would be whatever he needed.

Ollie grabbed my hand, and I followed him to the bed. We both lay on our sides, quiet and still. My back was pressed against his torso. He found my hand and held it out in front of me as he twisted the ring around my finger—a promise made not too long ago. Was my mistake grounds for allowing him out of it?

He moved the hair off my shoulder and neck, and kissed my shoulder blade, his lips lingering longer than usual.

He wanted one more night.

He was giving *us* one more night.

TWENTY-FOUR

"I'm yours, and you're mine,
and that's all I'll ever know."

OLIVER MASTERS

"*Meet me in the library -OM,*" the note beside my head read. When I woke, Ollie was gone. My sore eyes were raw from the day before as I tried blinking the sun away. The nausea had already set in. If I didn't show up, he wouldn't have a chance to end us. Avoiding him would be better for me, but not for him. I'd done enough damage. I had to give him this.

After showering and brushing my teeth, I headed for the library. Taking the stairs slowly, I walked toward the end of the route of us. If I could have, I would have been crying, but I was all tapped out of tears. I had on the same clothes I'd worn my first day here. My shorts and "Cute but Psycho" tee. It only seemed fitting. This was the girl I'd been when I arrived, but ever since I'd been touched by Ollie, I would never be the same. Even though I dressed the part, I was forever changed. Even if I wanted to, I could never build another fucking switch—not after him.

After turning the corner, I stood at the end of the hallway. Ollie waited right outside the library door with his back slumped against the wall. His gray pair of sweats hung perfectly around his hips, and his white shirt made his inked skin more dramatic. He lifted his head and squinted down the hall. No smile formed, but his eyes still held the same look he always had for me. The one that never went away after four months. He looked at me as if he got lost and found in me all at once. My presence still affected him, and his eyes grasped on to me—clinging for life—in case I disappeared.

He straightened his posture as I walked down the hall of shame.

When I approached him, he bent down and picked up the two cups of coffee, handed me mine, and lifted the brown paper bag off the floor— still nothing, not even a smile. His face carried hurt, but his battered green eyes held a glimmer of hope and a spark of wonder.

"Thank you," I said quietly. Ollie nodded and opened the door for me before walking me through the maze of books until we reached his spot.

It was our spot, but now it was back to only his.

We sat side by side in the nook. Ollie dropped the brown paper bag between us and let out an exhale. "Mia ..." He paused and cleared his throat. "I ... *Dammit,* Mia ..." he choked out.

His strength dulled, his face unreadable. Looking into his wounded eyes, I knew I had done this to him, and I hated myself for it. There was nothing I wanted more than to carry all the pain he felt. Pointing blame at a girl who no longer existed wouldn't ease the betrayal. Instead, I wanted him just to come out and say it. He chewed on his lip, fighting the tears, and finding the words I earned to hear.

"Don't let me down easy, Ollie. I don't deserve easy." I sat the coffee down beside me. I couldn't stomach anything. "Please, just say it."

Ollie pinched the bridge of his nose and shook his head slowly.

He couldn't look at me.

Please, look at me.

"Mia, that's not with this is."

I was shaking my head now.

He pressed his back against the bookshelf and tilted his chin to face me. "Do you know how hard it was for me to not run after you yesterday? I wanted to, Mia. After finding out, I still wanted to run after you, and the only reason I didn't was because it wouldn't be fair. I was still angry, and I needed to think. But then I couldn't even think straight. Not without you near me.

"Ollie—"

He raked his hand through his hair. "No, let me finish. I have to get this out, alright?"

I nodded.

"So, when I went to your room and saw you still hadn't come back, I felt sick about leaving you like that and walked outside to get you. I just know what we have is stronger, Mia. For fuck's sake, I can't picture you with anyone, not even my brother. I'm not in denial. I know what happened, but I can't bring myself to picture it. What happened with you two should be making me sick right now. It should be haunting me, but I can't fucking see it because I'm yours, Mia, and you're mine, and that's all I'll ever know and see.

"Last night confirmed it for me. I didn't want to hear your explanation at the time. I didn't want to say something stupid I didn't mean. I only wanted to feel what we have. I wanted to make sure you being with him didn't taint that fucking feeling, and it didn't. Not for me, anyway." Ollie exhaled and closed his eyes. "I should have told you he worked here, but the only reason I didn't was because I wanted to keep the two of you separated. I didn't want him finding out about you and I didn't want you confronting him. I couldn't take the chance." Ollie moved my trembling hand from my lap to the back of his neck. "Jake said you were throwing up …"

I moved my head rapidly from side to side. "Only because I hurt you…I hurt you in the worst possible way, and it made me sick to know I was the one who did that to you."

Ollie drew in a shaky breath and ran a palm down his face with his empty hand. "Remember, I told you nothing worth it would be easy?"

"Yeah, I remember."

"Things will get difficult, but nothing is going to change the way I feel for you. I won't allow it. My heart won't allow it. Every breath I take is wasted if you aren't in my life, and I know my brother, Mia. My brother doesn't walk away from a girl. My brother gets a slice of something, and he doesn't stop..." Ollie's eyes fell on mine, tears falling, and he did nothing to wipe them away. "He hasn't stopped with you, has he? That's the reason for your panic attacks?"

My mind couldn't wrap around what was happening. Ollie was looking past this. He wasn't allowing it to come between us. He was more concerned about my panic attacks. "He said no one would believe me," my voice rasped out.

I don't deserve him.

"I would've believed you. All you had to do was talk to me."

"You would have done something stupid to jeopardize your future."

Ollie swiped his eyes across his sleeve. "Dammit, Mia. What has he done?" He looked up again, more tears gathering. "How long has this been going on?"

My eyes were dry, and my lips cracked. The insides of my nose burned along with the ongoing ache in my chest. All my mental strength was completely depleted. "The last time I ... was with him in that way ..." I couldn't even say the word, afraid to break him even more. "Was before you and I had ever kissed. He was only the trainee at the time. Then, when I got back from psych, he came on to me, and I tried pushing him away." I moved my head back and forth frantically. "He says he owns me. He would have his way with me, and no one would believe me. He taunts me in the halls, and he shows up in my dorm. He waits for me when I walk out of the shower. Ollie, I'm terrified of him and what he's capable of ..."

"Has he touched you?"

"Ollie ..."

"Answer me, Mia. Has he touched you since we kissed?"

"Yes, but he threatened to take me away from here. He threatened to send me to the mental institution. Said he read my file. First, it was over clothes, but each time he takes it a little further. I tell him, no, Ollie, I tell him to stop." When I thought I had no tears left, more found their way down my cheeks and into my hands. "I just don't know what to do anymore."

Ollie pulled me over his lap and wrapped his arms around me. "I've got you. I told you, I'll never let you go through anything alone, alright? *Fuck.* I knew you were suffering, but I thought I was helping you get through it. I thought it was your past. I'm sorry I didn't see it before. I'm so sorry I failed you." He lifted my head from his neck and wiped his thumbs under my eyes. "It's you and I, alright?"

I nodded before he pulled me close again.

Somehow, we walked out of the library stronger than stone. For so long, I had allowed my past to brew inside me. I'd let it dictate me, control me, let me become a cynic of the world and the people in it. And yes, life was cruel, and people were vicious, but if I'd never took my guard down, I would have been blinded to the beauty and how people could surprise me.

And people did surprise me.

Ollie had surprised me; all I'd had to do was step outside my comfort zone, and it was scary as hell. I wondered if I would have appreciated his light if I hadn't been through the dark. And the funny thing was, I would never know. But what I had learned was it wasn't about what had happened in my past. It was how I'd let it affect me. There would be dark with the light, good with evil, lose with the win, and love with hate. How could I appreciate when I was up if I never felt the pain of the down? Each moment, beautiful or ugly, was never a wasted moment. Each moment was there to mold me: a lesson.

A purpose.

I accepted my past with my head held high, because it had led me here, and there wasn't any other place I'd rather be.

"New Year's Eve fireworks through the window at midnight, mate? What do you say?" Isaac asked Ollie in the community bathroom after dinner. Standing under the shower head, washing the soap out of my hair, I listened as Isaac, Bria, and Alicia made plans for tonight. Jake was in the stall beside me, singing "Pony."

"No, not after what happened the last ... I don't know, every time we all get together drinking. Fuck. No," Ollie slowly said after turning off the faucet. Through the mirror's reflection, Ollie noticed a gap in my curtain, turned, and closed it.

"It's fucking New Year's, Masters. We have to celebrate." Isaac wasn't letting it go.

"I can't come tonight, I have a hot date," Jake said from his stall, and my eyes went wide.

"What? What about Bryan?" I asked over the water.

"Bryan and I agreed on an open relationship while I'm gone."

"I can't go, either," Alicia said from another direction.

"What you think, Mia?" Isaac asked from the other side of my curtain.

Turning off the water, I wrung out my hair and grabbed the towel from the hook to dry off. "I don't know ..." I said, getting into my panties and pulling one of Ollie's shirts over my head. Before opening the curtain, I stepped into my plaid pajama shorts. It would be nice to see Ollie tonight for New Year's. Having a New Year's kiss wasn't something I'd ever wanted in the past. Something about a fresh new year with Ollie by my side made me giddy inside.

"Come on. I got a proper bottle for tonight." Isaac punched Ollie in the shoulder, but Ollie's lips never moved. "It will be laid back."

Ollie glanced at me and back to Isaac. "Coming on strong, mate. Why do I get the feeling you're up to no good?"

"Am I ever up to any good?" Isaac wiggled his brows. "Plus, I can't see the fireworks from my window, so it's either your or Mia's room. I'm showing up one way or another."

"Fine," Ollie caved.

Isaac applauded.

Bria squealed.

And I spit out my toothpaste thinking this was going to be a good night with Ollie, or things were going to go horribly wrong.

During the holiday, the security checks had diminished, but the automatic doors still locked right on time. I'd been spending every night with Ollie. Him not wanting to leave my sight, and me not wanting him to. He insisted on walking with me everywhere and told me about the things Oscar had done in the past. Told me how bad it could get, and how dangerous he was.

It was ten minutes until midnight when Isaac and Bria fell through the vent hole of Ollie's room. "Let's do this!" Isaac said as soon as his feet hit the floor with a bottle of liquor in his hand.

Ollie grabbed the bottle from Isaac and examined it. "Where did you get this?"

"A hookup, Masters. You need to relax," Isaac said, taking the bottle back from Ollie.

Ollie was on edge. Heat flared from his skin as he laced his fingers through mine and turned to face me. "Something's up, Mia. I can feel it."

Isaac popped open the top and poured some into Bria's mouth. "Yeah!" he cheered, then came between Ollie and me and held the bottle over my mouth. "Come on, Mia."

Shrugging my shoulders, I opened my mouth, tasting the bitter burn in my throat. It warmed me instantly. If there were one thing I'd come to learn about the students here, they were consistent. No one took "no" for an answer, and the badgering would only continue.

Bria grabbed my hand and pulled me aside as I swallowed the rest I was holding in my mouth. Her breasts bounced in her cropped shirt as she skipped to the corner and spun me around. "I'm doing Isaac tonight." Her determined smile verified she was on a mission.

"Here?"

She nodded excitedly. "Yeah, where else am I going to have him?"

298

I smacked my hand to my forehead. "Oh Lord, I don't want to see that."

"I'm sure you and Ollie will busy yourself."

Rolling my eyes, I said, "What? You think this is an orgy?"

Bria laughed. "Wanna?"

"Hell no," I said through a laugh. "Not going to happen."

Bria made a pouty face, and I slipped away from her before her ideas clouded her best judgments. Isaac encouraged the alcohol on Ollie and Ollie finally caved, taking a few gulps before wiping his mouth with the back of his hand. I checked the clock above the door. Two minutes before the fireworks.

"One minute!" Isaac called out, and Ollie wrapped his fingers around my wrist as he pulled me in front of him toward the window.

His breath was minty and laced with alcohol as he pinned my back to his torso. "You ready for a new year?" His words danced in my hair as his breath worked small bumps across my skin.

"I'm so ready."

We stared out the window. Past the rolling hills and the darkness, the city lights sparkled as if all the stars in the sky had gathered and hovered around one location. Since Ollie only started three months before me at Dolor, we both had half the school year down, and only one and a half years to go. We could make it.

"Ten!" Isaac and Bria said, counting down. "Nine ... eight ..."

Ollie leaned into my ear. "Close your eyes, Mia."

I spun around to face him. "Why?"

"Six ... five ..."

Ollie wrapped his fingers around my chin and brushed his nose to mine. "Just close your eyes, my love. Pretend we're far away from here and I'm holding you in the middle of the city under those lights."

"Ollie ..."

"Two!"

"Do it for me." Ollie dipped his head and kissed my objection away. I gripped his sides to keep from falling back as he held my head in his hands.

His lips melted over mine, soft and captivating. His hand traveled to my neck as he swept his thumb along my jawline. Our tongues crashed, and all my senses kindled against his fervor.

He pulled away slightly and brushed our mouths together as I inhaled his sweet breath. "Happy New Year, love," he whispered, his lips turned up into a smile against mine.

"Happy New Year."

Turning around in Ollie's arms, I looked back out the window to see the firework display as Ollie slowly swayed me back and forth with his long arms tight around my waist. Shades of red, purple, and white glowed in the distance, shooting from a nearby city, creating designs in the velvet black before sizzling into a stardust rainfall.

Closing my eyes, I pictured being under those colors, inside Ollie's arms, with the night wind in my hair. Ollie pressed his lips to the back of my head before resting his chin over it.

"Happy fucking New Year!" Isaac shook Ollie from behind and the moment dissolved as quickly as I had created it. "Let us drink!"

The bottle hooked around us and appeared in my face. I grabbed the bottle and took a swig before Bria pulled me from the window.

"Isaac kissed me," she whispered. I gave her two thumbs up after she took the bottle from my possession.

"See! You can do this." I smiled. She had no reason to be nervous. She had already screwed the guy more than once, but she was right. Tasting feelings of my own, I understood how nerve-wracking it could be—especially the first time. It was like losing your virginity all over again.

I couldn't have drunk much, maybe three shots at most, but my vision distorted as if I were trying to see through a pool full of chlorine, and each time I tried to stand on my feet, the floor moved from under me.

I blinked rapidly, and Bria and Isaac came into focus. Bria was completely nude across the floor, her breasts bouncing as Isaac had his way with her. But she wasn't moving. She wasn't saying anything. Her eyes were closed.

"What are you doing?" I called out. "What's wrong with her?"

But Isaac didn't respond. He never turned around. Was I even talking?

"Ollie?" I called out. "What's happening?" I sat at the edge of the bed, leaning, almost falling over, or already lying down. *How did I get here?* Nothing was making sense.

After finding the strength to turn my head and look behind me, my eyes found Ollie sleeping against the wall over his mattress. He'd had one sip; how was he already passed out? Had I passed out?

I had.

I tried to crawl my way to him, but my limbs were useless.

Fear gripped me entirely.

"Ollie, wake up," I tried to say.

Suddenly, someone dragged me to the foot of the mattress by my feet. "Oh, no you don't." My eyes went wide when I noticed it was Isaac. "I need to get you good and ready." I shook my head as Isaac cocked his head at the door. "Shit. He's late."

"What are you doing?" I tried kicking my legs, but nothing. There was no strength, no movement. The ability to resist and refuse failed me.

He dropped my legs over the edge of the mattress and returned the bottle to my lips. "Open up, Mia." He pushed my cheeks together with one hand and poured the liquid over my face. The liquid burned the inside my nose and my eyes as I tried freeing myself from his grasp. His hold became forced as the alcohol hit the back of my throat. Isaac laughed as he glanced over in Ollie's direction. "No one is saving you tonight. Ollie's out, and he's not waking up for a while."

Struggling to keep my eyes open, sounds muffled around me and through me. The door bolt unlocked, and the outline of a side profile blurred as someone came through the door, but I knew it was him.

It was Oscar.

"Blimey! You already fucked this one, yeah?" he asked, moving Bria to the side with his foot. *Don't touch her.* My lids fought to stay open as Oscar took a few steps toward me. "You haven't touched her, have you?"

"No, bro. We had a deal."

Oscar looked behind me to Ollie and nudged his head. "My brother take a good bit?"

"No, I had to take your advice and knock him out." Isaac ran his hands over his hair. "I don't get it, man, he's your brother."

"And he's your mate." Oscar's evil glare landed back on me. "We have a rule. Oliver knows this. She was mine first. This will show him never to take what's mine."

"Whatever, man. Did you bring what I asked for?"

Oscar dug into his pockets before withdrawing a bag full of pills and handing it to Isaac.

Ollie. "Ollie …" I think I moaned. My tongue felt fuzzy—numb. "Ollie." All I saw was Oscar and Isaac. All I felt was the numbness, the cold, and the darkness.

"He's out like a light bulb." Oscar laughed.

There were two Oscars and two Isaacs in front of me, blurring together and spinning and I tried to reach up to grab hold of Ollie's legs, but suddenly, I was moved around like a rag doll as the room shifted.

"Damn, such a fine pussy right there. Ever been with her?"

"No way. Ollie would fucking kill me."

"I'll let you get her wet for me." It was the sound of his haunting laugh and the belt coming off that had me clawing at Ollie's legs. Digging my nails into his flesh in desperation, I silently cried until Ollie's voice blessed my ears.

"Mia …"

"Good, it's about damn time. Watch, brother. Watch me fuck your girl."

The bed moved around me, and everything disappeared. "Get the hell off her!" Ollie's voice boomed. Sounds came from me, and I couldn't see him. My head couldn't move to either side. *Darkness.*

"Mia ..." A blanket consumed me before everything went dark.

TWENTY-FIVE

"Damn, baby.
Take a moment,
look in the mirror,
see how strong you are."

OLIVER MASTERS

"Ollie?" My stomach stirred, and I threw my body over the mattress just as someone pulled a trashcan under me. "I'm right here, Mia. I got you," Ollie whispered, stroking the back of my head. "You have to get this crap out of your system."

Hardly able to lift my heavy, pounding head when I finished, Ollie pulled me back onto the mattress. It was warm here, in these clothes, and... I turned my head. "Bria," I whispered. She lay helplessly beside me.

Oscar.

Isaac.

My body flinched as the memories flooded.

"They're gone. They can't touch you." Ollie moved the trashcan and crouched down beside me. "You have to drink some water." He held a bottle in his hand, twisted the cap, and brought it to my lips. The water instantly soothed my throat. "There you go."

"What happened? Why aren't you …"

Ollie dropped his head to his chest for a moment, and when his eyes met mine, I was met with a bruised face.

"Ollie, your face." I reached out to touch him, but he grabbed my hand before it made contact.

"I'm fine. Don't worry about me." Ollie forced a small smile. "You need to get some rest."

"Why aren't you …"

Ollie shook his head. "I was only knocked out. I'm fine." He kissed the palm of my hand. "Promise."

"Did he?" I winced at the thought. But it wasn't me I was worried about; I was afraid of what Ollie had witnessed. What exactly had he seen? Had I been touched? Raped? I couldn't seem to remember.

"No, love. You made sure that didn't happen." He showed me the claw marks on his ankles. "See how strong you are? You woke me up, and I took care of the rest." He pressed his lips to my forehead and sat at the edge of the bed. "I'm sorry, Mia. I had no idea Isaac would betray me. I should have known better."

"It's not your fault."

Ollie's gaze slid over to Bria then back to me. "I need to get her to the nurse, and I don't know what to fucking do."

"Go get Jake."

"I don't want to leave you."

"I'm fine. Go get Jake."

It didn't take long for me to fall back asleep, and when I woke up again, Bria was gone.

"Take it easy." He pulled the trashcan up again as I emptied my stomach into it. The convulsions strained my eyes as tears ran down my cheeks. My brain was still foggy and pounded against my skull.

Falling back against the pillow, I moaned. My mouth was dry, and my entire body felt like it had been run over by a semi. *Twice.* "Bria okay?" I opened my eyes, and Ollie sat on the edge of the bed again with his hands in my hair.

He nodded. "I think so." He removed his hand and ran it down his face. "You've been sleeping for twenty-nine hours now. You have to eat something. You have to get up, take a shower, and soak this up with some proper food."

Twenty-nine hours? It only seemed like four. "What have you been doing this whole time?"

"Reading." He ran his hand over my forehead and through my hair. "I can't leave you, Mia. I can't turn myself in, either. Not until you're better."

"Turn yourself in?" I sat up, but with the help of the cold concrete wall to support me. "You didn't do anything! Why do you have to turn yourself in?"

Ollie only shook his head. "Bria was raped. In my room. You guys were drugged, Mia. The only way I'll be able to find justice in all this is to tell the Dean what happened. The only way to get Oscar away from here, away from you, is to be honest." He dropped his hand from my head and rubbed my back. "Already thought this through, it's the best option, so don't try to change my mind." He forced a convincing smile, but there was fear behind his exterior. "Now, come on. You have to get in the shower, change these clothes, and brush those teeth."

Ollie stood to his feet and gathered a pile of things at the end of the bed and stuffed them under his arm. He held out his hands to help me to my feet.

It was dark outside. "What time is it?"

"A tad past six in the morning."

We walked down the corridor toward the community bathroom. The only security guard on duty would have been Oscar, who wouldn't dare show his face. It was quiet. Eerily quiet. Even our footsteps made no sound as we walked barefoot. The bathroom was empty. Ollie turned on a shower as I focused on not falling over.

As we waited for the water to heat up, he stood before me, our eyes locked on each other in a comforting silence. He wore his usual black V-neck and those amazing thin joggers I could see the outline of his length through. The bruise over his eye looked like a watercolor tray of greens and purples. His hair was in disarray from the number of times he'd presumably clutched it in the last twenty-nine hours.

"Mia?"

"Yeah?"

"This is all fucked up, isn't it?" he asked, and I nodded. "Promise me we never tell our children about how we met."

"Promise," I said, forcing out a small smile.

He took my hand and led me behind the curtain.

"Can I touch you, Mia?" he asked, his voice coming from his throat, but having an unintentional crack mid-sentence. He cleared his throat. "You need help out of your clothes."

I nodded and lifted my heavy arms over my head. Ollie peeled off his shirt I wore before withdrawing his own. His eyes stayed on me, watching every expression, studying every detail in my frozen face.

He dropped to his knees before me. His eyes still held my gaze as he tugged off my pajama shorts, my panties coming off along with them. He gripped my hips and pressed his lips to my hipbone before standing to his feet, his eyes never leaving mine.

His joggers and boxers were gone, and he steered me under the water, tilted my head back, and submerged my hair under the stream. "Let me do this for you." Ollie grabbed the bottle of shampoo and massaged it into my scalp. "You'll feel better afterward."

"I don't want you to turn yourself in." It was all I could think about. He would be taken away as well. I couldn't survive here without him. "You promised me—you and me, remember?"

Ollie grinned and rinsed my hair out under the stream, focusing on getting all the soap out. "I am doing this for you and me."

"Stay with me, Ollie."

"I am with you … always."

No. I wanted to cry, but my body was too weak to do anything. Ollie squeezed soap into his hands, rubbed them together, then ran his palms over my shoulders, down the length of my arms, and over my back. The warm water beating against my skin loosened my aching muscles, and Ollie's hands over my bare skin erased the painful memories of Oscar away. He dropped to his knees again, running his soapy hands over my legs and between my thighs, and over my bottom. I held on to his shoulders to keep myself steady.

"Do you remember anything?" he asked me as he gripped the backs of my thighs. "They said they didn't touch you … Did they touch you?" His hands felt amazing as they came around to my front and up the middle of my thighs. My brain couldn't think about anything else aside from Ollie's hands over me. "I'll fucking kill them."

"No, I don't think so."

Ollie drew in a deep breath and got to his feet. He wrapped a towel around me and propped me against the wall as he finished showering himself. Ollie quickly washed his hair, his body, and rinsed off before turning off the water. He dressed me in a big shirt that hit me mid-thigh.

"I'll go to your room and get you some knickers," he said and ripped up my old ones before tossing them in the trash.

We brushed our teeth before walking hand in hand down the hall back to his room. The halls were still empty. Dolor was quiet. He closed the door behind us and stripped his bed completely before I lay back down. He kissed the top of my head. "I'll be right back."

My mind was murky—unable to develop a single thought aside from everything Ollie had done for me in the last twenty-nine hours with guilt in his eyes. He'd washed me, the worried look in his eyes the entire time, and I wondered if he was scared to touch me. The last thing I ever wanted to lose was his constant need for me, and I felt it slipping away.

Ollie came back with my blanket and a change of clothes. "We're borrowing this," he said through a smile and threw the blanket over the bed beside me. When I didn't smile, his face fell. "What's on your mind, Mia?"

"You're so scared to touch me. Like I'm fragile. I don't like it." Ollie took a step closer to the bed and ran his hand through his hair as I continued, "I'll be fine, and I don't want you to treat me differently."

"It's not that ..."

"Then what is it?"

"I'm terrified you'll leave me."

"I'm right here, Ollie."

Ollie shook his head. "No, I'm talking about in here," he said, pointing to his head.

"Touch me," I pleaded. It was all I wanted to feel.

Ollie paused over me. His eyes searched my face.

I lifted his shirt I was wearing over my thighs, over my vulnerability, over my stomach.

His lip twitched as his eyes scanned my body.

"Mia ..." he whispered in a warning.

"Ollie."

"Mia."

"Touch me, Ollie. I need to know you still want me."

Ollie's face twisted as he pulled his brows together. "What are you talking about? I always want you."

"You haven't touched me since you found out what I did," I stated as a matter of fact. And it was true. Ollie hadn't. He'd said whatever had happened wasn't tainted. But he had yet to touch me, and this engulfed me with insecurity. I needed him to take my insecurity away.

Pulling the shirt back down, I felt like a fool. I rolled onto my side, away from him.

"Nothing has changed." Ollie rolled me to my back again. "I want you so fucking bad right now, but you were drugged not even two days ago. I'm trying to respect you."

"Okay," I muttered and dropped my gaze.

"No." He lifted my chin, forcing me to see him. "Don't shut me out." Then he grabbed my thighs and turned me around in a swift movement, bringing me to the edge of the mattress. "I worship you, Mia." He lifted my legs and pulled them apart unapologetically. His lust-filled eyes soaked me up like it was a privilege. "What are my limits, love?"

"You have none."

With sin in his smile, he leaned forward, pulling my shirt up and over my head. I arched my back against him, his body becoming the magnetic pull mine was always drawn to. He withdrew my shirt from over my head and kissed along my jawline before grazing my lips with his tongue. "Just lay here and let me take care of you, then," he whispered against my lips. My body trembled through each word as he ran a palm over my breast and down my side. "Don't move, and just feel me."

Ollie pulled away and stood before grabbing one of my legs. He massaged my foot, to my calf, to my thigh until his thumb brushed my sex. He set my leg down off to the side before grabbing the next leg and repeating the deep massage, giving me everything I didn't know I needed. He dropped my leg off to the other side before collapsing to his knees. With two handfuls, he grabbed the insides of my thighs while his thumbs massaged around my entrance. "You're soaking wet. Is that what I do to you?" My hips involuntarily swayed against his movements, and he pinned me down. "Stay still."

I whimpered as his thumbs continued to tease. Ollie wet his lips, taking one thumb to my knot, making slow unhurried circles, and two fingers of his other hand to keep me spread for him to see all my details. He loved everything about me. And his craving for me drove me to the edge and off the cliff into a land of rapture.

Starting from my entrance, he licked me from bottom to top with pressure, heat, and need before his lips covered my clit, applying forceful flicks against the nerves. Then he went lower to his favorite spot of mine, and the place he knew drove me insane. The spot he did own now, just like the rest of me. But *this* spot. He showed no mercy as his tongue drove inside, scraping along the walls at my entrance where he branded his name.

Subtle moans escaped him as his fingers caressed and kneaded me around his mouth, stretching me so he could have more—digging me into the mattress, opening me up, feeding on me into climax.

My legs shook uncontrollably as his hands slid up and down both sides of my sex around his mouth until one hand found my knot again. "Ollie," I whimpered, the sensation mind-blowing, but begging for more. He did it again, and my hips bucked against him. "Hold on a little longer. Don't let go, baby. I'm not done with you yet," he said with a smirk and dove back in to do it all over again.

My hands found their way to his hair as I pulled, and pinned him against me in a dire need. Ollie's moans vibrated deep within me, loving me entirely from the inside out. The feeling of a thousand sparklers lit, pushing me closer, each lick sending me deeper, each suck taking me higher until I finally cried out. But this didn't stop Ollie. He brought me to the extremity only to capture it for as long as he could. His eyes stayed on mine as he kept me spread and steady, relishing in my pleasure as I came into his mouth. Each time I pushed his head away because it was too intense, he fought harder against me, driving his tongue deeper, pinning against me harder.

But then he did pull away when he knew he had me reeling in a boundless orgasm. Only he knew how to do this. His pants and boxers were already gone when he stood before me. His lips glistened as he watched me come undone.

"Come here," he breathed, and sat on the edge of the mattress, moving his hands to my hips as he pulled me on top of him. My legs trembled as he wrapped them around his waist. "You don't have to do anything except hold on to me."

I wrapped my heavy arms around his neck as I straddled him.

He had complete control of me.

Always.

Ollie pushed my thighs apart as he looked down with hooded eyes. His two thumbs spread me wide as he eased his hard length inside me slowly. Our bodies melted as his eyes screwed shut. "I fucking love that, Mia." He kissed me. "I literally can't move for a second … you're swollen around me, pulsing, thumping. It's the second-best feeling in the world."

He grabbed the back of my head, and his mouth claimed mine. Greedy yet gentle, our tongues flowed as I rolled against him. Ollie moaned as his hand ran up my side and grabbed my breast. His other hand grasped my bottom as I circled over him, taking him deeper.

He dropped his head into my neck, and I took advantage of his weakened state and pressed against his chest until he was lying flat on his back. His green eyes scoured my face and body as I slowly rolled my hips against him, taking him deep and sending his head back.

He gripped my thighs. "*Dammit*, Mia …" he moaned. Ollie tensed as his hands pinned me still, breath held as he pulsed inside me until his body went slack and his eyes clenched shut.

Ollie's chest reached for air underneath my fingertips, and he opened one eye and squinted. "Seven days is too long because that was fucking embarrassing for me." He chuckled and gripped my wrist, bringing me on top of him. My chest crashed against his, and Ollie moved the hair from my face and looked into my eyes. "I love you, Mia, and I'll never not want you."

"What did you mean 'the second-best feeling in the world'?"

Ollie pressed his brows together as his forehead wrinkled. "I tell you I love you and you're stuck on that?" I nodded, and he smiled. "The best feeling is the way you look at me." He shook his head as if nothing he could say would measure up. "The way you look at me makes me feel like I'm someone important, you know? Someone you appreciate, and I'm deserving of you in return. I'm someone you're in awe of, and that feeling is the best feeling in the world, and I'll gladly spend forever making sure I'm worthy of that look."

My flushed cheeks dropped into the curve of his neck. "You read too many books," I said through a laugh.

He rolled me over to my side and held my waist. "Oh, come on now, love. It wasn't even a line. It came from my mind."

"Uh huh … you're a poet, and you didn't even know it?"

Ollie laughed. "That was genius … as skilled as my penis …"

"No, you didn't just say that …"

"Don't deny it, love, because you can't get enough."

"Okay, stop, Slim Shady."

"Alright, alright, I'm done. That was fun." He laughed out. "Shit, why can't I quit?"

Smiling, I pressed my lips to his to help him.

TWENTY-SIX

"If reality becomes unbearable, close your eyes.
We were made with an imagination."

OLIVER MASTERS

School would resume from the Christmas holiday in precisely three days. One more day was all I had asked from Ollie before he told Dean Lynch everything. Only one more day. His only plan was telling the truth about what had happened in his room. *Truth.* Not only would this take away our nightly get-togethers, but this was grounds for punishment for the four of us.

With what happened to Bria, I sounded selfish. Our nightly get-togethers didn't hold a candle to what this could mean for Ollie and his future, or Bria's future, but Ollie was very adamant about being an honest man.

"How can I continue to love you if at the end of the day I can't even love myself?" he had asked me the night before. *"And if I don't do this, Mia, not doing the right thing turns into regret, and regret turns into hate, and the hate will slowly grow*

into resentment, and I never want hate or resentment to reside in either one of our lives, no matter the outcome."

And no matter how quickly I could forget what had happened in his room after midnight on New Year's, I knew this was something he could never forgive himself for if he chose to stay quiet.

It was breakfast time, and Zeke acted strange as he rocked back and forth in his chair. "Ollie will be here soon," I said to him, trying to ease his nerves, but it didn't seem to work.

Ollie had gone to visit Bria at the nurse's station early this morning. Jake and Alicia sat at the old table, and I hadn't seen Isaac's face since New Year's. I couldn't say I wasn't relieved.

One good thing about Ollie coming clean: I would never see Isaac or Oscar again.

I couldn't bring myself to see Bria yet, but there was one thing I never was good at—being there for others when something terrible had happened. Over the last ten years, if someone had a loved one pass away, I'd steered clear of engaging in conversation. Empathy had never been a strong suit of mine, and in my defense, I hadn't had feelings, so really, I'd been doing them a favor. Though I had feelings now, I'd become socially awkward—never knowing the right things to say. I'd learned words were like swords. Once the words left your mouth, they couldn't be taken back. They couldn't be erased. Words, once they were in the air around you, would forever leave marks—imprinting the world.

Sometimes the best things to say was nothing at all.

I lifted my eyes in time to see Ollie turn the corner and enter the mess hall. His boyish grin appeared as his green eyes lit up like they always did when he saw me. Ollie wore his black tee, gray joggers, and Converse. He'd finally had his hair cut at the nurse's station, so he was able to style it again like he used to.

Ollie took the seat beside me and immediately acknowledged Zeke before pressing his forehead to the side of my head. "Good morning, love." He kissed my head and squeezed my thigh under the table as I leaned into him. His small gestures were always capable of making my heart flutter inside my chest. "I'm going to get breakfast," he said before excusing himself.

As soon as Ollie stood, the sight of Dean Lynch walking into the mess hall made the entire room go quiet. Two security guards walked behind Lynch with a police officer to follow. They walked toward us as Ollie followed my gaze and turned around.

"Oliver Masters?" the officer asked, and I frantically looked back and forth between Ollie, Lynch, and the officer's face for any indication of what was happening. My chest tightened, and my flutter turned into a hammer.

"Yes, sir," Ollie replied, but hesitation clouded his tone.

"This is him," Lynch confirmed.

"Masters, you are being arrested for the rape of Bria Nielson and possession of an illegal substance. Please turn around and put your hands behind your back," the officer said, twisting Ollie's arm and pinning him against the table.

"Dean, I didn't do this." Ollie shook his head. "You have to believe me."

Chaos befell as Zeke broke out into a scream and threw himself out of the chair.

"That wasn't Ollie! This wasn't his fault!" I cried out, standing to my feet. One of the guards tried to manhandle Zeke. "Don't touch him. You can't touch him!" My brain went haywire. My senses strung out. Zeke's screams pierced the room, the guard yelled, and the officer threw Ollie into the table.

Lynch averted his eyes from Zeke. "The only thing to help you right now, Oliver, is your cooperation."

"This is bullshit, and you know it." Ollie shook his head and looked up at me, the betrayal and shock in his eyes, but he still held on to the tiny bit of strength he had. "Mia, look at me and listen …" My vision fogged as my gaze darted between Zeke and Ollie. "Don't trust anyone. Keep your head down—"

"No, Ollie ..." I said, shaking my head, denying this was happening at all.

"Just bloody listen." He struggled for a bit to give us more time. "Whatever happens, don't turn it off. You have to stay even when I'm gone, alright?"

"Alright," I whispered through tears as he flinched under the officer's applied pressure at his wrist.

Ollie took in a deep breath as he held my gaze. The suffering pricked in his eyes, but it wasn't the physical kind. This was a suffering I'd seen when he struggled to fight back his emotions. "Close your eyes, Mia."

I closed my eyes, giving permission for my silent tears to fall. I gripped the table in front of me to keep me steady, and I never wanted to open my eyes again. I knew once I opened them, the reality of all of this would hit, and I would never be ready for it. So, I kept them closed tight, imagining every moment Ollie had created for us. Him and me on a typical Sunday morning. I fought to smell the coffee and feel the sun, the warmth of his body beside mine as he read to me. Us walking a boardwalk hand in hand. The two of us watching the sunrise with our feet in the sand and the salty breeze in my hair. The hot tears spilling down my cheeks was the only constant reminder that if I opened my eyes, none of it was real.

A hand against my back turned me and Jake wrapped his arms around me. I kept my eyes closed as I cried into his chest. "He'll be okay, Mia." His hand against my back did nothing to soothe me as he held me tight, attempting to take my pain away, but it was only Ollie who held that power.

And Ollie was gone.

"You need to tell them the truth, Bria. You know damn well Ollie isn't capable of this." It was the first time I'd seen Bria since New Year's, and she lay in the hospital bed, still recovering. Pacing back and forth in front of her bed, I was desperate. She was his only hope.

Bria was as shocked as I was. "Mia … I … I tried telling them. I told them everything I know. One minute I was drinking, the next I'm waking up in the nurse's station."

"Did you tell them Isaac was there? That Oscar was there?"

"Oscar was never there, Mia!" My stomach did a one-eighty before launching up my throat. "And, yes, I told them about Isaac being there, but I really don't think Isaac would rape me. Especially since I was more than willing to have sex with him. You know that. He knew that…"

"You're kidding me, right?" I placed two hands beside her as I leaned over. "I saw it with my own eyes, Bria. You were on the floor, butt-ass naked and unconscious. Isaac raped you."

"Then why didn't you do anything about it?" she sneered.

I threw my hands in the air. "I couldn't move, or else I would have!"

Flashes of Oscar kicking Bria out of the way like a ragdoll flooded my mind, and I couldn't believe Bria was so naïve. Ollie was being set up, again, by his brother. It was the perfect plan, but this time, he had me.

Pushing off the hospital bed, I took one last look at Bria, who lay there defeated. "I'm sorry this happened to you, but you know Ollie wouldn't do this. You need to open your eyes. Who is the only person who has come to check on you since you've been here? I bet Isaac never fucking came in here." The look on her face twisted and though I couldn't read it, I knew she was a lost cause. I turned and walked away, heading straight for Ollie's dorm.

Ollie's things were already packed up and gone like he'd never been here. I collapsed over his mattress and closed my eyes. The rage boiled, and I could feel it first in my fist as I dug my nails into the palms of my hands. I jumped off the mattress, the same mattress we'd fallen asleep on so many times before. The same mattress where he'd read to me. The same mattress where we'd made love. Adrenaline pumping through my bloodstream, I grabbed the side of the mattress and threw it across the room as I cried out.

My face fell into my hands as I sobbed. My legs buckled as I collapsed to my knees. "What did Ollie ever do to you to deserve this?" I asked out loud, desperation in my tone, heart, and soul. Was I so desperate, I had turned to God? I had to be going insane. As I shook my head, the cries only deepened, coming from the pit of my stomach. "What the hell am I even doing ... You never listened. You never helped. We're your little puppets on a damn string as you sit on your throne and toy with people's lives. Well, you know what? You're fucking sick!"

Dropping my head, my eyes landed on Ollie's phone in front of me along with *The Notebook*. It must have been under the mattress.

My cries faded as I held the phone in my trembling hand. The phone was on, but it only had a quarter of its battery life left. Gathering to my feet, I stuffed the phone into my back pocket and swiped the book off the floor before heading back to my room.

It was day two without Ollie. The fog from the day before had lifted, denial dissipated, but it hadn't taken me along with it. I was stranded and alone, and all I could think about was what he must be going through. Where was he? Was he even still on campus at all?

I finished *The Notebook*, and I wondered if Ollie had noticed the same similarities in the story as I. It was Ollie who always reeled me back in, to fight for me, to wake me up, to bring me back, to remind me, like Noah reminded Allie. Ollie never did anything without a purpose. Every word, every action, every movement was carefully considered. He'd known since we first opened this book what it would take to find me inside my walls. He'd known this whole time how difficult it would be, and he allowed himself to love me, anyway.

Day three wasn't any better, only worse. I ate, but only because I had to stay, and stay strong. I showered and spent the entire Sunday in the library because it was the place I could feel closest to him. Jake and Alicia tried to talk to me, but Ollie's absence didn't disrupt their lives as much as it corrupted mine. They couldn't understand.

Zeke was my silent rock.

It was the first day back in classes, and I showered in the morning, ate breakfast, and attended the first class of my new schedule for the second semester. The halls reverberated, bodies bumped into one another, and I pushed my way back toward my dorm after my second class before I was pulled away from the hall and into a closet.

Black eyes sliced into me as Oscar backed me into a corner. The bulb hanging from the ceiling swayed back and forth, casting shadows and lights over Oscar's face. "Hi, pet," he sneered—a smirk forming on his face. If I didn't have anything left to lose, I might have been scared, but I wasn't afraid anymore. I knew it was only a matter of time before he would try to flush me out and get me alone. "Have you been keeping your pretty mouth shut?" He ran his fingers over my lips as he took a step closer.

"I don't remember much, anyway." I may not have been scared, but I was done being stupid.

"Aw, what a shame. I was about to make you feel really good before my little brother got in our way. Fucker broke my nose."

I bit the inside of my cheek. "You must have deserved it, then."

Oscar smiled. "Deserved it, yeah?" The evil in his black heart corrupted his smile quickly when his eyes narrowed. "Let's get one thing straight. Oliver should have never taken what was mine. He knows better."

"Is that why you drugged us? To take what's yours because you can't have me any other way?"

"I didn't drug you. Isaac did."

"Did you rape Bria?" I knew he didn't, but I needed to keep him talking.

"Does that bother you, Mia?" He wrapped his arm around my back, reaching for my bottom, but I quickly moved his hand to the front of me. "Did it make you jealous?"

"A little." I lifted my shoulder in a half shrug as Oscar undid the button on my jeans. "So you or Ollie never touched Bria? Only Isaac did?" His eager hand applied pressure over my jeans. I didn't flinch. All I wanted was his confession.

"You want me to tell you how I fucked that little slut? Will it make you want me more?"

"I want to know the truth."

Before Oscar could pull my jeans down, I slipped the phone from my back pocket and set it high on a shelf beside me with the recording still on without him noticing. "I don't want you after you've been with Bria."

Oscar's hooded eyes searched my face as he grabbed my chin. "I didn't bloody touch her. Your boy Isaac did, but for you—" He tried to kiss me, but I pulled away.

"For me what? What did you give me and what were you going to do?"

"Just a little something to help you relax." He smiled, then yanked down my jeans. "See how tense you are without it?"

Okay, now I was getting scared. I had what I needed. I had Oscar's confession. "You need to go, Oscar." I couldn't run out of here. I needed the phone. I couldn't leave it on, or it would die. I'd been waiting this entire time for him to confront me, and this moment was here. I'd never thought about what would come next after getting the confession.

"I'm taking what you owe me." He gathered my panties in one hand and moved them to the side when I spit in his face.

"I don't owe you shit."

A sudden force whipped my head around, and my face slammed against the side of the shelf. My hand immediately shot to my face from the initial burn on impact.

"You hit me," I whispered in shock. A man has never hit me before, and suddenly I couldn't feel the pain from it. I pushed against his chest, but he gathered my hands in one of his and slammed my face forward into another wall.

Something came over me, and I screamed at the top of my lungs before Oscar threw his hand over my mouth. I bit his fingers and screamed again until he covered them. He threw his weight against me, pinning me to the wall and pressing my face against it as he threatened me. But his threats were useless now. He had nothing to hold over my head anymore. Ollie was the only card he had left, and Ollie was already gone. Tears fell from my eyes as my screams muffled against his hand.

The doorknob jiggled on the other side. Someone was trying to come in. Oscar's entire body tensed against me as he held his hand tight over my mouth. He waited for the jiggling to stop and then I felt a blow to the back of my head.

It was almost midnight, but the string lights all around me lit up the sky before the fireworks could. "Mia!" someone shouted. "Can you believe we're here? We're in fucking London of all places! New Year's, baby!" The girl handed me a drink, the liquid splashing over the rim and onto the cobblestone ground beneath me. My freshly manicured nails got my attention. They were pink. "Mia, come on. It's almost midnight." The happy girl with big brown eyes and brown hair grabbed my hand as she pulled me down the path. People buzzed all around us. Smiling faces, lights, a Ferris wheel. The crisp winter air took my breath away as we ran through the street. Laughing, music, and conversations blurred together as this happy girl shouted against the wind and noise. "We're almost there!" We stopped along the edge of the water line as the smells of boat fuel, salty ocean, and fried food filled my nose.

I leaned over the railing and looked down below into the black sea as soon as the fireworks went off overhead. The reflection of the colors bled across the surface of the black ocean, and I lifted my head when the lights sizzled into waterfalls, cascading in the night sky. The fireworks dimmed, leaving a trace of smoke before new colors took their place.

"Beautiful," a slow, deep voice said beside me. I turned my head to see bright green eyes—eyes more captivating than the fireworks. My entire body turned to face him. He had his arms folded over the railing, hunched over, but his head turned toward me with an awe-struck grin. He wore a white sweatshirt, black Converse, and his jeans were faded and ripped at the knees, and fit him perfectly.

I found his eyes again. "Yeah, it is," I whispered.

The guy shook his head and chuckled. "No, love. I wasn't talking about the fireworks." Heat rose in my cheeks as he turned his whole body to face me and leaned into his side. "Tell me your name."

"Mia," I said in reflex, unsure of how the words were able to leave me as I'd forgot everything else I'd ever known.

The guy held out his hand. I reached to shake it, but instead, he grabbed my hand and spun me around before pulling my back against his chest. His hands returned to the railing as he caged me in, but I didn't mind. He didn't scare me.

He pressed his head against the side of mine and whispered, "I'm Ollie. You know what tonight is, Mia?"

"New Year's?" My response was accurate, but I felt foolish for saying it.

"Tonight is the night we'll be telling our kids about one day. The night my life changed."

A relieved smile washed over me as another firework blasted from the charter boat off in the distance. My eyes followed the rocket up into the sky, and as soon as the colors burst over us, a gust of wind smacked me in the face. He pulled me closer against him, wrapping his long arms around me to keep me warm. He smelled of nostalgia and marine breeze, with a hint of cologne. I closed my eyes to take in this moment.

"No, Mia. Now open your eyes."

"Mia, wake up. Open your eyes." My eyes sprung open to see the nurse hovering over me with a flashlight pointed directly in my eyes. I squinted against the light when she said, "Oh, good. Now follow my fingers."

The nurse held a finger between us and moved it from side to side. I did as I was told, still confused to where I was and what was going on.

She dropped her finger and her head all at once. "Do you remember what happened?"

My eyes blinked rapidly. "Ollie," I said. *Oscar.* The phone. I stumbled to my feet with the nurse's assistance.

The nurse looked me up and down. "You're going to have to come to the station."

I looked down to see my jeans down to my ankles. Shaking my head, I reached up for the phone and exhaled when I felt it beneath my fingers. "Please, I need to see Dean Lynch. It's important."

"You will definitely have to talk with the dean, dear," she explained as she pulled up my pants, and I clutched the phone in my hand.

TWENTY-SEVEN

"And suddenly, when all is lost,
she becomes an explosion of home."

OLIVER MASTERS

"Good news is, I don't see any evidence of rape," the nurse said as she took off her latex gloves and rolled her chair over to a wastebasket to toss them. "But you have a mild concussion." The nurse released my feet from the stirrups and set my legs out flat in front of me. She rolled her stool to the side of my bed, and she looked at me with the most delicate eyes a strong woman like her could have. "Mia, who attacked you? Who did this?" She genuinely cared.

The phone clutched in my hand burned a hole. "I need Dean Lynch," was all I could say. She probably knew Oscar, and they were most likely acquaintances or possibly had lunch together. I couldn't trust anyone.

My angel of a nurse sighed as I pulled the white sheet higher over me.

"Dean Lynch and an officer are already on their way to take a statement."

I was able to exhale, calmer than I had been since Ollie was arrested. "Thank you for finding me." I would have looked up to tell her, but the bright lamp above me was blinding.

"I didn't find you. The janitor found you in his closet and came and got me. I'm only doing my job." She patted my leg and stood. The way she said *"I'm only doing my job"* made her either humble or aloof. Nurses shouldn't say things like that. "Now try to stay awake. I'll flip on the telly to keep your brain occupied, yeah?"

"Yeah, okay," I mumbled.

Fifteen minutes into a British soap opera, the Dean and an officer walked in. It was a different officer, not the same one who had taken Ollie days before.

Dean Lynch introduced him as Officer Scott. The blue-eyed and dirty-red-haired man in uniform seemed less threatening than the one who had taken Ollie away from me. He was young, as if he was fresh out of the academy. He looked at me, and his face fell. You could tell he was new at this and didn't quite know how to handle himself. "Now, Officer Scott here is going to take your statement. Do you feel comfortable with me staying in the room?" Dean Lynch asked.

Yes. I prefer it. But, "Where is Ollie?" was my reply. Maybe I shouldn't have asked. I didn't want Lynch to assume my only mission was to get Ollie out. Somehow, it made my story a little less credible by bringing up Ollie so soon.

Lynch adjusted his suit jacket before crossing his arms. "Ollie is being held here in solitary confinement, but we need to talk about what happened to you." The vague answer, then re-direct tactic. He must have learned that in training.

I looked over to Officer Scott, and his eyes set on mine. He examined my face, but my gaze didn't hinder him. I brought my fingers to my face, and there was a slight sting under my eye. There must have been a bruise or a scratch. I hadn't looked in the mirror yet. "Oscar," I said.

Lynch's arms tightened against his chest as his brows furrowed. "My security guard Oscar?"

"Oscar is Ollie's brother," I informed them. "Did you know?" I was angry at the fact the Dean could know this and put Ollie in this situation in the first place.

"No, I didn't know." He sighed.

"You should do more extensive background checks." Lynch shook his head, and I continued, "Oscar did this to me. Isaac was the one who raped Bria, and Oscar and Isaac were the ones who drugged us." He shot me a skeptical look, and I held up the phone. "Here is Oscar's confession."

Together, Lynch and Officer Scott listened to the recording. Officer Scott's eyes darted back and forth from me to the phone. Lynch's nostrils flared, and his eyes only grew bigger after each word that came from Oscar's mouth. Furious, he excused himself immediately.

Officer Scott bagged the phone for evidence, but he stayed behind.

"Mind if I ask you a few more questions?"

"Sure," I said and adjusted in the bed. "Has anyone ever told you that you look like Prince Harry?"

He chuckled. "More than you know." He rolled over a chair and kept a safe distance from the hospital bed as he rested his pad and pen on the bedside table. "I know what you're thinking, I look young, but you can trust me."

"What makes you believe I don't trust you?"

Officer Scott raised a brow. "I can see it on your face, and I can't even begin to understand what you have been through." He paused and drew in a breath. "My younger sister was," he stopped, shook his head, "Look, I know the nurse said you weren't raped, but I'm trained to follow my gut, and my gut tells me you haven't told the entire story."

His blue eyes wouldn't turn away from mine; they held on, shouting at me, telling me he was sincere, and my eyes watered. "My story, Officer Scott, would keep you here for a couple of hours."

He didn't smile. He didn't flinch. "Please, call me Ethan. I'm still not used to people saying Officer Scott quite yet."

"What do you want to know?"

He pulled up his chair an inch closer and relaxed a bit. "Start from the beginning."

It was the first time I had gotten through my whole story without crying. Ethan listened intently and never once reached for his pen to take notes. He had to close his eyes a few times to lessen the blow I was sure was all too familiar with his sister he almost mentioned. He was kind, and by the end of our conversation, he slipped me his card to call him in case I would ever need it.

Examining his card, I knew I wouldn't have a chance to call him if I ever needed help. "I think you forgot where I am."

Ethan dropped his head into his hand and shook his head. "Sorry, I get lost in the routine of things." He let out a small sigh. "To be honest with you, you're making me nervous."

"Why do I make you nervous?"

"You just told me your whole story, and I'm sitting here thinking how much I admire your strength." He stood and fixed his shirt. "I wish my sister could have been here to hear your story. There are a lot of young girls out there who feel they're alone. Maybe if they had someone to talk to who went through similar experiences, they would feel a little less pain and a little less alone."

"You can always bring your sister here. I'd love to talk to her."

"I appreciate that, Mia, but she left this world nine months ago now. I didn't protect her when I should have, and I'll spend the rest of my life making up for it." I nodded, but my heart felt the depth of his sorrows as if they strangled me. "Anyway, thank you for your time. Call me if you come into any more trouble …" He rubbed his forehead and rolled his head back. "I keep forgetting … Don't call me, Mia. Well, you can if you can, of course." He shook his head. "Okay, I'm just going to walk out the door now."

He turned, and my fingers shot out to stop him. He paused mid-step and turned back to face me. "I'm sorry about your sister, Ethan. She would be so proud of you."

Ethan had moved me forward two steps in the last hour, and he would never be able to understand how he'd been a part of putting two more pieces back into their original places. He'd helped me, and all he'd had to do was sit there and listen.

"Thank you," he sincerely said, and squeezed my hand before walking out the door.

Ethan was right. So many people who went through the same trauma as mine, and it would be a waste if I didn't share my story and help others out of their darkness. If no one was there to hear them, to understand them, to carry them, I wanted to be that one.

I was discharged the day after with instructions from my Nurse Angel to take it easy. "You'll experience headaches, but don't hesitate to stop in and I'll give you something to ease the pain," she explained. "You will resume class tomorrow."

As I walked through the halls back to my room, the oversized gray sweatshirt and drawstring pants draped over my body. It was the only clothes the nurse had. Maintenance maneuvered their way, dorm by dorm while everyone was in class. They checked vents, and filtered through belongings. I was sure everyone would hate me, but I didn't care. All I cared about was clearing Ollie's name.

During lunch, gossip spread like wildfire. Isaac had been taken into custody while I had been recovering, Oscar was still M.I.A., and Ollie was still locked in solitary confinement. Bria sat in silence at her table with Jake and Alicia, her attention trained on the tray before her, but she wasn't eating. Even though Bria was in denial about what had happened, I knew it wouldn't be long before the aftermath of what Isaac had done to her would kick in. It wasn't the fact she may never remember, but it was the knowing, and eventually, the knowing built walls without the need for memories. It was only a matter of time.

"Hi, Zeke," I said as I sat across from him. "Sorry I wasn't here yesterday."

Zeke grunted and looked around. A part of me believed he was looking for Ollie. He wanted to see Ollie. I wanted to see Ollie. "He should be back soon."

And that was how the rest of lunch went.

My appointment with Dr. Conway wasn't canceled along with my classes. I was still required to see her. After I walked into her office, I avoided eye contact and took a seat on the leather couch. Our visits since Maddie's return had fallen into a redundant routine: me being vague, and her being intrusive.

"I was going to visit you at the nurse's station, but you were discharged before I had the chance," she immediately explained.

It was an hour past noon, but shades of gray were smeared across the sky. Dr. Conway's window faced the front of campus, and sitting in front of the building was a police car.

"Mia?"

"Yeah?" I lifted my head in time to see Dean Lynch and Officer Scott—I mean Ethan—exit the building and walk toward the police car.

"Do you want to talk about what happened?"

They shook hands, and for a split second, I caught Ethan with a smile. I had never seen his smile. It was hardly there, but the corner of his mouth lifted slightly, and my heart slowly unraveled from his sorrowful strangle.

"Ah, Ethan Scott … he's got good genes."

Cocking my head at Dr. Conway, I said, "You know him?"

"I was introduced. He starts here next week."

"I thought he was a police officer?"

"He is. After what happened with Oscar, Dean Lynch found it necessary to strap down on security. He feels police presence is crucial for the safety of our students, and I couldn't agree more, but don't get any ideas. He's a good one."

"Afraid I'm going to corrupt him?" I smirked.

Dr. Conway peered down at me with an all-knowing glare.

"Relax. It's not like that, anyway." I turned back in the leather chair after Ethan got into his car. "I met him while I was in recovery. He told me about his sister, and it was the first time I think I comforted someone. I don't know. It sounds ridiculous." She was staring at me, wide eyes and smiling now. "*Crap*, I forgot I'm not talking to you. I'm still mad at you."

Her smile disappeared as she narrowed her eyes. "What did I do?" I looked back at the window and watched the police car leave through gates. "Mia, now you're being ridiculous."

My head snapped back in her direction. "Why did you bring Maddie back?"

"You know I can't talk about other students with you. That's not fair."

"She's manipulative. She's lying…She isn't even taking her medication, you know."

Dr. Conway crossed her legs and leaned her elbow over the desk. "This has been all about Maddie? You know, if you just would have talked to me about it, it wouldn't have had to go on this long, and you wouldn't have over-analyzed this whole situation."

I didn't respond, so Dr. Conway continued, "One thing you need to learn, Mia, is you need to start getting it out. You have too much going on inside your head, and if you don't let it out, one of two things will happen. Either you will have a panic attack, or your volcano will erupt like the time in the bathroom or the time you punched the wall."

"What's the point if you won't even explain to me why you brought Maddie back?"

"Because if you never ask, the answer will always be no. A rejection is better than a regret. You can learn to live with rejection, but regret haunts you for the rest of your life."

I fell back into the cracked leather and held my head in my hands. Exhaustion swallowed me entirely. My limbs were weak, my mind was mush, and all I wanted to do was cry, but I was too tired to deal with the tears.

"When was the last time you had a full six hours of sleep?" she asked, reading my mind and body language all at once. It had been a week since I'd had a full six hours. Since Ollie was taken, I hadn't been able to sleep more than two hours at a time.

"My brain is fried. I can't think past five seconds ago."

"Go to your room and get some sleep, Mia. Oscar can't get into Dolor. He can't hurt you anymore."

For four days, I debated whether or not to waltz into Dean Lynch's office. Each time I paced my room, I played out the entire conversation in my head—what I would say, and whether or not I should take no for an answer. Dean Lynch had Oscar's confession. He didn't need Ollie anymore. Ollie was innocent. Why wasn't Ollie with me this very moment?

It was morning, and Lynch was always in a better mood in the morning. Not a good mood, but a better mood. My palms were sweaty and my knees went weak as I walked down the wide spiral staircase. It smelled different on the first floor in the morning. The smell was new, a beginning, a million opportunities hiding behind a glass wall, ready for someone to break it. The crisp scent was like a dare.

The handle on his office door was cold to the touch as I opened it after knocking. The smell of coffee instantly wrapped around my tongue and watered my taste buds. Lynch didn't show any signs of how my unexpected presence affected him as he offered for me to sit.

"Why hasn't Ollie been released yet when we both know now he didn't do this?" I immediately asked as soon as I took the seat.

Lynch leaned back into his chair, and his face struggled to react to my question. He stared at me with sunken eyes. "Miss Jett, you can't show up unannounced and demand answers."

"I announced myself when I'd knocked on the door. What is keeping Ollie in solitary?"

Lynch looked down at his tailored suit and rolled his shoulders as he fixed his jacket. He probably thought this was going to be one of those days. He snapped his wrist and glanced at his watch. *Yes, Lynch, it's too early for this.* "I shouldn't be telling you this. Oliver had a … setback while in confinement. He will be released as soon as he is cooperative and agrees to go back on his treatment plan and take his prescribed medication."

Were we talking about the same Ollie? Ollie wouldn't risk a setback. "What did he do?"

"I'm not at liberty to say." His voice was clipped and direct. He was already over the conversation. He had other pressing matters to take care of. Ollie wasn't one of those important matters, but Ollie was *my* important matter.

"Please, let me see him. I can get through to him. He'll listen to me." He had already said too much, and now I was overreaching at this point. The air around me changed. It grew thicker, and too much oxygen was being shoved down my throat.

Dean Lynch chuckled as if my request disrespected him in a way. Though he chuckled, it was only because my request was absurd and the tension suddenly ignited. "Absolutely not."

"Dean Lynch, with all due respect, this is a reformatory institution meant to help people, not to destroy them even more. Now, you had him arrested when he did nothing wrong, shoved him into an isolated room for a week, and now he's probably scared and lashing out because he feels no one is on his side."

Lynch, his mother, his brother, and Isaac were all supposed to be on his side, and each one of them had failed him. Ollie had to know I wouldn't fail him. I was on his side. He wasn't alone.

"Excuse me, Miss Jett, but he is in no way innocent in this, and neither are you. He may not have raped or drugged anyone, but he has broken more rules than one."

Lynch had a point. We'd broken the rules. "I understand. Really, I do. But if you could just let me see him, I can talk to him, convince him to take the meds, he can get out and go back to his normal routine. Please. Give me five minutes with him."

Lynch stared at me for a long hard moment. I held my breath as he stood from his chair and walked toward the door. I closed my eyes, waiting for his words of dismissal. "Well, come on, then."

We walked through the corridor and down a flight of stairs to the basement—another security checkpoint. I'd been down here once before. It was quiet and bitter. There were three rooms on each side of the hallway. From experience, I knew nothing was in those rooms. The walls were padded much like my room, and there was no window, bed, or furniture. The rooms were meant to break you into submission.

Ollie wasn't created to be broken down—he was created to burn bright.

Lynch stopped before one of the doors. "Five minutes," he stated without looking at me, then stepped back as a guard unlocked the door.

After the door opened, my heart immediately caved. Ollie sat on the floor in the corner with his long legs bent at the knees. His head hung over his folded arms, and I couldn't see his face. When the door closed behind me, he lifted his head, and his whole face changed when he saw me. At first, it was a look of denial, as if his mind played tricks on him. The lump in his throat moved when he swallowed, and then he blew out a shaky breath.

"Ollie?"

His whole body reacted to my voice, and his shoulders shook. He clenched his eyes, and my heart broke for him all over again. Suddenly, he pinched the bridge of his nose as the tears fell.

I collapsed on my knees before him, gripping his legs. Ollie had reached utter ruin, and he was ashamed as he held his face in his hands and lowered his head into a silent cry. He was rendered powerless, stripped. *Gutted.* Ollie arrived at his rock bottom, and I had never wanted anything more than to switch places with him.

Ollie had never prepared me for these kinds of tears. The overwhelming ones when seeing the one you love carrying so much pain, with the entire heavy world pressing down on you.

"I'm right here," I choked out through staggering tears. I was scared to touch him, but couldn't bring myself not to. I gripped his hair, and he dropped his head into my neck.

"I've never had so much hate in my heart," were his first words. He pulled back, and his eyes were clouded with mist, his long lashes soaked with tears. His chin trembled. "I'm so angry, and I'm going fucking mad. I want to kill him, Mia." Ollie's breath wavered as he tried to get it under control. "I don't know what I've done. What is it about me others seem to hate so much. All I've done was try to do the right thing, make sure everyone was happy, and in return, I get this"—he threw his palms in the air—"shoved in a bloody corner and hated on." He turned his head away, not wanting me to see him like this. His cheeks puffed as an unstable breath blew from his lips. "And now I even hate myself for what he did to you."

The words seemed so foreign from his lips.

"Look at me," I pleaded, and Ollie shook his head. I grabbed his face to force him to see me. "I love you so much. Give me your hate, let me carry it all for you because I have enough love to crush your burdens. There is so much, and there is nothing anyone can do to diminish that. I'm right here, Ollie. You don't have to be strong anymore. You only have to hold on, okay?"

Ollie's hardly used frown line between his brows deepened. "He raped you!" he whisper-shouted. "He stood right out there and bragged about it, wanting me to hear every bloody word."

"No, Ollie. He didn't. He never got the chance. He hit me. I had a concussion. I wasn't raped."

His eyes fixed on me for a moment as my words set in, and then he exhaled. His once weakened body went rigid. "He fucking hit you?" His voice was full of guilt and remorse as he looked me in the eyes.

"It's over now. I got Oscar's full confession recorded. You can leave here, Ollie."

Ollie shook his head. "Please don't tell me you put yourself in that situation on purpose."

"No, of course not. I knew it would have only been a matter of time before Oscar tried again. So I carried your phone with me just in case, everywhere I went. I had to have proof it was him."

There was a sudden lift in the air when Ollie wrapped his arms around me and finally pulled me to him. He reached for the back of my head, and even though I was supposed to be the strong one, I melted in his hold.

"The only way they'll let me out is if I take my medication," he said into my neck.

I pulled him away to see him. "What did you do?"

"I was so angry after I heard that, and when my door opened, I didn't care who was on the other side. I fucking lost it." Ollie fell back against the wall and ran his hands through his hair. "What do you want me to do, Mia?"

"I convinced Lynch to let me see you. I told him I could convince you to take your prescription so you'll get out of here, but I can't be selfish. I can't tell you to do something you don't want to do. It wouldn't be fair. I just want you to be okay."

"I'm so scared of what will happen to us if I take it. I know how I was before, and you will hate me, Mia. I'm certain of it. I was dead. No conscience. On the meds, I just didn't care about anything. I was numb."

My heart was in my throat. The panic of the possibility consumed me, but Ollie loved me. The small voice in the back of my head convinced me he couldn't possibly be capable of making me hate him. "It's not possible. We can't be tainted, remember?"

"We can if it's no longer *me*," he stated with confidence. There was a long pause, and the worry grew bigger and bigger. "And when I take the meds, and they let me out of here, you have to promise you will bring me back, alright?"

Bring him back? Bring him back from what? What did the medication turn him into? None of this was making sense. As I remembered our conversation about what had happened with Maddie, I'd always thought it was because of how insane she was, not because of Ollie's side effects from his pills. "How do I bring you back?"

"You have to remind me. You have to find a way." He was so sure this would happen that there was no doubt in his tone. He didn't even want me to have an ounce of hope. From the look on his face, he was telling me he would, in fact, change, his feelings for me would, in fact, change, and there was nothing he could do about it.

"Let's go, Mia," a voice said and I turned to see Dean Lynch with his head popped through the door.

"Shit." Ollie sighed as we got to our feet. "I love you, Mia ... always. You have to remember that, alright?"

I nodded, and he looked past me to Lynch as he ran his nervous hand through his hair and gripped the ends.

Another tear fell from his eye as his breathing turned jagged. "Fuck it," he said and crashed his mouth to mine in a last attempt of desperation to convince me, or remind himself, or give himself something to hold on to, or all of it. He grabbed my face as he pressed his forehead to mine and his warm tears transferred to my cheek as he gasped for air.

"Close your eyes, Ollie," I whispered, bringing my hands over his and removing them from my face. Ollie clenched his eyes closed as more tears shot down like dying stars.

I took one last look at him, hoping the next time I would see him, nothing would change. We were stronger than any pill. It seemed extreme, what medication could turn people into, and maybe he was overreacting. Medicine couldn't come between us. He was confident it would, but I was confident what we had could conquer anything.

TWENTY-EIGHT

"There's a villain in all of us.
Some are just better at deceiving."

OLIVER MASTERS

They found Oscar. I wished I was more relieved than I was. Dean Lynch showed up to my dorm before breakfast one morning to tell me the news, and relief hadn't quite washed over me yet. It wouldn't until I saw Ollie again, and it had been another tormenting week since I'd left him in solitary confinement. I wondered what was taking him so long. Had he changed his mind on taking the medication?

I went through the same routine, waking up as soon as the automatic doors unlocked, took a shower, brushed my teeth, read in my dorm for another hour until breakfast. I'd hated to read before, but getting lost in a novel was the only way to get by. It wasn't the same as when Ollie read to me, but I still found comfort in it—even if it was a little. I held on to the small part of happiness until I could wrap my arms around it.

Holding on to the possibility of a future with Ollie did not succumb with each passing day. I only held on stronger, fought harder. The vision of seeing his eyes light up when he met new people, seeing him cry with them through their pain, being a part of his growth, success, and his poetry … I wanted to be a part of it all. And now I had found my purpose; I also wanted to be there for girls across the world who were scared and alone. Learning to become empathetic was a whole new thing for me, and Ethan, the police officer, had introduced me to a side of myself I hadn't known I was capable of, never fathoming how much it would touch me.

Today, I wore Ollie's hoodie over my Dolor shirt. The temperature on campus only turned colder. His scent of freedom left unscathed as I pulled it over my head. It was the first time I smiled as the drifting scent in the air hugged me.

There was a gloominess in the mess hall without Ollie's presence.

"Care if I sit with you and Zeke today?" Jake asked as he stood beside me in the lunch line. His smile was gone, too, but I doubted it was because of Ollie's absence. "Alicia and I are in a tiff."

This thing between Jake and Alicia seemed to be happening at least once a month. "Maybe you two are on the same cycle."

Jake tilted his head, and his forehead wrinkled as we moved along the buffet line. "Bloody hell, maybe you're right. What's it called? Sympathy period?" Normally, he would have giggled, but he didn't. It was because of Ollie. He was gone, and he'd taken his bright light over everyone with him.

I shrugged. "Don't forget to acknowledge Zeke."

"Yeah, yeah … I know the rules," Jake muttered.

As we left the lunch line of the breakfast buffet, my legs came to a standstill, and I suddenly forgot how to breathe. My heart beat in my eardrums, and the quickening of my pulse traveled down to the tips of my fingers.

Ollie stood in the entryway of the mess hall under the curved arch. My eyes scanned the outline of his silhouette of his side profile. His hands were stuffed deep in his pockets. He wore the same white tee, black jeans, and

Converse. His hair was perfectly styled into his backward wave. Paralysis prevented me from dropping my tray right where I was standing, and run toward him. I couldn't move.

Frozen.

"What's wrong?" Jake asked, but I couldn't respond.

I waited for Ollie to find me as he talked to another student—one I didn't know the name of. Why wasn't he looking for me?

Find me, Ollie. Lift your head and find me.

"Ollie's back!" Jake called out.

Ollie turned his head at the sound of his name, and our eyes met. It was no longer the same eyes I had looked into so many times before. Now, only an emptiness resided where a wistful vulnerability used to collide with wonder. I had never seen his shade of green so dim, and it caused my stomach to fall into the same somber eclipse, spiraling faster and faster with no end, no walls—only darkness.

He didn't even smile as I stood frozen—wasted. I waited for that smile. It seemed like forever as I anticipated in misery, but his lips never twitched. His Mia-smile was gone. I had been waiting for two weeks to see his smile. I had closed my eyes, dreaming of that smile. And now it was all a memory.

He'd warned me this would happen.

And then he averted his gaze. The walls in the room slowly caved in around me, suffocating me. The oxygen in my lungs, the blood in my veins, the flesh from my bones—all of it crumbled, breaking into small pieces yet still holding on by a thread. The thread being my heart. It still pumped on auto-pilot as if it couldn't associate with the rest of my body. Thumping sounded in my ears, and I wished it would stop, but my heart was not ready to let go. It continued with the same steady pump, refusing to give up what was right in front of me. I was drifting, barely existing because he was gone—and that meant I was gone. We were gone. But my heart was still going, and now I hated it.

I hated my heart.

Maybe my heart believed his eyes would return to mine. Maybe my heart believed the light would shine in his eyes again. And I waited. Like I had a choice. Two seconds passed ... then three, waiting as my body weakened from his disconnection, and my heart continued to pump. Four...

And then his back was to me. Whatever we'd had no longer existed, but I remembered everything clearly, and it wasn't fair. He was detached, and it wasn't fair. Why hadn't he taken me with him? *"Are you going to forget me or take me with you, love?"* he had asked me once before. *"Take you with me,"* I had said, but I forgot to ask him the same question in return.

I should have asked him.

Could I ever learn to accept the hollow in his eyes over the wonder and vulnerability? Surely, anything he had to offer would be better than nothing. If only he would turn back around. Had he even noticed me? *"Promise me you'll bring me back,"* he'd said to me, but I was frozen. *"You have to remind me. You have to find a way."*

And then he took a step in the opposite direction. He was gone, left in obscurity, but my heart still maintained a steady beat, pumping along to a rhythm of crimson hope. *"Stay with me,"* he would say over and over. Who would have thought he would have been the one to take a step into oblivion? Inside, I screamed. Inside, I crumbled. Could he hear me?

Why couldn't *you* stay with *me*, Ollie?

Even though he was only twenty feet away, I missed him, and it hurt so bad. It was quite possible he would wake up and turn back around, or I would wake up. Either way, it was a nightmare.

Each step drew more distance and less of a chance of him coming back. The darkness wasn't better. I saw and felt his light with my own eyes and my own heart. I knew what was on the other side. He was the light. And now he was in the dark. And now I was left in the memory of it, and it wasn't fair to be standing here alone.

The only warmth left was the water gathering in the corner of my eye, and no matter how hot it felt as it ran down my skin, I still shivered in his cold.

Dropping my tray onto Jake's, I ran after him. My feet moved despite my inability to feel my legs. I breathed too hard, or not at all. I wasn't quite sure, and I didn't care. Words stuck in my throat as I tried calling out his name. His back was to me, and his shoulders were recognizable, and his stride was familiar, but he'd looked at me only moments ago like I was a stranger.

I grabbed him by the arm and turned him around, forcing him to look at me, forcing him to see me. He seemed confused as he looked down at me, and then he smiled, but it wasn't the same smile I had grown to love. This smile was different. It was fraudulent. He ran his hands through his hair as I waited, dangling over the edge of a cliff.

"I don't know what to say," he said, looking past me and not at me, and there was something he was trying to hide.

"Say anything." I grasped for hope, but he stood before me, unreachable. I grabbed his hand, but it was cold, and he pulled away before stuffing his hands into his pockets.

"You fucked my brother. I should have never allowed it to go on as long as it did."

His words sliced through me. They cut me up, stuffed me into a blender, and he pressed the "on" button.

"Allowed what to go on?" *Don't say it, Ollie. Don't you dare say it.*

He took in a deep breath and looked at the ground as he exhaled. It was the most extended breath he had ever taken. "You and I."

You and I.

Those were bullets. Three of them. One to the stomach, one to the heart, and one to the head. Before, when he'd said those words, it was all that mattered. *A promise.* Now it sounded like a past time, a regret. Another tear fell down my cheek, and I was trying to be strong for him when strong was all he was now. He still wouldn't look at me, and my hands trembled at my sides.

"Ollie, it's the medication. You don't mean it. You promised me," I held up the ring for him to see. "You fucking promised me, remember?"

Ollie removed a hand from his pocket, but only to lower mine with his cold and bitter touch. "Don't curse, darling. It's a turnoff."

My eyes went wide as I searched his face, but he looked at everything else but me. He exhaled, and I could tell he was about to pull away, so I stepped in front of him. "Tell me what to do, Ollie. How am I supposed to remind you?"

"You can't. It's over. You have to let me go."

I shook my head as I felt the color drain from my face. Everything told me I should walk away, but I couldn't. All I wanted was to stay with him. I brought my hand to his face, and he froze under my touch.

"Please look at me," I begged, and his eyes slowly lifted to mine. The hollow he had described to me so many times was there, but he was still there also, lost in his newfound darkness. He laid his palm over my hand, but he didn't pull away. It was all I needed to keep going.

Lifting myself on my toes, I kissed him lightly. I'd never been so scared. He opened his eyes.

"Mia …" He gasped as if it were his last breath, then kissed me back with his hands on my face, our lips holding on desperately, yet dangerously. But as quickly as it had started, it was gone.

Ollie pulled away and dropped his forehead to mine. He wet his lips as he slowly shook his head back and forth. He was slipping away before my eyes, and I didn't know what else to do. "It's your turn to stay with me," I whispered.

Ollie pulled away from my hold and took a step back. The hands that once couldn't stay off me were now in his pockets. The lips that once always wanted to be on mine, weren't, and the eyes that used to always see me, couldn't.

"I'm such an idiot." He pushed out a harsh laugh that quickly dissolved. Looking me up and down, he took another step back. "Stay *away* from me, Mia."

Then he left me alone in the hallway.

And those words knocked me to my knees. Each step Ollie took away from me propelled another blow to my soul, impelling more tears from my eyes, provoking every outcry, and only intensifying the pain in my chest.

He never told me to close my eyes.

But I closed my eyes anyway.

EPILOGUE

Ollie

Since five in the morning, I'd been awake. Everyone had left around four, and I'd had too much to drink. It was a rare occurrence, me drinking, but Oscar always gifted me with bottles. Half of me wanted to believe he felt terrible for pinning the crime on me, so he dropped the bottles off once a week in my dorm; the other half of me was certain it was all a ploy, another way to control and manipulate me. *Either way, fuck you, Oscar.*

She couldn't have been real, though—the girl from the mess hall. It happened instantly, my heart and soul coming to an automatic agreement, promising their all to her, and frankly, I have too much.

Too much heart and too much soul.

But last night, Jake and Alicia confirmed her existence. They said her name was Mia. How could a three-letter word sound better than poetry? *Mia.*

She'd sat at the table against the window, couldn't have been more than thirty feet away, but my body had liquefied and turned into lava, wanting to flow in her direction. Everything had stopped. Though, she couldn't have been real. No one could've physically affected me the way she did. It had to have been a dream—a mirage—a reflection of what I'd been waiting for. *She wasn't real,* I'd kept reminding myself.

But she was. Her name was Mia, and she was fucking real.

They had invited her, but she hadn't shown up last night.

I couldn't get her out of my head.

The doors automatically unlocked and I grabbed my plain white shirt (the collar on the Dolor shirt was constricting), my black jeans, and fresh pants before heading out, slinging them over my shoulder. The morning was my favorite time of day. I'd always been a morning person. The smell was different in the morning. The air felt different in the morning. I breathed differently in the morning.

I always felt the need to beat the rising of the sun. A sunrise was different from a sunset. When the sun rose, it spoke of new beginnings. When the sun set, there were no words to follow.

My head pounded—*bloody hangover.* Walking into the bathroom, I rubbed my fingers over my eyes. Another shower stall was already turned on. The water beat against the tile. Steam built across my skin. Something slowly changed inside me. I felt it before I saw it.

Her presence, it was overwhelming.

My hands dropped to my side.

Mia.

I only saw her, and she saw me.

Her eyes on me kept me steady. Her eyes on me allowed me to exist. Her eyes on me made me important. She made me feel like I was something to be in awe of. Something to be worthy of.

A somebody. Her somebody.

A rush of emotions washed over me as I stopped in my tracks. My feet were useless and unable to move. I felt lost, utterly lost, and I suddenly didn't know where I was or how I had ended up here. I felt found, discovered by her, and I never wanted her eyes to leave mine. I felt scared, fucking petrified, if we lost this eye contact, she would disappear. I felt peace, undeniably calm in her existence. I felt resurrected, awakened, and I didn't know how I had lived this long without this privilege of being in her presence.

The pounding of my heart was the only sound as everything else went silent. It beat so loud. Could she hear my heart beating? It was speaking. It told me I had found her.

There.

She.

Is.

There was the girl I had been waiting my whole life for.

I was so weak, it was embarrassing. Staying on my feet became a struggle, when all my body wanted to do was fall to my knees.

Dammit, Mia, I already fell for you.

And suddenly, everyone was wrong. Except for Thomas Mann. *Thank you, Mr. Mann, for you gifted me words for everything this moment had brought me. Will Mia be okay with naming our first son after you? Little Thomas Mann Masters.*

No matter how hard I tried, I couldn't force away the stupid smile on my face. I was smiling, and it was the first bit of movement my muscles were able to overcome since the shock.

If I didn't speak now, I would scare her away, but I had forgotten how to speak. It was right there, just one word. *Bloody hell.* It came up from my chest. The word pumped from my own heart. The heart she now owned.

"Hi," I breathed. *Oh, good, I was breathing.* I wasn't fucking dead.

She smiled, and I fell all over again. Her top lip thinned out when she smiled, but the bottom lip kept its perfect shape. I loved her smile. I wanted to kiss her smile. I wanted to wake up to her smile every blessed morning.

Morning.

I knew I liked the mornings for a reason.

This was the beginning of a brand new day for her, but for me, this was the beginning of our lives together. She just didn't know it yet.

"Hi," she said, and the one syllable engulfed me entirely. I swam in it. I drowned in it. I wanted to say something more, but my heart was still recovering. Though, I doubted it would ever recover. Nothing about me would ever be the same after her.

I was certain of it.

We stood staring at each other, and I was not sure how long it had been. I took all of her in. Her eyes, though we were five feet away, were golden brown. Yesterday, they had been dark brown. Today, they were like coffee with two—no, three—tablespoons of creamer. Did she like coffee? She was American, so of course she did.

God bless America.

Her hair was wavy, but straight at the ends. Her hair was brown but lighter near the ends. It was like God couldn't decide. I didn't blame him for it. Despite his indecisiveness, she was a masterpiece.

But it was not the almond shape of her eyes, or the style of her hair, or even the way her lips moved when she uttered the simplest word causing my heart to stop. No, it was how I was finally home. *It was not love at first sight, Mr. Mann.* She had always been a part of me. My soul already knew hers, and it was now, in this fucking moment, when we were finally reunited. And there she stood, the girl I belonged to. I was no longer homesick. I was complete.

She turned away, and my heart suddenly crippled. It crippled because her eyes weren't on me. I needed her to see me. I didn't exist without her eyes on me.

I took steps toward her, and I never wanted to take another step unless it was in her direction. We were so close; I was careful not to touch her. *God, did I want to touch her.* I leaned over to grab a towel, making sure to keep a distance, but the distance was the last thing we needed. My skin was inches from hers, yet the beauty radiating from her soul penetrated everything. Me. My body. My heart. Everything. Her warmth was ecstasy, and I wanted to fall asleep in it every damn night.

Switching the water on in the stall next to hers, I didn't know what to do with myself. I couldn't scare her away. I walked up to the sink beside hers and turned it on. I could have given her space and chosen the next sink over, but my body wouldn't allow me. My eyes found hers in the mirror. She was my reflection. She was my other half. She was everything I wasn't. She completed me. She was home.

Words came out of my mouth, and I was certain my voice shook, but I had to hear her again. I had to keep talking to her because if I didn't, I might've exploded. "Mia, right?" The name sounded so amazing coming from my lips. When I said "Mia," I instantly became a poet. I never wanted to speak another name again. Nothing else would feel right coming from my lips. She looked into my eyes in the mirror, and though I wanted to keep them on me, her presence pulled my body in.

"Yeah, that's right," she said, but an ache crept behind each word.

Turning to face her, I leaned into the sink because if I didn't, I would have fell. She looked into my eyes. She looked deep into them, and I looked deep into hers. We saw each other. There was so much her eyes said, I couldn't keep up. She was scared. She was screaming. She wanted me. *No.* She needed me. I needed her more. She was trapped. *I hear you, Mia. I'm right here.* I wanted to comfort her. I wanted to hold her, but I couldn't bloody move.

What happened to you, love?

What was happening to me?

I extended my hand because that was what people did when they met, but I had a need to touch her, to soothe her, and there was a chance she would find comfort in that. "I'm Ollie," I said, but I wanted say so much more. Usually, I had no filter, but with Mia, I had no words. I wanted to tell her everything. I wanted her to tell me everything.

Fucking gobsmacked.

Her hand connected with mine, and I didn't shake like I usually would; I only held on. I held on to this feeling possessing me. The warmth. Our completeness. My breathing calmed, but my heart pulsated like a drum. Did she see what she was doing to me? Her little hand fit perfectly in mine, and her touch only confirmed all my beliefs. We were meant to be together.

My stupid smile returned.

Though I didn't want to pull away, I did. *Fuck.* I needed to get ahold of myself. I fidgeted with my toothbrush and razor, scattering things on the sink when I finally got a glimpse of myself in the mirror. Holy hell, I looked like a bloody mess. I frantically ran my fingers through my hair, but nothing tamed. Not my hair. Not my mind. Not my heart.

"Great first impression, yeah?" I tried to laugh away the fact I was a post-drunken mess with the unruly mop on my head. My gaze slipped to her, but hers was fixated at the sink.

"How can I get one of those?" she asked, and I loved her voice. I loved her American accent. She was looking at my razor, and I was looking at her—always.

"You haven't got a razor?"

She shook her head a smidge, and I loved the way her hair fell around her face when she did, and I forced myself not to move her hair behind her ear as I had read in so many romance novels. I had never felt the need to do that before, but it was all I wanted to do now. I wanted to feel her hair through my fingertips and tuck it behind her ear—girls in books liked that. But I didn't do it. Something told me she was not like every other girl. Instead, I slid my razor to her.

"You can have this one. It's fresh. I haven't used it."

Take my razor. Take my body. Take my heart.

You can have it all.

"Thanks," she said, and we shared a smile. Damn, her smile. With a smile like that, she should always be wearing it, and I would always be here to appreciate it.

Nodding, I turned away, so I didn't seem like a creep. I went into the shower and undressed before stepping under the water. She did the same with only a thin wall separating us—fucking torture. She was beside me naked. *Naked!* I had to turn my back to the wall, like that would have made a damn difference. I had to shut my eyes, but by closing my eyes only left my mind to its imagination. Her head was probably lifted slightly under the water, soaking her hair. The water was falling down her face, her neck, collarbone, breasts, curves. *Fuck.* I had to focus on everything aside from Mia naked so my knob wouldn't get hard.

I looked down.

It was too late.

Dammit, Mia.

I hurried because if I didn't, I knew I'd punch a hole through the wall and claim her in every way imaginable. Everything inside me already couldn't handle being only inches away. The space. The void. I wanted nothing between us—not even air.

I hurried.

After turning off the water, I quickly dried off and pulled on my pants. Then I tucked my knob into my waistband, so she wouldn't notice. I wanted to tell her it was her fault. I wasn't always like this. Instead, I said, "I would suggest hurrying if you want to avoid rush hour." But all I wanted was for her to come out here and see me, to talk to me. But, she didn't say anything. I pulled my shirt over my head and took one last hard look in the mirror at the bloke who was forever changed by her. "Only giving you a heads up," I added. It came out more like a plea.

I forced myself out of the bathroom, and I couldn't breathe. We were too far apart, and that's when I knew I was doomed. I wasn't sure how to feel about it, but there was a recognition my heart could no longer be without. She was lost, but I would find her.

I'm right here, Mia. Stay with me.

To be continued in...

Even When I'm Gone

According to the RAINN-Rape, Abuse & Incest National Network
(the largest anti-sexual violence organization in the US)

On average, nearly 934 people are sexually assaulted each day in the
United States alone. During one year, this equates to more than 340,991
men, women, and children. This is in one country.
These are reported cases.

Most sexual abuse cases are unreported.

If you or a loved one has been sexually abused
please call the RAINN Hotline

1-800-656-HOPE

or visit
https://rainn.org

ACKNOWLEDGMENTS

Thank you to every reader who has given my debut book a chance. Because of you, my words haven't been left unread. I am forever grateful and hope I've touched a place in your heart as you've touched mine.

Jumping into the intimidating sea of independent authors, and the talent that surrounds me, I'm honored and blessed to have met lifelong friends of bloggers, designers, editors, bookstagrammers, authors, readers, etc. this early on in my journey. Between taking the time to read my books, answer questions, receiving feedback, promoting my work, and so much more, words cannot express how much I appreciate you and the time you have given. You all hold a special place in my heart and I adore each and every one of you.

There are three people who've made sacrifices while helping my dream come true. A huge thank you to my husband, Michael, for being patient while I spent hours in front of my laptop and phone, supporting me, answering every one of my "Michael, what's the word for…." For working eight hours to only come home to pick up my slack, and allowing me vent and also celebrate with me. I love you forever! Thank you to my daughter, Gracie, who is my biggest cheerleader, also checks in on how my writing is coming along, helps around the house without me asking, and says she can't wait to read my book, and me always replying "not until I'm dead!" Thank you to my son, Christian, who has been so patient and has learned to do everything himself. I love all three of you!

Tina (Mom), thank you for your constant reminder that I need to get out of the house and feel some fresh air. You know me more than anyone, whether I'd like to admit it or not. Thank you for believing in me, dragging me places, and always asking if there is anything you can do to help. Thank you, thank you, thank you. I love you!

A huge thank you to my three rocks, Amanda, Kaylee, and Danielle. Amanda, my other half, you have been the first one to ever read a word I've written. Thank you for always pushing me and supporting me. I'd seriously be lost without you. You've listened to every idea, struggle, and success. Thank you, Kaylee, for always celebrating even the smallest of victories and rooting me on. You are my biggest inspiration. Thank you, Danielle, for being the second person to read my work (lol), though you don't like to read. The fact that you took time out to support me, going to events, and showing interest means the world. I have the best sisters anyone can ask for, and I love all three of you with everything I have!

A Florida-sized thank you to Kassandra Dosal McLendon aka Kassy aka my angel! Words haven't been invented yet for how much you mean to me. You always find a way to bring me back to solid ground when I find myself getting wrapped up in the negatives or doubting myself, and I love you for it. I never thought in a million years when I messaged you, our relationship would turn out the way it did, and now I don't know what I'd do without you. Thank you for spending endless hours on the phone with me, most times 'til four o'clock in the morning (my time, lol), calling me every time you know something is bothering me, working out all my kinks, smothering my insecurities, and lifting me up. You've made this experience that more enjoyable, and to be sharing this journey with you is a dream come true! (I promised myself I'd make your "thank you" shorter than my husband so he wouldn't get jealous, but I failed) I love you!

Thank you, thank you, thank you, Allison Dublin with Wasted Life Books for being my everything—my PA, my confidant, my bright side ... I could go on. It was fate for us to meet, but you're the reason I'm here today. A year ago, you read my very first project, and believed in me. Thank you for taking a chance on me, for listening to all my crazy ideas in the *Stay With Me* series, bouncing ideas around, getting me off the ground, and everything in between. You are my knight in shining armor and I honestly don't know how you do it all. My gratitude to you is endless, and I'm so incredibly lucky to have you in my life. I can't wait to ride this rollercoaster, but with you by myside, at least I know I won't fall off of it!

A huge thank you to my betas aka my lifelines, Faith Flores, Mia Kun (my Mia!), Junior, Lym Cruz, Magali, Amy Terry, Shanna, and Jennifer. You guys are freaking amazing! Your feedback is invaluable, and your unwavering support is priceless. Thank you for making Stay With Me what it is today. I'm so happy I met each and every one of you and couldn't have done this book without you.

A never-ending thank you to my best friend Diana Wallwork. No matter how many miles we are apart, you always make sure you are there when I need you. Thank you for always checking in, asking about progress, offering to help with anything, and for just being you. I love you!

Thank you, Murphy Rae for your creativity, researching items I failed to look up, and edits I so desperately needed. I have come to the conclusion I'm addicted to commas, em dashes, and ellipses …

With all my heart, thank you to my readers, my LOVELIES! You took a shot reading a book by a new indie author, and I am forever grateful for each and every one of you. I cannot wait to show you what I have in store.

A special thank you to my amazing family and dear friends spread all over the world. Without your support, I know I wouldn't have been able to get this far.

ABOUT THE AUTHOR

Nicole is the author of the Stay with Me series and Amazon's #1 Best Selling Author in Gothic Romance for her debut in Urban Fantasy, Hollow Heathens. She lives in Florida with her husband, two kids, and lazy Great Dane, Winston.

Her writing style is *"insanely romantic"* and *"wildly addicting,"* striving to push hearts and limits. When She's not writing, she's either listening to crime podcasts, watching horror flicks with her kids, traveling, or planning her next book adventure—with one hand on her laptop and the other balancing a mocha latte.

I LOVE HEARING FROM YOU!

Facebook: /nicolefiorinabooks
Instagram: @authornicolefiorina

SIGN UP FOR THE NEWSLETTER, NF STORE, & MORE:

www.nicolefiorina.com

nicole fiorina

Printed in Great Britain
by Amazon

78320375R00207